LAST

OF THE

INDEPENDENTS

LAST OF THE INDEPENDENTS

VANCOUVER NOIR

SAM WIEBE

DUNDURN
TORONTO

Editor: Laura Harris
Design: Jennifer Scott
Cover image: © zennie/iStock
Cover design by Carmen Giraudy
Printer: Webcom

Library and Archives Canada Cataloguing in Publication

Wiebe, Sam, author
    Last of the independents / Sam Wiebe.

(Vancouver noir)
Issued in print and electronic formats.
ISBN 978-1-4597-0948-5 (pbk.).--ISBN 978-1-4597-0949-2 (pdf).--ISBN 978-1-4597-0950-8 (epub)

I. Title.

PS8645.I3236L38 2014   C813'.6   C2013-908353-7   C2013-908354-5

1 2 3 4 5   18 17 16 15 14

We acknowledge the support of the **Canada Council for the Arts** and the **Ontario Arts Council** for our publishing program. We also acknowledge the financial support of the **Government of Canada** through the **Canada Book Fund** and **Livres Canada Books**, and the **Government of Ontario** through the **Ontario Book Publishing Tax Credit** and the **Ontario Media Development Corporation**.

Care has been taken to trace the ownership of copyright material used in this book. The author and the publisher welcome any information enabling them to rectify any references or credits in subsequent editions.

J. Kirk Howard, President

The publisher is not responsible for websites or their content unless they are owned by the publisher.

Printed and bound in Canada.

Visit us at
Dundurn.com | @dundurnpress | Facebook.com/dundurnpress | Pinterest.com/Dundurnpress

Dundurn	Gazelle Book Services Limited	Dundurn
3 Church Street, Suite 500	White Cross Mills	2250 Military Road
Toronto, Ontario, Canada	High Town, Lancaster, England	Tonawanda, NY
M5E 1M2	LA1 4XS	U.S.A. 14150

For my parents, Al and Linda,
and my brothers, Dan and Josh

Acknowledgements

Thanks to my editor, Laura Harris; everyone at Dundurn and the Crime Writers of Canada; Jess Driscoll; Mercedes Eng; Mike Stachura; Andrew and Lauren Nicholls; and Mel Yap.

All errors are mine, all resemblance to real people or events entirely coincidental.

"It is the struggle of all fundamentally honest men
to make a decent living in a corrupt society."

— RAYMOND CHANDLER

Business Is My Trouble

The younger Thomas Kroon leaned forward on the clients' bench and said, "There's no real polite way to say this, Mr. Drayton. Someone's fucking our corpses and we'd like it to stop."

"The sooner the better," his father added.

I stared at them across the table that served as my desk, past a half-eaten sandwich and a cold cup of tea, past the keyboard, past the day's filing and the week's accounting, and over the mountainous sinkhole of despair that was the Loeb file. The two Thomas Kroons wore identical broad-lapelled suits with the same gold, silk diamond-patterned tie. They had the same mahogany-coloured hair, though I suspected the senior Thomas Kroon's was the result of chemical treatment. Neither looked too encouraged by the furnishings of my second-floor Hastings Street office. When one of them shifted on the cinder-block-and-plank bench, the other had to hurry to find a new equilibrium.

At the word "fucking," my assistant, Katherine Hough, stopped typing. I waited for her to resume before I said, "This has happened multiple times?"

"Four," Kroon the Younger said.

"Three that we're sure of," his father corrected.

"And how did you deduce that this wasn't some sort of …," I struggled for the word, "…indigenous secretion?"

"I know what ejaculate looks like, Mr. Drayton."

"It's not exactly easy for us to sit here admitting this," the younger Kroon said. I'd started to think of him as Thomas Junior, even though he'd prefaced our consultation by stating that he wasn't named Junior, hated being called Junior, and anyway it was inaccurate because he and his father had different middle names. "Like the Bushes," I'd said. The comparison hadn't been well-received.

"The first one was just over two months ago," Elder said. "The 27th, a Monday. I normally open by myself during the week, but Thomas was with me. We came in early that morning to get started on draining a young woman who had arrived Sunday night."

Kroon the Younger added, "Draining fluids for embalming, he means."

"We found ejaculate on the outside of the bag, and when we opened the bag up, more ejaculate in the woman's oral cavity."

"Which wasn't there when she arrived," Younger said. "I was there when the Removal guys dropped her off Sunday night. The bag was pristine."

I took notes. "What was the woman's name?"

"Ethel Peace," Elder said.

"And what'd you do?"

"Cleaned her up, of course." Elder indignant.

"He means did we call the cops," Younger said to him, turning to me for a nod of confirmation. "We wanted to, but I felt, if that kind of thing ever gets out, we're finished. Bad news travels at warp speed in the funeral business. So we put up a camera over the freezer, figuring next time we'd catch this person."

Elder inclined his head toward his son. "Someone kept forgetting to turn it on at the end of the day. Two weeks later,

Violet Thorvaldsson, same modus operandi, as you folks say."

Us folks. I said, "Did you get footage of the other incidents?"

"There was only one other attack," Elder said. "Two days ago. Maureen Lennox. Some of the ejaculate happened to land on an adjacent bag."

"You don't know that," his son said.

To me the father said, "Think it's safe to say he wasn't interested in both Mrs. Lennox and Donald Peng."

"But there's no video of the incident or incidents?" I said.

"The cameras were on," Younger said. Anticipating his father's interjection he added, "I set them, I'm sure. They'd been switched off from the office. Someone entered the password and exited the program, then restarted it about an hour later."

"How many people know the password?"

"The two of us alone," Elder said, readjusting his weight on the bench so that Younger had to scramble to stay poised on the edge.

"Well, he says that," Younger said. "But our tech guy Jag has it, and I'm sure Carrie, our secretary, has it, which means it's probably written down somewhere, which means anyone in the office could find it." He snorted. "There's the right way, the wrong way, and how the secretary does it. I'm sure you deal with the same thing."

Without looking up, Katherine said, "I'm not his secretary."

Younger shrugged, whatever. "There's about eight people in the office. Some of them know. We want to pay you to put a stop to this."

"You could just change your password and leave the cameras running 24/7," I said.

"To give you the straight deal, Mr. Drayton, we don't know what to do when we catch this person. If it comes out we didn't report the first four —"

"First three," Elder corrected.

"— we'd be put out of business. We can't turn this person over to the police."

"But he must be made to understand this can't continue," Elder reaffirmed.

"You want me to find him and give him a stern talking to?"

"Or geld him," Younger said. "Whatever keeps him from fucking our corpses."

"I don't geld," I said. "But I'll find who he is and confront him with the evidence, if that's what you want." Nods of affirmation from both Kroons. "Three hundred dollars a day plus expenses and equipment fees."

"Sounds equitable," Elder said.

I dredged up a contract and two boilerplate liability waivers. The Thomas Kroons read them and signed.

"Any pattern to these attacks you've noticed?" I asked them.

"Always Mondays, or the first day back after the weekend," Elder said.

I looked over at the vintage car calendar nailed to the wall above Katherine's computer. Today was Wednesday, the 2nd of September. September's car was a '50 Ford painted a milky orange hue. The colour of peach yogurt when it's been stirred up.

"I'll come by Friday, talk to your staff," I said. I rose out of the chair and shook both exceedingly dry right hands.

Thomas Kroon the Elder said, "Would it be all right if we introduced you as a security consultant rather than a private investigator?"

"As you like. You're open weekends?"

"Three-quarter days," Younger said.

"I'll need a key and your security codes when I come by on Friday. I've got my own equipment, and I might have someone stay overnight. Keep this between the two of you."

"No worry about that," Younger said. "Believe me, this isn't the kind of thing we like to advertise."

* * *

After the Kroons were gone I slid my sandwich forward to the edge of the table. "So what do you think?"

Katherine swiveled around in her chair. A high-school rugby player, now a student at Langara College, Katherine was stockily built and only feminized, in the traditional sense of the word, in the light eye shadow she wore, the berets in her black hair, and the layer of foundation she used to hide her freckles.

She had become the second employee of Hastings Street Investigations eight months ago, doing four hours of clerical work a week. When her course load lessened in the summer, I'd brought her in Monday to Thursday. I'm proficient with computers but I hate them, and worse, am the type of person who tries to pass this hatred off as a distinction rather than a deficiency, the mark of a genius whose intuition is hamstrung by binary code and random access memory. So much of modern investigating is simply knowing which database to search. I was happy to turn much of that work over to Katherine, freeing me up for the kind of jobs my antiquated skill set was better suited for. Like camping out in the basement of a funeral home, waiting for a necrophiliac.

"I'm just glad my grandpa went through Forest Lawn," Katherine said. "Can you imagine the audacity, them not telling the cops?"

"It would ruin them."

"Maybe they should be ruined. How'd you feel if that was your aunt, or if it was you?"

"It's dead tissue at that point." I finished my sandwich, wadded up the wrapper and missed a three-pointer into the wastebasket next to the door. Through the window, the afternoon sun was making one last effort to break through a chalk-coloured sky.

"So you wouldn't mind, after you're dead, someone having their way with you?"

"I couldn't mind because I wouldn't be there."

"But the family, Mike."

"I doubt the Kroons will tell them."

"Then I guess that makes it a victimless crime," Katherine said.

"The Kroons are the victims."

She rolled her eyes, one of her handful of annoying tics that meant "I give up, I can't reason with this idiot." She returned to her search. I finished typing my meeting notes and forwarded them to her. I was passing her the contract when the buzzer rang. Katherine looked over at the television monitor to her left and said, "Your friend is on his way up."

"Which one?"

"How many do you have?"

A moment later Ben Loeb crashed through the door and collapsed wheezing on the clients' bench. He shed his jacket and took several gulps of air before saying, "I just saw the weirdest pair of twins."

"Father and son," I said.

"Clients?"

"Can't really go into it."

"They run a funeral home and someone's having their way with the corpses," Katherine said. "And your hero here thinks it's no harm, no foul."

"Undertakers. That's why they looked so weird." Ben dug through the pockets of his sweater, found his notebook, and jotted something down. "They did have that Bonasera vibe. What did they want? Did they entreat you to beat someone up for them?"

"Obviously they wanted the corpse-humper stopped," Katherine said.

"That's about the gist of it," I said.

"And you took the job?" When I nodded, Ben's head sank.

"What?" Katherine said. "You don't think necrophilia is a serious crime? You'd be happy with someone defiling your lifeless body?"

"It's kind of flattering," Ben said.

Not only did she roll her eyes but her head followed, and her body followed her head, as she turned back to her screen, done with us, muttering, "Peas in a fricking pod."

Ben looked at the Loeb file on the corner of the table, and the Loeb file looked into Ben. Five years ago nine-year-old Cynthia Loeb had walked four blocks from her home on Seventh Avenue into a 7-Eleven where four witnesses saw her. Her exit was on the security tape, but she had never been seen again. There had been bogus sightings, anonymous tips, a scrapbook's worth of news clippings, dozens of VPD and RCMP bulletins, spots on local and national news. Dozens of serious-voiced blond anchors had intoned, "The search continues for," "Months after the disappearance," and "The family continues to hold out." All that was left now were numbers and names.

Cynthia and Ben's father had died of angina, a condition which existed before the disappearance but caused their mother to state that he had died of a broken heart. He may very well have. Mrs. Estelline Loeb hired me thirty-two months before that day with the Kroons. I had failed her, her husband had failed her, the police and the media, the support groups, the talk show hosts, and her son, Ben, had failed her. Her optimism never faltered. Her hope never waned. The Loeb file grew to Jarndyce and Jarndyce proportions, a labyrinth of dead ends. I nicknamed it "The Impossible Case." I stopped accepting her money. But the first of every month I received a phone call from her. We'd discuss what witnesses needed to be re-interviewed, what agencies hadn't been contacted recently, whether a fresh round of flyers should be put up. She never cried or fell into hysterics, or emoted at all beyond cheerful, blind optimism. To fail her so consistently, so spectacularly, had broken my heart.

Her son Ben was different. He'd been twenty when his baby sister disappeared — there was a middle child, Izaak Junior, who had died in infancy — and after two years of brooding and sulking, overindulging in every vice he could find, Ben's life, according to him, went pretty much back to normal. Not that he wasn't moved every time he saw the file, but he'd resigned himself to his sister's absence in a way his mother hadn't and couldn't.

"Benjamin Loeb," so an article in *GamePro* read, "is one of the hottest video game writers to come on the scene in the last decade, bringing the sensibilities of William Gibson to the world of Hideo Kojima and Drew Karphyshyn." Ben kept a laminated copy of the article in his wallet. He'd been blocked since developing the third installment of *Your Blood is a Drug!* — a role-playing game he'd written about a dystopic future where the majority of people volunteer to undergo the chemical equivalent of a full-frontal lobotomy. The series was wildly successful, spawning a line of merchandise that included a fully poseable Magnus Kane action figure (the brooding, leather-wearing, curtain-of-black-hair-across-his-forehead antihero, the one person in Neo Vancouver immune to the effects of the drug) and a T-shirt that said PROUD SLAVE OF THE PARAGON CORPORATION. Ben was wearing one of those shirts underneath his jacket, stretched and bunching in an effort to contain his amorphous trunk.

He spent more time in the office than Katherine did. Perhaps in the cobbled-together furniture and the high-tech gadgetry he saw the clubhouse or the neighbour's tree fort he'd been excluded from. My office has that effect on some people. Most, though, like the Kroons, find the outside world an immensely desirable place after fifteen minutes in the cramped second-storey shoebox that houses my business.

"Talk to your mother lately?" I asked Ben.

"Why? Anything develop?"

"No."

"So why bring it up?"

"She likes to see you."

"What she likes is to run me through the gauntlet of her disapproval," Ben said. He affected an elderly lady's voice. "You know, Benjamin, I'm not one of those mothers who hover over her children nitpicking every last detail. But would it hurt you to wear some lighter colours, even a white, for heaven's sake? And while I wouldn't say you're fat, let me remind you, your father had to do an hour's worth of cardio every day to keep his figure. Tell you what, Benjamin. I'm going to send you home with a nice case of lentil soup."

"Imagine that," I said. "A nice old woman wanting to make sure her son takes care of himself. What an unreasonable bitch. Anyway, she asks about you. Try to fit in a visit this fiscal quarter."

Katherine pushed back from her desk, stood up, and picked pieces of chair stuffing off her ass, compliments of a ripped seat cushion. I made a mental note to duct-tape the chair tomorrow.

She said, "Gordon Laws says thank you, says his son's on the next plane home. You can pick up the check on Monday."

"He should thank you; you're the one who found him."

"In under an hour," Katherine said. Her searches were usually only tangential to the case. Laws's son David was the first person she'd located. I'd been waiting all week for her to ask for a raise. I was planning on countering with a piece of the business, meagre but steady. Instead she said, "Just to let you know, school's back next week."

"Thought it wasn't till —"

"— After Labour Day, which is next Monday."

I looked again at the auto calendar, the unchanging centre placard reading MORRIS CARGILL'S ACCOUNTING AND TAX PREPARATION: WE CHARGE BY THE HALF HOUR!

"So it is," I said. "What about nights? Weekends?"

"No nights, have to study. Saturdays yes, no Sundays. A possibility of Wednesdays if I can switch French labs, but I won't know till the second week when people start to drop."

"*La langue de l'amour,*" Ben said.

"More like the language of government service," Katherine said. "You know how much better your prospects of a government job are if you're bilingual?"

Ben said, "What I like about you, Hough, is that you're a starry-eyed idealist. You really set your sights high."

"Let me know about Wednesdays," I said, as Katherine smoothed the collar of her wool coat. She nodded her good-byes, slipped into the straps of her backpack, and began her descent. I watched her on the monitor as she reached the bottom of the stairs, threw open the front door, and stepped out into green-tinted sunlight.

"Developing a thing for her?" Ben asked me.

"It's employer-employee concern," I said. "I've never had underlings before. It's empowering."

"Who's Gordon Laws?"

"A wealthy man with an estranged son. After a twenty-year lost weekend, he finds himself owning a couple of car dealerships, wonders what happened to his family. His son took his ex-wife's ex-boyfriend's last name. Katherine found him on one of those social networking sites. Amazing how much info people will volunteer for public scrutiny."

"They all think they'll be famous," Ben said. "Not realizing, of course, you have to be famous *for* something, even if that 'something' is being a contemptible prick. Gordon Laws and his offspring sound like raging bores."

"You don't know the first thing about either of them."

"I can spot a raging bore. Hundred dollars says I'm right." Ben stood and walked to Katherine's chair and sat down, the torn cushion emitting a wheeze. "I've got a case for you."

I nodded at the Loeb file. "You're telling me."

"Something else," he said.

While we were talking I'd been drafting an email to a woman's shelter in Toronto, sending them age-enhanced photos of Cynthia Loeb and requesting they post them and keep an eye out. She'd be fourteen this year. Some of the photos had been aged ten or twelve years to account for possible amphetamine or crack addiction. The combination of drug-damaged skin and a little girl's eyes and smile was unsettling. I fired off the email and turned my attention to Ben.

He said, "I don't have all the details, but the guy sounds like he's in dire need of a private eye."

"Is the melodrama necessary? Out with it."

"Remember the choices I had for community service?"

"You parleyed your way into attending Pastor Flaherty's group."

"Right, Coping Without a Loved One. The Father invited my mom once. You can imagine how that went. Anyway, I showed up, got the signatures, figured we were finished. The good Father, however, turns out to be a big video game fan, and he keeps in touch. We were talking one day and you came up."

I leaned back in my chair until my head touched the wall. "Oh?"

"He thinks highly of you, despite your attitude to him."

"'Attitude' meaning the fact I don't give discounts to people of the cloth?"

"'Combative to people of faith' is how he described you."

"And what did you say?"

"I said, 'Apt.' Like that's not true?" Ben stood and grabbed his jacket from the bench, pulled from its pocket a flyer folded lengthwise.

"Yesterday he asks to meet me for coffee. I'd given him some back issues of the spinoff comic. I figured he wanted to take me to task for the blood and gore and godlessness. Instead he hands me this to give to you and asks if you'll meet with this guy to discuss taking over the case."

I spread the flyer on the table. A black-and-white school photo of a slightly-disheveled, dark-haired boy, defiantly unsmiling. I could almost hear the photographer coaxing him, aware of the two hundred other brats she'd have to shoot that morning, telling the kid, "Don't you want to look nice in the yearbook?" The kid thinking, "Hell no."

Above the photo were the words

DJANGO JAMES SZABO.
TWELVE YEARS OLD.
DISAPPEARED MARCH 6TH.
MISSED BY HIS FAMILY.
IF SEEN, CONTACT VPD MISSING PERSONS
SO WE CAN RETURN DJANGO TO HIS FAMILY.

Phone number and email address followed.

"He's been on the news off and on," Ben said. "He's not the most photogenic kid, and the dad's six kinds of crazy. It never became the big news story it should've."

"The dad goes to those meetings?" I said. "After six months?"

Ben said, "No, but Pastor Flaherty is campaigning for him to come. Mr. Szabo mentioned he was unhappy with the people he hired, so the Pastor asked me to ask you if you'd see him. Will you?"

"I don't know yet," I said. "Who did Szabo hire first?"

"Aries Security and Investigative Consultants."

"There's ten grand down the toilet," I said. "Tell the Pastor I'll meet him tomorrow morning at the mission, nine if he can make it."

The new door I'd put on my grandmother's house was wedged in its frame. The book on household carpentry I'd been following recommended shaving the frame down half an inch, but in my wisdom I'd thought I could get a more perfect fit by only shaving a third. Now that winter was slouching towards us the wood was expanding. The crown moldings I'd installed in the living room had cracked and the banister on the basement stairs had started to warp. The doorframe was only the latest casualty.

I wrenched the door open and found myself enfolded in the smell of chicken and pipe smoke. She was asleep on the couch, her TV trays in front of her, a separate one for the ashtray and clickers. Some asinine game show silently emitting from the TV.

I found a plate waiting in the oven, baked chicken, boiled and buttered potatoes, green beans, and corn. Everything cold, waiting for me to flick the dial on the oven.

The pile of dishrags and dirty laundry in the middle of the floor raised its head and whimpered in my direction. I put down a plate of dry kibble moistened with chicken juice. The dog made no move to get up. I took the cold plate from the oven and headed downstairs.

Despite the water-stained concrete and exposed ceiling beams, the basement was comfortable, warm. Everything

I'd taken from my apartment that had survived the breakup had found a place in the long low-ceilinged room. I put some McCoy Tyner on, cracked a beer from the mini-fridge, and sat on the corner of the bed, eating dinner and reading part of an Elmore Leonard western. The plot seemed familiar, either because I'd read it before, or I'd seen the movie, or a character in one of Leonard's crime novels had read the book and used it for inspiration. Eventually the dog joined me, hobbling over to the stiff-bristled mat. I scrolled down my iPod from Tyner to Sam Cooke, lay on the bed, and drifted off thinking of Django James Szabo's Missing flyer, sitting on my table in the shadow of the Loeb file.

Last of the Independents

Pastor Titus Flaherty had fashionably cut hair, black with a white streak that ran temple to sideburn on his right side. His teeth were widely spaced and jutted at odd angles, and when he spoke he vivisected you with enormous, soulful John Coltrane eyes.

"Cliff Szabo is a difficult person to maintain a friendship with," he said as we crossed the parking lot in the direction of the mission.

I drank some of my London Fog. "I'm not trying to marry into his family," I said. "Long as he's somewhat close to sanity, I can work with him."

The rain had abated by the time we started back from the café. The Pastor had ordered a pumpkin soy latte and a whole grain fudge bar without a hint of shame. Vancouver. Water droplets from leaky awnings hit our shoulders as we walked along Cambie Street.

Over my shirt and jeans I was wearing a tan trench coat that had been liberated by an ex-girlfriend from the wardrobe department of a local television show. Due to a romance that ended with the girl abandoning her possessions and fleeing to the Maritimes, I'd inherited the coat of the show's tough-as-nails, murder-solving coroner. Forget that in the real world coroners don't usually solve murders — neither do private investigators. The coat had taken a beating over the years, and I'd lost the belt, causing it to billow out unglamorously as the Pastor and I walked into a strong wind.

"I didn't mean to imply Cliff isn't a good-hearted person," Pastor Flaherty said. He rolled up his sleeve and tapped the face of a large-dialed, numberless watch that looked out of place on its simple leather band. "My father's. When it was stolen Cliff tracked it down and paid for it out of a pawn shop window. He wouldn't let me reimburse him."

"Almost like giving to the poor," I said. "If he called the cops he could've got it back for nothing."

"That's what I'm getting at. Cliff can be suspicious. Truculent. Especially with agents of authority. He will scorn your help. He will make this about anything other than the matter at hand. Just bear in mind, Michael, whatever he says comes from a man dealing with unfathomable heartbreak, pain, and guilt."

"Guilt?"

"I'll let him tell you, if he decides."

The mission took up both floors of the leftmost building on a block of similar-looking grey rectangles. I stood under the canopy on a walkway of crushed stone while the Pastor went inside to find Mr. Szabo. I read the list of activity groups and meetings booked into the top-floor common room for the coming week: NarcAnon, AlAnon, Overeaters Anonymous. Coping Without a Loved One met Monday afternoons excluding holidays. I flung my tea bag into the rusted ashtray mounted by the door.

Szabo came out alone. A short man, bald, with a dark beard and thick dark eyebrows. He wore a light grey polo shirt and slate grey slacks, polished black shoes, and a cheap digital watch. He glared at me for a moment.

"Mr. Szabo," I said. He nodded. "My name's Michael Drayton. I'm a private investigator."

He nodded again. We'll see.

"I understand from Pastor Flaherty your son is missing and you're thinking of hiring someone to look for him. I've a certain amount of experience in this."

"In kidnappings?"

"Beg pardon?"

"Django James wouldn't run away. He had to have been taken." The earnest expression on his weathered face challenged me to disagree.

"By whom?" I asked.

"If I knew that, would we be talking?"

"How do you know?"

"I don't know my own son?"

"You're saying he was too obedient to run away?" I thought of adding, "Ever heard of puberty?"

"Django was waiting in the car," he said, as if summoning every part of his will to remain calm. "When I came out of the pawn shop, the car was gone. You think I'm lying?"

"I don't know you."

Emphatic nods from Mr. Szabo. "Or my son. Just like the other vulture, Mr. McEachern, you don't care. You're here for your chance to pick the bones."

"I don't work like McEachern," I said.

But he was on a roll now. "You smell blood in the water. You say you can help; only you need money first. You take the money and you ask questions. You get things wrong, you don't listen. Then you don't find him and you say, sorry, I have other ideas but they cost more money."

He paused and lit an American cigarette. It smelled harsh and good in the morning air.

"Do you know what I do for a living, Mr. Drayton?"

I shook my head.

"I buy and sell. Gold, electronics, bicycles, anything. I buy for cheap, fix and clean, sell for more. I support my family on this. You think that's easy?"

"Couldn't be," I said.

"Damn right. I pay attention and I have an eye for scams. I know the difference between gold and gold-plated, between an American Stratocaster and a Korean. I've seen every fraud. I even pulled off some, when I was younger." He sucked on his smoke and stared at me through a yellow cloud. "But I never made money off a missing child."

"Your mind's made up," I said. The cigarette smoke had awakened old urges. I downed the cold dregs of my drink and placed the cup in the ashtray.

"You people exploit grief for money. You sell false hope. I can't believe I let Mr. McEachern convince me to trust him. You people are all smiles while the wallet is full."

"I've heard about enough," I said. "I didn't take your kid and I'm not after your fortune. If you manage to swallow that wad of self-righteous bile lodged in your throat, you can find me in the corner office on Beckett and Hastings. Mira Das with the VPD will vouch for me."

I took out one of my business cards and tried to hand it to him. He made no move to take it. I set it on the edge of the ashtray. The card gave my address and company name in bold, and in cursive the motto *Last of the Independents*. Katherine had insisted the old cards looked too plain. Szabo stared down at the card but didn't move.

Before I left I added, "Whether I hear from you or not, I hope you find your son."

I crossed the street, leaving him there, feeling bad about letting down the Pastor, but not that bad. There was nothing else to be done. Clifford Szabo needed angelic intervention, not a PI.

* * *

Instead of going to the office I went home. Self-employment has its privileges. I made a chicken sandwich and sat on the back porch, eating and reading and every so often tossing a grey tennis ball across the overgrown yard. My dog limped after the ball and dutifully retrieved it, less enthusiastic about the game than I was.

It had been two weeks since the diagnosis. Cancer of the lymph nodes. Before that she'd had laboured breathing and the odd rectal discharge. Physically, she looked deflated, as if someone had let a third of the air out of her. I had a talk with a very nice vet who recommended treatment to postpone the end. I said of course, how much? She quoted me a figure in the mid four digits. I told her I was twenty grand in debt already and was there any other option? She told me I'd have two months at best and that some time before that, "When you think it's right," I should make another, final appointment.

The dog had flawless bowel control before lymphoma. Now she rubbed her ass on the carpets compulsively, looking ashamed of herself as her body continued to betray her. In addition to ruining the rugs on the upstairs floor, a stool softener had to be inserted every morning. Dawn usually found me cradling her on the porch while one hand pushed a spongy red capsule of Anusol into her rectum. As vile as that chore was, I would've done it happily every day for the rest of my life.

"He's right here," my grandmother said, banging through the screen door to deposit the cordless phone into my hand.

"Drayton," I said. My grandmother stood over me, arms crossed.

"Mr. Drayton? Gordon Laws. Talked to your secretary a couple minutes ago. Nice girl. Listen, just wanted to extend my thanks personally. My son and I, lot of water under the bridge, but on account of you we have a chance to go forward as a family. My wife is thrilled. Also wanted to tell you, check's ready for pick up, and we decided to give you a nice little bonus."

"That's very generous. My assistant, Katherine, she's the one who did the lion's share of the work."

"Well, make sure she hears that we're happy."

"Will do."

"Take care."

"Same to you."

"All right."

"All right then."

"Christ," I said, handing my grandmother back the phone.

"Something the matter?" she said.

"No, I just owe Ben a hundred dollars."

She shrugged and pointed at the dog. "Looking a pretty sorry spectacle."

"She still gets around the yard," I said.

The only way my grandmother would coexist with a dying dog was a promise from me that once the cycle was over, I'd refinish the main floor in real hardwood. My grandfather and his brothers had built the house on Laurel Street. During renovations in the late seventies, on my grandmother's whim, they installed pink shag carpeting in all the bedrooms. Her sinuses had had to live with that decision for almost forty years.

"You will never catch me letting someone put their hand up my bum," my grandmother said. "I'd rather be dead than that."

"If it was Antonio Banderas's hand, you'd look forward to it all day."

She scowled, shook her head, collapsed the phone's antenna and took it back inside. I rolled the ball underhand along the shadow of the clothesline. The dog, resting on the lawn, raised her head and watched the ball roll past, as though deciding if it was worth the effort.

* * *

At the office I found Katherine and Ben in the midst of an argument over some film, Ben making the kind of sweeping statement that I doubt even he believed, but said to enrage others and make himself feel edgy.

Ben vacated my chair and moved to the other side of the table. His hands were busy slicing one of my old business cards into strips.

"How'd it go?" Katherine asked.

"Ever date someone who was on the rebound, and they try to hold against you everything their ex did to them? Well, Mr. Szabo hired Aries Investigations, and based on that, he's decided not to pursue a relationship with us."

"Poor guy," she said.

"Settle this for us, okay?" Ben said to me. "Orson Welles: genius or fraud?"

"Genius," I said, settling into my chair.

"Correct. But would you watch his movies?"

"Sure."

"But *do* you watch his movies?"

"Once in a while I'll put on *Touch of Evil*." I turned to Katherine. "Why, who was he saying was better? He never makes one of those grand dismissals without an equally absurd replacement."

"I don't know the name," she said. "The guy who directed *Speed*."

"Not what I said, I said it was a better film than *Citizen Kane*." Ben rolled the strip of cardboard into a makeshift filter and affixed it to a slim joint he produced from his pocket. I scanned my table carefully and found particles of bud, mostly stems and seeds.

"Go outside to do that."

"Not till you hear me out on *Speed*," he said. He began counting the virtues on his fingers. "It's got at least as many fully-developed characters. It's better paced. The effects are better. It's got as many memorable lines of dialogue. It obeys the laws of Aristotelian unity. It's better acted."

"Better acted," Katherine said. "Keanu Reeves?"

The buzzer saved me from responding. On the monitor I saw Cliff Szabo start up the steep stairs. "Troll somewhere else," I told Ben. To Katherine I added, "The bonus for the Laws job is yours provided you pick up the check from him."

"Why so generous?" she asked, as Ben ducked out of the room, pawing his pockets in search of his Zippo.

"You did the work."

"That the only reason?"

"It's not the highest paying job, I know."

"How about fifty-fifty?"

"Where I come from we don't turn away money."

"You just did."

Cliff Szabo stepped past her. Katherine shut the door as she left, shooting me a look that was equal parts "thank you" and "you're insane."

Szabo tested the bench before sitting down. "I overreact," he said by way of apology.

"I'd like to help," I said.

"I'm still not sure," he said. "What can you do the cops can't?"

"Nothing."

"Nothing," he repeated.

"That's right. The police have resources and connections I can't begin to compete with. They're your best hope to get your son back. Any PI who's not a fraud will tell you the same."

"So why hire you?"

"Because, statistically speaking, the more people looking, the better. And because sometimes people get lucky."

I gestured at the kettle. Szabo shook his head.

"Most missing persons the police find, or they come back on their own. Of the three I worked where that wasn't the case, I found two. And both were due more to luck and patience than skill."

"You said three."

I nodded at the Loeb file on the corner of my table.

"I want you to understand," I said. "The best I can do is work this efficiently and diligently. I can't make your son appear. When you feel that what I'm doing isn't helping, say so, but know going in that it's expensive and time-consuming, and there are no guarantees."

He stood up and walked to the table. He produced a thick roll of twenties, stretched the elastic around his wrist, and began counting out piles of five.

"You don't have to pay up front," I said.

He didn't reply until there were six piles of five, fanned across the table like a poker hand.

"Six hundred is all the money I have," he said.

We both looked at the money silently.

"I can also pay you ten percent."

"Of what?"

"My business," he said, his posture perfect, dignified.

I was going to object, because I didn't want his money and because it wasn't nearly enough. It was an insult to say anything either way. I nodded and created an empty file on the Mac.

"Tell me everything," I said.

"Friday, March 6th was the day he went missing. I pulled Django James out of school to take with me. I had things to sell. An Ampex reel-to-reel, some coins, and a BMX bike. He was very fond of the bike. He helped me clean it, paint it, replace the chain. The previous owners hadn't cared for it, even though it was a Schwinn Stingray, the Bicentennial model. I let Django choose the new colour. He chose blue."

"The cleaning et cetera happened prior to that Friday?"

"Yes. We loaded the car in the morning. I sold the Ampex around ten to a music studio. Twelve hundred dollars. Cost me ten dollars fifty cents."

"Name of the studio and address?"

"Enola Curious. Broadway near Cambie, a couple of blocks from the Skytrain station."

"Who did you sell to?"

"Amelia Yates, she owns the studio."

"Is that Yates with an A or Yeats with an E-A?"

"I'm not sure," Szabo said. "She's bought from me in the past. We finished about 10:45, then Django and I went to some coin shops Downtown, but I didn't sell anything else."

"Let me stop you for a second," I said. "Why exactly did you pull your son out of class?"

"To show him."

"Show him what, exactly?"

"How the world works." He sat down, not on the bench, to the left of the desk in Katherine's chair. I watched him flex his left knee several times.

"School is important, of course," he said. "He has to get an education. But school doesn't tell you how to make money. How to survive. They teach you Tigris and Euphrates. Tigris and Euphrates is good, but try and pay the Hydro with Tigris and Euphrates."

"You pull him out often?"

"Once a month, usually. We go on holidays and Pro-D days as well."

"After the coin shops?"

"Lunch," he said. "We went to Little Mountain. He rode the bike around. He wanted to keep it. I told him we had to sell that bike, but we'd find another. Bikes are easy to find, but original BMX bikes are too valuable to keep."

"And he was upset over this?"

"Not upset. He's very well-behaved."

"Disappointed? Bummed out?"

"Yes, a bit. When I went to the bike store he sat in the car."

"What time was that?"

"One."

"One," I repeated, typing it into the file. "And after you sold the bike?"

"I didn't sell it," Mr. Szabo said. "The bike shop low-balled. Times are tough, he said. Not tough enough to give away a Stingray Bicentennial for chicken feed."

He waved his hand in dismissal of the owner.

"After, we went to a pawn shop, and that's where it happened: Django and I went into the store. I was talking to the owner. Django asked could he wait in the car. I gave him the keys. I made a deal with Mr. Ramsey who owns the shop. I came out and the car was gone." Anticipating my question he said, "2:43 p.m.," and repeated "Friday, March 6th."

"The car was never recovered?"

"No, it wasn't."

"Make and model?"

"Brown Taurus wagon, 1994. Transmission not so good, few dents in the passenger's side door. Previous owner practically gave it away."

"What happened then?"

"I was in shock for some time. I checked my watch. I looked around to see if I had parked somewhere else and forgot. I went into the store. I told the owner and his daughter my son had been taken. They smirked like I was joking. I kept saying it until they saw I was serious. They called the police for me. I repeated to them what happened again and again. An officer named —" He dug through his wallet, shuffling through business cards and creased scraps of paper. "Sergeant Herbert Lam." He offered me the card. I waved it away, aware of who Lam was.

"Any phone messages after?" I asked. "Any response to the news stories?"

"Someone said I should check a house on Fraser. Three tips said that, but it turned out to be the same person each time. Sergeant Lam said the woman had a problem with her neighbour and was trying to get the police to arrest her."

"Sounds like my grandmother."

I saved the file as *Szabo-prelim.txt* and sent it to the LaserJet.

"I'll need all the missing persons data, including a full description of Django, what he was wearing, dental charts if you've got them, the plate and VIN numbers from the car."

"I'll bring them tomorrow."

"Make it Monday," I said. "Give me time to run some of this down." I brought out the client and contract forms. "And I'll need everything McEachern worked up."

Mr. Szabo looked at the door. "I don't have that," he said.

"McEachern didn't give you a copy?"

"He did, but I was angry. I threw it at him. I told you, I overreact."

"I don't blame you," I said. "I'll talk with him."

We shook hands. On his way out Cliff Szabo turned back and said, "I love my son, Mr. Drayton."

"Never doubted it."

"They'll tell you I didn't," he said. "I'm not good at sharing such things. But I do love him," he reiterated, and was gone.

In my brief time on the job, I'd met few cops better than Herbert Lam. He'd been one of the legends of the VPD, up there with

Kim Rossmo and Al Arsenault, Dave Dickson and Whistling Smith. Lam was probably responsible for half a dozen missing children ending up back in the arms of their loved ones. A legacy to be proud of.

One evening in July, Lam and his family were driving home from Spanish Banks. A semi-trailer crossed the median, flipping the car, killing Lam and injuring his wife and daughter. I found this out from the front desk of the Main Street station. The news floored me. I wasn't Lam's age and I hadn't worked with him on the job, but I felt a sense of loss. In the movies the great detectives are obsessive geniuses. In real life, too often they're hard-working family men and women who don't deserve the ends they meet.

When Katherine came back at half past four I was on the phone trying to figure out who had taken over Lam's workload. I'd negotiated through the VPD phone maze to Constable Gavin Fisk's desk, only to get his voicemail. Fisk I knew. I'd gone through training with him. We'd once been friends.

Katherine read through the file while I waited for Fisk to pick up. He didn't and the call went to message. "Gavin, this is Mike Drayton. Concerning the Szabo kid. You have my number."

I hung up and tried Aries again, to no avail.

"He's so precise about the time," Katherine said.

"What does that tell you?"

"I guess it's possible he looked at his watch just before he noticed Django was missing." She studied my expression. "Is it possible he's lying?"

"Is that ever impossible?" I hung up the phone. "Sometimes an abundance of details means you're trying hard to convince someone something is true. More likely, though, after being grilled by the police several times, being interviewed by the press, not to mention McEachern, Szabo probably committed his best guess to memory and now repeats it as fact."

"So what does that tell you?" Katherine countered.

"That he's more concerned with emotional truth than empirical truth, as most of us are. Facts have to cohere into a story of some kind before we can deal with them."

Katherine had placed an ATM envelope on the corner of the table, currency visible through the holes. "What's that?"

"Five hundred dollars," she said. "Half of Laws's bonus. I couldn't take it all once I saw how much it was."

"It's yours," I said. "You earned it."

"When I worked at White Spot, management took a portion of the tips. Take it. Or put it into the business. Upgrade some of this shitty furniture."

I took the money. "What's your schedule for this semester?"

"I'm yours Tuesdays and Fridays starting next week."

"Drop out of school and come work for me."

She laughed. "Seriously?"

"I need the help."

"You want me to drop out and do this for the rest of my life? On what kind of wage?"

"You just got five hundred dollars."

"Is that likely to happen again?"

"We can negotiate," I said. "This isn't about money, it's about you fulfilling your calling."

She smirked. "Which is what?"

"Every person has a purpose to serve. This —" I swept my arm majestically around the room, Charlton Heston style "— is yours."

"And what's your calling, Mike?"

"I'm here to make sure you don't squander another three years on a bachelor's degree, and then the rest of your life in government service. Smart as you are, why the fuck would you want to work for the Canadian government?"

"Money. Security. Benefits."

"That's the language of fear."

"No, Mike, that's the language of adults."

I said, "Work here."

She said, "I'll think about it."

The Blessed Peacemakers

In the lobby of the Cambie Street police station, above the plaques commemorating the dead, is stenciled an excerpt of witness testimony from the Sermon on the Mount: "Blessed are the peacemakers, for they shall be called the children of God." Every time I step inside I'm drawn to that wall. I look from the scripture to the plaque beneath the word *peacemakers*. I stare at the bottom row. I find the photo of the clean-shaven man fourth from the end, and I lock eyes with him.

It's a photo my grandmother doesn't display. He is so eager to do good. His is the expression of a man who has never reckoned with deep uncertainty. His world is one where the law, the Sovereign, and God are perfect and infallible and in no way contradict one another. It's hard to look at that face and believe he would know anything about living in the world today.

My grandfather, Jacob Kessler, was born the year of *Stagecoach* and *Gone with the Wind*. A rawboned Mennonite from Moosefuck, Manitoba, he rebels, runs away from home, gets drunk, and enlists. After a stint in the navy he moves west, joins the Vancouver Police, meets a thin, sharply beautiful girl with a glint of prairie poverty in her eye. They have a son and a daughter: a nuclear family in the nuclear age.

The son eventually hangs himself. The daughter meets the draft-dodging scion of the Drayton & Kling Paper Products empire. They're together twelve years before they have a kid. The pressure gets to Jacob's son-in-law and he splits for an ashram in Southern California. His daughter follows as soon as she sheds the pregnancy weight. The kid only knows them as abstracts.

Around the house, Jacob was a dark presence, a stoop-shouldered, apelike, Victor McLaglen-type who drank lemon juice during the afternoons and Crown Royal in the evenings; who watched hockey scores and *Hee Haw* and owned three long-playing records, all of them Merle Haggard. Doted on me, took me camping and hunting, always teaching.

As a cop he never sought advancement and hated the brass. He stayed CFL, Constable For Life. In the seventies, his heyday, he was part of an anti-gang unit charged with taking the neighbourhoods back from the local gangs. Rumours abound about members of the H-Squad descending on the East Vancouver parks, preying on the predators, beating them senseless or worse. He didn't talk much about those days.

Six weeks before mandatory retirement, Jacob rousted a drunk who had passed out after rubbing fecal matter on the cenotaph in Victory Square. The drunk stabbed him in the throat with the broken-off handle of a sherry bottle, then high-tailed, taking his gun and radio.

Legend has it Jacob completed the walk to St. Paul's Hospital, passed out at the door, and never woke up.

Four years later, the moment I'd met the recommended minimum of post-secondary education, I dropped out of college and applied for the job.

It didn't work out. Which is why, on a cool Friday in September, three days before Labour Day, I was staring up at my grandfather's face, a stranger amid the day-to-day traffic of the Main Street station.

Gavin Fisk had said he'd be down in a minute. Seventeen minutes later he strolled out of the elevator, a hockey bag slung over his shoulder. A tall, muscular white man with a stubble-dotted head, wearing grey sweats and a shirt that said POLICE: THE WORLD'S LARGEST STREET GANG.

He grinned and grabbed my hand in an alpha-male hand-shake. I upped the torque of my own grip. Rule one for dealing with people like Gavin Fisk: never show weakness and never back down. Otherwise you'll spend every morning handing over your lunch money.

"Encyclopedia Brown," he said. "What'd you want to see me about?"

He didn't wait for my response but kept moving. We walked out of the station, down Wylie to the high-fenced lot beneath the Cambie Street Bridge that contained the motor pool and the staff parking.

"One of Lam's Missing Persons cases from earlier this year. Django James Szabo?"

"Lunatic father," Fisk said. We stopped by a white F350 spotted with gull shit, parked over the white line so it took up two spaces. He unlocked the canopy and hefted his hockey gear into the bed.

"I talked to him," he said, "took him through his story a couple times. He was real calm till we get to the questions nobody likes — did he hit his kid, did he fuck his kid, and I'm being diplomatic as hell — then out of nowhere he overturns the table and lunges at me."

"He was distraught."

"Yes, Mike, I guessed that too."

"You look into his story?"

Fisk unlocked the door of the cab and propped one foot on

the running board. He rolled down the window and threaded his arm through.

"If I remember right, he'd dragged his kid to a bunch of junk shops. They all remembered him, frequent customer or seller or whatever he was. He sold some old junk to a music studio. The hot piece of ass that owns the studio said the same thing, though I grilled her very thoroughly on the subject."

That wolfish grin. "What about the pawn shop?" I said.

"Not much to get out of them. Store tape shows the kid goofing around, his dad sending him to the car. Dad leaves, comes back, acts upset or a reasonable facsimile. They call the cops, the cops show up."

"Anything suspicious on the tape prior to their arrival?"

Fisk's good humour chilled a few degrees.

"No," he said. "'Magine that, no one walked in with a sign round their neck saying 'I plan to take a kid.' Has the dad unloaded his conspiracy theories on you yet?"

"He thinks it's a kidnapping."

"Of course. Because the idea his kid took off on his own is hard to take."

"You think he ran away?"

"From that nutjob? Wouldn't you?" Fisk sat and pulled the door closed. "Herb Lam had the same thought. Know what clinched it for me?"

Anything other than facts, I thought, but shook my head and said nothing.

"Szabo taught the kid to drive. Lanky kid, he could reach the pedals with the seat all the way forward."

"So nothing ever came up, no evidence someone might have taken the car with Django in it?"

He shook his head and started the engine.

I shouted, "You or Lam ever run down a list of carjackers?"

He shifted out of park but the truck didn't move. His gaze had frosted over.

"There's no way in your mind we could be right about this, is there?"

"I have to check either way," I said.

"You talk to Roy McEachern yet?"

"Won't return my calls."

"Drop my name if it helps." His warm, predatory smile flashed through. "You know Mira and I moved in together."

"Tell her I've still got her Jeff Buckley record if she wants it back."

"I'll make sure to tell her that. Take care, Mike."

The pickup peeled out in reverse, launching into traffic with a guttural roar of exhaust.

I walked back up Main to where I'd parked the Camry, wondering if Gavin Fisk was right, if I did want him to have made the wrong call so I could wave his failure in his face. *Any chance I was that petty?* I asked myself. *Maybe a little.*

Ben lived a block off East Broadway in a standalone building leased by reasonably-trustworthy Bohemians. The street-level storefront sold pottery and hand-carved African djembes. Four or five people lived on the second floor, sharing a kitchen and bathtub and toilet. "One of those old claw-footed tubs," Ben said with obvious pride. "The kind that pop up in novels about struggling artists in Manhattan lofts."

"Oh those kind," I'd said.

Today he was waiting on the corner across from the Fogg'N Suds, dressed in a black raincoat and matching vest, navy slacks and a pearl-coloured shirt and red and black silk tie. Except for the vest, it was the same outfit I was wearing.

"Jesus," I said. "Do I have time to go home and change?"

"Company uniform," Ben said.

"Why don't you stay home and brainstorm like you're supposed to?"

"I was," he said. "I had three pages of ideas this morning. I was working on a prequel game about Rosalind and Magnus before they met, showing how they were always just missing each other as they chase the same assassin. The player would alternate characters on each level. But the logistics sunk it. Too many coincidental near-misses and it becomes cute. And my audience hates cute. They want to see them tear someone's larynx out, not narrowly avoid meeting each other like some bad Robert Altman movie."

"I'm no expert on anything game-related," I said, aiming the car toward Kroon & Son. Up Granville then left on Marine Drive, then right into a cluster of industrial parks. Midday traffic on Granville was slower than usual, and I saw why: up ahead, flaggers in hard hats and reflective vests were funneling traffic down to one lane.

"You were saying?"

"Sorry?" My thoughts had been on the Szabos.

"You were saying," Ben said, "that you're not an expert on games."

"I'm not."

"But?"

"But what?"

"Weren't you getting ready to upbraid me about not working?"

I made the left. Marine Drive was no less busy, but traffic flowed more efficiently. "I don't get why you don't just write game three, you know? Like we were discussing the other day, how *Indiana Jones* is better than *Star Wars* 'cause at least the series moves forward. No one gives a shit about stuff that already happened."

"That's your entire job, isn't it? Telling people things that already happened?"

It was a fair point. "But yours is to tell people what happens next," I said. "So why not pick up where you left off?"

"I can't," Ben said, exasperated at the question. "It has to be note perfect. After three years' hiatus, if it's not note perfect, exactly the right blend of wisecracks and philosophy and gore —" He shrugged. "It'll let down the fan base."

"Hell with the fan base."

"But I'm one of them," he said. "We're Legion. It's got to be true to the original vision. If it's not, I've let myself down."

I ticked off the street addresses as we passed them, eyes out for 851. "You were seventeen when you had this quote-un-quote original vision? Nineteen when game one came out?"

"Your point being?"

"You're not a teen anymore. Few years you'll be thirty. What people like changes. I haven't listened to Screaming Trees since high school, and back then I didn't know about Stax Records or Blue Note."

"Your point being?" Teenager-sulky.

"Stop moping and come up with some new shit."

Silence until we pulled to the curb at the end of a long line of hearses. Of course it wasn't that easy for him. His work had ground to a halt in the years after Cynthia disappeared. Getting back to work frightened him. I didn't understand that. In the years after leaving the job, I'd have been happy to have work to cling to as everything else crumbled. Learning the ins and outs of private investigation had consumed a lot of nights that could have been spent self-destructively. In times of grief, the work is always there. I hoped one day I could make him see that.

As we exited the car, Ben said, "*The Young Indiana Jones Chronicles* went backwards."

* * *

The younger Thomas Kroon ushered us into an office that was tastefully accoutered, the huge brass-rimmed desk and the wall panelling a matching walnut. The word *sumptuous* came to mind.

"Pop can't make it," Younger said. "I'll give you a tour, introduce you as our security consultant. Then you'll have the run of the place."

I nodded my head at Ben. "My secretary here has never seen a decomp. You by any chance have some Vaseline?"

Younger looked at Ben. "Maybe he should avoid the back rooms," he said.

The outer office had two facing desks and a smaller empty desk behind, and an entire wall given over to a dry-erase board covered in inscrutable shorthand.

Carrie, a cheerful woman of about forty, handed a sheaf of papers to Kroon the Younger. Together they loaded the Xerox. At the opposite desk a portly young man worked the dispatch lines. He nodded at us as we passed.

"She did have the code," Younger said as we passed out of the offices, down a grey carpeted hallway to a wood door. Even before he opened it, the death-smell filled our nostrils. I looked over and saw Ben rock as if slapped in the face.

I dashed back down the hallway to the office. "Anyone smoke here?"

Carrie held up a pack of du Mauriers. "Down to my last three."

I broke a smoke in half and ripped off the filter. I handed Ben the two halves and instructed him how to wedge them into his nostrils. We followed Kroon inside the back room. A decomposing body has a cloying, tangy odour. There were several in the room, on gurneys, in bags. A wide-hipped black woman sat at the embalming table reading a Walter Mosely novel while the fluids drained out of a Caucasian lady, green-skinned by now, weighing conservatively five hundred pounds.

"Meck," Ben said.

I noted the camera above the door, its red light on. The wire ran down to a plug to the left of the basin. "Back up power source?" I asked.

"The battery is supposedly good for eight hours," Younger said.

"Guh," Ben said.

We toured the freezer, the storage room, the freight elevator. The crematorium was in a separate building out back. The burying ground and all-purpose chapel was a few blocks east.

"Keys to the back door?" I asked.

"Pop and Jag and Carrie and I. Though I assume anyone could duplicate them."

"What about the elevator?"

"Locked at night."

"Chuh," Ben said.

"Rest room?" I asked.

"Hallway, second door on the right," Younger said. Ben took off, sprinting.

I held out my hands apologetically, what can you do?

"Good help is hard to find," Younger said.

Back in his office I said, "I'd like to put the building under physical surveillance. That means staying overnight. Most of these people work Monday to Friday?"

"Except Vonda, our part-time embalmer, and Kurt the dispatcher. And my father and I."

"I'm going to disconnect the red LEDs from the camera," I said. "I want you to tell everyone just before closing, tonight and tomorrow and the next, that the camera isn't working and that the system will be down for the next few days. Remind them to lock up."

"I could tell them there have been vandals in the area, which is why we're upgrading security. I could even advise them to take all their valuables home."

"You could mention it," I said, "but don't overdo the theatrics. We don't want this to look like a trap. Best to just add a few words to the bottom of a memo or post it in the break room."

"Understood," Younger said. "You'll be here tonight?"

"After closing."

"I'll inform Pop."

I stood up. "I'll let myself out."

Ben was leaning on the hood of the Camry, vest off, shirt unbuttoned, a touch of sick around his mouth.

"Can you bring the car back for seven tomorrow?" I asked him as I unlocked the trunk.

"You're really going to stay there overnight?"

"Looks that way."

In a nylon tech bag in the trunk I keep a laptop and a pair of battery-operated wireless cameras. I also keep an overnight bag. Depending on the situation, I sometimes bring a gun.

I opened the suitcase, pulled out enough clothes so I could fit the tech bag inside, and covered it with a toiletries kit. Ben looked like he needed some encouragement.

"You get used to it," I said. "It's like if you lived near a rendering plant. You stop minding after a while."

"How long is a while?"

"It's less of a shock every time."

"When'd you see your first?" Ben asked.

"August, year before I graduated high school. Victim died of exsanguination, meaning he bled out from a neck wound." Adding the inevitable, "My grandfather."

"Oh," Ben said. "Hey. Sorry."

"You didn't kill him."

I took out the suitcase and closed the trunk. "I've got two hours to kill. Drop me at the Wendy's just up the street." Then, to lighten the mood, I added, "You know the sound maggots make when they're gnawing on soft tissue?"

"No."

I simulated it.

Ben doubled over and puked straight into the gutter.

Later, in the silence and darkness of the office, with the cameras up and trained to cover the perimeter of the embalming room, I sat back in the sumptuous leather chair in the Kroons' sumptuous office and dialed the number for Aries Security and Investigations.

"May I ask who's calling?" the office manager said.

"Bill Billings. I'm phoning on the recommendation of Constable Gavin Fisk. Would it be possible to speak to Mr. McEachern, please?"

"Just a moment, sir."

The dominant sounds in the still evening were the hum of the freezer in the adjacent room and the whir of the laptop's hard drive. No movement in the embalming room.

"Roy McEachern speaking. Mr. Billings, is it? What can I do for you?"

I said, "You could have the courtesy to return a fucking phone call."

"Is that Michael Drayton?" McEachern laughed, staccato bursts that taxed the phone's speaker. "Well, Mike, you got through. I have to hand it to you."

"You blocked my caller ID?"

"We had several offensive crank calls from that number."

"What a pity. That robot who answers your phone must be quite distressed."

"We could go back and forth all night," McEachern said. "My time's too valuable, I don't know about yours."

"I've inherited an ex-client of yours named Cliff Szabo."

More of McEachern's easy laughter. "Mike Drayton and Cliff Szabo — a match made in heaven right there. Did he try to pay you with ten percent of his business?"

Ignoring him I said, "He was your client from April till August."

"Off and on, depending on when he felt like paying us. When he laid that ten percent scheme on me I told him I'd love to work for free, pal. Just convince my ex-wife and two kids in college. All seriousness, Mike, don't allow a client to gyp you out of dough just because he's got a sad story. Sad stories are free."

"I'd like an overview of what Aries did for Mr. Szabo. Who you interviewed, what information you gathered."

"All in the report we prepared for him."

"Which he left in your office."

"After tossing it at me."

"He was distraught."

"Sure," McEachern said, "but not about his poor little kid, about paying us the nine grand he owed us."

"He'd like his copy of the report."

"That ship has sailed."

"I'd appreciate it."

"You I like even less than him," McEachern said. "Only reason I haven't told you to go fuck yourself yet is on account of your grandfather. Tell you what, though. Szabo comes up with the nine he still owes us, I'll c.c. you all the copies you want."

"Any media coverage he gets he'll be speaking about the investigation," I said. "You want me to recommend he tells the CBC that you took his money and were no help to him?"

"You really think you'd come out ahead in a PR war, Mike?"

I took a breath through my nostrils and held it until I could pick out the Pine Sol and the death-smell and the lingering aftershave of Thomas Kroon the Younger.

I said, "How about for a few minutes you not be a prick and email me the report so we can maybe find this kid?"

"Fuck yourself, Mike."

Click.

Enola Curious

The next morning I gave myself a whore's bath in the cramped washroom of my office. I plugged in the plastic kettle and traded my suit for black jeans and a blue flannel shirt, loose-fitting and faded: the two best qualities in a garment. I made a pot of Earl Grey and stood out on the narrow wooden balcony watching the clouds douse Beckett Street and listening to Blind Willie Johnson.

The night had been uneventful. The elder Kroon had opened up around six. When I told him nothing had been disturbed, he said, "Maybe we're done with all this awfulness."

Ben had only been half an hour late and I was back at the office by 7:15. I could've gone home, walked my dog, taken my grandmother out for a scone. I could've gone to sleep. But I felt like doing exactly what I was doing, which was, or amounted to, nothing.

The buzzer buzzed. On the monitor Cliff Szabo climbed the stairs carrying a milk crate full of papers. I held the door for him, directed him to put the crate on the table.

"Here's everything," he said.

It didn't amount to much. A comprehensive missing persons report with dental charts and a description of the boy's clothing, the full report of the brown Ford Taurus with VIN and license number, an inventory of the car's contents, including a photo of the repainted Schwinn Stingray. Szabo had also collected press clippings and copies of the flyers. I moved the Loeb file onto Katherine's chair so I could spread the Szabo clippings out.

"You taught Django how to drive?" I asked him.

"I let him drive around parking lots." He drank from a bottle of water he'd brought with him. "People are so stupid when they drive, he should start now so he doesn't become like them."

"Fisk seems to think he took off in the car."

"Where would he go?"

"No idea," I said. "Is he close to any of your relatives?"

"His mother died when he was two from an embolism." His pronunciation slowed around the last word. "Her parents are dead. My sister lives with us. When you want to talk to her she's there."

We drank our beverages. The office was cool, owing to the fact that I'd left the balcony door open a crack. A car with an overdriven subwoofer passed by, hip hop trickling down toward Cordova. Saturday, September 5th. Almost seven months from the date of disappearance.

"I spoke to Fisk and I spoke to McEachern," I said, hitting print and standing to wait for the pages to land in the LaserJet's tray. "So far all I've heard is a bunch of bullshit. Which means we're starting at square one."

Szabo's expression didn't change.

"I'm going to re-interview everyone, starting with the people who saw Django that Friday. Then everyone who knew him from school. Then your neighbours. Losing McEachern's files isn't setting us back all that much, because I'd do this anyway."

"Good," Szabo said.

"We'll make up new flyers and get them posted around the city, and if we can afford it, take out some ads. There are online groups dedicated to getting information out. Pastor Flaherty might be able to help us finagle some press coverage."

He nodded, following me.

"I'll also contact all the police agencies in B.C., Alberta, and Washington State, have them check any unidentified remains against the description. If you have anything with your son's DNA —"

"The sergeant took some things of his." Same level expression.

"If you've got others, keep them handy, though your own DNA will do in a pinch."

I handed him the two pages, listing the addresses of the shops he and Django visited and the day's itinerary up to the hour of disappearance.

"Can you think of any place you went that's not on this list?"

Szabo unfolded a pair of flimsy reading specs and went over it. "Seems to be it."

"If you think of anywhere else," I said.

"I'll tell you."

"Good. Let's meet every Friday for the next month or so. Anything else you think of you write down, no matter how trivial."

"I will."

"Last thing: Fisk said you overturned a table during your interview."

"I was upset," he said. "Like I told you, some —"

"— times you overreact, got it. Not anymore. From here on out you are the model of restraint. We can't afford offending anyone else. What's more, I need you to apologize to Fisk. I know that sucks, but we need him to pity you."

"I don't want anyone's pity."

"It's not for you. Apologize, kiss his ass, get him to work with us."

"All right," he said. "I suppose I should do the same with Mr. McEachern?"

"No, fuck him," I said, then checked myself. "No, you're right, it would help to be on good terms with him, too."

"All right."

"See you next week, then."

"All right."

He'd reached the door when he about-faced and placed a fistful of bills and change on the table, spreading it out so I could count it. "Seventy-three dollars," he said. "Ten percent."

I put the music up, reused the teabag for a second pot, and worked my way through the Szabo file. Quarter past ten Katherine came in. She shed her soaked peacoat, hung her umbrella on the balcony rail, and said, "Don't ever ask me to do that again."

"She appreciated it. And you said you liked animals."

"The front ends of animals, Mike. The cute, cuddly ends."

"Least in this job, unlike, say, government service, your exposure to assholes is brief and irregular, pardon the pun."

She looked at the overturned crate and the papers on the table. She noticed the Loeb file on her chair. "Should I file this?"

"No, it's important it stays out."

"Where?"

"I don't know. We'll move it when we get back. Did your boyfriend lend you the van?"

"His mother's minivan," she said. "With express instructions it's back by noon."

"We won't be any longer than that."

"Damn right we won't."

"But we do have some stops to make," I said.

* * *

I love Staples. It's an irrational love, but genuine. Only book stores and the Army & Navy inspire the same level of ardour. I love the ten-dollar packages of parchment and the locked display case of ballpoint pen refills. I love the bins of cheapjack school supplies, dollar-ninety-nine plastic hole punches, thirty-nine-cent cahiers. I love the row of overpriced lockboxes and safes and the solitary Brother typewriter in the last aisle next to the ribbons and correcting tape. Every item in the store seems both necessary and frivolous, and the store itself seems aware of this paradox. The cashiers will find any justification you come up with entirely reasonable, even if you yourself don't believe your business really requires a tri-coloured stamp set that says *Welcome!* in eight languages.

By the time we'd circumnavigated the store I'd bought a stack of folding chairs, two stainless steel filing cabinets, and a year's supply of alligator clips and legal pads. Katherine had added an ergonomic keyboard and a CO_2-powered dust remover. She circled back through the furniture section to re-examine a pleather-covered office chair.

"Look," she said, using the lever to raise herself incrementally and then with one depression sink till her knees were above her waist. "We should get a matching pair."

"Not me. I need four legs and wood so I can tip it back against the wall."

"You could get hurt doing that."

"I live on the edge, Hough."

She grinned. "Well, I'm getting one. And a ridged plastic office mat to go underneath it."

"Oh, you have to get the mat."

"It's more of an investment then an accessory, really."

"Have to spend money to make money."

After doling out my debit card to the cashier, we ran through the rain, pushing our purchases down to where we'd parked. We folded down the van's seats and squeezed everything into the back, abandoning the shopping carts on the curb.

As Katherine inched out of the parking spot, I said, "How many government jobs let you pick your furniture?"

"You know," she said, "there are always going to be other students looking for part-time work."

"It took a long time for me to get used to your many short-comings. I don't want to go through that every year."

"What you mean to say is, it's hard to find someone gullible enough to administer a suppository to your dog."

"Is that what I mean?" The dashboard clock read 11:40. I brought out Django's itinerary and gave Katherine directions to Enola Curious Studios.

"We'll be quick," I promised.

The studio was on the third floor of a yellow building just off Broadway and Quebec. Katherine parked beneath an overhanging maple tree behind the property, her boyfriend's mother's silver Odyssey slotting between a beige Vanagon and a custard-coloured Mustang.

The studio's double-door back entrance was locked. We walked around and caught the front door as a skinny beret-wearing kid was exiting. He looked grateful for the help as he maneuvered his upright bass through the doorway.

On the landing, three forty-year-olds in punk regalia were passing around a joint. Two of them leered at Katherine. The third leered at me. Only as we reached the last flight could I hear soft music from inside. As I opened the hallway door the music got louder, and by the time we were standing at the studio entrance I recognized the song as a thrash-metal cover of "The Way You Look Tonight."

"Get it? Because it's ironic," I said to Katherine as I knocked on the door.

The music cut off. I knocked again. Bare feet padded across the carpet. The door opened and a woman ushered us in. Before I could ask if she was Amelia Yates or Yeats she had disappeared through a glass-paned door at the end of the hall.

On the left side of the hallway was a live room with a piano in the corner, patch-cords snaked across the floor, and a drum kit in the centre surrounded by a forest of microphones on boom stands. The walls were covered with ribbed foam. Movable baffles had been set up around the kit. The right side of the hall led to smaller rooms: a storage closet containing, among other things, a Fender Rhodes and a sitar, two isolation booths with ancient-looking Koss headphones hanging off music stands, and a break room with a pink-upholstered couch.

"Must be worth a fortune," Katherine said.

From the glass room the music blasted out, stopped, blasted out, stopped.

I opened the door to the central booth. The woman was facing away from us, staring at a pair of computer monitors each bigger than my grandmother's television. Her crescent-shaped mahogany desk was flanked by speakers, no doubt positioned equidistant from her ears. A half-finished bottle of Diet Dr. Pepper with a pink straw stuffed inside sat next to the office chair.

"Miss Yates?" I said.

"Just a sec, just a sec." She manipulated a wave form on one of the screens, pulled down a menu on the other. She held up her hand, gesturing for us to wait.

The walls were decorated with framed photos, a gold record, a letter of nomination from the Juno Awards, an official thank-you from some fundraiser. I was looking for clarification on the Yates-Yeats question, but the documents were evenly split. I picked out faces in the photos. The crème de la crème of Canadian music superstardom: the bald guy from the Tragically Hip, Randy Bachman's brother, one of the bald guys from the Barenaked Ladies, Dan Ackroyd in his Elwood Blues get-up, Randy Bachman's son, Colin James, Avril Lavigne, the bald guy from *Hard Core Logo*, and Randy Bachman. And on the door, a very nice signed photo of a young Amelia Yates or Yeats in between the Wilson sisters from Heart.

"Look," Katherine whispered, nudging me no doubt to inspect one of the photos. Instead she pointed to Yeats's chair. "Same as the one I just bought."

"Then you've got a lot in common."

"Okay, sorry," Ms. Yates said, swivelling to face us. "Just have to bounce this down for those creeps in the hall."

The song started up again and we were forced to endure the entire two minutes and fifteen seconds. When it finished, she said, "How's it sound?"

"Fine," Katherine said with exceeding politeness, or at least her version of it.

"I'm sure The Man will feel it's been suitably stuck to him," I said.

"Punk's not my thing either," she said, "but you have to admit those drums sound lethal."

She was unnervingly beautiful. To give a laundry list of her attributes with a poetic rendering of measurements and hues would miss the quality that made her that way — brown hair, brown eyes, brown skin, purple slacks, and an oversized Joan Jett tee exposing one perfect shoulder. Mussed hair swept back from her face. She was the kind of impossible thin that we decry in polite company, before retreating to privacy to think about lithe hips and small high firmly sculpted breasts. She didn't look fragile, though, or arrogant. Just preoccupied.

The tray on her computer ejected a disk. Amelia Yates handed the disk to Katherine. "Could you run this over to them?"

Katherine balked but took the disk and left the room, shooting me a what-a-bitch roll of her eyes.

"Ms. Yates," I said. "First, is it *Yates* as in Rowdy or *Yeats* as in 'Rough Beast?'"

"Either or," she said. "It's a made-up name. My dad always spelled it A-T-E-S because it seemed more American. But he was born in the West Indies, spent most of his childhood in London, and the last thing he wanted was to be reminded of anything or anyone British."

"Irish," I said.

"Same difference. So pick a spelling."

"I like E-A," I said. "My name's Mike Drayton, I'm a private investigator."

"Cliff hired you."

"Right," I said.

"He told me this morning you might be coming by." She pointed to a large grey box in the corner of the room, its empty reels like owlish metal eyes. "That's the reel-to-reel. I asked him if he had a source for new two-inch tape. He's working on it. He's a good guy to know. I'm so sorry about Django."

"Could you take me through that Friday?"

She nodded, uncapped her soda. "He got here about ten with the Ampex. I had the money for him. We dickered for a little bit." She shrugged, exposing more of that shoulder. "And then he left."

"Django was with him the whole time?"

"Pretty much. He likes to bang on the drums, so he did that while Cliff and I discussed price."

"He seemed okay?"

"Django?" She smiled. "He's a great kid. I gave him a CD of his namesake, which he seemed to appreciate. He didn't seem like he got many gifts."

"You think the relationship with his father was ..." I let her finish the sentence.

"I don't know. Cliff seems like a good dad. Just strict. But then Cliff could've been worried he'd break something expensive. I told Cliff it's fine, let him play the drums. It's just stuff, right?"

I asked her more questions just to ask her questions. When Katherine came back to tell me we had to go, Amelia Yeats was telling me about the studio.

"I named it after a band I started in grade ten with a girl-friend of mine. We'd do Heart and Zep covers, as well as our awful originals. We were playing up that are-they-lovers angle. Got us an opening slot on a Bif Naked tour. We were never as good live as we were in the studio, since Alison was always nervous singing in front of an audience. But it was the first time I did something musical that didn't have anything to do with my dad."

"We really have to go," Katherine said over my shoulder.

"Your dad was who?" I asked, standing up but keeping my back to the door.

"He still is," she said. "Chet Yates. The producer."

"Wow," I said, not recognizing the name.

"Yeah. When your dad's photo album has pics of Hendrix and Syd Barrett, you're kind of in the music biz whether you want to be or not." She gestured at the room, the studio, the building. "But I've done all right for myself."

"Who've you worked with?" I asked, but Katherine insisted and I let myself be dragged from the room. Amelia Yeats waved and walked us out, trailing behind to lock the door.

"Any other questions, call," she said.

In the confines of the van, Katherine said to me, "It's ten past one."

"Yeah."

"I'm late getting the car back, Mike."

"Yeah."

"What a self-centred ass."

"Her or me?"

"Both."

"I thought she was all right."

"No kidding," Katherine said.

V

Puritans and True Believers

Eyeball three parts Canada Dry club soda, add one part President's Choice red grape juice, a thimble's worth of lemon juice and the same of lime. It's important to add the ingredients in that order, as the grape juice is heavier and won't mix properly if added first. My grandmother took these tonics medicinally at two in the afternoon and again at seven, claiming they levelled off her blood sugar and took the place of a diuretic. When she called down to ask if I wanted one, I was as dead to the world as one of the Kroons' customers. I mumbled a yes instead of asking for tea.

I'd spent Saturday night back in the funeral home, and had the same to look forward to tonight. I'd lasted about thirty hours tweaked on caffeine and a disappearing-reappearing Yeats-inspired erection. I took a shower in the basement stall, then dressed and headed upstairs.

My grandmother had set up one of her TV trays on the back porch. We sat and looked at the carnage wrought by last night's windstorm. That morning, when I'd delivered my dog from the throes of constipation, the laurel bushes that served as a fence between us and our neighbour had been rocking ferociously. Now, as I ate half the tuna sandwich my grandmother made, I watched the dog inspect the fallen branches and root beneath the laurel leaves that carpeted our backyard.

"You sure you don't mind doing the yard?" My grandmother's way of introducing a chore she wanted done.

"No big deal, Gran."

"And the doorframe, you'll take care of that?"

"I'll get it done."

"I know. You've just been busy. Like your grandfather, always working even when you're not."

We watched the dog toy with the slack clothesline, fumbling a clothes-peg about the yard with her snout.

"Too bad that's not a power line," my grandmother said.

At 3:00 a.m. I woke up behind the desk in the Kroons' office, bathed in the glow from the laptop. I could hear what sounded like plastic being dragged across concrete. The screen showed no movement in the nearby rooms. I stood up, conscious of the bulge in my pants, thinking if I'd attended to that and ignored the yard work, I probably wouldn't have fallen asleep. I was glad there wasn't a camera on me.

I trained my Mag-Lite on the carpet, walked to the door of the embalming room, and threw the door open. It slammed off the wall. I hit the lights. Nothing.

The sound had stopped. I killed the lights and shut the door. Down the hallway and back to the room, silence except for my own footfalls. At the door to the office I heard the same scraping sound from the break room. I trained the light through the glass door and saw a mouse beat a swift retreat to the darkness of the space behind the cupboards.

I relaxed, thinking, that's exactly how the situation plays out in a horror movie, right before Jason Voorhees appears and eviscerates some unsuspecting co-ed.

I went back to the office and sat down behind the desk in the darkness and the silence. I turned off the Mag-Lite.

"Guess there's nothing to be afraid of," I said, hoping it was true.

Monday afternoon I stumbled sleep-deprived into my office, collected my notes and the list of questions I'd prepared, and headed out to interview the proprietor of Imperial Exchange and Pawn, the last place Django James Szabo had been seen. I was at the door when I remembered to dump the receipts I'd just collected on the table and Katherine's package on her desk (a special-delivery box that contained some kind of sex toy she'd been too embarrassed to have sent to her home because her father opens her mail). As I did this I chanced to look up at the car calendar and noticed it was Labour Day, a statutory holiday, and nothing was open. The only person foolish enough to be in their office on this fine rainless afternoon was me.

Tuesday I was outside of Imperial Pawn at 9:54 a.m. I spent the minutes in my car sucking back a London Fog and holding Thorstein Veblen's *Theory of the Leisure Class* in front of me and trying to make sense of the letter-like markings within it. It was the kind of book where you have to read every sentence at least three times to figure out what's going on, and by then you've forgotten the context. I try to alternate reading something educational with reading something fun, a sort of Nabisco Frosted Mini-Wheats reading program. I'd finished the Leonard on Monday; before that it had been Eric Hoffer's *The True Believer*. I liked Hoffer: every other sentence read like it could have been on a fridge magnet. The Veblen was harder going. Occasionally, though, you'd come across something like this:

> As has been indicated in an earlier chapter, there is reason to believe that the institution of ownership has begun with the ownership of persons, primarily women. The incentives to acquiring such property have apparently been: (1) a propensity for dominance and coercion; (2) the utility of these persons as evidence of the prowess of their owner; (3) the utility of their services.

I was struggling with that when I saw a hairy arm twist the sign on the door to WE ARE OPEN. A moment later, the neon sign flickered to life. It was 10:02 a.m.

Imperial Pawn was located on the corner of a strip mall. There were a few parking spaces in front of the shop, and a larger lot around back. Cliff Szabo's Taurus had been parked on the side street. I'd looked the area over when I arrived, as if the months between the disappearance and now might have left some trace. But of course there was nothing to see. No traffic cameras, no nearby stores. Across the street were a Value Village and a large, empty parking lot. Doubtless the people there had been grilled by the police, but I made a note to ask them again once I finished with Imperial Pawn.

An electronic bell dinged when I entered the store. "Morning," I said to the corpse behind the counter. He was sitting on a stool behind a cash register, arms crossed as if daring business to shows its face. Thick beard and thick eyebrows, a Chia Pet growing on each arm. A flattened Roman nose. He gave the slightest of nods.

Glass counters ran nearly the length and width of the

store. Under the glass were cameras and iPods and Xboxes and paintball gear and jewellery. A shelf of DVDs stood in the middle, a CD tower in the corner. Shelves bolted to the wall held TVs and computer monitors, the odd turntable or snare drum. The cement floor around the shelves was reserved for power tools and speaker wedges. Behind the case was a door, open just a crack, leading to what looked like storage. In the corner above the cash register was a camera, trained on the exit.

"My name is Michael Drayton. I'm a private investigator. I'm sure you remember Cliff Szabo and his son."

Recognition in his eyes. He said nothing.

"I'm also sure you told the events of that afternoon to countless people — the police and the media, and maybe other investigators. But I'd like you to tell it again, if you don't mind. What can I call you, sir?"

He seemed reluctant to answer, but at last he said, "Ramsey."

"Mr. Ramsey, okay. And do you own the store, Mr. Ramsey?"

No response. He stared at me, unblinking, a statue of diffidence.

"Were you working here on Friday the 6th of March? If so, were you in the store when Mr. Szabo and his son were here?"

He shook his head.

"But you do know who Mr. Szabo is?"

He nodded.

"You do business with him every so often?"

Nod.

"How would you characterize Mr. Szabo?"

No response.

"What's he like? Good guy?"

Ramsey cleared his throat. "Good guy, yes."

"And his son Django?"

"A good guy, yes."

"How often did Mr. Szabo come in?"

Pause. "Three times."

"Including March 6th?"

"Four times."

"You saw him on the 6th?"

"Yes."

"Did he usually buy or sell?"

"Both."

"What did he bring in to sell on March 6th?"

"I don't know."

"You can't remember?"

"I wasn't there."

"On March 6th."

"Yes."

"Who was tending the store?"

"Tending?"

"Who was sitting where you are right now?"

He blinked. "My daughter."

"She dealt with Mr. Szabo on that day?"

"Yes."

"What's her name?"

Hesitation. "Lisa."

"When will Lisa be in?"

"Not today."

"Tomorrow? Thursday?"

"Thursday."

"I'll be back Thursday then." I closed up my notebook, the page empty. While we'd been talking a dreadlocked white kid in cutoffs and sandals had entered the store and started perusing the racks of dusty Nintendo games. I thanked Mr. Ramsey for his time. He didn't respond.

* * *

Tuesday, 2:50 p.m.

Place: Brahmin Stamps Coins and Collectables, 3rd Street.

Speaker: Germit Gil, owner and proprietor

"Yes, I've done much business with Mr. Szabo. I believe he is a good man. I like his son very much. At least once a month I'd see him. Sometimes he brought his son. I liked them very much. They seemed happy. He sold me some silver coins that day. I still have them. A very good man. I'm very sorry for him."

Wednesday, 10:45 a.m.

Place: Coin Land, International Village Mall

Speaker: Bill Koch, store manager

"Cliffy, yeah, he did stop by that day. Sucks for him, huh? He'd bring the kid but usually send him to the food court with a dollar. A single dollar, like four quarters. What can you buy with that, a packet of ranch dressing? He never seemed cross with the kid, but he's not an affectionate guy. But then I knew a guy in the service, nicest, most brave guy I ever met. They found two hookers buried under his house. Goes to fucking show you, doesn't it?"

Wednesday, 12:10 p.m.

Place: Diaz Bicycles and Sporting Equipment, West Broadway

Speaker: Arturo Diaz, co-owner

"You know how I know Django ran away? 'Cause whenever they came into my place Cliff would tell him not to go anywhere, not to touch anything, and Django would usually do both. We'd look around and he'd be gone. Then we'd find him downstairs trying to pedal one of the ten-speeds. Just the kind of kid he was. No, Cliff never hit Django that I saw, but maybe he should've. My dad tuned me up a few times. That's how we learn."

Wednesday, 2:00 p.m.

Place: Mumbai Sweets, Cambie Street and 49th

Speaker: Ashraf Dillon

"Don't remember, sorry. Lots of people bring their kids to eat. Rice or naan?"

Wednesday, 3:45 p.m.

Place: Emily Carr Elementary School, King Edward and Laurel

Speaker: Henrietta Chang-Clemenceau, seventh grade teacher

"It was so horrible, so sad. It's why I changed schools. No, I never noticed any physical abuse, bruises and such. Believe me, if I had I would have spoke up then and there. But I'm pretty attuned to moods and attitudes, and Django was troubled. He'd rarely write in his Classroom Journal, and when he did it was about looking forward to the next Friday when his dad would take him out of school. I had words with his father about that.

"I guess that seems counter-intuitive, that you would look forward to spending more time with someone who treats you poorly — and believe me, I did witness Mr. Szabo treat Django like that several times, snapping at him to get his coat, expressing frustration when he didn't move fast enough. Have you heard of the Stockholm Syndrome? You may think it's bull, but I've seen it.

"Between us? What's so horrible, Mr. Drayton, is that I can't shake from my head the idea, the feeling, that Mr. Szabo killed his poor son."

Thursday I hung back until half past eleven. I'd made about fifty pages' progress in the Veblen, decidedly less on either of my cases. I'd met with the Kroons and we decided to give the Corpse Fucker two more months of weekends: if he hadn't reappeared by Hallowe'en, we'd leave the cameras up but forego the nightly watch. That meant resigning ourselves to another attack. No one was happy with that. Everyone agreed to it.

When I walked into Imperial Pawn I saw Mr. Ramsey seated on the stool showing unpolished jewellery to a lanky East Asian woman of about forty. They were the only two people in the room.

"Afternoon," I said. "Is your daughter in?"

Ramsey looked at me as if he'd never set eyes on me before, and wasn't all that impressed now that he had. He turned his attention back to the woman, helped her with the clasp on a bracelet.

I leaned over the counter close enough so the two of them were within arm's reach. "Did some tragic illness befall her? A seventy-two-hour virus, maybe?"

"I like this one," the woman said. Ramsey nodded.

Looking between them I said, "I don't understand why you're not more cooperative, considering you and your daughter are two of the last people to see that child before he went missing."

The woman looked up, looked at me, looked at Ramsey. "What child?" she asked.

I took a flyer from my coat pocket and unfolded it. Two Django James Szabos stared at her, the petulant expression from the school photo and a lower-quality image blown up from a birthday photo taken by his aunt.

"He disappeared just out front, parked in a car on that side street." I pointed through the wall. "Mr. Ramsey hasn't been much help. I'm not really sure why." I turned to Ramsey and gave him an expression of innocent puzzlement. "Do you not want the child to be found, Mr. Ramsey?"

"I don't want to get mixed up," he said in explanation to his customer, who had withdrawn from the counter, leaving the bracelet.

"You put your own convenience over a missing child?"

"I don't know anything."

"Not what he said on Tuesday," I told the woman.

She said something to Ramsey that I didn't catch, but couldn't have been too different from "I want nothing to do with you, asshole."

After he had buzzed her out, Ramsey turned to me, dull fury written on his face.

"She looked like a good customer," I said. "That would've been, what, a four-hundred-dollar sale?"

"Get out of my store."

"Where's your daughter?"

"She doesn't know anything. Go."

"We both know you were there," I said. "You think Szabo didn't tell me? Or that the cops wouldn't back him up, I ask them?" I picked up the bracelet and let it fall. "The fact you tried to game me tells me something."

No answer, just a sullen, unblinking stare. I pounded my fist on the table, causing the jewellery to rattle and Ramsey to wobble on his stool. He was squat and solid-looking, but age and a sedentary lifestyle were working against him. Once he regained his balance he was quick to sweep the jewellery back into its display box.

"See, I don't think you'd hurt a child. You have one of your own, which generally means you have some degree of empathy. But why run interference for someone like that? Kind of parent does that to another parent?"

"I know nothing," he reiterated. I could tell by his expression the words sounded false even to his ears. I could also tell that he'd cling to them as long as he could.

"How 'bout you talk to me and let's decide that together. Doesn't have to involve the law or anyone else. Or you could talk directly to Mr. Szabo."

The door to the back room opened. If Ramsey had wavered at all during our conversation, at the sight of his daughter his will was re-forged. Lisa was about my age, pear-shaped, with a face buried under bronzer and red lipstick.

"You get the hell out of here," she said to me. "He's not talking to you. Ever. Understand?"

"He said you were the one who dealt with Szabo."

"You're a police officer?"

"Private detective working for —"

"I don't care," she said. "Get out or I call the real police."

I nodded and walked to the door to wait for her to buzz me out. Propping the door open, I turned back to hurl some scathing putdown at them. I started to point out that between the two of them they had one pair of eyebrows, but it was too much of a mouthful. I drove home alternating between coming up with better insults and telling myself I was the bigger man for holding my tongue. The perfect ending for a day/week/month full of mistakes, false starts, and what-could-have-beens.

Thursday, 7:30 p.m.

Place: Szabo residence, a small house with a wide paint-stripped back porch.

Speaker: Agatha Szabo, aunt of Django James.

"I can tell something about you, Mr. Drayton. I can tell you were a lonely child. So you know what it's like. I was like that. So is Django. Cliff? No, he was always too angry to be lonely.

"Django is quiet. He sees everything — that he gets from his father. It's hard for him to fit in.

"I know what his teachers think — that he was unhappy at home, or that Cliff was a bad father. It's not true. He's strict about business, yes, but he loves his son. And Django loves him. When Django was younger, Cliff would read to him every night.

"Since he's been gone, Cliff has become short-tempered. He's angry at himself. His business has been slow, and he makes mistakes he never would have before. He was distraught when Marisa died, but it was easy for him to know what emotion to feel. He's lost now.

"The policeman, Fisk, seemed to think Django might have taken off in the car. I don't believe it. He wouldn't leave his father and I. He was very well-behaved.

"What do I think happened? I haven't said it, even to myself. It's too horrible to say. But I think it all the time. My beautiful nephew.

"I dream about him often."

VI

The Ethereal Conduit of Madame Thibodeau

"He's been sleeping for the last two hours," I heard my grandmother say as she led someone down into the basement. I imagined them in single file, proceeding cautiously down the stairs, the only light my grandmother's torch. And me, lurking in that basement like some cut-rate Cthulhu, waiting for the seals on my sarcophagus to be broken.

The expedition reached the lower depths of the household. I emerged from my room stumbling and rubbing my eyes. I saw Katherine and Ben, noted their reactions, and debated whether they'd think less of me if I turned around and retreated back into my room.

"Did you forgot Monday's a work day?" Katherine asked.

"I didn't forget." I took the mail from my grandmother. "Just felt like taking a personal day."

"Usually you phone in and tell the office."

I tore up the flyers and subscription renewal warnings. "Usually Mondays the office is empty."

"Would you like some lunch?" my grandmother asked me.

"I'm fine," I said.

"Well, would you mind putting on some pants?"

I stepped into a pair of jeans, turned on the light and ushered them inside. My grandmother retreated to the sanctity of the upstairs. I sat on the bed, motioned Katherine into the threadbare love seat. Ben stood against the wall. Usually he needed to be at the centre of any discussion. Today he held back.

"So what's going on?" I said, groping behind the headboard to find my moccasins.

"You tell us," Katherine said. "Mr. Szabo dropped off some money. About sixty bucks in change. I put it with the rest."

"Good," I said. "Any other developments?"

"Like what?"

"No messages?"

"None," she said. "Oh, except for that skinny record producer chick. What was her name?"

"Amelia Yeats," I said. "What did she say?"

"Just that she really enjoyed meeting a famous detective and wanted to have dinner with you tonight. I told her you were busy."

"Really?"

"And afterward you might want to come back to her place and share a nice bubble bath. Come on, Mike."

I collapsed back onto the bed. "So sorry for having a dick."

Ben had begun inspecting the room. "You have a Sega," he said.

"If you listen closely you can hear his fanboy-itis wearing off," Katherine said to me.

"No, it's a nice room," Ben said. "It's fine. It's just —"

"Not very glamorous, is it?"

"Well," he said, "you live with your grandmother."

"She lives with me," I said. "And it beats living above a djembe store."

"Smells kind of funny," Ben said.

"It does smell awful," Katherine agreed.

"It's the dog," I told them. That prompted an explanation

and medical history. By the time I'd finished, the dog had clambered down the stairs and buried her face in Katherine's crotch. She pushed the dog away firmly and crossed her legs.

"What's her name?" Ben asked.

"When she was a baby we called her Babe — real creative, I know. Years later we decided she needed a real name, so I named her Odetta, after the blues singer. Only she doesn't look like an Odetta and she doesn't answer to Odetta, so I went back to calling her Babe. But she's not a baby anymore and that doesn't fit, and because it's been so long, she doesn't come to that name either. So I just call her 'dog', or *the* dog if I have to differentiate her from other dogs."

The dog in question walked to her corner and with a laboured wheeze collapsed on her mat.

"Poor girl," Ben said, stooping over to rub two knuckles against the dog's skull.

"Anyway," I said, "there anything else going on?"

"I just drove here because he asked me to," Katherine said, pointing at Ben. "If it was up to me I'd've let you sleep."

"Are you pissed at me?" I asked.

"Of course not," she said, in what she probably thought was a convincing tone.

I turned my attention to Ben. "Out with it."

"Not a big deal, really. It's just my mother wants to hire someone else."

"I see," I said, leaning back against the head-board. I hoped at least it wasn't McEachern. "She's entitled to do that, of course. Tell her I understand."

"No, she doesn't want to replace you." Ben held up a card, pink with blue script. "It's just that someone told her about this and now she can't get it out of her head. I was actually hoping you could talk her out of it."

I looked at the card. MADAME THIBODEAU, ETHEREAL

CONSULTATIONS followed by an address near the foothills of Burnaby Mountain.

"She's serious?"

"'Fraid so."

"Who told your mom about her?"

"No idea." His expression turned strangely credulous. "It's all bullshit, right?"

"What do you think?"

I got up and walked to the washroom and splashed cold water on my face.

"I know your mother," I said. "The more we try to talk her out of this the more she'll want it. So let her book the session."

"She already did. Sundown tonight."

I sat back down on the bed and started buttoning my shirt. "If it's one session and your mom is willing to waste the dough, there's no real harm. But some of these people are lampreys. They'll string her along, week after week, with nothing to show for it."

"And that's our job," Katherine said. Immediately she added, "I'm kidding, of course."

"We'll go and see," I said, ignoring her. "And if Madame Thibodeau starts with that 'To find your daughter you must purify your bank account' shit, we'll call her on it." Looking at Katherine I added, "After all, we can't have her honing in on our turf."

Before the illness, when I took the dog to Douglas Park, she'd take off across the field, ruining ball games, harassing little children and stalking the wildlife. Now when I loosed her collar and tossed her ratty tennis ball, she loped after it as if the activity held no pleasure for her, like it was a huge favor to me. The next time she ignored the ball and squatted behind the home team dugout. I watched a crumbling deuce fall from between her legs.

"Lovely," I said.

I was sitting on the bleachers on the Laurel Street side, watching the convoy of SUVs and minivans pick up kids from Day Care. I watched the vehicles recede down the block. An assembly line of similar kids and similar cars.

I thought about Cynthia Loeb. I do that often. I know more about her than anyone except her mother, more even than Ben. I'd read her journal eight times. I knew the seating plan of her second-grade art class. I could draw her dental charts from memory. I felt like the host of some sort of virus.

My last girlfriend, Mira Das, walked out after seven months of listening to me babble about time tables and partial license plates. She told me she'd slept with Gavin Fisk just to feel like she mattered in some way to someone. What kind of a non-entity do you have to become to make a woman feel like that?

But at least with the Loebs I'd exhausted everything. With Django there were the pawn shop owners. They weren't speaking, though that could be due to healthy distrust rather than conspiracy. That left me at an impasse. The Ford Taurus wasn't recovered. Ditto the bike. I'd exhausted a comprehensive list of people who knew Django or saw him that day. Everyone else thought Django had run off or Cliff had been complicit in his disappearance. I didn't believe either scenario.

Eventually the dog brought the ball to me. I stood up and pocketed it. We started home to get ready for the psychic.

I expected the parlor of Madame Thibodeau to be dusty and low-lit, the shelves crowded with occult knicknacks. I was half-hoping for a crystal ball. She ushered Ben and Mrs. Loeb and I into a sparse eggshell-coloured room, drew the teal drapes and sat us on a pair of L-shaped couches that formed a U facing the Madame's rattan throne. The Madame herself eschewed kerchiefs and beads in favor of a teal pants suit with silver hoop earrings and a half-dozen silver bracelets on her left wrist. Her hands were soft and she had honey-coloured press-on nails. Her hair was blonde and swept back from a puffy pink face with a hefty amount of concealer. Her expression was earnest.

"I'm not a fortune teller or a prognosticator," she said. "I think of myself as part of a conduit. What comes through the conduit depends on what is put in."

Mrs. Loeb, perched on the edge of the sofa cushion, nodded. She held clutched in her hands a folded photo of her missing daughter. Ben sat on her other side, stealing glances at me over his mother's head. I fiddled with my wallet.

It was a slick pitch, delivered directly to Mrs. Loeb's heartstrings, ignoring the scoffs of her son and the disinterest of their family friend. The Madame cautioned her on what not to expect, in a way that would produce in Mrs. Loeb's mind a strong hope for the miraculous without making any claims to it. At the end of the spiel Mrs. Loeb handed over her daughter's picture and an envelope containing five hundred dollars. Madame Thibodeau did not accept checks.

Before she could stow the money in her pocket, my wallet slipped out of my hands, spilling business cards across the floor. The Madame used the toe of her slipper to scoot a pair of cards towards me. Each card said MORRISS CARGILL, INVESTMENT STRATEGIST. They'd come with the calendar.

"We'd like to speak to Cynthia," the Madame said. "We'd like to talk to someone who knows her. This woman is her mother. She must be allowed an audience."

Ben looked at his mother, who had closed her eyes, and at me, who shot him a look that said: patience. Madame

Thibodeau did not close her eyes, but kept them trained on a corner of the room, at the juncture of walls and ceiling. I could almost imagine a disembodied torso floating there.

"Someone is telling me that your uncertainty is almost at an end," the Madame said. "They want me to tell you to be strong. That hope is one of the most powerful forces in the universe."

"How powerful?" Ben said.

His mother shushed him.

"They are sending me an image of water."

"It was raining the morning Cynthia disappeared," Mrs. Loeb said. The Madame nodded knowingly.

"The image is of two silhouettes in the rain, a larger silhouette and a smaller one. I can't make out their faces."

"Can you tell where they're heading?" Mrs. Loeb said.

"They are two shadows in the darkness and the rain. They are moving through the darkness and the rain towards a green light."

Her eyes settled on Mrs. Loeb's.

"I've been given a glimpse," she said. "It takes time and patience to interpret what comes through the conduit." She patted Mrs. Loeb's hand. "I know you're eager. This will take some time. But I'm willing to make your daughter my highest priority."

Mrs. Loeb nodded gravely, thankfully.

"I believe two sessions a week would be the most productive. I will consult the literature and try to find out exactly who is trying to contact us."

"What will that work out to a week?" I asked. "A thousand dollars? Is there a punch card for a free session with ten of equal or greater value?"

Madame Thibodeau never looked at me. "Some people," she said to Mrs. Loeb, "simply can't understand or won't accept the science of what I do."

"What science?" I asked her. "Cold reading and five minutes on the web searching the kid's name would've given you every detail you just fed us."

Mild annoyance stoked to anger. "My gift is to ask questions of the spirit world."

"I don't dispute that, just that the spirit world answers you."

"I can sense your frustration," she said.

"Not exactly a divine revelation, is it?"

Madame Thibodeau said, "When you dropped those cards a moment ago, I knew your heart wasn't open to this experience. No doubt you expected me to use the information and pretend it came to me supernaturally. I don't know what your name is and I don't claim to be clairvoyant. As I explained, I am just a woman who is open to what pours forth from the conduit. People who are deaf to it can't help but be jealous, but I sense frustration from you, also. You have exhausted your abilities and the poor girl is still missing. I can't guarantee a result, but isn't it only fair of you to let Mrs. Loeb decide whether or not she wants to employ someone with a different set of skills? Aren't you letting your jealousy and prejudice stand in the way of what's best for Cynthia?"

The Loebs looked at me, anxious for a response. Madame Thibodeau drew herself up in her chair and rotated some of her bracelets. Feline satisfaction seemed to radiate from her, but her face remained meek, her eyes imploring me to relent, to forgive, to apologize. Her words were not without effect. She'd used the same word I'd thought of back at the park. *Exhausted*. It was true. I felt a trickle of shame in my blood.

I said, "You've got some inarguable points there. You're perceptive. I appreciate that quality. I like to think of myself as the same. And I am frustrated."

She smiled sympathetically.

"I don't claim to be a great detective. Most detective work is drudgery. It's reading through a transcript for the umpteenth time in the hope that something jumps out, some overlooked clue. I'm also prejudiced against anything that takes a leap of faith. I hear you say to a woman who's lost her kid, 'I see two figures in water, give me five hundred dollars,' well, the hackles go up."

Madame Thibodeau began to protest but I held up my hand. My turn.

"Ten minutes before we walked in here I told them how this would go down. I explained to them what a cold reading was. How you'd single out the mother 'cause she's emotionally vulnerable, easy to manipulate. I told them you'd say something cryptic, wait for our response, then build on it. Fact is, the morning Cynthia Loeb disappeared there wasn't a raindrop in sight. But you built your story on that, keeping it just vague enough so you'd have an out."

"I never said her daughter disappeared during a rainstorm."

"You never said anything substantive. You're a fraud, how could you?"

I stood up. The Loebs followed suit.

I'd like to think my speechifying left the Madame torn up inside and repentant, but all I'd succeeded in doing was tearing off the last scrap of pretense. Our eyes met. I also like to think that beneath the mutual disdain and scorn, we shared an admiration, or at least an honest appraisal of the other's nature. But all of that might be romanticized, two worn-out hookers trying to claim emotions they had no right to.

"You're a bastard," she said.

"Pretty much. Mrs. Loeb would like her money back."

Looking up at us, Madame Thibodeau took the envelope and passed it to Mrs. Loeb, but not before withdrawing two of the bills. "Cost of doing business," she said, smiling.

I looked at Mrs. Loeb, who nodded, her stoic good cheer already returning. She knew she was getting off cheap.

"That should at least buy one fortune," I said as the Loebs headed out of the parlor. "Any sooth for me before I leave?"

The Madame remained in her seat staring at the portraits of Robert Borden on the currency, an absent glaze to her eyes. Without looking up she said, "How 'bout, 'beware the ides of March?'"

"Ah, it was worth a try," said Mrs. Loeb. She dropped me on the corner of Beckett Street. As I climbed out of the car, she killed the engine to rummage through her purse, coming up with the envelope which she offered to me. I waved it away.

"Your money's no good."

Ben had climbed into the front seat. Leaning with his elbow out the window of the Town Car he said, "That was a bravura performance, Mike. Really restored my faith in you."

"Shucks," I said. "Pissing off the clairvoyant is easy. They never see it coming."

He shook his head at the cornball joke. "It's always the ides of March you have to beware of, never the nones or the calends. The calends are my favorite."

"The calends are under-utilized," I agreed.

Alone in my office I made tea and answered an email query about my fee structure. I made the calls that needed to be made and fired off emails to people who deserved them. During our Staples spree I'd picked up a scanner, and I spent time making digital copies of the Szabo documents, including Django James's birth certificate and baby footprint.

It was dark out and the usual Hastings Street crowd was gathering under the awnings at the end of the block. Sex trade workers, homeless persons, a whole lot of substance abusers, some of whom encompassed both the other categories. We are all of us whores of one kind or another.

I worked until nine. When the mundane chores had been knocked off, I stood out on the balcony with the dregs of my tea and thought hard about the Szabos and the owners of Imperial Pawn. Ramsey and his daughter knew something. Theirs wasn't a silence built around staying away from the police at all costs. If you run a pawn shop in Vancouver it's inevitable you deal with the law. It could be gang-related: it's hard to make a store owner talk when the person they might finger has friends who enjoy playing with matches.

I wondered if Gavin Fisk sweated Ramsey or his daughter. I wondered if he gave a shit. About the Szabo case, about anything. I hoped he made Mira happy.

The day I moved into my office on Beckett Street I was struggling up the stairs with the table when a woman named Darla spotted me from the street. She held the door open for me and helped me schlep the table into my office. I knew who and what she was: not many occupations called for fishnet stockings and a faux-leather fanny pack. I also knew she was momentarily forgoing any solicitation in anticipation of a larger contribution to the Help Darla Get High Fund once the furniture had been stowed. So we acted cordial to each other and I paid her thirty dollars for her help, making her swear she wouldn't let the rest of the neighbourhood know I was a soft touch.

The next day she reappeared with a fresh pink and purple bruise on her jaw, her shirt stretched and ripped and her fanny pack gone. She explained that she'd cut ties with her pimp and was raising money for a bus ticket back to Banff. I suppose there are more obvious scams, but not many. I didn't so much fall for it as allow myself to get swept up in the story, because I like the idea of being a hero. By the time I'd realized the lie, I'd been parted from another fifty dollars, and Darla was on her way anywhere but to a Greyhound terminal.

That same evening I was on my balcony when she passed below me in the slipstream of a fiery little pimp juggling burner cellphones. A look passed between us not unlike the one between me and Madame Thibodeau. I'd been outgunned by a faster draw. Lesson learned.

A month later, on a July night when I'd succumbed to depression and despair, I found myself thrusting my con-dom-sheathed cock into Darla as she lay face down on the office table, the tendrils of her dirty hair draped over the Loeb file. A hundred dollars, the last currency that would ever pass between us, was clutched in her palm throughout the entire transaction.

One of my grandpa's favorite sayings: "When you've only got a hammer you treat every problem as a nail." Sometimes your options aren't limited by your tools so much as by the mindset you bring to them. But that doesn't mean that mind-set is necessarily wrong. Sometimes the problem really does call for a big fucking hammer blow.

On the balcony thinking of the pawn shop owners, I had an epiphany. I went to one of the new file cabinets and opened the bottom drawer. I had another camera like the ones planted in the Kroons' embalming room. I had parabolic microphones and some rudimentary bugging equipment. But I doubted I had enough to cobble together what I needed.

I phoned Amelia Yeats, using a number I'd gleaned from Cliff Szabo's address book. I told her why I was calling and reminded her who I was.

"I remember you, Mike," she said. That was heartening.

"I got a hunch that you're a night owl," I said. "Do you have time to meet me for coffee?"

"You know Kafka's?"

"Is that the place where you order coffee, it never comes, and the next day you're tossed in jail for an unspecified crime?"

"Funny," she said. "Eleven fifteen?"

"I'll be there."

I pissed out two pots of tea and sat and listened to Chris Whitley scrape his dobro on "From One Island to Another". Another brilliant musician who'd burned out early. I put my feet on the table and tipped my chair back against the wall.

It wasn't a simple plan but it was based on who people were. The hard reality was that I could never make the pawn shop owner and his daughter talk.

To me.

VII

The Hastings Street Irregulars, Part I

Kafka's was busy given the hour. The couches near the window were occupied by bearded, scarved screenwriter types, clacking away on their laptops. Women sat at the back tables, talking or texting on cellphones. Neither group paid much attention to the other. Fifteen adjacent bubbles of solitude. A pair of old men played timed chess at a table in the far corner. Another two looked on.

I was early; I'd brought my book but didn't need it. Amelia Yeats pushed away a crumb-covered saucer and stood up. She deposited the section of the *Province* she'd been reading in the recycling bin and led me back out into the night.

"We might as well grab dinner," she said. "There's a noodle house round the corner that stays open till two."

She was wearing a black warm-up jacket with an orange mesh lining, a magenta T-shirt with an indie band's logo on it, the name something long and literary-sounding. Black leggings tucked into calf-length brown boots and half-rimmed eyeglasses. I think glasses look sexy as hell on women. I may be alone on this. As we walked up Main she pulled hers off and slid them into a case, then dropped the case into her scale-covered purse.

Most of the buildings we passed were closed and empty but not dark. Secondary lights burned in the windows of a

Korean grocer's, a Legion hall, a gelato parlor with a fenced-off patio. People congregated under awnings to smoke cigarettes and talk hockey. Others hustled down side streets clutching brown paper bags or cases of beer with the receipt threaded through the handle. Main Street at night can be quiet and bustling and yuppie and traditional all at the same time.

The restaurant was low-ceilinged and required descending four stairs to reach the entrance. The menus and signs were in Chinese only. They were doing brisk business among a certain clientele: boisterous, drunken, middle-aged Asians. I was the only white person in there. Amelia Yeats ordered: duck feet, Chinese cucumber, a vinegary chicken dish, mushrooms, egg rolls and Cokes.

"What are you grinning at?" she said.

"I was telling someone earlier today that my job was mostly drudgery." I gestured around, as if to add, "And yet here I am."

"I get that sometimes," she said, missing my point. "Any job that's a bit off the path, people think it must be super-glamorous. You can't believe how often I have to tell people, it's not all about snorting coke with rock stars. Mostly it's me alone in the control room, trying to get the drums to sit just right in the stereo field." She cracked her Coke and jabbed in the straw. "Not that I'd ever want to do anything else. I bet you're the same."

"Working for myself seems to suit me," I said. "Any situation involving red tape or a holier-than-thou boss, I become a liability. I like to be left alone to do things how I see fit. There's not a lot of those type jobs left anymore. It's nice to have a niche."

"Isn't it?" She clinked her can against mine. "To everybody everywhere finding their niche."

After our food arrived I worked the conversation around to my plan.

"Let me put this to you," I said. "Unlike most people our age, I'm not tech-savvy. It took me a week of reading the manual to figure out how to hook two surveillance cameras up to my Mac, and those things are supposed to be idiot-friendly. I need someone with expertise recording sound."

"What do you want to record?"

"A conversation in a locked room."

"You want to bug someone?"

"Yes."

She smiled. "Is this legal or illegal?"

I waved my hand, *comme-ci, comme-ca*. "With these kind of people, I'm not sure that distinction really applies."

"Gangsters?"

"No, but if I'm right, they're connected to something they'd rather people didn't know about. What kind of gear would I need for that sort of job?"

She pinched a morsel of chicken from my plate and sucked it up the way the other customers were. I fumbled with a clump of rice and managed to get it to my mouth without getting any on my shirt. The kitchen staff, visible and audible through the glass partition in the back, matched the patrons in volume. Except for the cucumber, the food was excellent.

After thinking it over Amelia Yeats said, "You could run a bug through FM radio, but to guarantee sound quality, at the very least we'd need an interface, a wireless system and a battery-powered mic."

"It has to be impossible to detect. High-powered, enough to pick up low voices clearly. At least one of the speakers is a mumbler."

"How much time do I have to plant it?"

"Ten seconds, probably less. And I can't guarantee we'd get the chance to retrieve it."

She broke the last eggroll in two and slathered her half

in plum sauce. "High-fidelity, invisible, battery-powered and disposable. On what kind of budget?"

"What can you make do with?"

She started scribbling on a napkin. "I have most of the gear," she said. "I can probably pick up the rest of the parts at Radio Shack."

"You make your own microphones?"

She shrugged. "When I was thirteen I made a decent low-frequency mic out of a reverse-wired Kenmore woofer. I still use it occasionally for kick drums. Not exactly a Neumann U-87, but it serves a purpose."

"What'll it cost?"

Another shrug. "If it's to help Cliff, no charge," she said. Then looking up at me: "But I get to be the one that plants it."

I wanted to object. I started to. But the waitress buzzed by to clear the empty plates and ask if we wanted coffee or sponge cake.

"Just the check," I said.

"Like me to split it?"

"Please," Amelia Yeats said, but I handed the waitress two twenties. "I got this."

"What'd you do that for?" she said after the waitress was gone.

"It could be the only money you get out of this. Private detection isn't a thriving business."

"When will you need the mic by?" she said once the waitress had returned with the change. I left it on the table as we pulled on our coats.

"Tuesday work?"

"I can do that, long as the parts are in."

"Great." I slid my card across the table. "Tuesday at eleven, my office. Two-eight-eight-two Beckett Street."

"Should be fun," she said.

***

I crawled through another weekend in the Kroons' office.

Sunday I took my grandmother to the flea market in Cloverdale. The admissions girl found it funny I didn't want my hand stamped. As we pushed into the throng of poorly-dressed and irritable bargain-hunters, my grandmother said, "I don't see why we didn't just go to the one on Terminal."

"The one on Terminal's nothing but dealers and junk," I said. "This one's worth the drive. At least they don't get offended when you try to bargain. Plus it's near the Pannekoek House."

"You're taking me to breakfast?" she asked.

"I will if you don't piss me off." I squeezed her shoulder.

Later, as we walked through the parking maze, her searching her pockets for the keys and me carrying an azalea in a hanging pot, a pair of drapes, and a brass samovar, she looked at the latter and said, "I don't know what you need with that thing."

"It's for the office."

"Who drinks that much coffee? You don't even like coffee."

"Maybe I just like samovars."

She shook her head, ready to up-end her purse on the concrete if the keys didn't materialize. She checked the zippered side pouch.

"Your mother loved knickknacks and junk, too. She used to collect old typewriters. Never wrote a word on any of them. There!" She came up with the keys. "And do you know how hard brass is to clean?"

"A little CLR and water, good as new."

"I don't know where you get that stubbornness, Michael. Certainly not from my part of the family. That's a Kessler trait."

"What exactly are the Drayton traits?" I asked her.

"Oh, don't worry, you're not much like him."

Him.

91

"So all the virtues come from your side, and all the riffraff from the Draytons and Kesslers?"

She answered, "My side did quite well for itself. And we did it without ever buying a dirty used samovar."

I don't understand why people talk to their dogs, but that doesn't mean I haven't engaged in that practice myself. At the park on Monday night my dog shot me a look of admonishment, as if to say, "So you've added criminal invasion of privacy to your job description? And you think it's going to work out? Or stop there?"

I didn't have an answer for her.

Tuesday I picked up Katherine from her boyfriend's parents' house and Ben in front of the Djembe Hut. I swung by a Tim Horton's and bought an assorted dozen. At the office I steeped a gallon of tea in the samovar and cleared the table of everything except the Loeb file and a pad of graph paper. Katherine folded back the flaps on the doughnut carton and set out napkins in a neat square pile. Ben deliberately mussed up her pattern. We set up folding chairs and waited for the others to arrive.

They weren't long. Cliff Szabo was there at two minutes to eleven, Amelia Yeats at eleven ten. Katherine glared at her. Ben tucked the manga he was reading under his chair.

When they were seated, all eyes drifted to me. I'd never chaired a meeting in my life.

"Here's the situation as it stands," I said. "Mr. Szabo's son disappeared from outside Imperial Pawn. More specifically, Django was in a car that disappeared, along with the car's contents, including a bicycle."

"A Schwinn Bicentennial," Szabo clarified.

"It is entirely possible that the pawn shop owner, Mr. Ramsey, and his daughter Lisa, know jack-shit about this disappearance. But I don't get that feeling."

"They're liars," Szabo said. "Tried to cheat me every time."

"Then why do business with them in the first place?" Ben asked.

"I have options?"

"We're getting off track," I said. "They know something we need to know. They won't talk to us. I want to make them talk to each other."

Nods, silence. Katherine said, "Well if nobody else is going to have tea, I will." That prompted paper cups to be filled and passed out, and the box of doughnuts to make the rounds.

"So what's your plan?" Ben said.

"Bug them and make them frightened enough to talk," I said. "That requires someone to cause a distraction while someone else plants the bug."

"Which I'm doing," Amelia Yeats said.

"Isn't that up to Mike?" Katherine said.

"It's part of our arrangement." I flipped around the graph pad so they could see the sloppy floor plan of the pawn shop I'd drawn from memory. I pointed to the squiggle that stood for the back room door. "In there is where the bug has to go. Tomorrow Katherine will drop in and try to get a glimpse of what's back there, so we can hide the mic in something appropriate."

"Why me?" Katherine asked.

"Because they don't know what you look like, and if you pop up later it's unlikely they'll find you suspicious."

"Meaning I have a forgettable face?"

Amelia Yeats made the tiniest of shrugs.

Ben said, "I could do that."

"No you can't," I said. To Katherine: "On the day of, I want you to go in there with money and pretend to be shopping for something, maybe a camera. I need you to get lots of merchandise out on the counter, so the Ramseys' attention will be split between the merch and the customers. Then Mr. Szabo enters and yells at them. That way, even if they re-check the security tape, all they'll focus on will be the cluster of people around their high-end gear."

"What will you do?" Yeats asked.

Szabo had been sipping his tea, eyes gravitating to his son's face on the stack of flyers atop the cabinet.

"Mr. Szabo will storm in and accuse them, loudly, of knowing about Django's disappearance. I'll go in and pretend to wrestle him out of the store. My hope is, in the aftermath, the Ramseys will retreat to the back room and discuss things, maybe even contact whoever did it."

"Wouldn't it be easier to break in at night and plant the bug?" Ben asked. "You could do that yourself, when they're not around, then wait for them to bring up Django."

"Airtight plan," I said. "Except that A, I'm not a fucking ninja and I don't break into places, and B, I don't have an inexhaustible supply of manpower to listen to them for weeks and weeks. And C, if they know about the kid, I want to know now, not when they feel like talking about it. That's not something that comes up in day to day conversation."

"Okay," Ben said. "But if you think they might try to contact the guy, why not tap their phones?"

"Yeah, and I'll calibrate my infrared geo-satellites to peer into the store. And I'll hire Gene Hackman and John Cazale to record every word the Ramseys say."

I took a breath and a bite of doughnut.

"Fact is, if I get a name I'll be happy. A name is somewhere to start." I looked around. "Any other poorly conceived objections?"

"Do you know how much of this is against the law?" Katherine asked me.

"Ten percent?"

She rolled her eyes.

"It's academic because we're not going to get caught."

"Right," Amelia Yeats said. "The useless shitheads on the VPD couldn't help Cliff, so why worry that they're going to be able to catch us?"

"Most of the cops mean well," I said.

"Bullshit. They're thugs who beat gays and immigrants just for being different. Any excuse to shoot or Taser someone."

Katherine looked at me, grinning, like, "You're gonna take that?"

I said, "All we have to agree on is that this could help. Could. No guarantee. But I don't see any alternatives."

Whatever energy was in the room dimmed and the meeting was over.

"Someone want to take the rest of these doughnuts home?" Katherine asked as she swept up the coffee cups into the trash basket.

"I'm sure you do," Amelia Yeats said.

Katherine bit her tongue and looked away.

To me Yeats said, "Can I speak to you alone for a minute?"

Outside on the pavement she handed me the bug, which, with battery, was about the size of my thumb. "Twelve bucks seventy cents in parts, including battery."

I dug out my wallet as Cliff passed us, heading towards where he'd parked his car. We nodded at each other. I offered Amelia Yeats the money but she pushed my hand away.

"Anything for Cliff," she said. "Especially if he comes through with that two-inch tape." She lit a cigarette, offered me one, du Maurier Lights. "My friend's band's playing the Commodore next week. They're not bad for a tribute band, although the new rhythm section hasn't gelled yet. You're welcome to come."

"I'd like that," I said, trying to think of the last concert I'd been to.

"I can put her on the guest list too."

"Katherine? We're not together."

"Good," she said.

Both feet weren't in the office before Katherine said, "She is such a bitch."

"Yuh-huh."

"And her 'fuck the police' rant? I'd've clocked her there and then."

"Katherine's experiencing what the French call *l'espirit de l'escalier*," Ben said without looking up from his book. "Stairway wit. She's thinking of all the great comebacks she should've said ten minutes ago."

"I should've shoved her down that stairway," Katherine said.

"I had a talk with her about that," I said. "I straightened things out. It won't happen again."

"Good," she said.

The Hastings Street Irregulars, Part II

It rained Wednesday night. In the morning there was a rainbow over Cordova Street, its apex above the train yard along the waterfront. I didn't know what that could portend.

Katherine's boyfriend and his parents shared a condo on Wall Street. I parked behind their Odyssey and followed the walkway around until I saw their slice of ground-floor terrace. I leaned over the guardrail and tapped on the sliding glass door. The boyfriend looked up from his yogurt and reached over to unlatch the door and pull it open. I climbed over the rail and wiped my feet on the concrete before stepping inside.

I don't like Katherine's boyfriend, Scott Shipley. I'm not quite sure why. I get the feeling he doesn't like me, or doesn't approve of Katherine working with me. Tall and pasty with an over-pronounced Adam's apple, red stringy hair that comes over his brow at an obtuse angle, like Gyro Gearloose from *Duck Tales*. That morning he was wearing blue briefs and a two-tone long-sleeve shirt.

"How's your day going?" I asked.

"All right I guess."

"Katherine about?"

"Changing."

I sat down at the table and watched him spoon up yogurt.

"You're taking the van again?" he asked. "Do me a couple favors? First, could you please fill it up with gas if you drive it for any length of time? Second, in the future, when my mom says specifically to bring it back for noon, could have it back *for noon*, not two fifteen?"

"Reasonable requests," I said.

He nodded and resumed eating and scanning the newspaper.

I asked him, "How's that Flesh Light working out for you?"

I don't see how yogurt could catch in someone's throat, but Scott covered his mouth and coughed, his spoon clattering back into the bowl. I heard Katherine bounding down the stairs and I stood up.

"Sex toys are nothing to be embarrassed about," I said. "Personally I'm content with the hand, but some people like to explore the frontiers. And shouldn't we be glad to live in a pluralistic society that welcomes those differences?"

By the end of the coughing fit Scott's face had turned pink. Katherine strode into the kitchen, school bag over one shoulder. She pulled out a chair from the table and sat down to pull on her hiking boots. After a minute of pure silence she looked up and said, "What?"

"Nothing," Scott said.

"We're good," I said.

She insisted on walking out the front door instead of going over the back rail. Out of earshot of the apartment she said, "I don't know why you two can't get along."

"Jealousy," I said. "He's not the first to be driven to it. I have that affect on people. It's something I've learned to live with."

"You could be more considerate."

"True. But I bet you don't chide him the way you do me."

"We argue all the time," she said.

"Ah."

"Not what I meant."

At the curb I opened the trunk of the Camry and began shifting gear into the van. I folded down the Odyssey's back bench and took out one of the seats in the middle row.

"It occurs to me," I said, carrying the seat over to the trunk of the Camry, "that we have the opposite of a professional relationship, where you think being an employee gives you the right to criticize the boss."

"Is it criticism to ask you to observe the bare minimum of etiquette?"

"I paid to borrow the van," I said. "If I'm a couple minutes late and I forgot to top up the tank —"

"So a 'please' and 'thanks' are out of the question, Mike?"

She settled into the driver's seat, me sitting shotgun with an eye to the gear in the back. She made a left to get us onto Hastings.

I said, "Please convey to the Shipleys my immense gratitude for the usage of their conveyance."

"More like it," Katherine said.

We picked up Ben. Then we swung by my grandmother's house. I ran inside and came out cradling my dog. I connected her leash, handing it to Ben before letting her down onto the floor of the van.

"You can't bring that thing with us," Katherine said.

"She's good luck." I caught Ben breaking off a piece of muffin. "Do not feed her that."

Katherine had reconnoitered Imperial Pawn Tuesday after the meeting. She'd measured the distance from the entrance to the back room (eight strides to the counter, two more to the back wall, five at most to navigate around the counter and the floor junk). She'd seen into the back room. It was dark but she was sure she'd seen a box full of blue VHS cases. So that was what we encased the bug in. Amelia Yeats had taken an old head-cleaning tape, scooped out the guts, and mounted the bug inside. I'd visited four Salvation Army stores before finding an identical blue plastic VHS case. The cashier had registered shock when I forked over two quarters for *Don Cherry's Rock'Em Sock'Em Hockey Volume Four*, only to dump the cassette and the cardboard insert in the trash and walk out with the case.

The jump-off point — it had taken all of a day for *Mission: Impossible* lingo to invade the office — was two blocks up the street in the parking lot behind a Ricky's. Cliff Szabo and Amelia Yeats were waiting for us. They hunkered down on the floor of the van while I outlined the order: Yeats first, then Katherine, then Szabo and I. I would drag Szabo out, Katherine would linger, Yeats would leave after us as soon as seemed reasonable.

"What about me?" Ben said.

"Stay in the van and don't feed that muffin to my dog. If someone comes by, move the van."

"I'll set the mic up now," Yeats said, "but someone will have to make sure it's working till I get back."

"Show Ben," I said to her, then to everyone: "So we all understand what we're doing?"

Szabo nodded, Yeats and then Ben.

Katherine said, "I can't."

Turning around in the driver's seat she said, "I know what you're trying to do, and I'm not saying it's wrong, Mike. It might even be noble. But I can't be a part of this. If there's even a chance we could get in shit, from the cops or whoever, that's too much of a risk." She looked at Szabo. "I'm sorry."

"Understandable," he said.

"How would you feel about staying in the van, making sure the mic's picking up properly?"

"I can do that."

"Good." I said to Yeats, "Show her what she needs to do."

I turned to Ben, a streak of melted baker's chocolate on the corner of his mouth.

"That means you're up."

Amelia Yeats had been in the store five minutes when we unleashed Ben. Szabo, nervous and looking for a distraction, opted to walk the dog around the block. Katherine and I shared the pair of Koss headphones Yeats had supplied. We watched the waveforms on the laptop screen. The bug was picking up the ambience from the pawn shop perfectly. Ben opened the door and climbed out of the van's back seat.

The overcast sky had been growing progressively darker as noon approached. The threat of rain hung in the air, keeping pedestrians to a minimum. The thrift store's parking lot across the street would have been ideal, but it was too empty, our van too conspicuous. From where we'd parked, we had a good diagonal view of the storefront.

Over the headphones I heard the *dunh-donh* of the electronic door chime as Ben stepped inside:

"Afternoon, sir," Ben said. "I'm here today to buy something."

I didn't look over but I knew Katherine was rolling her eyes.

Ben: "What I'm actually looking for is a camera."

Ramsey: "Okay."

Ben: "I don't know anything about cameras."

Ramsey: "Okay. Well —"

Ben: "— Other than, y'know, you point and click. At least I think that's the order."

Ramsey: "Right."

The sound of tapping on glass.

Ben: "That one looks nice."

Ramsey: "Yes."

Ben: "Can I see it?"

The sound of a key chain being rifled through, a lock being slid back, the case drawer sliding open, and presumably a camera being plunked down on the counter top.

Ben: "Looks pretty good. How many, um, megapixels?"

Ramsey: "It says right here."

Ben: "Right. So is eight good? I mean, is it enough?"

Ramsey: "Depends for what."

Ben: "Nature photography. I take a lot of footage of squirrels and the like. The odd chipmunk. I like squirrels better than chipmunks, even though chipmunks have the better PR. Alvin, Simon, Chip, Dale. Like raccoons. Ever see a raccoon that wasn't eating garbage or murdering cats?"

Ramsey: "I don't know."

Ben: "And yet they're beloved. Chipmunks are the same. You have a preference, chipmunks or squirrels?"

Ramsey: "No."

("Thinks he's seventies DeNiro," I said to Katherine.)

Ben: "Weird how some animals get the cartoon stamp of approval and others don't."

Ramsey: "This is a nice camera."

Ben: "Does it shoot video?"

Ramsey: "No, but this one—"

Ben: "— Let's see it. No, don't put that one away, I might get both. And do you have any accessories?"

Lisa: "Can I help you with something?"

Amelia Yeats: "No, just looking, thanks."

Ramsey: "Tripods in the corner."

Lisa: "Well if you need anything let me know."

Ben: "What about flashes?"

Yeats: "I will, thanks."

Ramsey: "Flash is built in."

Ben: "On both?"

Ramsey: "Not on the video. But you can adjust —"

I took off the headphones as Mr. Szabo came around the front of the van. We lifted the dog inside.

"Ready?" he said.

I handed Katherine the leash and gave her a hesitant thumbs up. She returned it. I nodded to Szabo.

"I'll be thirty seconds behind you."

I put the cans over my ears. I'd counted twelve Mississippis when I heard *dunh-donh* and Mr. Szabo say in a frozen razor of a voice, "I know you know who took him."

And everything that had been fun and unreal about the plan fell apart. I bolted for the door.

On the tape both Ramsey and his daughter start to speak in low, placating voices, before Szabo screams, "Lying mother-*fuckers*, tell me where he is." And louder, "Tell me where my son is." And even louder: "*Where is he?*"

On the tape this is followed by a hard click and the tinkle of glass, and the door chimes ringing yet again. Through the door I saw Szabo clock Ramsey on the jaw as he came around the counter. Ramsey fell back, one of the cameras still in his hand. The hand with the camera smashed into the display counter.

Szabo swung again but by that time I was through the door, behind him, and I snapped him back from Ramsey and pulled him across the room, catching the closing door with my foot as Lisa charged at him. I maneuvered Szabo out as Lisa swiped my ear and chin, drawing blood.

Leading Szabo up the block I said, "What the shit was that?"

"Lying motherfuckers," he said. I spun him around to face me, saw the tears.

"He's going to phone the cops and we're going to jail," I said, which was an exaggeration of my concerns. What really went through my mind was: *I'm out of business.*

After we turned the corner and were out of sight I slowed our pace. "Did you see if she planted the tape?"

Szabo shook his head.

We climbed into the van. Katherine was sitting on the floor, headphones on.

"What happened?" she said, speaking louder than necessary. Wearing headphones for long periods of time has that effect.

I shook my head and leaned over to take the phones.

"You should get out of here, Hough, maybe take a bus or a cab."

"I'll stay," Katherine said.

I heard Ben's voice saying, "No, seriously, that dude was out of it. You want me to testify or anything just say the word. My uncle's a barrister, we could sue. Do you know that guy?"

"No," said Lisa. "Some crazy."

Amelia Yeats had joined us in the van. She unplugged the phones so we could listen on the laptop's speakers.

"Anyway I'll let you get cleaned up," Ben said. I heard them buzz Ben out.

The silence in the van mimicked the silence in the shop.

Ben opened the side door, decided it was too crowded and sat up front. The dog had worked between the two front seats and had her snout shoved into the muffin's waxed envelope.

I was conscious of the breathing of every organism in the van: Katherine's, steady on my left; Yeats's excited and quickened as she leaned over me from the right; Szabo's frenetic and uneven; Ben, already bored and impatient; me, all of these things; and beneath us, the leaky bellows of the dog.

I picture them in a back room with a "Closed" sign on the front door. Ramsey's hand has been bandaged, his body language betraying the shock of unexpected combat and trauma. Lisa paces in front of him, clicking her broken nails on the door frame. Their breathing is audible on the tape.

"What does he know?" Lisa said.

"What could he know?" Ramsey said. "Not everything."

"No, he couldn't know everything."

There was a sound of running water and crumpled paper.

Ramsey: "Or else —"

Lisa: "Or else he'd call the police."

Ramsey: "So."

Lisa: "So what does he know?"

Ramsey: "He knows about Zak."

Lisa: "Not for sure he doesn't."

Ramsey: "He has to know something."

Lisa: "Say he does. What do we do?"

Ramsey: "Do? He's a sad old man."

Lisa: "He's dangerous. That man he's with —"

Ramsey: "— The detective?"

Lisa: "He's smart. He probably set this whole thing up."

Ramsey: "Set up the old man punching me?"

Lisa: "Is that so hard to imagine?"

Ramsey: "What does he get out of him punching me?"

Lisa: "Perhaps it scares you into talking."

Ramsey: "He said he already knew."

Lisa: "He could've said that to trick you into talking to him, Papa. Like, if you're hiding money and I say I know where it's hidden, and you look over to the bathroom where you hid it."

Ramsey: "Why would I hide money in the bathroom?"

Lisa: "You see my point though."

Ramsey: "Dangerous."

Lisa: "Possible. How's your hand?"

Ramsey: "Fine."

Lisa: "How's the camera?"

Ramsey: "It probably needs some parts."

Lisa: "Not a problem."

Ramsey: "But who do we go to for them?"

Lisa: "I'm sorry it was Cliff. I wish Zak had been later or earlier."

Ramsey: "It's a strange and cruel world."

"Was that what you wanted?" Katherine asked me.

"Don't know." To Szabo I said, "You know a Zak?"

He shook his head.

"But it's something to go on, isn't it?" Katherine asked me.

"Sure," I said. "I can take it to Fisk. How long will the battery in that bug last?"

"A few days," Amelia Yeats said. "But the laptop has to stay in this area."

I pointed through the tinted window at the Waves café across the street. "Can you get a signal from over there, least until I bring my car back?"

"Long as you bring a charger with you."

"I think you all owe me an apology first," Ben said.

Katherine shook her head. "What on earth for?"

"For stepping in at the last moment and selling the shit out of my part. I've always considered acting kind of an unworthy profession. But now I see the allure of a life in the theatre."

"You played a longwinded doofus who didn't know what he was talking about," Katherine said. "What a stretch."

"Some are born to tread the boards, others to hurl insults from the safety of the balcony."

He hadn't meant to remind Katherine of her choice, but her mood sank. Later, once Cliff and Amelia had gone and Ben had been dropped off, and the laptop was charging off my Camry's lighter, I leaned in the window of the Odyssey and said, "Actually worked out better this way, all things considered."

"I'm sorry about that," she said. "I feel like I let you down.

And when I heard the fighting I thought of coming to help but —"

"It worked out fine."

"How's your ear?"

"My —" I touched the crust of newly formed scab. "Right. Got to get some antiseptic on that."

"I could bring you that."

I shook my head. "Your day's done. When they close shop I'm heading to the Kroons'. I'll pick some up on the way."

"Night," she said, starting the engine.

I'd already been lucky, but I waited in the car another four hours hoping to give Zak a last name, a description, or a base of operation. All I got was a few mumbled g'nights as Ramsey and his daughter locked up and went their separate ways. Luck provides no encore.

IX

Near-vana

I'd been giving the Corpse Fucker short shrift, putting in my hours but leaving all kinds of stones unturned. I made up for that in the last weeks of September. I interviewed the office staff under the guise of taking suggestions for improving security. I uncovered very little. Carrie knew about the situation, but had no idea who it could be or how they were getting in. Jag was in the dark. The dispatcher, Kurt, had only heard rumors. The Kroons were more concerned with preventing another defiling than catching the culprit. To me those seemed like the same idea.

Spending three nights and four days on the Corpse Fucker subsidized the time I was spending on the Szabo disappearance. At least that's how I rationalized it. I hoped that splitting myself between the two cases wasn't adversely affecting them. It was tough to tell. Both were moving on glacial time.

Tuesday afternoon Tish at the front desk of the Cambie Street Station told me Gavin Fisk was off that day. I looked up his home address, an apartment within walking distance of the Science World dome. I fed the meter and walked over the Cambie Street Bridge, enjoying the view of the boats and barges rocking on the choppy grey water below.

Fisk's apartment was a white shard of crystal jabbed into the skyline. Given his pickup and his shit-kicker persona, I'd expected a less cosmopolitan dwelling. As I rang the buzzer I wondered if he had white wall-to-wall carpeting in his flat. Maybe a tiger's pelt draped in front of a fake fireplace.

A woman's voice, a familiar woman's voice, asked who it was.

"It's Mike," I said. "To see Gavin if he's around."

"He's not," Mira said.

"Will he be home soon?"

"Come up and wait for him if you like."

She met me outside the elevator on the third floor, the door to the apartment held open with the bent-back latch. Padding down the carpet in slippers and a terrycloth robe, tendrils of hair spilling from the towel wrapped around her head. Sometimes after seeing an ex you think, *Thank God I dodged that bullet*. Sometimes it starts a pain in your guts because she looks so beautiful, so at peace. That wrenching of the innards is the knowledge that her happiness is predicated on not being with you. With Mira Das I felt neither, though a sex impulse reared its head as I scoped her contours through her robe. What I felt was a loss without a longing. Sometimes you reread a favorite book, particularly one you treasured when you were young. You meet the same golden characters who utter the same witty banter and jump through the same startling and pity-evoking hoops. The book's brilliance hasn't diminished on rereading, but you are different. You've moved outside the circumference of the book, and you know that as much as you may admire it, you will never recapture the feeling that the book was translating yourself to you as you read. So that even knowing it by heart, it feels strange. That was the feeling she evoked: we were beyond each other now, and contentedly so.

We sat down on sections of a black-upholstered sofa. Only the barest of traffic noise petered through the double-glazed windows. Grey wall-to-wall Berber carpeting, scuffed enough that I didn't feel bad leaving my shoes on.

Mira had her hands folded in her lap. "I should have offered you something to drink."

"Not too late," I said.

"Tea? I probably have some Twinings Earl Grey."

"You remembered."

"I remember being dragged out of perfectly good restaurants that didn't serve it. That was before you started sneaking it in."

"Creature of habit," I said. "I'm less particular now. I've become addicted to these London Fogs — teabag, steamed milk, shot of vanilla. Each one costs half a week's pay, but it's worth it."

Mira laughed. "What else has changed?"

"I'm learning to work with others, trust people a bit more. This is turning into a therapy session. What about you? You moved in with Fisk?" I didn't mean it to come out as a question.

"I moved in in August, after months of debate."

"He didn't want you to? I'm sure he had great excuses. 'Y'know, darling, for two people to really appreciate each other they need space.'"

"Actually I was on the fence," she said. "Gavin wanted me in from the start."

"So why'd you cave?"

"I didn't 'cave,' I decided. Why would I have to cave?"

"Because you're not in love with him and he's not in love with you."

We heard the click of the plastic kettle shutting off. She brought the teapot in, set it on the glass coffee table. "You were saying?" she said.

"You're too smart to consider him an equal and he's too much of a cunt hound to settle on one woman."

"You're still a prick," she said, her childhood in London evident in her voice.

"You asked. Two fuck buddies want to delude themselves they've found true love, that's their business."

"How's your love life, Michael?" she asked.

"Arrested," I said. "I mean, there's someone."

"Which is it?" Enjoying watching me squirm.

"Well, we're friendly. She's rich and gorgeous and self-employed and talented as hell. And I get the feeling she's into me. But every so often I get a look from her like she's Queen Elizabeth and I'm standing in her throne room wearing a coxcomb."

"What's her name?"

"Yeats. Amelia."

"The producer?" Mira stood up and walked to the large maple bookcase on the far wall, the one I'd built for her that matched the two in my bedroom. She reached to the top shelf and pulled down a CD by some B.C. band. How could I tell they were Canadians, let alone from British Columbia? In the cover photo of the band, the kick drum head was painted as a Canadian flag, green bars instead of red, a cannabis leaf substituted for the maple. Only an alt-rock band from Vancouver would find that clever enough for an album cover.

The blurb at the bottom of the back of the CD read: "Tracks 1, 5, and 7 (*) produced by Bob Rock. All other tracks produced by Amelia Yates. Mixed and Mastered at Enola Curious Studios, Vancouver."

"Won a Juno last year," Mira said, her voice losing the accent. "I watched the show. I think she had a boyfriend."

"Could be," I said. "Didn't stop you from trading down."

The door rattled and Gavin Fisk walked in, carrying two cloth bags full of groceries. He wore track pants and an MMA T-shirt with silkscreened images of barbed wire and diamond plating. He nodded at me, stepped over to Mira for a peck on the cheek.

"Beverly Hills Buntz," he said. "Returning that Jeff Buckley CD?"

"Came to talk to you about the Szabo case."

He put the groceries on the counter of the kitchenette. "Want to start dinner?" he said to Mira. She nodded and began unpacking cauliflower and jasmine-scented rice, as if a sound-proof wall had sprung up between them.

"You know the dad phoned me out of the blue to apologize?" Fisk said, flopping onto the couch.

"He's a good guy."

"You put him up to it." He shrugged. "Doesn't make much of a difference."

"Did you come across anyone named Zak? Maybe connected to the Ramseys and Imperial Pawn?"

To his credit he thought it over. "Can't say I did because I didn't. Why?"

"I heard the Ramseys mention him."

"In connection to the kidnapping? How'd you work that?"

"Do you really want to know?"

He grinned. "Mr. Right and Wrong is beating confessions out of people now?"

"Only a cop thinks 'right' and 'lawful' are synonyms."

"Which you're not anymore."

"Will you ask about Zak? Maybe run the name through CPIC, see if anyone with that name has a sheet with car thefts or kidnappings?"

"It's not exactly lawful — or right — to run searches for civilians," Fisk said.

"Not like you can't find an excuse."

"But I don't have a motive."

"Solve a case that's still on the books? Reunite a kid with

his father? What do you want, a kickback?" I poured three dollars in quarters, leftovers from the meter, onto the coffee table. It was the wrong thing to do.

"What I'd like from you, first off, is a bit of fucking respect. We're not co-workers, Mike. You're not on the job anymore. Maybe you haven't clued in to that. If you were in my place — and you *know* this, Mike — and some pain-in-the-ass amateur approached you with a first name and he's in no hurry to tell you how he got that name, you wouldn't hop to it like you expect me to." He mock saluted. "Yes, sir, Mr. Private Citizen, sir. Thanks for enlightening me how to do my job. By the way, you want to tell me how to take a shit, too?"

"Just treat it like a tip. If a stranger came to you with the name Zak —"

"I'll take it under advisement."

"Go fuck yourself, Gavin."

We stood up. He gave me a "you-want-some-of-this" stare. I stepped past him towards the door, our shoulders grazing. I looked at Mira in the kitchen, chopping cauliflower to make aloo gobhi. I left them to each other.

Saturday afternoon I laid things out for Cliff Szabo.

"My guess is that Zak is primarily a car thief. I don't have too many contacts in that world, so if you know anyone who runs a chop shop or fences cars or car parts, I could use a steer in their direction."

"I'll find someone," Szabo said.

Before he left he put fifty four dollars on the table and apologized. It had been a slow week.

* * *

The night of Friday the 24th: no Corpse Fucker.

The night of Saturday the 25th: no Corpse Fucker.

The night of Sunday the 26th: no Corpse Fucker.

Tuesday night I met Amelia Yeats at the Commodore for her friend's concert only to lose her in the multitude for two hours. I stood at the bar and drank exorbitantly priced Jack Daniels. I was handing over my tag to the girl at the coat check when Yeats tapped my shoulder, asked me how it was.

"Good. Tribute bands weird me out a bit, but at least they were more about the songs than just looking like the musicians." No worry that her friend's band would fall into that category: while "Near-vana: a Tribute to Kurt Cobain" boasted a guitar/vocalist with the appropriate dirty blond hair and red-and-black horizontally striped sweatshirt, the rest of the band included a five-foot tall female Krist Novoselic and a Samoan Dave Grohl. "It was nice to hear 'Down in the Dark.'"

"Wasn't it? Zoltan has a decent voice, but he's a stellar guitar player. I keep telling him to get some originals together, maybe get another singer. He's more comfortable, I guess, doing Cobain than himself."

We crossed Granville to the Mega-Bite, found a table, ate potato pizza off of paper plates.

"So is he your boyfriend?"

"Zoltan?" She wiped her mouth demurely. "Not since forever. Why?"

"Why do you think?"

She shrugged, smiled. I leaned over and kissed her. Hot sauce, potato, cigarettes, rum.

"My ex says she saw you at some awards show," I said after some silence.

"Your ex. She leave you or you leave her?"

"I moved out. She moved on."

"What'd you do, cheat on her?"

"Lost myself in work. Missing child. Ben's sister, actually. Cynthia Loeb."

"You ever find her?"

I shook my head. The demons that the night off had dispelled crowded around, demanding entry. I willed myself to enjoy the moment.

"No leads?" Yeats said. "No hunches?"

"All likelihood she's dead," I said. "But I can't tell them that."

"You lie to them?"

"Never. But her mom won't hear it and her brother doesn't need to."

"Horrible."

"Yeah. And here we are eating pizza."

"What does that mean?"

I shrugged. "Just that nothing stops on account of tragedy. I still have to get up every day, make tea, walk the dog, earn some money. So does Mrs. Loeb. And Cliff Szabo. You try to remain vigilant, but most days there's nothing you can do. You can't make the kid materialize out of thin air. The hard thing is getting accustomed to your own uselessness." I finished my pizza and balled up a napkin with my fist.

"So why do it?"

"I have some bad tendencies that come out when I work for other people, or when I'm not working at all. This way I'm always busy and I have a measure of control."

"It's the same with me," Yeats said. "If I can't tell the people I'm working with to fuck off I go nuts. Not that I want to tell them that, just that I want the ability to tell them that."

"To disengage. At your discretion."

"Right."

"Come back with me," I said.

"Can't tonight. I have to mix Zoltan's demo for some contest he's entering. How about Friday?"

"Working. Monday?"

"Let's leave it open," she said.

Thursday afternoon Cliff Szabo told me to meet him outside a body shop on Kingsway. A Vietnamese man shook Cliff's hand and led us into a back room, where a half-dozen men in smocks were disassembling a Cabriolet. I spent a couple minutes with each one, heard a similar smattering of evasions, non-answers, and lies. Outside the shop I said to Szabo, "How do you do business with them?"

His answer: "Their English is better when money is involved."

The night of Friday, October 2nd: no Corpse Fucker.

The night of Saturday, October 3rd: no Corpse Fucker.

The night of Sunday, October 4th: no Corpse Fucker.

I'd started to bring my dog to the office in order to keep her out of my grandmother's way. On dry days she'd lie on the balcony, letting out the odd disgruntled woof at passersby.

Katherine was spending more time at the office, studying in the evenings for her midterms at the end of October. I saw less of Ben, who would stop in, try to goad one of us into an argument and finding no takers, announce that he was heading to the Comic Shop or Golden Age Collectibles for intellectual stimulation. Aware that even this last comment was his way of starting an argument, we ignored him. For Ben, after the high of the bug planting, lingering in an office watching two people write emails to other people in other offices was a letdown. Part of me agreed with him.

I'd become embroiled in a minor legal dispute with a private school in New Westminster. The principal had hired me to ascertain whether or not one of their Social Studies teachers was a pedophile, after an unfounded rumor about a locker room peep show reached some concerned parents. After two weeks of stakeouts I'd concluded that he wasn't a pedophile, at least not a practicing one. His taste in porn ran to the exotic but legal; I found this out by staring into his apartment window three straight balmy days in July. I could see the back of his head and the monitor of his computer through the bedroom window, while in the living room his wife watched the daytime soaps she'd recorded earlier in the day.

The principal was relieved, said the check would be mailed after the mandatory two-week processing period. Mid-September I received a sheaf of paperwork, including an employee records form, federal and provincial tax sheets, two workplace safety checklists which I had to sign after reading the accompanying booklet, a direct deposit form, a questionnaire about my marital status and whether or not I smoked, and a release for a background check. I wondered who they'd hire for that. Even though I don't have a home computer, I was glad my bedroom had no windows that looked out on the street.

I'd made Katherine fill out all that crap and run interference when they phoned to get a photocopy of my driver's license and SIN card. The afternoon of Wednesday the 7th, I'd just finished dashing off a "More-in-sorrow-than-in-anger" type missive informing them that if I didn't have the three grand and change on my table, in cash, by Hallowe'en, I'd take them to court, when Katherine told me someone was coming up the stairs.

I didn't need to look at the security monitor to know who it was. The dog jumped up with more verve than she'd mustered in the last two weeks. She was sniffing at the office door when Mira Das opened it. Not even in the room yet, Mira squatted down and accepted a lick on the face.

"Missed you too, Babe," she said. Looking up at me she said, "How's she doing?"

"Better for seeing you." I stood and introduced her to Katherine. "Constable Mira Das of the VPD. Katherine Hough."

"Pleasure," Mira said.

"Same," Katherine said. She picked her coat off the balcony. "I'll go get lunch, let you two talk. Want anything from the sushi place?"

"I'm not picky. Improvise."

When she was gone Mira settled into one of the clients' chairs. "The last time I was in here you didn't have furniture. Or a secretary."

"She's more of a junior partner than a secretary," I said. "Hildy Johnson to my Walter Burns. As for the furniture, it's getting better. Although part of me kind of liked that ramshackle look."

"You need a piece of art for the wall behind you," she said. "Or a fish tank."

"How about a great big tactical map with colour-coded pushpins?"

"Lovely."

The dog leapt onto Mira's lap and nuzzled her neck.

"I have something for you," Mira said, producing a creased piece of paper from one of the pockets of her uniform. She pushed it across the table to me.

Unfolded, the type read:

> *Zachary (Zak, Zack) Atero*
> *5'7" Caucasian*
> *Brown and Brown*

Tattoos: 'Shawna,' left bicep. 'Devo,' right wrist.
Prior arrests for controlled substances, vandal-
ism, vehicular theft.
No current record of employment.
Last Known Address: 412 Crookback Drive,
Edmonton, Alberta
Sibling, Theodore (Theo) Atero, lives on West
60th

"Just don't tell anyone you got it from me," she said. "Especially Gavin."

"Won't leave the room," I said. "Thank you."

As I moved to take my place behind the table, she stood and kissed the dog one last time before heading to the door. "Take care of him," she said to the dog. To me she said: "Behave yourself."

X

The Impossible Case

Often the trouble isn't a lack of evidence but a deluge. If you post ten sentences a year online, in forums or on social networking sites, FAQs or blogs, you've left ten clues to your location, personality, activities and mindset. And how many people post ten times that much over the course of a day?

Zak Atero wasn't a particularly garrulous net user, but he'd kept an online journal for a few years. That led me to an automobile message board he frequented, though all of his posts were at least two years old. His forum responses ranged from "UR A FAG" to detailed, considerate advice on repairing the fiberglass bodies of vintage Corvettes. Sometimes in his posts he would give himself credentials he didn't have, in order to make his opinions seem more authoritative. Once, after another poster claimed to have worked on the Sunfire, Zak claimed to have met with Ford officials and offered them "tens of suggestions" which the company used in designing the new Mustang.

Getting into Zak Atero's social sphere was slightly more complicated. Hastings Street Investigations employs two fictional people for the purposes of making friends with strangers. Ned Freen and Melissa Abandando don't exist, but through them Katherine and I can find information denied to our real selves. As Melissa, Katherine friended two of Zak's former high school buddies. One of them had configured Zak's posts to appear as updates on the friend's side. By scrolling back a few years, Katherine could view Zak's most popular comments without being authorized. I would struggle to think of something like that, which is why I keep my own internet profile almost nonexistent. For Katherine it came instinctually.

After reading through his journal, I knew seven important things about Atero. I wrote them down in a list:

Atero:

- Is passionate about cars and very little else. His father was a mechanic and his brother shares his passion.
- Moved from Alberta to B.C. about the time he'd stopped posting to be close to his brother and to get better drugs.
- Went through a string of jobs in Alberta, quitting for various reasons: the manager was a dick, his co-workers accused him of stealing gratuities, the muffler shop wouldn't give him a week off to go to a car meet.
- Lives with his brother now.
- Does something illegal for money. While he didn't talk about it, he wrote an awful lot about how he wasn't allowed to talk about it.
- Was responsible for the death of a woman when he was nineteen. According to his journal, it was entirely her fault. Zak was obeying the signs, and actually under the speed limit. She was walking along the shoulder, a grey mass in his peripheral

vision. Her feet strayed over the line. The accident left him "bummed."

- <u>Had asthma as a kid.</u> In recent pictures he looked thin-chested, furtive, utterly unobtrusive. He'd never go for your throat, but he wouldn't forgive an insult, either.

Before I braced Atero I wanted to know him well enough to predict him. That meant finding and following him. Easy enough, though Atero's schedule clashed absolutely with mine. Except for weekends when I was stationed in the Kroons' building waiting for the Corpse Fucker, I was usually in bed by midnight and at the office by eight. Atero woke up between one and three in the afternoon and usually went to bed after sunrise. Disrupting my sleep schedule is part of what I get paid for — except of course I wasn't getting paid. Cliff Szabo's tithes would barely cover Katherine's salary.

Financially, then, the Kroons were subsidizing the Szabo case. I had other means of making money if I needed it. Odd jobs came up, favors for out-of-province lawyers and PIs. If my finances were dire, and they tended to reach that point at least once a year, I could subcontract to a security firm. The pay was shit, the hours long, the uniform itchy and confining and as fashionable as clown shoes, but it allowed me to keep the business going. That was everything.

Thomas Kroon the Younger came to the office around noon on Friday. I was dialing Ben to see if he wanted to tag along while I followed Atero, but his phone went straight to message. I'd tried him twice so far.

Kroon sat down in one of the client's chairs, thankful he didn't have to balance on the old bench. "Place looks better," he said. "A comfy chair makes all the difference."

"How's your father?" I asked him.

"Sick with the sniffles, though if you talked to him he'd make you think it was dengue fever. How 'bout your associate with the weak stomach?"

"Not answering his phone," I said, hanging up.

"Anyway, Mike, I won't take up too much of your time, but I do got to let you know there's a financial situation at the home."

"Is there?"

He nodded his reddish-brown square of a head. "'Fraid so. Lease on our facility has been renegotiated. It's costing us a couple more points. Nothing drastic, understand, but it makes it hard to justify certain expenses."

"I see."

"We're not talking about termination, just putting an end date in place. An exit strategy, if you will."

"Sort of like our neighbours to the south and their Middle Eastern adventure."

Kroon shrugged. "Pop thinks you do a hell of a job. I'm right there with him. But the Corpse Humper seems to have vamoosed, making you standing guard a bit redundant."

"I see."

"So let's scale things back to Saturdays and Sundays, and let's say at the end of the month we call the game."

"Reasonable," I said.

"You disagree?"

"With the scaling back? No. What I object to is giving the Corpse Fucker — Humper, whatever you want to call him — a pass. My other associate, Katherine, almost insisted the police be involved. I was content to keep them out knowing that, if pursued long enough, eventually we'd put an end to the incidents."

"That's what we all want," Kroon said.

"I don't consider a dead body particularly sacred."

"Neither do I."

"But it's wrong for the bodies to be violated. If dropping this could lead to another incident, then I do object."

"How can you if you're working for us?"

"I object morally."

He grinned. "Hard to put noggin to pillow knowing the big bad Corpse Humper's out there, uh? I'm right there with you. Difference between us is, for me, no question about it, finances top morals. You willing to work gratis, order to catch this guy?"

"I can't," I said, thinking but not adding that I already had my charity cases, and both of them trumped the Kroons'.

"So how can we come to an accord on this?" Kroon the Younger said. "Some way we can do business and part friends?"

"Give me till Remembrance Day," I said.

"You can catch him in that time?"

"Yes."

"You guarantee it?"

"Of course not."

"Remembrance Day is what, the 11th?" He turned it over in his head. "Yeah, I can do that."

He stood and extended a lanky arm across the table. "Glad we got that squared away."

As Kroon left I dialed Ben again. On the sixth ring a subdued voice said, "Yeah?"

"Where've you been?"

"In the bath."

"For the last three hours?"

"I'm fine, Mike."

"Out with it."

"I got some news, okay?"

"Bad?"

"Bad, yeah. And no I don't want to talk about it."

"Someone found your sister's body?" A white wall appeared on my mind's peripheral. Pain, relief, gladness, sorrow, and the exuberance of knowing that finally these emotions could be expressed.

But Ben said, "Not about her," and the wall sank back below the horizon. "I don't want to go over it on the phone."

"Fair enough. Interested in coming with me on a stakeout?"

"I guess."

"You've only been begging me for months."

"That was then," he said.

I closed up the office, set the alarm. The trees had begun to drop their multicoloured burden, clogging drains and sewers along the side streets that I took to get to Ben's building. Some of the houses I passed were already festooned with Hallowe'en decorations, corpses and mummies. A few even had their Christmas lights up.

I drove with the windows down, savoring the last few days of the year before the lack of heat became noticeable. Fall is the best season, and in Vancouver, at least, it seems the shortest.

I kept thinking about Amelia Yeats. I found it hard to keep my bearings around her. What threw me, and I only clarified the thought while pulling into a parking space in front of the building next to the Djembe Hut, was that Yeats was the most self-sufficient person I'd ever met. Mira had been strong, but she had needs, for companionship, for sex. Yeats didn't seem to need anyone. If she went with me it was out of desire or whim. My worry was that she'd take to me briefly, like a new toy, only to lose interest when another novelty came into her field of vision. I wondered what that would be. A performance artist? A human spider who climbs buildings with suction cups? I was already pondering the dissolution of our relationship, and being aware of this made me think I'd blown the kiss out of proportion. It had been a chance occurrence, with no guarantee to repetition. I didn't know what it had been. In relationships, I am the last person to spot the obvious play.

Ben wasn't waiting by the curb. I locked the car and took the staircase at the side of the building, banged on the door at the top. A Jamaican woman holding a baby opened the door. She nodded to the end of the hallway behind her, a door with a cardboard skeleton thumbtacked to it. "Ben in there." Smells from the kitchen, chicken and peppers. I pounded on Ben's door and made the brass-jointed skeleton dance.

"Come in."

Ben sat on the edge of the bed, dressed in cords and a hoodie, sneakers laced and tied. A cigarette burned between his fingers. He'd been crying.

"You need to tell me about this," I said, leaning on the doorframe.

"All right. In the car."

But in the car he didn't want to talk, either. I drove to a Subway where we ordered sandwiches and I filled my Thermos. I keep a case of water in the car, along with a Costco-sized box of granola bars, the nutritive kind, not the ones with chocolate coating. In the event that following Zak Atero kept us car-bound for the next twelve hours, we wouldn't suffer for food.

Following Zak proved more challenging than that. At five he came out of his brother's house and peeled out of the cul-de-sac in a white Eagle with a Jesus fish bolted above the rear plate. He was an impatient driver, cutting people off, making snap turns without signaling. When he made a right off Granville I nearly lost him. By making the next right and crawling back, I found the Eagle in the parking lot of a Save-On. Someone was in the car with Atero.

After a moment the two men climbed out of the car and crossed the lot to a Cold Beer and Wine. They were inside for seven minutes before Atero came out carrying a flat of beer and the other man, stocky, Chinese, clutching a paper bag.

"Some sort of payoff," I said.

"How can you tell?" Ben asked me.

"The paper bag."

"Alcohol comes in paper bags, case you weren't aware."

"The bag wasn't shaped to a container or bottle. It's half rolled-up, creased, so it wasn't new."

"Do you know who the Chinese guy is?"

"No."

Atero placed the beer in the car. The other man held onto the bag. They pulled out of the lot, headed east, made a left on Cambie. A few blocks north they pulled into a strip mall of predominantly East Asian shops. Atero idled while the other man dashed into a Mumbai Sweets and emerged moments later with another wadded-up paper bag.

They made four other stops before Atero dropped his partner at a parking garage near the Chapters on Broadway. The man walked down the ramp as Atero sped off.

"Here's my guess," Ben said, upright in his seat now, a bit of his vigor restored. "My guess is they're the world's least efficient garbage removal company."

Atero was picking up speed as he dashed through lanes and ran stale yellows. I got caught behind a light and he was soon out of view. Moments later I was two cars behind, and we went over the Granville Street Bridge together.

"Drugs?" Ben asked me.

"Or protection money. Could be anything."

"Think they do this every week?"

"I wouldn't be surprised."

"I bet they don't reuse those paper bags," Ben said. "I hate to think of them piling up in some landfill."

"We could ask him," I said.

"What does any of this have to do with the disappearance?"

"Beats me."

Zak Atero took a circuitous route home, over the Granville and back up the Cambie by way of a few one-way streets and alleys. It was a route designed to lose a tail, but he drove it mechanically, with no heed to what cars were in his proximity. I kept back for the most part. When he went down the alley I hung a right and then a left so that I was in front of him when he came out. I waited for him to pass me. Despite my best moves, if Atero had been looking he would have lost me easily.

He parked in front of his brother's house, a grey and brown Vancouver Special that had survived half a century without attaining much in the way of dignity. Atero went around the back. I parked in the alley with the lights off and watched through the kitchen window. His brother was beefier, his hair fairer and thinning, but they had the same axe-blade of a face, close-set eyes and narrow, high-bridged nose. The house could stand a re-siding, the eaves were clogged with mucilage from the backyard trees, and the deck, which sloped towards the alley, was in need of buttressing.

At eleven the lights in the upstairs went off, but the basement lights still burned. Through a gauze of curtain I saw Zak Atero flopped on a couch watching sitcoms, a crack pipe resting in a wooden bowl on a burn-pocked ottoman. I saw no signs of anyone else in the house.

I parked out front and set the interior light so it wouldn't come on when I opened the door. Every hour I'd walk around the block and peer over the fence to make sure Atero hadn't moved. He was comatose by midnight, the television still aglow.

At two we had our sandwiches. My window was open just enough so the windows wouldn't fog. We drank tea to keep warm.

"The glamorous world of private detection," I said, keeping my voice low. "Kind of makes you want to get back to video games, doesn't it?"

"You kidding?" He took a bite of a sloppy meatball sub that hadn't aged well. "I'm having a great time."

"Feel like telling me what got to you earlier?"

"It's business related."

"I'm in business."

He sighed. "I met with what's left of my development team. The others split for greener pastures. I don't blame them — I mean, not everyone made what I made off *Blood 2*. They wanted to meet to discuss the third one, whether we're gonna go through with it or disband."

"And you disbanded?"

"Worse," he said.

"You came up with an idea but it's not what you wanted."

"Even worse, because I didn't come up with it. Mahmoud, the project leader, brought in this twenty-one-year-old, Felipe, straight out of the Art Institute. He pitched this idea of, instead of a sequel, making a spinoff first-person shooter using the same characters." He sniffed. "Mahmoud says it's the only way to keep the team together."

"So?"

"So it's not right," he said. "Magnus and Rosalind aren't kill-crazy psychopaths. It's not a game where you pick up little white health kits, for God's sake. There's depth and poetry to it. And I know you're not an artist, or a big video game guy, but *Your Blood is a Drug!* is important to people. They'll see this FPS and think, 'Oh, Loeb doesn't care anymore, he'll license anything. He's got his paycheck. Now he just wants to piss on us.'"

"Didn't hurt those plumbers, being in a few subpar games."

"But that's a brand," Ben said. "I'm talking about a world that I created, that I wrote. You see the logo and I want you to think of more than just entrails flying at people. You think Felipe with his newly minted degree gives a shit about maintaining that legacy?"

"Not so loud."

"Sorry, okay? Sorry."

I handed him a napkin that was free of mustard stains and listened to him blow his nose. The light from the small basement windows winked out.

"I've never heard of anyone actually refer to their legacy," I said. "Let alone someone under thirty. Not every book's got to be *Moby-Dick*. If it makes the kids happy, and everyone gets paid, who gives a shit?"

"You wouldn't understand," said Ben.

"Probably not." I refilled one of the mugs I'd brought and handed it to him. The tea had already lost most of its heat.

I said, "You know that question, what'd you rather be, rich or famous? Well you've got both. Granted, you're not famous to anyone who doesn't read *PC World*, but it's still a kind of fame."

"But I want to be famous for the right things."

I shook my head. "This is like talking to a guy who won the Lotto and wonders why it couldn't have been eight million 'stead of six."

"Maybe," he said, depositing the snot-filled napkin out the window.

We watched the dark house. After fifteen minutes by the dashboard clock we packed it in. As I drove Ben home he said, "If you had your choice what'd it be?"

"Between?"

"Fame and fortune."

"I'd settle for solvency and a clean conscience."

"But if you had to choose," he said.

I looked at him like he'd been sneaking hits off Zak Atero's pipe. "You're not serious."

"So money then."

"Course."

"I could just give you some."

"You should."

"I mean it," he said. "I don't have much to spend it on. Not like I have a lot of friends. How much do you need?"

"Why be stingy, how 'bout half?"

"Seriously, Drayton."

"I'm not taking anything from you, Loeb."

"Well, Drayton, that makes me think you're full of shit. I'd've given you twenty grand here and now, and you said no. That means money's not as important."

"No," I said, "it just means money's not *most* important. There's a difference between fame and self-respect."

"All right, but say we flip the polarity. What'd you rather be, horribly in debt or have everybody hate your guts?"

"I'm already in debt."

"Say it was a choice between insurmountable, crushing poverty, and being as hated as Hitler."

"Debt, probably. Least with a good name I can earn."

"But that's my point," Ben said. "If you're the kind of person who doesn't care what they're famous for as long as they get moved to the head of the chow line, that's one thing. But if we're talking about reputation — people knowing your name stands for something, rather than just knowing your name — that's a fame that's worth something."

I paused for a beat. "You're right."

"I know."

Moments later, at the curb in front of the Djembe Hut:

"Twenty grand, huh?"

Ben grinned as he climbed out of the car.

XI

His Countenance Enforces Homage

Thanksgiving I was up early to prep the turkey. In point of fact I hadn't gone to sleep, though I'd spent a few hours lying on the bed with the dog curled around my feet, feeling the intake and release of her ribcage on my shin. I sautéed onions, celery, and sausage, added this to breadcrumbs and sage. I salted the cavity — one more hand up one more animal's orifice — and stuffed the bird. Then I rubbed a pat of butter into the turkey's hide so vigorously that I could sense the nipples of Julia Child's ghost getting hard.

I had my first Jack and Ginger of the day and watched Kurt Russell defeat aliens until my grandmother came down to make the pie.

Family-wise I think of myself as alone except for her, though she has a sister with three children and six sullen, Nintendo-addicted grandchildren. I view them as acquaintances, conventioneers who I put up and put up with for one afternoon every year, plying them with mashed potatoes and gewurztraminer and sending them on their way so that the other 364.25 days can be free of relatives. For their part, I'm sure they feel equally obligated to descend from their comfortable homes once a year to check in on the Widow Kessler and her peculiar grandson. What does he do again? Some kind of security guard or something. Oh, right. There any money in that?

Sunday night marked the first interesting occurrence in the Corpse Fucker case since the incident with the mouse. Three days previous, a member of a biker gang had been gunned down on Gaglardi Way in Burnaby. His name had been Marc Moulette. I'd arrested him once.

He'd come out of the Gentlemen's Club on Main and Powell drunk and loud, staggered across the street, colliding into a homeless man's shopping cart full of dead soldiers. Mira and I had answered the complaint. We'd turned the corner onto Carroll and seen Moulette launch an empty bottle of Stoli at a bus.

Mira had been senior. She talked to him while I made an effort to put myself between them. Moulette was bald with a long fringe of brown hair, and wore his vest with the gang rocker and patch over a grey long-sleeved shirt covered in coffee stains. He was two inches taller than me, shoulders developed but waist paunchy, clean-shaven so the tattoos on his throat would be visible.

"What's the problem, sir?" Mira said. Five foot seven and dwarfed by the beast in front of her, and not giving an inch.

"You're a cunt," Moulette said. "You're both cunts."

"Now now." Mira had her hand on her Taser. "You're going to stop the name calling and the bottle throwing and come with us."

His hand went to the cart for a fresh bottle. His eyes were on her. He didn't see me close the distance. I cracked him across the head with my collapsible baton, hard enough so that the stick would never collapse properly after that. Moulette hit his knees hard enough to rip the denim. The second shot might have been excessive, but felt almost as good as the first. It left him sprawled on the pavement, face-down, dazed.

Later Mira and I had argued about it. She said I'd undermined her authority. I said I'd saved her life. In truth I simply wanted to hit Moulette because of what he'd called her.

There had been a brief investigation which cleared us, and the threat of a lawsuit that never materialized. And here was Marc Moulette, 47, reduced now to a sack of festering, foul-smelling organs encased in a grey reptilian skin, a hole in the back of his head and most of his face contained in a separate bag, an autopsy Y-scar hacked into his chest. Below that, a steroid-abuser's shriveled testes and a stubby blue-veined prick, a tag on his ankles with his particulars. His son was coordinating the burial. Closed casket. A big deal for Roman Catholics, apparently.

Moulette would have stood trial in November. It was a safe bet his own people had taken him out.

Killed by one family, buried by the other. As I sat watching *The Thing* I wondered if the shooter and I were the only two people to ever get the best of an exchange with Marc Moulette. I wondered what Moulette would have given to at least have been able to see his killer.

At noon I went to the store for a can of whole cranberries and a carton of whipping cream. When I came back the street was packed with minivans and station wagons. I parked in the alley and once inside I ran the gauntlet of relatives, letting them pinch and smooch to their hearts' content. "He's gotten so tall." "What do you do again, Mikey? Hunh. There any money in that?"

By a quarter past four I was mildly sloshed and had retreated to the basement to play *Mortal Kombat* with my seventeen-year-old second cousin, Kaylee. She'd recently gone through a retro-punk phase, and the holes from the multiple piercings in her nose were still visible despite the absence of hardware. Before that she'd been a goth, and a stoner before that. I couldn't say what she was now, except that with her striped arm socks and matching stockings she looked vaguely like a Dr. Seuss character. Even with one hand petting the dog she was kicking my ass.

My cell went off just as Kaylee performed Sub-Zero's spine-rip finishing move. I was good sport enough to concede before picking up the phone, though fifteen years ago if I'd lost to a girl I would have pretended the ringing had distracted me. "Drayton," I said into the phone, turning down the stereo so I could hear over Ozzy's wail.

"Can you come here?" Amelia Yeats's voice, agitated and tense.

"Sure," I said, envisioning a late afternoon fuck atop her mixing board.

"Do you know where my dad's place is? The big mansion close to UBC?"

"Give me the address." She recited a house number and gave me the code to the front gate: one nine six seven.

"Fifteen minutes," I said, hanging up.

I looked down at Kaylee, who'd ingested nothing all day but cigarettes and root beer. "You driving yet?" I asked her.

"I have my learner's."

"Feel like a jaunt?"

From upstairs, on cue, came a cackle of laughter from her grandmother.

"Fuck yes," Kaylee said. "Get me away from these people."

Only when Kaylee punched it in at the gate did I apprehend the significance of the four-digit code. 1967, Summer of Love. The gate enclosed an acre of manicured lawn, dotted with sculpted mounds of bark mulch that supported an assortment of flowers, most of which had withered and lost their colour. A large oval of driveway led up to a great house at the top of the incline. A Packard, a Rolls, and an Austin mini were parked near the double-sized front doors, along with a black panel van and further down, Amelia's pistachio-coloured Jag. The property stretched another football field behind the house.

When it came time to park, Kaylee slipped it in neutral and traded places with me so I could maneuver the car between the Jag and the van. I told her to wait in the car. I strolled up, peering in dark windows, looking for signs of activity. I was reaching for the lion-shaped brass knocker when I heard the first shot.

I dashed back to the car and told Kaylee to keep her head down, feeling awful for bringing her into whatever this was. I reached through the window and popped the trunk as the second shot sounded, a thunder crack unmuffled by the house. The source was around back somewhere.

I opened the trunk and cinched up my Kevlar vest. *Stupid*, I thought, *you're not a cop anymore, you don't even have a gun with you*. I started to dial the police when the third shot drowned me out. I tossed the phone to Kaylee, told her to keep down, give me ten minutes and then phone.

At the edge of the house I saw a lush varicoloured garden, burnished reds and oranges providing a carpet of leaves and nettles over the mulch. Above and to my left was a long second-floor veranda with a roof of corrugated green plastic. I saw Amelia Yeats and a Filipino woman crouched behind an overturned table on the gazebo, thirty yards from where I stood. Assuming they were the targets, that put the shooter on the veranda.

The house had been added to over the years, and signs of unfinished renovation were still evident. Walls had been added and torn down, a second floor had been built above the garage, and the stately brown paint was newer here than on the far side by the solarium. I broke a window on the newer annex and dropped down into the basement.

Immaculate inside. Ivory-coloured carpeting in the garage with maple flooring leading up the stairs. Maple walls, decorated with every music award possible. Grammys, Junos, a Best Original Song Oscar nomination letter. Photos of Chet Yates with Sinatra, George Harrison, some of the Jacksons. I double-took when I saw Yates next to Miles Davis, a rare smile on the Dark Prince's face. Yates had a fearless fashion sense, a lot of purple suits, Holstein-patterned shirts, eccentric headware and all manner of jewellery. He was average height, round faced and curly haired like his daughter. Handsome, with a smile helped along by some sort of narcotic. If a fourth shot hadn't rung out I would have stayed to look at everything. I went up the stairs to the main foyer and treaded on marble tile until I saw the sliding door leading out to the veranda.

I could hear him before I could see him. His hair was silver now and close-cropped. He'd traded the electric suits for a terrycloth robe and Bermuda shorts. Some kind of Aztec sun had been tattooed on his gut. As I watched he aimed a nickel-plated .38 at a spider plant hanging from the roof of the veranda and blasted it. Soil and white chunks of calcite sprayed the deck.

"Jesus Christ, Daddy," Yeats called from below.

Her father grinned, held the gun to his temple.

"I'm getting tired, love. I'm tired all the time now. Don't 'spect you to understand." He spoke in a cockney-accented baritone. "Just know that your daddy — motherfucker, what are you looking at?" He took aim at a hummingbird feeder, still rocking wildly from being hit with a shard of the planter. He missed, the bullet sailing in the direction of the garden, though thankfully not towards Yeats and the other woman.

Six shots means he's empty.

I slid open the door in a crouch but my eyes saw the empty brass jackets by his feet and the open box of ammunition on the plastic table. Chet Yates took aim at the feeder and pressed the nozzle up to it and pulled the trigger, shattering it. Amelia Yeats screamed.

I went through the door, thinking in headlines, FOOLHARDY P.I. SHOT BY ECCENTRIC RECORDING LEGEND. He saw me as my fist closed on the gun. I tapped him in the face with my elbow just hard enough to cause him to break his grip on the revolver. He fell to the deck, landing on his ass. Tears in his eyes, snot and blood cascading from his nostrils.

I opened the cylinder and dumped the ammunition into my hand. "He's okay," I shouted to Yeats. I checked the brass. Two live rounds, four expended.

I looked over at Chet Yates, holding the cuff of his robe to staunch his nosebleed.

"Any other ordinance?" I asked.

He shook his head.

As we waited for Yeats and the other woman to approach he pointed to the gun and said, "Gift from Colonel Tom Parker, that was."

"Yeah?"

"The King had given it to him, is what he told me, anyway. Had a thing for guns, Elvis did." He grinned nostalgically.

"Ever meet him?" I asked.

"Just once," Chet Yates said. "A sweet man. A bit gormless, but sweet. Colonel Tom was a bit of a wanker, though."

Roanna, the Filipino woman, was the old man's live-in nurse. She sedated him and helped him to bed while Yeats and Kaylee and I gathered up the bullets and casings and dirt and shards of plastic. I'd pocketed the gun.

"He's always been weird," Yeats said, crouching with the dustpan as I swept. "He gets agitated once in a while and has these freakouts. But I've never seen him with a gun before."

"Am I wrong in thinking he was a heavy drug user at any point?"

She looked at me like the answer was self-evident.

"Of course he partied back in the day. Lately though, he's been withdrawn. He plays a lot of Nina Simone and Joni Mitchell records, and sometimes I catch him muttering to himself, 'It's all over,' or, 'They're all gone.' Ro and I want him to see someone, but there's no way to convince him to go."

"Hear that?"

From outside came the sound of a policeman's knock, patient but firm.

"The pigs," Yeats said.

"I just told them to come," Kaylee said. "I didn't say why."

Patting my pocket, I said, "Where can I dump this?"

"Basement, maybe? There's a pool down there."

I squeezed myself down an incredibly narrow and orna-mented spiral staircase as Yeats admitted the officers. I heard her talking to them in a placating tone, explaining that some neighbourhood kids had set off M-80s in the backyard, upset-ting her father, who had just been put to bed.

The pool room of Yates Manor was marble-tiled, brightly lit and dank. Both the pool and hot tub were tiled in orange with a design in blue and white on the bottom that I couldn't make out. The water was scummy and undisturbed. I flattened myself on the cold tile, reached in and opened the cage around the filter. I put the gun and shells inside and withdrew my arm, slick and clammy.

I came upstairs and backed up Yeats's story.

* * *

It was seven by the time Kaylee and I got back to my grand-mother's house. Most of the relatives had dispersed except for my Great Aunt June, Kaylee's grandmother. The two old women were watching equestrian and killing the last of a bottle of white wine.

"Where've you two been gallivanting about?" My grand-mother said.

"Work."

"On Thanksgiving?"

"Is there any food left?"

"Want me to heat it up?"

"I can manage with cold," I said.

"I thought you were in the basement playing those computer games," Aunt June said to Kaylee. "Your cousin been keeping you safe?" To me she said, "She hasn't been a nuisance, has she?"

"Furthest thing from it," I said, lifting Saran Wrap off the turkey platter.

Kaylee smiled, a tinge of pride in her pale face.

After dinner, with the grandmothers asleep in front of the tube and the two of us hunched over the dining room table, Kaylee said, "That was fucking badass."

"It was fucking badass, wasn't it?"

"Don't worry, I won't tell anyone."

I uncorked another bottle, the last of the case, and she pushed her mug forward expectantly. Here I was presented with the moral dilemma of the cool adult: do I cut her off for her own good, losing her trust, or do I continue to supply a seventeen year-old with liquor, staying cool and turning a blind eye to the consequences? I thought of myself at seven-teen, thought, *hell with it*, and filled her glass to the brim. If that was her first drink, she was overdue.

"So is that kind of stuff usual?" she asked.

"No."

"What mainly do you do? Spy on people?"

"Sometimes."

"Like catch cheating wives?"

"That racket hinged upon obscure divorce laws from mid-last century," I said. "Nowadays anyone can get a divorce for any reason. But occasionally you do get someone with an issue of trust."

"Do you own a gun?"

"Two. Handgun and a shotgun. And they're locked up at the office, case your next question was, 'Can I hold them?'"

"Ever kill anyone?" Smiling drunkenly, ashamed a little at the childishness of the question.

"Several," I said. "Once a year at least, just to keep in practice. You?"

"Not yet," she said, "but I'm a quick learner. What kind of equipment do you use?"

"Eighty percent of it can be done with a computer."

"And the other twenty-five, I mean, twenty percent?"

"Legwork, mostly."

"Tell me about some of your cases."

I told her in general terms about the Szabos.

"Sucks," she said. "There's no, like, leads or anything?"

"There's a car thief who might know something."

"You haven't talked to him?"

"Not yet."

"You haven't tried?"

I drained my mug, topped it up, pushed the bottle towards her. All the wine glasses were in the dishwasher, so we used Aunt June's Christmas gift from two years ago, a matching pair of coffee mugs with embossed horse heads on the front and horse-themed literary quotations on the back. Kaylee's read, "His neighing is like the bidding of a monarch, and his countenance enforces homage." Mine said, "There is something about the outside of a horse that is good for the inside of a man."

I told her, "If I talk to him, he'll know he's being watched. I figured I'd eschew direct confrontation till I can get a bead on him."

I watched Kaylee struggle with the bottle. I reached over and steadied her pouring hand.

"Why not go to the cops? I mean the pigs," she said, recalling Amelia Yeats's term and giggling.

"Same reason," I said. "If the pigs are involved — the cops — he'll give us nothing. And if there's even the slightest chance the Szabo kid is alive, I don't want the kidnapper suddenly concerned about leaving evidence."

"You think he's dead?"

"Almost certain."

"Szabo," she said, turning the name over. "I remember seeing him on a flyer. If he's alive, where do you think he is?"

"Obviously if I knew that —"

"No," Kaylee said, "what I mean is, like, what kind of place would he be? Someone's home?"

Anywhere from a home to a hole in the ground, I thought, then realized with disgust that I'd said it out loud.

Her black-rimmed eyes teared up. I passed her one of my grandmother's neatly-triangled linen napkins.

"You can't leave him like that," she said.

"No."

"You have to find him."

"I wish it were that easy, cos," I said.

"Yeah." She stared at the inscription on the back of the mug. "'His countenance enforces homage.' The fuck does that even mean?"

I let her have the bed and watched with amusement as the dog, gorged on giblets and table scraps, curled up next to her. I sat in the old armchair with headphones on listening to Koko Taylor until I couldn't take it and picked up the phone.

I was exuberant from helping Yeats, chastened by my talk with Kaylee, and more than a little drunk, but mostly I was overconfident. I'd helped a damsel and I'd seen the body of an old enemy. For a brief moment I felt like I was more than a poor bastard whose best-case scenario was not adding too much to the misfortunes of others. It was time to Do Something.

At the office I had a small file on Atero, but I kept the original sheet that Mira had given me in my wallet. I pulled it out and smoothed it, then looked up Theo Atero's phone number. I asked for Zak.

"Who's calling?"

"Mike," I said.

"One moment." Clump-clump-clump down the stairs, a brief back-and-forth between the brothers.

Then: "This is Zak, man. What up?"

"My name's Drayton. Your contact info was in a cellphone I found on the bus this morning."

"Don't know no one that takes the bus. Turn it in to Lost and Found, man."

"To be honest with you, Mr. Atero, the phone was in a jacket pocket on the seat next to me. In the other pocket was a paper bag containing a rather large sum."

"Really."

"Yes. You can understand my reluctance in turning this over to Lost and Found."

"Totally," Atero said. "What'd you say your name was?"

"Michael Drayton. Let me give you my office address. Could you come around tomorrow afternoon and pick it up?"

He could.

XII

Ko Business

Knowing Atero didn't rise until late afternoon didn't make me less anxious to get to the office early. By seven I'd quieted my stomach with a pot of tea, deposited an Anusol where the dog needed it, and warned my grandmother I might be late. I was at the office by 7:30. The lights were already on.

Inside, Katherine was at her desk, head lowered so her forehead almost touched the textbook. She looked up groggily at me.

"Biology," she said.

I set the kettle to boil and lifted off the wall panel behind the door. Behind it was a wireless hard drive that backed up both computers, a fireproof document box, and a smaller wooden box that held my Glock 31. I brought out the pistol and set about cleaning and loading it. After handling Chet Yates's Elvis revolver, the automatic felt like a toy.

"I started at five this morning and I think I'm dumber now," Katherine said. "Bio stinks. The midterm is straight memorization, a hundred terms. Prokaryotic and eukaryotic. Kingdom Phylum Class Something Family Genus Species. I can never remember what the 'on' stands for in 'kids play catch on the farmer's green shed.' Organism? That can't be right."

"Can't help you there," I said. "Straight B-minuses in everything that wasn't English or Crim."

Her monologue of academic despair continued as I fed .357 shells into the gun's clip. Eventually she got around to asking what I was doing.

"Getting ready for my meeting with Zak Atero," I said.

"Here? When?"

"We agreed on this afternoon. By Zak's sleep schedule that probably means four, but he could show earlier."

"This is a person who might have kidnapped a child."

"We don't know anything for sure. Hence the meet."

I tucked the box away, replaced the panel. I sat at the table with the Szabo file in front of me and the Loeb file like a hillock to my right. I placed the gun in the file cabinet by my side.

"You're not worried that he knows where to find you?" Katherine asked me.

"Anyone with an internet connection knows where to find me."

She sighed. "You could have told me beforehand."

"I did. You've got hours before you should be out of here."

"That's what you want me to do, is it?"

She rolled her fancy chair over to the table so we were eye to eye.

"Can I be frank? I feel like you're putting me in a box."

I pushed the monitor and keyboard aside. "We're going to have *this* conversation, are we?"

"Every time you do something like this I either have to agree with you or become this shrewish feminine stereotype who poo-poos anything the boys want to do and ruins their fun. And I don't want to be in that position."

"You're taking a Gender Studies course, aren't you?"

"Don't shut it down like that. It's helping me articulate what I've been dealing with since I started working with you." She squared her shoulders. "At times you can be like the guy who makes sexist jokes in the workplace, and when someone calls him on it, says, 'Why can't you women have a sense of humour?'"

"I defy you to name something misogynist I've done or said to you, ever."

"It's not about you, Mike, don't get defensive. It's about our relationship." Quickly adding, "At work. This is the second time you've put me in a position where I either have to put myself in harm's way, or else have you think I'm a ball buster. And don't say it's because you care so much about the Szabo kid. I know your intentions are good. This is about the way you do things, not what you're trying to do."

"Okay," I said, trying to act like my main objection hadn't just been kicked out from under me. "You know I respect your opinion — least I hope you know that. Why else would I want you to stay on? Far as putting you at risk, you're not supposed to work today. Last thing I want is to get you in any kind of jackpot."

"Thank you."

"I'll admit that this confrontation with Atero could be a mistake. I took a shot with the pawn shop and I'm taking one here because I don't see any options. And I hope you appreciate that."

"I do," Katherine said.

"And I can't promise you that however this resolves itself, I won't head right into another pile of shit. It's how I work. It's not a perilous job but it does have its risks."

She was nodding, ready to reply, but I was fired up now.

"And I'll tell you something else," I said. "I like that part of my work. Yesterday I disarmed a lunatic, put my cousin at risk, almost got myself shot."

"On Thanksgiving?"

I nodded. "Best holiday I've had in a while. I'm not an adrenaline junkie, but I won't deny that part of me wants to push things. I like putting people under pressure and seeing what happens. And I like being put under pressure. You learn things that way. My grandfather was like that, and I can see my cousin's going to be, if she isn't already. So maybe it's genetic."

"And I'm not like that, is what you're saying." Katherine withdrew her hands from the table. "You don't even know me, what I've been through."

"It's not about you," I said, quoting her. "It's how you react. Me, I jump into the fray."

"Or start the fray."

"Right," I said. "And you're more staid. More prudent. But we seem to work well together."

"Occasionally."

"So how do we make this work? Do you want out?"

"No," she said. "I don't want out."

"Do you want to stay?"

"I don't know."

"You should decide that soon."

So often after a blow-up, the easiest way to go on with things is to act as if it never occurred. Katherine studied and I sent out emails to the various groups and agencies that make up my Monday morning mailing list. Weekly emails aggravate some people, but most are sympathetic to a missing-child inquiry. I worked through the list for Django James Szabo and then ran the same list for Cynthia Loeb.

I had a message from Pastor Flaherty saying he'd set up an interview for Mr. Szabo with the local news. He asked if I wanted to be present. I wrote him back saying that if Mr. Szabo requested it, I'd be there, but otherwise no. I hate being on television — I look greasy and eager, and since I don't censor myself with any consistency, I tend to say the least helpful thing.

At ten past ten, three people came through the door, none of them Zak Atero. Two looked to be in their sixties and all three were Chinese. We shook hands. When they seated themselves, the elderly couple sat across from me, while their grandson or nephew interpreted. The elderly man wore a blue short-sleeved dress shirt, red and black tie, dark blue pants with a sharp crease, and a digital watch with orange buttons. His wife wore black slacks and a green padded jacket, and sunglasses she never took off. Their grandson or nephew wore hip hop brands, cutting edge, but out of deference to his elders, his jersey was tucked in and his baseball cap was spun brim forward. His name was Frank, and the family name was Ko.

Their story was a straightforward custody-related trace job. The Kos' youngest son had married a white woman and they'd had a child, named Michael of all things. The son had flown to Taiwan on a business trip a year and a half ago. He'd been killed when his taxi was broadsided by a bus. In the aftermath, his wife Rita managed to piss away her share of her husband's life insurance, from what I understood not an insignificant sum.

As Frank told it, Rita had made unreasonable financial demands on the Kos, which had been turned down. A month ago, in retaliation, she took her son out of school, cleaned out her condo, and skipped town, leaving no note and no contact information.

It sounded to me like a leverage move rather than a genuine attempt to sever ties. Rita seemed to be hoping that the family would be more supportive if she denied them access to Michael for a time. My suspicion was that she'd moved out to the suburbs, or possibly the Island, and was living under her maiden name, Riley. Sure enough, when I found them a week later, they were subletting a basement suite in an area of Fort Langley called Walnut Grove. Rita was working part-time in a strip mall electronics store, shtupping the evenings-and-weekends manager while little Michael languished in daycare.

When Frank and the Kos had signed the contract and left, I said to Katherine, "You plan on moving to Montreal when you graduate?"

"Haven't thought about it," she said. "I guess I'd go if a job was there. Why?"

"You're learning French."

"You might not be aware, Mike, but Canada is a bilingual nation."

"French won't help you much if you stick around Vancouver. Why not learn Mandarin?"

"Why don't you learn Mandarin?"

"I'm sitting here thinking that myself," I said. "Might increase my client base, give me an edge. Learning French is like learning Latin, least if you live in B.C. Aside from reading the back of a Cheerios box, it's of little practical use."

"I'll inform the millions of Francophones you feel that way."

"You do that."

A while later she said, "You don't know any French?"

"'*Est-ce que je peux aller aux toilettes?*' is about the sum of it."

Katherine left at one to catch a bus to the college. I pretended it was a work day like any other and sat at my table fielding emails. After a point preparation becomes counterproductive. The readiness is not all.

Atero appeared on the stair camera at four. I was on the phone with Cliff Szabo finalizing plans for the interview. The journalist had talked his station into filming a news segment on Django James, replete with a rundown of the case, interviews with the principles, and probably a lot of shots of Django's father walking the streets alone, turning his grief-stricken visage off-camera and sighing wistfully. Horseshit, yes, but that's what it takes to get on the box.

I made Atero wait on the landing until I'd concluded with Szabo, then ushered him in. He took in the room with brief sweeps of his head, nodding hyper-actively. Tweaked, possibly. I sat down and motioned for him to do the same.

Up close Zachary Atero exhibited several signs of drug use, most obvious being the grey pallor to his skin. He clasped his hands, rubbed them, turned his wristwatch and fiddled with his cellphone, all before we even began to speak.

"So, yeah," he said, rubbing at his temple.

I tipped my chair back. "So."

"You got something for me, is what you said."

"Did I?"

"Some sort of paper bag, I think it was." He sniffed, ran his hand under his nose reflexively, caught himself, and wiped his hand on his sequin-covered hoodie.

"Is that why you're here?"

Perplexed and grinning, Atero said, "You called me."

"But why are we here?"

"Why are you —"

"Why am I sitting behind this table, across from you? Why would I want to do that on a Tuesday afternoon?"

Grinning still, all a misunderstanding. "How exactly would I know, dude, when you're the one that set this up?"

"Guess, Zak. Guess why I'm talking to you. What I want from you."

Eyes narrowing, cagey. "You're a cop?"

"I'm a botanist," I said. "Answer the question. What could I want from you?"

Snorting, sniffing, standing up. Pushing back from the table, glancing towards the door. His movements circular, hesitant.

"Not sure 'zactly what you want me to say."

"Django James Szabo."

One eyebrow raised. "What's that?"

I pushed Django's Missing flyer across the table. Atero took a step forward, looked down, then back at me. Dead-eyed, trying his best to keep me from reading his reaction.

Child abductor, I thought.

"I don't fucking know anything about a missing kid," he said.

"Who would you suggest I ask?"

"Man, how would I know? I look like I should have a kid around me?"

"No," I said.

"So why ask me?"

"I figured you might know."

"Well I don't." He moved towards the door, then spun back, angry. "And I shouldn't be made to answer questions like a common criminal and be treated like that. It's against my rights."

Now I stood up and came around the table and looked down into his hatchet face. "Why, 'cause you're a bag boy for some dipshit bookie?"

Grinning and pulling back, he said, "You don't have a clue who I represent, do you?"

"Ask me if it keeps me up nights."

"Lloyd Crittenden. Know who he works for?" A broad smile, about to play his trump card. "Tony Chow."

The name resonated. "He's incarcerated."

"Doesn't mean he doesn't know what goes on," Atero said. "Or that he won't stick up for his boy."

"And you're his boy?"

"Like this," he said, folding his middle finger over the index.

The grin lost its voltage as I stared at him, a standard police issue eye-fucking, driving his grand rebellion back down to a petulant defiance.

"This Crittenden," I said, "he's your boss?" Making it sound demeaning.

"We work together," Atero said.

"You work for him?"

"Yeah."

"Take me to him."

Eyebrows shooting up. "Pardon?"

"Let's go see him," I said.

"I can't just do that."

Reaching to the table without breaking eye contact, I picked up one of my cards and handed it to him. "Give this to Crittenden," I said.

"Michael Drayton Hastings Street Investigations Last of the Independents," he read without inflection or pause.

Atero turned the card in his hand, probably weighing the pros and cons of tearing it up and throwing the scraps at my feet. Eventually he nodded. "I'll tell him." He left, pausing at the top of the stairs for one last scowl before the descent.

It took me hours to unclench. When I got home my grand-mother was watching some sort of crime drama on TV, the kind that adds a gloss of titillation to the weekly rape-murders before wrapping everything up by 7:58 sharp.

I fixed dinner and then dragged my dog for a walk. I tried to tell myself, and the dog, that I'd actually done something to advance the case. Neither of us seemed all that certain.

Snake's Eye

Crittenden waited until Friday to contact me. Cliff Szabo had come by that morning for our weekly meeting, and I'd given him a rough account of what I'd been up to, omitting Crittenden and Zak Atero for the moment, which meant I told him nothing. Better nothing than not enough was my thinking: after his reaction to Ramsey, I was reluctant to give Cliff any provocation. All I had was a tenuous thread connecting a pawn shop owner to a car thief and the thief's boss. Adding an irate father to the mix wouldn't help anyone.

When Crittenden phoned, I was leaning back in my chair, mind on Amelia Yeats. Ben was chewing Katherine's ear about the superiority of Christian Bale's Batman to all others. I took the call on the balcony, trying to distance myself from the conversation in the office and the steady hum of my own dirty thoughts.

"Mr. Drayton? Michael Drayton?"

"This is he." Up the block two silver-haired cops were talking to a woman with a shopping cart full of liquor boxes and camping gear.

"You've been expecting a call from me."

"Mr. Crittenden."

"Do you know me?"

It seemed a strange question to ask. "I know you're married to the niece of Anthony Chow, who owns property around the Lower Mainland, some of which might be legitimate."

Laughter over the cell-to-cell static. Up the street the cops were trying to calm the woman down and help her collect the mess of tent pegs and string which had fallen through the grated bottom of the cart and wound around the rear axle.

"You've done your homework," Crittenden said. "In point of fact Anthony is chiefly a restaurateur, and I oversee a few of his establishments."

"Making Zak Atero, what, delivery boy?"

"How about we continue this conversation in person?" Crittenden said. "Do you know Blue Papaya on Richards? I can send a car for you."

The cops up the street were moving on, leaving the shopping cart lady to work out her own problems.

"I can walk it," I said.

"If noon works, I'll see you then."

It was 10:14 a.m. by the computer's clock. In the time I was on the balcony Ben and Katherine had resolved nothing.

"Can I be honest?" Katherine said to him. "Much as I love elaborate theories about different incarnations of Bruce Wayne, know what I like better? Getting my work done so I can study. Some of us have jobs that require we do them." With a false smile she turned back to her keyboard as if the matter were settled.

"Did your first-person shooter problem resolve itself?" I asked Ben, settling into my chair so I could view the clock without straining my neck.

Ben shrugged. "They're going ahead with it. Evidently I don't have as much clout as I thought."

"None of us do."

"Anyway," he said, "I was asking Hough what she was going as for Hallowe'en, and that prompted me to recall the most traumatic incident of my pre-teen years. Do you want to hear it?"

"God no," Katherine said without looking up.

"Well in that case," Ben said, and launched into his anecdote.

I was weighing the idea of taking my gun with me. I decided against it. I decided if Crittenden wanted a shootout he wouldn't have invited me so cordially, and if he wanted to threaten me, then possessing a gun wouldn't tip things in my balance. Better he saw me as a civilian.

Ben said, "It was right after the *Animated Series* came out, and guess what I wanted to go as for Hallowe'en. I remember they had an amazing costume at the mall, utility belt, cowl, the works. My mom said we couldn't afford it."

"What a hardship," Katherine said.

"I begged and pleaded, and eventually Mom said she'd make me one. Her mom was a seamstress. Mom didn't carry on that tradition — too bourgeois for her when she was growing up — but she had all the sewing stuff, her mom's Jay-gnome and the rest."

"It's pronounced Ja-no-me," Katherine said. "Janome. In Japanese it means 'snake's eye.'"

"Anyway, day and night Mom worked on this costume. I think she actually had to start over again because the first one was too small. Day of the class Hallowe'en party she let me try it on. I was so stoked."

While Ben spoke I thought, *I am scared shitless*. I put that thought under glass and examined it, like a fresh specimen on a lepidopterist's table. I decided that instead of the gun I'd bring my fold-out pocket knife. Useless in a fight, but it worked well enough as a totem. I ran my hand over the wood handle with its steel fasteners and felt a little better.

Ben said, "My Mom's costume, God bless her, was a mess. The cowl was a toque with floppy triangles stitched on. The cape was safety-pinned to a pair of my dad's long underwear.

Brown long underwear. A utility belt made of yellow felt, and for some reason, fingerless gloves. I mean, just picture a fat kid in that getup."

Katherine was laughing despite herself.

"So I get to the party and of course there's eight other Batmen, all in their badass store-bought costumes, and me, looking more like the piano-playing dog from *the Muppets*. Believe me I got my ass kicked. I put it all on my mom. She was so upset she swore off sewing. When I think back I remember the physical beating, then the anger at my mom for trotting me out in that sacrificial lamb costume, and then the shame from years later over how bad I made her feel after she worked so hard. 'It's the thought that counts' doesn't fly with kids. That is trauma."

"I went as a spider one year," Katherine said. "Cotton batting web draped around my real arms to hold up the two fake ones, and yes I know a spider has eight, but mine had four. I remember everything coming loose and unfurling, and some poor girl, I think it was Sarah Whitehead, tripped over it and sprained her ankle."

"Homemade costumes are the worst," Ben said. He turned to me. "Any horror stories?"

"I went as a cop for seven years running," I said. "One year, though, I was big into pro wrestling and I went as —"

"Macho Man?" Katherine asked. "Jake the Snake?"

"Worse. Bret 'the Hitman' Hart. Pink leotard, drug store shades, Intercontinental championship belt made of aluminum foil. Now *that* was an ass-kicking."

"Dear God," Ben said. He made the sign of the cross over me as I mimed being dead.

The tinted windows of the Blue Papaya had been trimmed with paper pumpkins. A gauze cobweb hung over the door.

The inside was lit partly by blue neon, and the chairs and table-cloths were black. Sarah McLachlan emoted from the speakers flanking the bar. I nodded to the hostess, a bottle blonde of advancing years, and followed her through the swinging doors into the muggy kitchen.

Off to the right, down a narrow hallway made narrower by two freezers, was an office, little more than a doorless cubbyhole. A cigarette-burned desk held an old beige and grey computer and an even older dot matrix printer, which spewed out faded type in intermittent screeches. There was room for two chairs. One of these was taken up by a stout dark-haired woman with an inscrutable face and eyes that sized you up and dismissed you without registering the slightest emotion. If I'd stuck out my hand and said "My name's Mike, what's yours?" her response would have been at most a shrug of indifference. Probably not even that.

"Crittenden," I said.

"Not here."

"Where would he be, then? He asked to see me."

She glowered. Behind me a server ran past with a steaming platter of noodles and seafood. The kitchen smelled of bean soup. Clouds of flour and starch drifted through the beams of harsh light from the neon overheads. The floor was tacky.

We held each others' gaze until I sneezed and she shot back in her chair, in a way that might have been warranted if I'd unholstered a gun. Her chair hit the back wall, dislodging papers from the wobbly shelf behind her head.

"Sorry," I said. "Haven't felt like myself since that last trip out to my brother's swine and chicken farm. Think I might've picked up some type of flu." I coughed, bringing my hand to my mouth seconds too late, then wiping my mouth and using that hand to prop myself in the doorway. "Any chance you could find Crittenden for me?"

She sprang out of the chair and squeezed past me. I watched her weave through the crowded kitchen and head up a tight spiral staircase in the corner behind the deep fryers. As she ascended, she was wiping imaginary germs off the sleeves of her fur-lined leather overcoat.

Eventually she came down trailed by a thin caucasian with silver-blond hair. He wore a herringbone sweater, navy slacks, thin gold chains around his neck tucked inside the collar of the dress shirt he wore beneath the sweater. He had rough hands and a creased face. His silver and bronze beard was a week's growth past being well-groomed, which may have been the fashion he was shooting for. His grey eyes regarded me benevolently. Behind the manners was an indifference that gave me the sense that Lloyd Crittenden had killed people, deliberately and up close.

"You're early," he said. "Would you like to talk up in my office, or would you prefer a booth in the restaurant? Have you eaten yet?" He turned towards an Asian man who was dumping a box of frozen squid into a deep fryer basket. Crittenden said something in Chinese to the man. Then he touched my sleeve and motioned me back to the dining room.

He sat in the corner booth facing the street and I took up the chair across from him. With easy cheerfulness he said, "How do you feel about a nice single malt?"

"I'm more of a bourbon man," I said. "But it's like Faulkner said: between Scotch and nothing I'll take Scotch."

He grinned. "I think we can accommodate you." He pointed past my head to a bottle on the shelf behind the bar. The barman nodded. Turning back to me, Crittenden said, "Faulkner fan, are you?"

"Not particularly, but I went to college."

"One of my great regrets," he said. "When your father's a commercial fisherman and his father's a commercial fisherman, you don't put as much value in education as you should. I did have an aptitude for history. I could have been good at it, I think."

"You're fluent in Cantonese," I said. "That's a feat. Just the other day I was thinking I should learn Mandarin."

"It's the business language of the future," Crittenden said. "My family's from Macau, so both dialects are second nature. One of the benefits of colonialism."

"At least for the colonizers."

The barman abandoned his post long enough to bring over a decanter of amber whiskey and a carafe of water. Crittenden himself built the drinks.

"Basil-Haden," he said. "The Reserve. What should we drink to?"

"The confusion of our enemies," I said.

He held his glass up to mine. "That could be a tall order, Michael."

"Long list of enemies?"

"No," he said, "only that there might be some overlap between one's enemies and another's employees or friends."

I took a sip of bourbon. Christ, it was good. Lloyd Crittenden knew how to mix a drink.

"I don't think it has to go that way," I said. "We're both here to make a buck. There's no reason everyone can't come out ahead."

Crittenden nodded as if seriously considering this. "At whose expense are we profiting?"

"My client's. Atero knows something about a missing kid. My client's a well-off family member who wants to see the kid returned."

I dug in my pocket, aware that this garnered the attention of the two men in the booth to my left. I came out with Madame Thibodeau's card and flipped it onto the table.

"I work with this quack psychic," I said. "She snags grieving relatives, puts them on the installment plan. I supply details that she can pull out of thin air. Some of these marks she strings along for months, even years."

Crittenden nodded. "It sounds lucrative," he said. "How does Zachary Atero fit in?"

I explained what I knew about Django Szabo's disappearance and Atero's connection. I said, "This rich relative's starting to think my partner's a fraud. She went to the metaphysical well one time too often, and now he's saying there's no more dough without results."

"There will be others."

"He's also saying the reward for the kid is a cool seventy five."

"Thousand."

"Maybe that's chicken feed to you," I said, "but say I get him up to a hundred fifty? Or higher?"

Crittenden finished his drink. "How exactly would you accomplish that?"

"Simple," I said. "Atero turns the kid over to me. I mail one of the kids' garments to the rich uncle, maybe douse it with a little red dye first. We make the uncle think the kid's in dire peril, then arrange it so it looks like I saved the kid at the last minute. Once I get the money, we split it between us and go our separate ways."

"You, me, your partner, and Zachary."

"Long as I get mine, I'm happy leaving my partner out. How you divide your and Atero's shares is none of my business."

Crittenden nodded. "It sounds lucrative," he repeated. "Unfortunately, Michael, I'll have to pass. Another drink?"

"If you're having one. Why exactly do you have to pass?"

"Because," he said, "I don't believe a word of what you've said. I don't believe Clifford Szabo could be called a 'rich relative' by even the most generous definition of the term. I don't believe you'd seriously entertain any kind of partnership with this psychic, and if you had, you wouldn't locate your office in such a ramshackle building, with such little attention paid to looking legitimate. And," he said, setting the refreshed drink in front of me, "pardon me for offering a judgment of your character based on the short time we've been conversing, but you're not capable of that kind of deception. I didn't go to college, but I'm a great reader of faces. I can tell from yours that you're neither a killer nor a scoundrel."

I drank my bourbon, trying to mimic the calm Crittenden exuded.

"Not that you'd be a pushover if it came to a quarrel," he added. "I don't doubt that you'd be formidable. But you don't enjoy hurting others."

"And you do?" I asked.

"Not especially," he said. "Like you, I want to make a living with as little interference as possible. But I have come into contact with that species of cruelty. Do you know Gregor Hess?"

I nodded.

"Gregor is a lifelong friend of my wife's uncle, ever since Anthony owned his first nightclub. Back when he was on the circuit, Gregor would come there after every fight to celebrate. When his pro career ended, Anthony made sure he was never out of work, and that Gregor's kids always had new clothes for school."

"Good to have friends like that when you're serving time."

"My point is," Crittenden said, "I've seen Gregor extract a man's eyeball from his skull with no more compunction than either of us would have taking an egg from a carton. Actions like that have a tendency to write themselves onto a person's face. You can look at Gregor and know instantly what he's capable of. Your face lacks that."

"Say it does," I said. "Say all I'm interested in is the safe return of the kid. Putting aside the bullshit, what would it take to get him back?"

"Frost on hell, I'm afraid."

I finished my drink.

"Zak Atero bragged about knowing you," I said. "It's been my experience that juiced-in people don't have to brag."

"An astute observation."

"Atero doesn't act like a sadist or a pederast. From talking with him I get the idea the kid's still alive."

"Could very well be," Crittenden said.

Could very well be.

"So what's the motivation for keeping him from his father?" I asked. "How do you benefit at all?" I threw my hands up and leaned back in the chair. "That's what baffles me."

"Your mistake," he said, "is in thinking I'm involved in any way." He gestured around the room. "As you said, what would it profit me? The whole business turns my stomach, as I'm sure it does yours."

"So?"

"I have no interest in becoming part of this. I don't know what Zachary Atero does in his off hours. I don't want to know. Between us, he's not the most intelligent young man, and he's fighting his battles with substance abuse. It's not my place to interject myself in his affairs."

"I can respect that," I said. "But I need to find out what Atero knows. So what we have to do is come up with a way for me to do my job without imposing on yours."

Crittenden shook his head. "I appreciate the overture, but I can't allow you to harass Zachary again."

"He can't be worth that much to you," I said. "Or the aggravation I'd cause."

"He's not. You described him aptly, someone on the fringes who likes to brag. But his brother Theo is a friend, among other things. Theo isn't a man who needs to brag." He rapped his knuckles on the table. "That is how things lie, and it's unlikely to change."

"You know I can't leave off him," I said.

"I'm afraid you'll have to."

"Or?"

He stood up, still smiling that avuncular smile. "Let's not demean ourselves by trading insults. Nice meeting you, Michael."

Crittenden shook my hand and passed through the kitchen doors. A large man with a shaved head held the front door for me. After knocking back the rest of my drink, I walked out into an afternoon downpour.

Nothing about Crittenden made sense. I couldn't shake the feeling there was something empty about his threat. Doubtless he had the muscle. He'd mentioned Hess and Chow, both tough men. But they were both in jail. How much juice did Crittenden really have? Was he under pressure from someone else?

It bothered me that I'd already assumed I'd defy him.

I stood outside and let the rain wash down the collar of my coat, dispersing the bourbon fog. As I enjoyed the regional pastime — getting wet — a black cargo van pulled up. It was tricked out with a grille, a winch, and a rack of lights. ARIES SECURITY was emblazoned on the door. Out stepped Roy McEachern, sandy-haired and square-jawed, an umbrella billowing out from his hand as he moved toward me.

"Cats and dogs, ain't it?" he said.

XIV

Ramrod, Wreckage, and Ruin

The inside of McEachern's van smelled of warm beef and garlic butter. He swept a pile of papers from the passenger's seat and placed his foil-wrapped lunch on the dash. I climbed in. As we reached the Granville Street Bridge I watched a group of joggers in matching red spandex pull up, huddle and start back the way they came, beaten by the downpour.

"How's your grandmother?" McEachern asked me.

"Doing good. She had a nice Thanksgiving."

"And how're things at the office?"

"It's still there," I said.

"Can't ask for more than that, now, can you?" He followed Granville to Broadway, taking a circuitous route to my grandmother's house. As we crawled up Laurel he veered left and circled Douglas Park, empty save for two kids in rain slickers and galoshes playing kickball in the empty concrete pool.

"Remember losing your trunks there one summer?" McEachern laughed. "Your granddad and me are sitting on the porch drinking Crown, and you come walking up that street stark naked."

"First of all I didn't lose them. Jenny Qiu told me her beret fell to the bottom of the pool. When I dove down to find it, she slid them off and hid them."

That patronizing smile. "Easy, Mike, not trying to make light of you."

"Exactly what you're doing."

He sighed, oh the young and their delusions. "Believe it or not, I had other reasons for coming to see you."

"Which I'm sure you'll get around to when you're ready."

Wind rattled the laurel bushes along the avenue. A sheet of water ran down McEachern's windshield. The wipers beat a stately 3/4 tempo on the glass.

"You met with Lloyd," he said as he passed Laurel and circled the park again.

"Lloyd. Yeah, I met with Lloyd. Is Lloyd a friend of yours?"

"I know him through his boss," McEachern said.

"Anthony Chow."

"I'm not hitting the links with him, but we do business, yeah."

"Knowing his business landed Chow in prison."

"That doesn't taint the legitimate work I do," McEachern said. "And it's not like it wouldn't get done regardless. There's a host of ex-cops eager to take my place."

"So if you don't feel guilty, then what are you doing here?"

"Keeping a promise," he said. "Or trying to, if you'll listen. You look at this with some sense of perspective, you'll find out I'm not the enemy, Mike."

"No," I said. "Just a guy who works for a guy who's keeping a father from his son."

McEachern's expression: sadness and disapproval and maybe a little pride. "So what did he say?"

"Crittenden? That if I pressed Atero he'd press back."

"He means it," McEachern said.

"You think?"

He pulled to the curb, leaving the engine running and the wiper blades pounding out their waltz. The lights in the Douglas Park Community Centre were burning. I wondered if they still ran karate classes there like the one I'd taken as a kid.

"Your granddad and I had run-ins with people who worked for Anthony Chow," McEachern said, "including Gregor Hess. Only man I ever saw your granddad size up like he knew he couldn't take him."

"And here you are years later," I said. "My grandfather's dead, Hess and Chow are in jail, and you're working for Chow's son-in-law. You ascribe that to cosmic irony or your own ability to raise the spirits of the people you work for?"

"I work for myself," McEachern corrected. "And I won't hear anymore shit from you. I do business with Chow companies — security, background checks. Why not? If I shunned every dollar that came from a somewhat shady deal, I'd be in the streets."

Twisting his body to look at me.

"Goddamnit, Mike, this superior attitude of yours. I offered to take you on, and not just 'cause you're Jacob's grandkid, either. Because I know you got the aptitude for it. You throw that in my face. Fine. I think, Okay, couple years of being on his own might do him some good. Might help him ditch some of the fanciful notions he's picked up. I got another eight years of this, tops. I know I could sell the business to Schuster or Sidhu, but I still hold out hope for you, Mike."

"Don't," I said.

"Right." He heaved a sigh and rolled his eyes the way Katherine sometimes does. "On account of your granddad is the only reason I don't put you out of business, and believe me, I could."

"Could you?" I opened the door. "Thanks for the annual lecture, Roy. Same time next year."

"Hold up," he said, touching the collar of my coat. I shrugged his hand away. "Listen to me," he implored.

I shut the door, folded my hands on my lap. Looked over at him expectantly, cocked my head sarcastically.

"I hit a similar snag with the Szabo case," he said. "Wasn't just financial, why I broke it off with him. I took a look at the paperwork behind Imperial Pawn, their business license, lease agreements. If you know how to read a paper trail, you can find things out you can't otherwise."

I nodded, cursing myself for not thinking of that. I made a mental note to write a real note for the office wall: JUST BECAUSE IT'S NOT ONLINE DOESN'T MEAN IT'S NOT OUT THERE.

McEachern said, "Turns out Lloyd's wife, Chow's daughter-in-law, sits on the board of a venture finance company which leant Mr. Ramsey a five-figure sum to renovate the store."

"So once you saw Susan Chow's name, you torpedoed the investigation?"

He shook his head. "I didn't torpedo shit. I worked it until I was out of options and Szabo was a month remiss. What I didn't do, Mike, is intentionally pick a fight with Lloyd Crittenden."

"I don't want anything to do with your friend Lloyd," I said. "But I'd like fifteen minutes in a locked room with Zak Atero and a phone book."

"Theo's brother," McEachern said, nodding, a spark behind his gaze. Despite himself he was taking an interest in the case. "You think Zak was the car thief, picked Django up by accident. It's workable, though why didn't he just dump the kid at the nearest gas station? What evidence are you going on?"

"Ramsey and his daughter were discussing whether to warn Zak."

"They told you that?"

"I heard it from them, yeah."

He shook his head, grinning. "You bugged the pawn shop. You devious bastard."

Despite myself I felt a little pride. "It was good, wasn't it?"

And then we looked at each other, and the grin and the pride faded, and we were adversaries again.

"Listen," McEachern said. It was becoming his catch phrase. "With Hess and Anthony behind bars, there's not much Lloyd can do if you cross him now."

"Good to know," I said.

"I said *now*." He tapped my shoulder with two fingers. "That's not to say that he'd just forget about you. One way or another he'll make you pay for crossing him. Maybe down the road, when Anthony is back on the street and Szabo's forgot about you. Then there's nothing to stop him from revisiting things. You willing to write that kind of check against yourself?"

I opened the door. "I have to go."

McEachern's paw slammed down upon my knee. "Your granddad and I promised each other, anything happens, we look out for our partner's kids. If it was me, I'd hope Jacob would talk to my daughters the way I'm talking to you. Help me keep at least that much of the promise. Leave them alone."

"Remember what you said to me when I asked you for the Szabo file?"

He shrugged. "I didn't want you on the case."

"But remember what you said? It was to the tune of 'go fuck yourself.'"

The righteous feeling of slamming the door on him and having the final word dissipated as I got to the front steps of my grandmother's house. I looked back. The van was crawling up the street, Roy McEachern hidden behind the tinted glass.

Waiting in the foyer of Yeats Manor for Amelia to come down, keeping her father company, made me feel eighteen again. I half-expected Chet Yates to ask me whether my intentions for his daughter were honorable. I'm not sure how I would have answered him.

Sitting in an uncomfortable Stickley, holding a cup of organic Earl Grey, the bergamot strong enough to render the brew undrinkable, I felt Chet Yates's yellowish eyes searching me. I wondered if he recognized me. His concern seemed to be whether I recognized him. I kept an uncomfortable smile on my face and let him direct the conversation.

"Where are you and Amelia headed?" he asked after wrapping up a long anecdote about the bassist of a band I've never heard of.

"Not sure, but I think it's the Media Club. A friend of hers is dropping a CD."

"I don't understand modern music," he said, not indignantly, but lamentably. As if his faculties were no longer up to making any kind of critical judgment.

He set his cup and saucer down on the arm of the settee. His eyes followed the row of photos along the wall. "I was lucky," he said. "I know I was. I dearly wish I could communicate more of what I learned to Amelia. But everything today is drum machines and Pro Tools and Auto Tune. What's worse is, instead of using these fascinating new inventions to explore, most people use them to cover up mediocrity."

"I don't know much about art," I said. "I've never really listened to pop music, I mean what gets on the radio. Nothing against it, it's just not my thing."

"What is your thing?"

"Townes Van Zandt, Howlin' Wolf."

"The Wolf," Mr. Yates said, lighting up. "I saw him in London once."

"Get the fuck out of here."

"It's true," he said. "I met a lot of those old musicians. Muddy, of course."

"The greatest."

"Sonny Terry and Brownie McGhee, Pinetop Perkins, Albert King, John Lee Hooker — I recorded the Hook with a bunch of European musicians in '86, no, '88. Spotty performances, but the old man still had it."

"What was he like?"

"Old," Chet Yates said, the word somewhat deflating him. "As we all get, sooner or later. I never got your last name, Mike."

"Drayton."

"Were your people British?"

"Protestant Irish on my father's side. The rest are Mennonites."

"Pardon my ignorance but what is a Mennonite?"

"Damned if I know," I said. "Deutschland by way of Russia, I think. It has something to do with buttons and zippers being Satan's handiwork."

"My paternal grandmother dabbled in Vodou," Yates said. His eyes went to the fireplace, a teepee of green kindling hissing and popping behind the grate. "Mind if I ask if you've been to this house before? Specifically on Thanksgiving?"

"What I saw isn't likely to become news any time soon," I said.

"I appreciate that. I feel out of it sometimes. Like I'm a spectator in my own life, watching myself on a projection screen. I couldn't tell you why I had that gun out."

"Your daughter said you were depressed. That's treatable."

"The symptoms are," he said. "The malaise goes deeper." A door closed upstairs. Chet Yates smiled. "I won't burden you with a laundry list of my frailties. I did want to ask you if there was something I could do to compensate you for your troubles."

"Not necessary."

"Maybe not for you. Can you understand my distaste in finding myself in debt?"

I thought it through. "There's a black van parked outside."

"Yours."

"I'd be interested in purchasing it," I said. "What would you take for it?"

"Whatever you feel comfortable paying."

"A thousand, assuming it runs?"

We shook hands on it.

Amelia Yeats walked down the left staircase. She was wearing a checkered skirt and a leotard below that, and a zipped-up bomber jacket that concealed her top. Her long curly hair was loosed from its normal ponytail and hung about her shoulders. Velvet boots and a touch of jewellery completed the vision. I felt woefully underdressed and unprepared, a monster from an old Hammer Horror film cobbled together in haste and brought to life prematurely to wreak havoc on some quaint European village. As if to drive the point home, when I stood up to greet her my shin grazed the glass coffee table, toppling it and shattering the top. Chet Yates tucked his legs onto the seat next to him as Roanna the housekeeper swept in to assess the damage.

"Awfully sorry," I said.

"It's just a table," Mr. Yates said.

His daughter leaned over him, careful of the glass, and pecked his cheek. "You're heading out now?" he asked her.

"Unless you want to bore Mike with more talk about how much better everything was back in the old days." To me she said, "That's my dad's favorite hobby. He doesn't even know who Daniel Lanois is."

"The actor from *Last of the Mohicans*," I said, trying out a joke that crashed even before takeoff. "We should probably go before I embarrass myself even more."

* * *

The CD release was another non-event. I hung out at the bar watching a bunch of dapper gents in scarves and homburgs, some of who were the band, co-mingle with women that ranged from awkward bespectacled fanzine journalists to bronzed and glittering groupies whose vanilla perfume I could smell long after they'd departed. I watched Amelia Yeats glide through the sea of them, at times seeming to belong, and then giving off a wayward glance that made me feel that she too felt out of place. I like people individually. In groups of a dozen or so they begin to act like a hydra, or at least that's how I see them, one big organism that tells the same stories and interjects the same one-liners and demands the same polite nods and chuckles. Even drunk I prefer the company of a small group, or solitude, to a place in the crowd.

The band played cuts off their album and then took the stage and played those same songs with much less artistry. I began to appreciate the amount of work someone like Yeats went to in order to sculpt a record out of the mushy soundwaves generated by a lousy band.

The smell of pot enveloped me. Some in the crowd danced. Most nodded their heads. A few held up their cellphones, capturing for posterity a moment they were already talking through.

At the intermission the bassist came down to man the merch table. I bought a CD out of politeness and used it as a coaster for the rest of the night. "Thanks for supporting local music," the bass player told me. I could picture him running a telethon. I couldn't see Yeats so I followed a throng of people outside to inhale cold air and secondhand smoke.

During the second set the band invited up guest musicians. Yeats's friend Zoltan took the stage for a pair of originals, both of which sounded vaguely like "Come As You Are." A dreadlocked girl got up and belted a Smokey Robinson and

"Kiss my ass."

I cleared off the student's desk that stood in the corner of the room and set up my kettle and grill. I lay down on the bed. My cast itched. I wondered what time it was in Reykjavik.

I'd dozed off on the bed with my shoes and coat still on. Fisk woke me when he opened the adjoining door. He looked over at the steaming kettle on the desk. "Planning on moving here?"

I sat up. He unplugged the kettle for me and looked at the other appliance. "That a George Foreman?"

"I was planning on walking down to the Overwaitea and buying the makings for grilled cheese," I said.

Fisk had a beer in his hand. "I thought we'd try out the famous Prosper's Point cuisine."

"I don't have money for that, and I can't stomach fast food more than once a day. You go ahead, I'll meet you back here later."

Fisk would have none of it. "I think I can put a couple of steak dinners on my expense account," he said. "Don't make me drink with Delgado alone."

Ace's had Molson and Bud on special. I forget what we ordered. By the second pitcher all was right between Gavin and Willie. They'd moved on to first names and were sharing war stories. We all ordered T-Bone steaks with fries. The two of them argued over who would pick up the check.

The autopsy had confirmed Dr. Boone's speculation: asphyxiation due to carbon monoxide poisoning, though she was waiting for test results on the carboxyhemoglobin-to-hemoglobin ratio in the dead woman's blood. No bruises on her body or any signs to suggest she'd been coerced. Moles on her left breast and both arms, a tattoo on her lower back of a

I'd pocketed a couple of bottles of Kokanee Gold for the ride home. We slugged back the tepid beer alone in our car of the train. We could hear a group of drunks in the next car, standing by the doors and squealing about the stupid bastard whose cellphone they'd just stolen. It was the kind of scene I hated to ignore, but there were four of them, I was drunk, and they were off the Skytrain two stops before us.

"Where's your mother in all this?" I asked her.

"Eastwood Park," she said. "It's a penitentiary in England."

"She's in prison?"

"She was part of a group called the Something Liberation Army, I forget what exactly. She and these other guys kidnapped an MP and his family. I think their plan was to hold the MP's wife and kids hostage and force the MP to kill the Prime Minister."

"Jesus," I said, because there was nothing else to say.

"Only the gags on the wife and kids were too tight and one of the kids threw up and choked on her throw-up."

"Jesus."

"Yeah. When the cops caught them they got one of the other kidnappers to confess. My mom had one of the longest prison terms handed out to a woman in that decade, which is kind of an honour." Tilting her head in lieu of a smile to acknowledge the necessity of a joke to deal with the horror of the event and the painful intimacy of sharing it. All of this was rehearsed and second nature.

"'Splains why you hate the police," I said.

"It's a corrupt, racist institution. They all are."

"I didn't see that on the job."

"Course you'd say that, you're —"

"White?"

"One of them," she finished. "Or were. And before you start thinking it's a race thing, my mom is whiter than you."

We got off the Skytrain at Waterfront and walked up to the lot where I'd stowed my car. A pint-size kid in a hoodie was tagging a parking sign. He took off at a long-striding walk as we approached, leaving a glyph in yellow paint dripping off a space of brick on the side of a building.

"When I was on the job," I said, "I always felt that, so long as everything I did squared with the spirit of the law, I had wiggle room when it came to obeying the letter."

"Beating confessions out of people?" Yeats said, equal parts curiosity and scorn.

"I wasn't a detective and I didn't handle too many interviews. Mostly I'd try to keep good people out of the system."

"Good people. Isn't it hard to figure out who the good people are?"

"No," I said. "If you're going about your life and not fucking things up for others, you're one of the good people. That doesn't mean everyone else is bad, just that for them, the system has to run its course."

"Sounds like you were one of the good ones," she said. "Good cops, I mean."

"There's some dispute around that."

"How'd you get kicked out?"

"I resigned, technically. The details aren't important."

"I told you about my mother," she said, mock-pouting.

"I could've found that out with a Google search."

"You're going to tell me," she said, "or I'll beat it out of you."

"Fascist."

"Tell me."

I shook my head. "I don't have perspective on it yet. I alternate between seeing myself as totally in the right and thinking I fucked things up completely. But I'll tell you why I wanted to become a cop."

So I did, recounting the whole lamentable story of Jacob

Kessler, his journey across Canada to work in Vancouver, and his even longer journey to St. Paul's Hospital, dying with every step.

"After work he'd take off his uniform and leave his clothing strewn about the house. Shoes by the door, cap on the sofa in the living room, jacket on the stairs. That's where he'd sometimes leave his gun and belt. His shirt and pants went into the basket near the basement staircase. I'd pick up different pieces and play. Obviously the gun was the best, but my second favorite was the hat. His name was felt markered on the inside and the band inside was always cool with his sweat. When he'd see me doing this he'd pull the brim down over my face. Didn't have a highly developed sense of humour, my grandfather."

I drove down the ramp and paid the outrageous parking tab. Traffic was thick for midnight, some sports event having recently ended, spilling fans out of the bars and putting questionable drivers on the road. I made it over the Cambie Street Bridge and hung a left.

"Anyway," I said, "I guess the point of that boring story was that I was trying to fill his shoes before I even understood the term. Being on the job meant ..." I trailed off.

"What?"

"Everything," I said.

"I feel like that about what I do," she said. "How does being a private eye stack up?"

"Better than most of the alternatives. Could stand with more income, but who couldn't?"

A man getting into the driver's seat of a car parked on Broadway took a step backwards into my lane. I weaved around him, catching the look of astonishment and irritation on his face as we passed him. "Drunk asshole," Yeats called back to him.

At her building we paused on the stairway. "Are you coming up?" she asked.

"Am I invited?"

She was two steps above me and leaned down so her weight was on my shoulders. Her hands met at the back of my neck. As we kissed I took a step up, put my hands on her back, a polite distance above her ass, the fragrance of beer and stagelight sweat on her. Her coat had bunched up and I ran my hand over the exposed small of her back, feeling the gooseflesh.

"You don't have to go?" she asked, a glimmer of welcome in her green-brown eyes.

"Hell with it. The Corpse Fucker can wait."

"The what?" Pulling back to look me in the eyes.

"Nothing," I said, kissing her, running my hands inside her jacket.

"Did you say the Corpse Fucker?"

"I'm guarding a funeral home from a necrophiliac. It's not a big deal. Got the keys?"

She withdrew, turning towards the door. "I should work anyway," she said. "Sounds like you should be there."

The smoke of our breath mingled. She pulled the keys from her purse and opened the stairwell door, kissed me, and pushed me back. I waited at the entrance. When the door had shut and the light had dimmed I went to work.

XV

Atero-Vision

After my stint at the funeral home I drove to the Atero household and parked down the block with a view of the front door. I unscrewed the lid of my Thermos and poured out the lukewarm dregs of last night's tea. The stereo played a compilation of murder ballads I'd picked up at Charlie's on Granville Street before it closed. Forty-four tracks of bloodlust and misfortune. Perfect music for the grey hours before dawn.

I'd pissed away days pretending I had any choice in the matter. Atero knew something I needed to know, simple as that. Getting that knowledge would put people I cared about at risk and invite a reprisal from Crittenden. Those thoughts were a pint of acid sloshing around the bottom of my stomach. I told myself I was doing this for the kid, and not because I balked at being told what not to do. Maybe it didn't matter. If the end result is good, who gives a shit how pure of heart the person is who brings it about?

I chewed a granola bar. Burl Ives was singing "Streets of Laredo." Odd to think of the snowman from the stop-motion *Rudolph* singing anything other than "Holly Jolly Christmas." I realized this would be the first Christmas without the dog. I finished my bar and stowed the wrapper in the ashtray.

Porch lights snapped on up the block as robed women dragged garbage cans and blue bins out to the curb. Zak Atero's brother Theo came down the front steps of his house and plunked a knotted green bag by the edge of his car. He wore red dotted boxer shorts and a brown tank top, showing tanned muscular forearms that connected to pale hairy upper arms thick with wobbly flesh. His horseshoe of hair stood at all angles. He was barefoot.

Theo disappeared inside. Leadbelly, Victoria Spivey, Dick Justice and Mississippi John Hurt took their turns on the car stereo. When Theo exited his front door for the second time, he was dressed in a pale blue short-sleeved dress shirt. He carried a brown suede jacket and a suitcase with gouges in its vinyl covering. He stored jacket and case in the trunk of a late eighties Mustang, its deep red paint scarred and flecked with rust. Theo started the car and let it idle a moment, kicking out enough black soot to suggest a problem with the exhaust system. Eventually he turned on his lights, swung the Mustang around and drove past me. I waited until the end of disk one before climbing out of my car with my gym bag and walking around to the back entrance of the Atero household.

The back door had a pet flap. I wondered when the last Atero pet had kicked off and what it had died from. I couldn't quite reach the handle when I put my arm through the flap, but the porch window was wide and low and unlocked.

I searched the upstairs and the ground floor, finding stacks of car repair manuals and plates covered with congealed grease and cheese. I found two thousand dollars in twenties and a .22 target pistol in the bottom drawer of Theo's armoire. His pay stubs, a messy pile on the shelf beneath his nightstand, showed he worked as a floor manager for a warehouse in Coquitlam. The other room on the top floor contained a queen-sized mattress stripped of coverings and boxes piled everywhere. I opened a few of them: knickknacks belonging to their parents, tax returns, old *Chatelaines* and *Car and Drivers*. Nothing to link them to Django Szabo, but I hadn't expected anything. Whatever connection existed would be found in Zak's room. I made sure the gun was empty, left everything, and took two flights of stairs down to the basement.

The television was running some early morning exercise show where a woman with a beatific smile put a class through yoga positions. Atero was asleep on the couch. I turned the television off and sat on the armrest by his feet so my shoes were resting on the seat cushion. My gym bag sat on the floor within easy reach. The room was dirty and bare, quiet except for Zak Atero's soft snoring. I stared down at him. He was wearing an orange shirt with an Atari logo, blue briefs with white trim. He was still wearing socks.

I prodded his stomach with my shoe. "Wake up, Zak."

He snorted and tried to roll over towards the back of the couch. I jabbed him in the ribs. His breath caught and his eyes opened. I waited for him to focus.

"What's going on?" he said through a yawn.

"Sit up and look at me."

He propped himself on his elbows, the situation starting to focus for him. I kept my hands in the pockets of my coat.

"You're the guy," he said, "from the office on Hastings."

"Two-Eight-Eight-Two, cross street Beckett, anytime you want to find me." Confident, easy. "I also make house calls."

His head sunk to the left and he stared at the clock above the TV. "It's five already? Shit, I'm late." His legs stirred, testing to see if I'd allow him to stand up. I shook my head.

"It's 5:00 a.m., Zak. Your brother won't be back for ten hours, you don't have anywhere to go, and we have a lot to cover."

"I told you already, dude —"

"None of this 'I told you already' shit," I said. "I want to know what happened on March the 6th. Leave nothing out."

"How can I tell you what I don't know?"

"Understand something, Zak." I looked down at the gym bag, made sure he saw me look at it. "Neither of us is leaving this room until you tell me what happened to Django Szabo. Now, I don't want to lay hands on you, which I'm sure you're not too keen on either. But I will beat you till you beg me for permission to die if that's what it takes."

I moved my leg to the floor and kicked the gym bag, hard enough so Atero could hear the clank of metal beneath the canvas. I grinned down at him.

His arm extended to the pipe resting on the ottoman. "I got to at least get a little high. You got to at least let me have that."

I booted the ottoman hard enough to send it rolling into the wall with a thud. The pipe, the bag, the ashtray, and clickers all hit the floor.

"Man —" he began.

"— Tell it and then you can get as fucked up as you want." He nodded.

"What happened was, a friend of mine had a similar car to the, whatever their names are, their car."

"Szabo. What kind of car?"

"Four-door Taurus wagon, brown, 1997 I think. Seven or eight. So anyway, their car and my friend's car —"

I swatted him on the side of the head. He looked up at me incredulously. "What'd you hit me for?"

"You lied to me. Don't want to get hit, don't lie."

"I was explaining —"

"You don't have any friend, Zak. You were ripping rides in front of the pawn shop."

He nodded. "So I walk by it and see one of the pegs is up. The door pegs, like for the locks."

"Go on."

"Car's empty, least I think that. I go around the block, come back, street's clear, I take another look, see that there's no club on the wheel. Not like I brought a slim-jim and cutters with me. I mean, I suffer from impulse control and this car's sitting there with a bow on it. So I open the door and start it up."

"How long till you realized the kid was on board?"

"I was almost at the handoff," Zak admitted. "I called Fat Rick, told him to meet me under the bridge at Marine, usual place. I'm on Cambie, within three blocks, and I see these little eyes staring at me in the mirror. Like to have a heart attack when I saw him."

"What happened at the handoff?"

"Didn't make the handoff," he said, shaking his head as if the wisdom of that decision was apparent. "Rick's not like that. I hand him a car with a faulty taillight I never hear the end of it. 'Magine what he does I hand him a car that's still got a passenger?"

"So you went where?"

Atero shrugged and snorted. "I don't remember."

"Where, Zak?" I raised my hand and he flinched.

"Hey, look." Eyes fixed on me, his version of sincere. "I look like a pedophile to you? Someone who hurts kids?"

"Prove to me you're not."

His head collapsed back onto the armrest. "I can't help you."

I said, "I can imagine a scenario where, you're driving, you see the kid, he's scared, you're scared, and maybe he's acting up in a way that's dangerous. Maybe you try to keep him still, in the interest of safe driving. And maybe the kid hit his head, or passed out and never woke up. Or you didn't know your own strength."

Atero's eyes were closed, tears forming in the corners, a bubble of spit between his lips.

"My point is, Zak, these are things the court would take into account were you to come forward and show remorse. But you've got to tell me where you stashed that kid's body. That's the only way you'll earn yourself a break."

"I wouldn't hurt anyone," he blubbered. "I just like cars."

I prodded him. "We're doing good being truthful to one another. Let's not louse it up now. Tell me where the body is. After that you can get good and high."

"I don't know."

"Zak, another second I'm going to start beating on you."

"Look look look," he said, scooting up to a sitting position, putting negligible distance between us. "Look, okay? I didn't hurt him. If anything's happened it is not my fault."

"Where's the body?"

"There's no body is what I'm telling you," he said.

"Meaning he's still alive?"

Zak Atero nodded. "I mean, far as I know."

Of course I'd considered it as a possibility, a hypothesis. Not every missing child turns up dead. Usually, though, the fortunate ones get fortunate within a few weeks. With runaways, sometimes they show up years later, living their lives, their parents forgotten or at least out of mind. Intellectually I'd entertained the possibility, but my gut sense of things had written Django James Szabo off as dead even before my first meeting with his father. I'd had the same feeling with the Loeb case.

What Atero told me sounded genuine. I'd heard every permutation of lie from him already. This was different. Determining veracity is not a science, but I'd stake my reputation that he wasn't lying when he said that Django passed from his hands alive and unharmed.

After he'd run through his story I unzipped the gym bag and removed a black metal tripod. I spread its legs, took an old-fashioned VHS camera from its travel case and threaded it onto the base of the tripod. I trained the lens on a medium closeup of Zak Atero.

"Tell it all the way through," I said, focusing and pressing play.

> My first thought was returning him, but I didn't know where the boy lived, and I couldn't just drive up and drop him at the pawn shop.
>
> I thought of the pawn shop owners, the Ramseys. They seemed to know the boy's father. How do I know the Ramseys? I work for a guy — don't ask me his name — and Ramsey has a deal with him. I try not to know the details about things like that. Ramsey and I also have a sort of side agreement with regards to his parking lots. I'm not saying I tell him when I take a car, but there's not much in his area that escapes him.
>
> So I phone Ramsey on a burner and tell him I'm swinging back with the kid. He says no good, he's not getting involved. Hangs up on me. 'Magine hanging up when there's a kid involved.
>
> Anyway, it's no secret I suffer from certain weaknesses. It was getting pretty bad and I was desperate to ditch the kid. It was a weird situation. He's sitting in the back staring at me with his little eyes. I'm freaking out more than him. He just kind of accepted it.

So I try to think where can I take him that's safe, that there won't be five-oh, and that I can get this other problem sorted out at the same time. I can't go home and I can't stay out on the road. There's this girl I know, Dominique, don't know her last name, couldn't swear that was the name she was christened with. She and a couple of girlfriends have this house over on Fraser. Big empty garage out back.

Yes they were hookers, but when I say that, understand I'm not talking about rock hos from Surrey. These are nice girls. No pimp. They get protection from the same guy I work for. They do their business in the first floor and live upstairs. The other two were dykes, I do remember that. Always bitching to Dom about having me over in *their* house.

I drive over there and one of the other ones comes to the door and says Dom's got a party, I should leave. I say I'm not going anywhere 'cause I need to get that car off the street, and I'm'a put it in the barn. She says no good, the john's car's in there. I'll spare you the whole comedy routine, but I get the john's keys and pull his car into the alley, then stow the Taurus inside. The kid's just sitting in the back seat all this time.

Far as I know the car's still there.

All the while the kid says nothing. Just watches me. I tell him come inside with me. He just nods.

Inside, Dom's friend, the older one, Barb I think her name was, she sits him down in front of the TV, starts asking him does he want a sandwich, juice, that kind of thing. Never offered me a sandwich, I've known her three years. I'm halfway thinking she's going to offer to take the little guy's cherry for him.

Anyway, Dom calls this guy she knows and we go pick up what we need to. When we come back the kid's still watching TV. The other girls are working, so Dom and I see to our business. Next thing I know it's the next day. I see the kid sleeping as I head out on account of some pick up I have to make. I'm careful not to disturb him.

That's the last I ever saw of that boy. Sure I've seen Dom and Barb and the other girl a couple times since, but never at their place.

Last time I saw any of them was two months ago. I ran into Dom and the other one at a club, might've been the Roxy, maybe the Commodore. I remember Dom was pissed at me, thinking I might have taken a bit more than my share of the dope, and that I was ducking her. Anyway, we made up.

Remember that freak summer storm that one weekend? Think it was July. Anyway, it's raining when I go into the club, and on our way out it's a righteous thunderstorm. Wind, rain, the whole bit. We went out to my car.

We attended to business, then we sat there, in the rain and thunder, counting the seconds between the flash and the rumble. The subject of the kid didn't come up.

XVI

Staring Down the Hydra

A melia Yeats answered her studio door in a long magenta T-shirt, hair clipped haphazardly out of her face. Seeing it was me at the door she pried open the clip and shook out her dark curls.

"I was just fixing this bass part," she said as we climbed the staircases. I rationalized the attention I paid to her ass as precautionary, since at any second she could slip and I'd have to catch her.

I put the gym bag down in the corner of her control room and pulled up a chair. Yeats worked the faders on the console and made some judicious mouse clicks. "Pro Tools is the necessary evil of what I do," she said. "Eli, the bass player, took seventeen passes on this song."

"That a lot?"

"Not if you're a perfectionist. All he has to do is play the root, but his tempo drags, he misses notes. Not every bass player has to be Carole Kay or James Jamerson, but I shouldn't have to cut and paste each note just to get a few bars I can loop." She sighed. "I hate people who don't love what they do enough to do it well."

She had assembled the equipment I'd asked for on the phone, a VCR and an old Sony Trinitron and a few cables. I hooked the camcorder up and began dubbing copies of Zak

Atero's confession. I had similar equipment in my office, but I was avoiding that place until I got the phone call. I'd told Katherine and Ben to do the same.

"Funny," she said, "I don't even know what kind of music you like."

"All kinds," I said.

"Everyone says that."

My iPod was in my jacket pocket. I surrendered it to her and fought the urge to justify every sound file on it with a lengthy explanation or excuse.

"Curious," she said.

"Is it?"

"Joe Strummer but no Clash. Iggy but no Bowie. I'd've thought you'd have more Rush."

"I don't really like Rush."

"But you're Canadian."

Zak Atero's mouth moved silently on the monitor. Yeats handed me my iPod back.

"It says your most listened-to song is 'That's What Love Will Make You Do' by Little Milton. In fact, almost all your Top Twenty-Five are blues or R&B."

"I like blues."

"What do you think of Canned Heat?"

I made a face. "Can't stand that guy's voice. Plus their big hit song is lifted from Henry Thomas's 'Bull Doze Blues.' Note for note down to the flute solo."

"I'm not their biggest fan," she admitted, "but you have to hear the double LP they put out with John Lee Hooker. Do you have a turntable?"

"Probably my grandmother does," I said.

"I've got one back at the house, I'll bring it by for you."

Once I had three copies I destroyed the original tape. I wiped my prints from each one. My hope was that using outdated technology would make it harder to trace back to me. Before I arrived I'd stopped at a PharmaSave and bought mailing envelopes and postage and a blue marker. I had Amelia Yeats address the envelopes: one to Gavin Fisk, one to Nate Holinshed at the *Vancouver Sun*, and one sent to my office. Once that was done, I cleaned up the mess and headed out to dump the garbage and mail the tapes.

"You have any kind of security in here?" I asked Yeats.

"I have one of these." She pointed to a rusty aluminum bat in the corner. "Alarms, cameras, et cetera."

"Don't buzz up any strangers," I said, feeling ridiculous saying it.

"Ever met a musician? How am I supposed to make a living?"

"You know what I mean," I said. "No unnecessary risks."

"Besides hanging out with you."

"That falls under the category of necessary risks," I said, squeezing her shoulder on my way out.

At the top of the stairs she stopped me. "I want to tell you something."

"Yeah?" Nonchalantly, which I managed only because her expression wasn't hesitant.

"I take drugs," she said.

"Yeah?"

"Coke. Sometimes others. I don't use needles and I'm not an addict. I don't score on the street and I don't fuck people for drugs."

"Okay," I said.

She swallowed. "And I wanted to tell you because last night I felt I had to hide it from you, because you're a cop, or were, and I didn't want to see that disappointed look on your face, and I didn't want to hear a lecture on how I should stop. But I figured you should know."

"Okay."

"I don't want us moving any further without you knowing that."

"Thank you."

We regarded each other. I couldn't recall seeing her exhibit any of the symptoms. Had I been so love-and-sex-obsessed, so infatuated, that I'd overlooked them? Or was her use so minimal and so regulated that she had it under control? Was that even possible?

"What do you think?" she said.

"You don't want to stop?"

"No."

I nodded. "Okay then."

"Is it?"

"I don't know." She seemed lucid, engaged.

"You should've known there was a downside to all this," she said, indicating her body with a self-effacing wave of the hand.

Seconds passed as I tried to formulate a response.

"My dog has cancer," I said, trying to think of something of equivalent importance to share with her, to let her know I accepted and appreciated what she'd shared with me, even if I didn't know how to deal with it yet. "I'm going to have to kill her pretty soon. I mean have her killed, obviously, but it amounts to the same thing. My grandmother thinks I should've done it a month ago."

"I'm sorry," she said.

"Why don't you have dinner with us?" I asked her. "My grandmother would like to meet you. Assuming you won't steal her cutlery."

I left the bags on the stairs and went back up to the landing to embrace her. I felt her body beneath the shirt, ran my hand over the trackline of her vertebrae. Her mouth tasted like blood.

My phone chirped. I freed an arm to check the number. CALLER ID WITHHELD.

"Cock-blocked by Nokia," Yeats said.

"This'll be good news."

I watched her lock the landing door and walk back to the control room before I took the call.

"Drayton speaking."

"Michael."

Crittenden.

"Afternoon; I'm at your office. The Atero brothers are with me. And your friends. I feel we should talk."

I told him I'd be right over, but I made a stop at the house to grab my grandfather's shotgun. I hoped it wouldn't come to that. A shotgun is a great persuasive tool, and great when the opponent is unarmed or unaware, but in a prolonged fight, the Glock would be more appropriate. The Glock, however, was back at the office.

Theo Atero's Mustang and a Lincoln that probably belonged to Crittenden were parked on the corner of Beckett, in flagrant disregard of the law to keep two meters' distance from a fire hydrant. Atero's car was empty. I pulled up across from the Lincoln so that the driver's side windows lined up. I saw Crittenden behind the wheel. Theo Atero sat next to him, tapping the butt of a stogie out the passenger's window. Zak sat in back. I put my foot on the brake and let them see the barrel of the Winchester.

"Afternoon," I said.

Crittenden nodded. Theo Atero scowled at the gun.

"Nothing's going to be solved by that," Crittenden said, nodding towards the shotgun.

"Where are the others?"

"Your friends barricaded themselves in the office. The girl was quite the pragmatist — she wouldn't let me in even when I explained we were friends of yours. The other one, the heavy-set man, had some unpleasant language for us."

"What were they doing there in the first place?"

"It's your office, Michael."

"Tell these two —" I indicated the Ateros "— to exit slowly, hands touching their ears, walk to their car, and drive back to your restaurant."

"Just who the fuck do you think you are?" Theo Atero said to me. "Break into *my* house, order my brother around?"

"We'll talk back at the restaurant," Crittenden said.

"Tell them to toss their guns before they exit. Put them on the dash where I can see them, two fingers on the butt."

"None of us came strapped," Crittenden said, enjoying the slang of the last word. "We came to talk, believe it or not, to come to some sort of amiable resolution."

"Not going to happen," I said. "It's in the hands of the cops and the press. If I knew how to convert that tape to digital, it'd be on YouTube by now."

"Listen to this mutt," Theo Atero said.

"You and your brother out of the car."

Out they came and walked back to their car. After lingering there for a moment, they drove off.

"Still want to talk?" I said, calling the office line with my free hand, getting a busy signal.

"I think that's best," he said.

I parked and together we went inside, the shotgun tucked into its leather carrying case. At the top of the stairs I rapped on the glass. Katherine sat in my spot, the Glock on the table in front of her. Ben stood by her desk, setting the phone back on its cradle.

I gave Katherine the thumbs-up sign through the door

and she unlocked it, stepped aside to let us enter, avoiding the polite gaze of Lloyd Crittenden.

"You're both okay?" I asked.

"Fine," she said. "Where are those other two?"

"Gone. Why didn't you phone me?"

"What do you think I've been doing?" Ben asked.

I held up my cell, showing him the lack of received-call messages on the screen. "What number were you trying?"

"Jesus," Katherine said. "You were trying the house line, weren't you?"

"Mondays my grandmother goes to the casino," I said. "The house line goes straight to message."

Katherine rolled her eyes at him. Ben shrugged. "You told me to try Mike's number, that's what's on the screen. Was I 'sposed to know that wasn't the right number?"

"You know the area code of his cell starts with seven-seven-eight, and the home line's six-oh-four. That didn't clue you in?"

Embarrassed at the infighting, I said to Crittenden, "It's nice to know we can all think on our feet during a crisis." To the others I said, "This is Lloyd Crittenden. He and I need to talk. You two should leave — though why you're here at all eludes me."

"Studying," Katherine said.

"Bored," Ben said.

"What subject do you study?" Crittenden asked her.

"Don't answer," I said, tossing Katherine the keys.

"Are you sure you're okay with him?"

"It'll work out."

"Nice meeting you both," Crittenden said on their way out. "Good luck with your studies."

Looking back at him briefly Katherine said, "If you hurt him —" She turned and followed Ben out, leaving the threat unfinished.

I put the shotgun behind me and pocketed the pistol. "Is this what it's got to be like," I asked, "guns and unfriendly visits?"

"You disobeyed me," he said.

"You didn't leave me a choice. And I halfway think you did it just to see what I'd do, as a form of amusement."

"I wouldn't take those kinds of liberties, least of all with work. Although it's been a while since someone fired a shot across my bow so blatantly."

"In any case it's done now," I said. "There's no profit in hindering the search for this kid, and whatever happens between us won't stop the police from following up."

"A stalemate," he said. He didn't seem angry, but his good humour had faded and with it the sense that he was toying with me. He remained a cutthroat despite his diction.

"If I told you the number and variety of responsibilities I have, you'd think I was an emperor. This was such a minor incident that I tried to remain impartial and let it sort itself out, realizing that whatever happens to the Ateros is of no consequence to me. Truth be told, Theo wanted to deal with you before your session with his brother. I felt there was no point in bloodshed."

"Do you know what the definition of a weak boss is, Mr. Crittenden?"

He leaned forward in his chair. "Are you calling me that?"

"I don't know you well enough to judge," I said, "but I know what it's like working for one. A weak boss doesn't want to get involved because he doesn't want to piss anyone off. He justifies his weakness as fairness. A shitty boss hurts everybody, but a weak boss hurts only the good and reasonable people. Two employees have a beef, 'stead of weighing in, he splits it down the middle, 'Well, you both have compelling arguments,' and so forth. That only encourages them to be less reasonable in the future. One guy says 'You owe me ten dollars, here's a receipt as proof,' and the other guy says 'Fuck your receipt, you owe me a million.' If a weak boss arbitrates, it's, 'Boys, let's not fight, you both have compelling arguments. Let's split this down the middle. You pay him five dollars, he pays you half a million. Nice talking to you fellows, I'll be in the coffee room if anybody needs me.'"

Crittenden had settled his claw-like hands on his knees. "I can't tell if you're trying to insult me or sympathize. Do you think I should have hurt you?"

"You should've helped me," I said. "Instead, you threatened me. With most people that would have been enough. But I'm not going away."

Crittenden sneezed into a black handkerchief and held the moist rag in his lap. Gesturing at the room he said, "It amazes me you'd risk this to talk to Zachary Atero."

"That's just how it turned out this time."

A droplet of blood fell out of Crittenden's left nostril onto the back of his hand. He dabbed at his nose with the handkerchief. "I get the occasional nose-bleed," he said. "Stress-related, I expect."

I pointed to the narrow door in the corner by Katherine's desk. "Washroom's in there if you want to clean up."

"Appreciated but not necessary," he said. "As to our business, I'll take the advice of my security consultant and wash my hands of the entire matter."

"Thank you."

"You shouldn't." Crittenden snorted back a trickle of blood. "I have some say over Zachary, but Theo keeps his own counsel. What he chooses to do is up to him. All I can promise is I won't involve myself. As far as I'm concerned, the matter is between you and the Atero family. I wish you luck."

He stood up, folding the handkerchief and tucking it into his jacket pocket.

"Cliff Szabo isn't a close friend?" he asked at the door.

"I don't even like him all that much."

"You don't seem to be involved for the media exposure, and I doubt he pays you more than a pittance."

"Less."

"Altruism?"

"I'm sure Freud could trace it back to my mother." I walked him to the door, pointing to my upper lip to signal him to wipe his. He shook out the handkerchief and held it to his face. He held out his other hand for me to shake, withdrawing it when he noticed the rivulet of blood run down the knuckles to the palm. I shook his hand anyway.

As he made his way down I said, "I had to guess, I'd say it's because I can't countenance what happened to Django Szabo."

"I'm sorry," he said, turning. "You can't what?"

"Countenance," I said. "It means 'Give approval to.' It also means about ten other things. I had to look it up in Oxford's."

Crittenden grinned. Condescension, admiration, pity.

"Look up the word 'Thanatos,'" he said. "That might come nearer the mark. We're an infernal mystery to ourselves, aren't we? Goodbye, Michael."

XVII

The Cat House

The tapes took three days to circulate. When mine arrived, I stashed it unopened in the bottom of the filing cabinet. I was alone in the office, waiting for Fisk's call. Outside, low charcoal-coloured clouds sped across a blank sky, threatening to burst into rain or hail.

The day before, I'd driven by the house on Fraser and spotted the graffiti-defaced, stand-alone garage. The street was clogged with cyclists and pedestrians. I walked up to the garage doors and peered through the sliver of light between them. A car was there. No child. Whatever else could wait for the police to cut the padlock.

That morning I'd run down a bogus lead on the Loeb case, forwarded the school's refusal of payment to my attorney, and dealt with the issue of the Ko family's relocated grandson. I asked the nephew over the phone to ask the grandparents if they wanted me to talk to the daughter-in-law. After a brief consultation he said no, they'd prefer to handle it themselves. I was prepping the invoice when Gavin Fisk phoned me on the office line.

"We need to talk, Encyclopedia Brown."

"You used that one already," I said. "You're running out of sleuths, Gavin."

"You made this tape?"

"Tape?"

"The one that came in the mail today while I'm having my McMuffin, that shows a guy named Zak Atero talking about jacking the Szabos' car."

"Great news," I said.

"Oh fuck off, Drayton. This has your pawprints all over it."

"Now that you mention it," I said, "something like that showed up in the mail today, no return address. Is that what yours looked like? I wonder who else might've got one?"

"Yeah I wonder. You do know this would never stand up in any court of law, don't you? You're not that deluded to think Atero's going to jail on account of this?"

"You think my primary concern is seeing him in jail?"

"Who knows what your concerns are," Fisk said. "Couple years ago I fucked your girlfriend and now it's any chance you can to make me look bad."

"The main concern is finding the kid. Making you look bad would be an ancillary benefit."

"So how long do I have till this tape finds its way onto the web?"

"My best guess? I'd say you probably have two to four days to talk to this Atero, 'discover' the car, and convince Mr. Szabo you're doing everything you can."

"And I'm sure you'll be real helpful in that regard, right, Mike? That cheap bastard already hates my guts. Imagine what nightmare scenario the two of you come up with."

I tipped my chair back to the wall, hanging a foot over a corner of the table.

"Far as I'm concerned, Gavin, you find the kid, I'll say you've been walking point this entire investigation."

Fisk voiced his appreciation by saying nothing for almost a minute. When he came back he said, "I'm on my way to the address Atero mentions. I guess it wouldn't botch things too bad if you came along."

"I'll meet you there," I said.

"You think there's a chance this kid's alive?"

"No," I said. The terribleness of not knowing.

"Me neither."

"Though if he made it into this Dominique's hands alive, and she's got no cause to harm him, then it stands to reason he'd be in that same condition."

"Possible."

"Maybe they fell in love."

"The kid and the hooker?"

"Puberty changes everything."

"How would you know?" Fisk said before hanging up.

Fisk was waiting in a patrol car across the street from the house. He climbed out of the passenger's side as I pulled in ahead of him. From the driver's side came Mira Das in her uniform and rain gear, her hat under her arm and a notepad and pen in her other hand. When I opened my door it brushed a thick pile of wet leaves away from the curb.

The street was residential and the condition of the houses varied from well-maintained to decrepit. Some houses had been subdivided into three, even four suites, with little attention paid to uniformity or symmetry. A bungalow-style dwelling had a second story of cheaper materials grafted on top, and other additions made to that. Dominique's was such a house, with two front doors facing the street and another along the side, each with a brass letter above the knocker. A, B, C.

We took our chances with the sagging paint-flaked porch. Knocking on the two front-facing doors yielded no answer. Mira rang the bell on the side door and we heard signs of life from the other side of the nearby window, through which I could see a tub of cat litter on the kitchen counter, along with an ice cream pail full of kibble, an overflowing ashtray, and two bottles of hundred-proof rum.

Fisk peered in and noticed the same things. "This'll be a fun conversation."

After two minutes of waiting and pounding and ringing the buzzer there was still no answer. I reached in the window, slid it fully open and began retracting the bent slats of the Venetian blinds. Two break-ins in one week — in the event the business ever went under, I could add cat burglar to my list of alternate career paths.

"We should probably try to get a search warrant," Mira said.

I handed her my trenchcoat and heaved my bulk onto the sill. "Just don't tell the cops."

I dropped down into a dining nook full of broken and mended furniture. Four litter boxes dotted the floor, all overflowing. I crunched cat shit, cat food, and cereal underfoot.

Every surface had a thick film of dust. A sour smell hung in the kitchen, distinct from the stench of the litter boxes. A cat made a padded landing off another windowsill and scurried by me, a bolt of orange and brown.

The kitchen cupboards were all open. Amidst stray cans and a bag of rice that had been clawed open and overturned was the corpse of a shorthaired grey.

I stamped to the door and opened it. As Fisk and Das filed in I said, "I feared the worst so I climbed through the window. Then I invited you both in."

"You're going to tell me how to write a report now?" Fisk said.

Mira tried two light switches. "Hydro's been turned off," she said. "The place has been empty for at least a few months."

"Possibly since the disappearance of Django Szabo," Fisk

said. He waded across the kitchen and opened a closet. "Think this is the result when some rich asshole dies and leaves everything to their cat?"

"Least when they left they had the good sense to leave a window open," I said, poking through an overturned garbage bag. A few pieces of junkmail addressed to MIRABELLA SWAIN OR CURRENT OCCUPANT. A slit brown government envelope addressed to BARBARA DELLA COSTA.

"No note on the fridge," Fisk said. He opened it, peered inside and slammed it shut. "Didn't bother cleaning out the milk products, either."

"So they didn't pack," Mira said, "which means either they weren't planning to be gone long or they weren't planning on coming back."

"The second, judging from the troughs of cat food." I swung open the bedroom door. Two sets of feline eyes, a used condom on the floor, a ratty-looking mattress, and a mouse carcass near a puncture in the drywall.

"That poor child," Mira said over my shoulder.

"We've all seen worse," Fisk said. "I don't see any trace of the kid."

"There's two other suites."

One of the cats nuzzled my ankle, not quite feral even after the months on her own. "I could use some air," I said. "How 'bout the garage?"

"How'd you get clued in to Atero?" Fisk asked me as we watched Mira attempt to unthread the rusty padlock on the garage doors.

"Do you believe in the divine conduit, Gavin?" I handed him Madame Thibodeau's card, which he read and flicked back at me in disgust.

"He and his brother work for some heavy money-lenders," he said. Mira had borrowed my knife to force the lock.

She scraped away a layer of oxidation, the blade slipping and catching the cuff of her jacket.

"Careful," I said. To Fisk I answered: "His employer wants nothing to do with this mess, but he made it clear he won't stop the Ateros from coming after me."

"Theo is a shylock when he's not unloading trailers at the warehouse. Zak's a bag boy who moonlights as a car thief, or vice versa." Fisk watched Mira tug on the lock and spat. "Point is, they're not going to let bygones be bygones. Whoever made that tape should be careful."

"If I find out who did it I'll pass the message along."

"You stubborn son of a —" Mira put her boot on the door and pulled. The chunk of rotten wood anchoring the bolts on the lock came away in her hand. Fisk and I wasted no time in ripping the doors open.

The floor of the garage was clean-swept, though a rainbow of machine fluids stained the concrete. Cliff Szabo's Taurus was inside.

"Nary a scratch," Fisk said.

I checked the passenger's door. The handle was broken. The brown core of a pear sat on the dash. The back was empty. No blue Schwinn.

"No bike," Fisk said, echoing my thoughts. "Could be a good thing, letting him take his toy."

The plastic panel beneath the steering column had been ripped away, exposing a coil of wires.

"If he'd only screamed when Atero broke in," Fisk said. "If he hadn't frozen up."

"Maybe if he had he'd be dead," I said.

"Assuming he's not dead now."

"Which we're not."

The three of us stared at the empty car before heading back to the prowler to call it in.

* * *

I left so they could cordon off the house and summon the technicians. Fisk told me he'd keep me informed, but I didn't hear back from him that night.

Thursday morning was cold and clear skied. I piled the dog in the car and took her to Jericho Beach. I gave her the full length of the retractable leash and watched her paw at driftwood and inspect broken seashells, working her way to the edge of the surf.

When we were back in the car I drove by the office. I didn't see either of the Ateros or their vehicles, though a car thief could be driving anything. The window of the diner across the street showed only the usual patrons. That was the logical place for them to set up, but then neither brother seemed to adhere to logic with any consistency. I did get the feeling that it was Theo who wanted to hurt me. Zak seemed either to hide behind his brother or not to care.

With the cameras and locks the office was a safe place to be, but the surrounding streets, with their dark doorways and alcoves, could hold any number of surprises. I made this clear to Katherine and Ben after my talk with Crittenden.

"You expect them to try and kill you?" Katherine said on the phone Thursday morning.

"No, but they'll try something."

The topic shifted to Hallowe'en. Katherine was going to some party with Scott, but she'd have time for dinner and drinks before. Did we want to celebrate?

"Depends if I can wrap up the Kroon job before then. Otherwise I'll be locked away in the mortuary."

"Kind of fitting," Katherine said.

"Course, if anything breaks in the Szabo case, that takes precedence."

After I checked out the office I drove to the vet's, which was on West Broadway, sandwiched between a taqueria and a Black Bond Books. In the waiting room a young woman sat texting while her terrier scampered and yipped. I signed in with the receptionist and sat on a hard plastic chair across from the woman. The terrier showed interest in my dog, who scratched her own shoulder and regarded the younger dog with irritation.

"Hi Mike," Deb the vet's assistant said, taking the leash from me and leading us into the examination room. It was well lit and decorated with posters of nutritional information and cat taxonomy. A beige travel cage sat on the floor by the examination table.

"Hi pooch," Deb said. "How's she been feeling?"

"I guess okay. Still some irritation, some leakage."

"Looks like you two had a nice walk on the beach. She's got sand on her paws."

"You should be a detective," I said.

Deb pulled down the dog's gums to inspect her teeth. "Rhonda told me that's what you do."

"Private investigator, yes."

"That sounds neat. Could you hold her front paws while I adjust her tail out of the way? There."

The dog whimpered as Deb prodded her sensitive area. The checkup was quick. The vet stopped in, she and Deb consulted, then they led me back to the waiting area, leaving the dog sequestered in the examination room.

"It's proceeding as expected," Rhonda the vet said. "In my opinion you won't get a better time to put her down. She's not in too much pain, she had a nice walk this morning. It's entirely your decision, but I want you to understand that things won't get better from here."

"You said the same thing a month and a half ago."

"She was in pain then. I recommended putting her down to spare her the intensification. Now, maybe the metastasis has been slower than anticipated, but that doesn't mean she's not hurting, or that the diagnosis was wrong. I'm spelling this out for you, Mr. Drayton, because I don't want you to entertain any illusions. She's very sick and she'll only get sicker. Now is the optimum time."

I sat down, rubbed my palms into my eyes. "So what's the earliest appointment you have?"

"We could fit her in within the hour."

I looked down at the dog. She wasn't meeting my gaze. I nodded to the vet. "Yeah, let's do this now."

She smiled conservatively. "Okay. Deb and I will get things ready. You and she wait here."

Deb carried the dog back to me and set her on my lap in the waiting room. The girl with the terrier had disappeared.

We waited like that for a half hour before Deb came back. She unhooked the leash and the collar and handed them to me. She guided the dog by the scruff of her neck. "Do you want to be with her?"

"No," I said. "Just tell me when it's done."

They went into a room at the end of the hall. I strapped the collar to my wrist like a tourniquet. I imagined Amelia Yeats doing this, tapping for a vein. But that was wrong, she said she didn't use needles.

I swung the leash, letting the hook hang like a pendulum. I thought of a great furnace somewhere in the barrens, where a soot-stained dwarf, face blackened, shoveled the corpses of euthanized pets, stoking the flames as thick clouds belched out towards the clean city, where the owners let their pets be taken away so that the animals' last moments were spent with strangers whose only interaction with the beasts was to kill them.

I bypassed the receptionist and opened the door at the end of the hall. The dog sat in a cage while Deb made an entry on her clipboard.

"Changed my mind," I said, opening the cage. "I'll let you know."

"Are you sure?" she said, but we were already heading back out to the street.

"How bad was it?" my grandmother called as I took my shoes off by the door. She appeared in the kitchen entryway wearing oversized floral print oven mitts, sleeves rolled up. The day before, I'd told her about having Amelia Yeats over for dinner. She'd been anxious to cook something. We'd stopped at Granville Island market for fresh produce and seafood. Her expression turned to dismay as she saw the dog, who skulked to the basement stairs without glancing at her food bowl.

"I thought this was the day."

"She looks better to me," I said. "Doesn't she move better? Not as stiff as a week ago. The doc said she misjudged the speed of the metasta-whatever-it-is."

"Michael."

I noticed the opened bottle of wine on the counter. I grabbed an old Slurpee mug from the cupboard and poured out a generous amount.

"Two weeks," I said. "The appointment's already made, I swear. How'd we make out on the pie crust?"

"There was enough dough left for a bottom," she said, her disappointment forgotten. "I did a brown sugar crumble topping. If your friend doesn't like it, tough."

I kissed her cheek and went downstairs to shower and change.

* * *

Dinner consisted of salmon steaks coated in flour and skillet-fried a golden brown, pasta with Duso sauce, steamed broccoli, tossed salad with lemon vinaigrette. Amelia Yeats showed up with wine and beer, and we consumed both. The women seemed to enjoy each other's company. Their conversation was pleasant. What do your parents do, dear? My dad used to produce records but he's mostly retired now. That's nice. And your mother? She's in jail. Sorry to hear that. It's okay. This salad dressing is excellent. That's because it's homemade. I'll get you the recipe if you like.

I made coffee and loaded the dishwasher. We had pie in front of the television, catching the last few minutes of *Jeopardy* before *Criminal Intent* started.

"She's half in love with D'Onofrio," I explained to Amelia.

"Oh piss off," my grandmother said.

"It was Jimmy Smits before that. I forget the others, but they all run to a type. A long line of Byronic heroes."

Amelia patted my grandmother's knee. "Jimmy Smits was hot," she said.

My phone rang at the second commercial break. I took the plates and mugs into the kitchen and tucked the phone between ear and neck.

"Satisfied?" Theo Atero said.

"With my phone bill, you mean? Is anyone?"

"This morning I'm at work, I find out the blues have rousted my brother out of bed and taken him downtown to answer questions about something he doesn't know nothing about. I got to lose a half day plus pay the cunt lawyer's fees to get him kicked. Now who do you think should be responsible for that?"

"*My Brother the Scumbag's Epic Tale of Woe* by Theo Atero," I said. "You could get shortlisted for a Giller."

"The hell's a Giller?"

"It's an award for a long, boring book that nobody reads."

Theo said, "I know you're sitting back laughing at this, thinking you got one over on some poor drug-addicted kid who wouldn't hurt a soul. Make my brother a laughing stock, get him harassed by the police. I'm sure you and that big dyke and that fat slob are having a good laugh. You know that can change, though. Hope you know that."

"Why don't you come by the office tomorrow, Theo? Personally I like to look the people I insult in the face."

"Watch your back is all I'll say."

"I know where you live too, Theo."

I brought my grandmother half a baby aspirin and her grape juice concoction. Amelia and I killed the last of the wine.

Over the credits I heard a car door slam and the car tear up the street, and then two shots. I dragged my grandmother off the couch, knocking over her glass. Next to me, Yeats followed suit. It occurred to me in the silence afterwards that the sounds were out of order, that the gunshots should precede the car driving off. I fetched the Glock from the coat rack, hit the porch light and stepped outside.

I saw three smoking firecrackers on the lawn and one in the gutter, and a woman righting her bicycle, and a pair of joggers, cellphones out, already dialing 911. My dog brushed my leg and shuffled out onto the porch, letting out a half-hearted bark. I felt Yeats behind me in the doorway.

"This is the guy you just talked to," she said.

"Most likely. Yes."

"What will you do about it?"

Good question.

•

XVIII

The Corpse Fucker

What I did was answer the uniformed cop's questions and then drive Yeats to her father's, stealing one long kiss before heading back to be with my grandmother. In the morning I installed a security camera over the door, along with flood lights, and hooked them to a motion sensor. My electrician skills make my carpentry look professional, but despite the unseemly wires, the system seemed to work. I devoted another hour to showing my grandmother how to work it.

Gavin Fisk wasn't answering his cell. I called Kroon and Son. I explained to the younger Thomas Kroon that I was ready to admit defeat. I'd be in later that afternoon to pick up my things and give a last brief warning to the employees.

"I want them all to understand basic security procedures," I said. "I'll sleep better knowing we're all on the same page."

"Sounds fair enough," Kroon said. "I'll warn you, though, it's our staff Hallowe'en party. You'll be talking to a bunch of nurses and Frankenstein's monsters."

"Just as long as everyone's there," I said. "If it's possible, could you make sure your father's there, too? Some of this he'll need to know."

"The old man never misses an opportunity to see Carrie in her police woman's uniform." Kroon added, "I think you're making a wise decision, packing it in now. Saves everyone a bit of grief, not to mention money."

"I just have too many other things on my plate," I said. "Monday I'll send off the last invoice."

While I was on the phone with Kroon, Cliff Szabo had phoned twice. I rang him back.

"I owe you a hell of a long explanation," I said, "which you'll get Sunday morning, I promise. For now, suffice to say there's a lead on your son, the cops are following that lead up, and we'll see very soon what pans out. If the press phones, stick to the basics — the cops are handling it, you've hired a PI, et cetera. No details yet."

"All right."

"Another thing: this suspect and his brother might make trouble, so take precautions." I gave him a brief description of the Atero brothers.

"Did these two take Django?" he asked.

"It's not quite that simple."

"I want an explanation."

"Sunday," I said.

By noon I got through to Gavin Fisk. "And the media shit storm begins," he said.

"Far as we're concerned, Mr. Szabo and I, the matter's in your capable hands."

"Real comforting," he said, a strange mix of sarcasm and gratitude. "I'll be in touch with Szabo later on."

"What'd you find in the house?"

"A lot of cat shit and no surprises," he said. "There's no forwarding address for any of these girls, though Barbara Della Costa has some relatives in Saskatchewan. Hookers always do. Their records of employment are also a bit spotty."

"There's no line on any of them?"

"We're not done looking," he said. "Sooner or later one of them will take a collar or, gasp, apply for a job that doesn't involve lying on your back."

"Keep me informed."

"Fair enough," Fisk said. Where he'd usually click off, he hesitated. "I ask you something, Mike?"

"Why yes, Gavin, you certainly can."

"You think Mira would like to go on a cruise?"

"Why ask me?"

"I'm racking my brain trying to think of a Christmas-slash-birthday gift she'd like. Big three-oh this year, should be something big. So how about a cruise? I know a chick who sent her parents to Mazatlan. They told her it was the best trip of their lives. What's your take?"

"Thinking back, Gavin, has Mira ever mentioned boats, sea voyages or Mexico with any particular fondness?"

"No."

"So what does that tell you?"

"Maybe she hasn't tried it yet," he said. "Is it true you're banging that music producer?" I didn't answer. "The ass on her, huh? Those tight little tits?"

"Just tell me when you get a line on those hookers."

"I sure will, Mike. Pardon me for voicing an opinion."

Phone calls all day. The vet, asking did I want to reschedule for today? Hell no. Estelline Loeb: she'd read an article about a child pornography ring busted in Fort McMurray. Remember that vice cop in Oklahoma who noticed the face of a missing girl in a batch of kiddie porn and reunited her with her family? I told her I'd check on it. The Kos' nephew phoned to ask if he could postdate a check for December 1st. I told him that was fine so long as it cleared. My lawyer wanted to know how to proceed on the school lawsuit. I told her full speed ahead.

At four o'clock I was nursing a hot water with lemon and honey in the breakroom of Kroon and Son. A boom box was playing a fifteen-minute mix of Hallowe'en music on repeat. I'd already heard Oingo Boingo's "Dead Man's Party" four times.

"Lame-ass party," Kurt the dispatcher said, perusing the cold pizza and warm sushi. He was dressed in a blood-stained version of his normal office attire. I agreed that it was. He leaned over and gave me a conspiratorial smile, then held his thumb and index finger up to his lips. "You want to smoke a joint?"

A former office manager now on maternity leave arrived with a basket of homemade samosas. Kurt came back from the parking lot. At 4:30, the younger Thomas Kroon gathered everyone in the main office. He made a banal speech full of generic attaboys, then handed the floor to me.

"My name is Michael, I'm a security consultant. For the last months we've been working to stop a security problem in this building. I wish I had better news, but the investigation has stalled."

"After a very thorough job," Kroon said, "which we all appreciate."

"All of you should be cautious until the new security measures are installed, which will be next week. For the next few days the building will be vulnerable. Be careful exiting and entering the building and make sure to safeguard your valuables." I swept a hand over the brochures I'd fanned out on one of the tables, *How to Protect Your Work Environment* and the like. "Feel free to browse the literature. There are some excellent steps you can take to feel safer. I won't take up any more of your time. Enjoy your party."

Polite applause. "What's that about?" someone asked.

"Corpse Fucker," Kurt whispered.

"Watch your language," the older Thomas Kroon said.

Carrie asked me, "What new security is going in?"

"Reinforced steel doors with electronic key cards which record who comes and goes from what room. Additional cameras and a few other surprises."

She turned to the Kroons. "And when was the office supposed to find out about this?"

"We'll discuss everything Monday," the younger Thomas Kroon said, peering at me with a raised eyebrow. The security measures were new to him. Before he could cross the room to ask me about them, he was waylaid by Supreet the former office manager. I made my escape.

"And here I thought you'd be the one to cheer me up," Ben said. He put his plastic tray down on the plastic table and squeezed his bulk onto the stool to my right.

"Just preoccupied," I said, stowing away my book. I transferred my tray to a nearby table, keeping the half-finished soda in front of me. From where we sat, with our backs to the kid's ball room, we could watch rush hour traffic battle inertia along Marine Drive.

Ben unwrapped his chicken burger, removed the top of the bun, set the tomato aside and squeezed a packet of ketchup onto the exposed patty. "So you don't want to talk about it?" he said. "Because unlike some friends, if you tell me you don't want to talk about something, I won't force you to." With a mouth full of food he added, "Unless you're really dying to, and you just don't want to seem too eager to unpack your heart. Then I might consider pursuing it."

My reluctance stemmed from the fact that I'd been

contemplating the Szabo case, comparing details with Cynthia Loeb's disappearance. The circumstances couldn't have been more different — years apart, one grabbed in her neighbourhood, the other in a commercial district, Django missing with the car and bike, Cynthia with the clothes she was wearing, a dollar seventy-eight in change and one of her mother's berets affixed in her hair. The similarities had to do with the effect the disappearances had on their families. Cynthia Loeb, Django Szabo. Cynthia Szabo, Django Loeb. Not the subject I'd choose to bring up with the brother of one of the missing.

I said to Ben, "I guess I'm disappointed in myself. I thought I'd been disabused a long time ago of the notion that everything has an easy and accessible answer. I recognize that some cases don't solve. Some of them you know but you can't prove. Others you know and can prove but no one's listening, or the ne'er-do-well perp's cousin is the Minister of Finance or some other bullshit. I know I have no reason to believe we'll find this kid alive, but I keep thinking, that's not good enough. I'm getting stupid, because I'm starting to believe that whoever's out there might actually be listening to me."

"Who's that?" Ben asked.

"I don't know. God?"

"Do you believe in God?"

"No. Do you?"

"No."

"But I'll tell you, if prayer's what helps get that kid back, I'd be first in line at the candle store."

"I'm pretty sure the church supplies those," Ben said.

"They wouldn't let you bring your own to — what's it called? Mass?"

"I don't know, I've never been." He balled up the burger wrapper and stuffed it in the empty french fry sleeve. "My family's Jewish if you go back far enough, but both my parents were free thinkers."

"Mine are cultists."

"There's a double date," Ben said.

Staked out a block from Kroon and Son, we talked about Ben's game design problems. More specifically, he talked and I listened. I kept my gaze on the door. At 7:30 the party broke up, and by nine the building was shut down for the long weekend.

"At least we all agreed to make the game a prequel," Ben said. "They're working from the backstory I established in the first two games and the spinoff graphic novel. I'd hate to put any important character developments in Choad Boy's hands. I admit adding vehicles was a decent idea. We could never make those work with the physics engine we were using. But his great storyline idea? Rosalind and Magnus break out of prison. I mean, that was old back in the days of *Wolfenstein*."

"You sound happier," I said.

"I'm not, I'm just ultra-busy making sure Choad Boy doesn't screw things up." He realized we weren't driving anymore and undid his seatbelt. "You're going to want to open your window."

"Christ," I said, as the smell of flatulence filled the car. I popped open the skylight. "Sure you're not one of the corpses in there?"

After hours, the industrial park was uninhabited save for the odd janitor or night crew heading to one of the warehouses. We were parked on a winding road with no curb, the car conspicuous but far enough from the doorstep of the mortuary not to arouse suspicion. Every car that passed us appeared first as a pair of headlights, giving us time to duck in our seats.

Everything I'd told the funeral workers was designed to flush out the Corpse Fucker, make him think he had a brief window to misbehave before the new security made sneaking in harder. That meant deceiving both of the Kroons, my clients. I was fine with that.

"Drayton," Ben said. "What was your gut reaction to the Szabo case? Did you think it would solve?"

"No."

"Why?"

"The state in which the kid disappeared tells you everything," I said. "Most missing persons cases are either runaways or custodial disputes. There was none of that with Django. His home life wasn't great but it was all he knew. He didn't have anyone to run to, and no relatives that would want to take him from Cliff."

Ben was silent. *Don't ask*, I thought.

"Is that the same feeling you got with Cynthia?"

"Course not," I said, mustering as much of a poker face as I could. Luckily it was dark and he was staring out his window.

"Really?"

"I still hold out hope," I said, which wasn't false. "So should you. Car coming."

We slumped down in our seats so we could just see over the dash. The sedan slowed as it passed the mortuary but didn't stop.

"It's just that what you said was similar to how it was with Cynthia," Ben said. "No reason to run away and no custody problems."

"Was she in a car that got swiped?"

"No."

"And was she in a high-crime area, like near a pawn shop?"

"Obviously not."

"So the circumstances are totally different, right?"

The lies felt like bile in my throat. *She's dead and you will never see her again. Accept it.*

"Don't confuse one case with the other," I said. "I wouldn't lie to you about this. In fact, next week I'm talking to a Vice cop who has a whole new angle on things."

"Really?"

"I'll tell you more when I know more," I said.

Ben was silent. I thought about his mother and Madame Thibodeau. I'd felt good about keeping the psychic from sinking her talons into Mrs. Loeb. And yet how was I any better? I liked to think I was different because I wasn't after her money, and because I tried to be honorable. In the end, though, I was another bullshit artist, plying her with false hope. I should tell Mrs. Loeb and her son that Cynthia was never coming back. Help to puncture the last of their delusions rather than bolstering them. That was the right thing to do. It was also merciless.

I remember my grandfather coming home one day after being first on the scene of a homicide. The victim, sixty-seven and asthmatic, lived on the first floor of a high rise. The killer had smashed through the sliding patio door looking for valuables, thinking no one was home. He'd tied her up, robbed her, raped her, and cut her throat. He didn't nick a major blood vessel and she remained alive for two hours, struggling and bleeding until giving up the ghost shortly after my grandfather arrived. He didn't talk to us when he got home that night.

Weeks later the woman's older sister requested my grandfather visit her in the palliative care unit of Peace Arch Hospital. I drove with my grandfather, we were going fishing after. The bed-bound woman demanded to know the particulars of her sister's murder. My grandfather obliged her.

He told it honest, from the defensive wounds on her hands to the damage to her face and eyes. The woman took it all in, nodding but otherwise blank, letting this information pour into her.

When he was finished, she thanked him for his candor. We made to leave. She called him back: "Constable." We paused and turned back to her but she said nothing. She had blue eyes and the pupils flitted from my grandfather's face to mine. Finally she said, "I'd like to think my sister wasn't in any pain when she passed."

What're you, an idiot? I remember thinking. I looked to my grandfather to see how he'd answer. Actually, ma'am, your sister was in a hell of a lot of pain and it lasted a hell of a long time.

But he said, "That's right. The coroner told me she didn't feel none of it."

I wondered whether it was strength or weakness that made him say it. Thinking back on the way she phrased that question, I'm sure she knew the truth. I think what she wanted was to be able to tell other people, "The police said she wasn't in pain." Maybe by repeating that, she could program herself to believe it was true, and in so doing, give herself and her sister some measure of peace.

Headlights in the rearview mirror. The same sedan coming back. It pulled into the mortuary loading area, a nondescript Cadillac, black in the lamplight. A company car.

The dashboard clock read 9:40 p.m. "We'll wait a few minutes," I said.

"He could do his business in that time."

"It'll take a couple minutes for him to wheel them out of the fridge," I said.

We waited in silence, which I was grateful for. At ten to ten the lights went on in the offices, then clicked off a minute later.

"Now," I said.

We walked up the path the car had taken, into the lot and around the side. I took out the key ring I hadn't returned and silently opened the doorlock.

I said, "Follow me. Hang back a bit. Don't say anything." I didn't look back to see if Ben had understood.

Single file we crept down the hall. I put my hand on the door to the embalmer's room, nodded one, two, three, and moved inside.

In the darkness I collided with someone. A slight figure, surprisingly strong. Off-balance, I struggled to keep a grip. The figure pivoted and my forearm shattered on the concrete wall. The burst of pain was accompanied by a numbness that meant something was broken. With my good hand I seized the figure and slammed it to the wall, feeling the body go limp as I repeated the gesture.

Ben hit the lights. I watched the older Thomas Kroon slide to a sitting position by my legs. I could see tears on the cheeks of the old man, his face contorted with humiliation and sorrow.

In the centre of the room a cadaver in a hospital gown had been laid out on a gurney. The dead old woman's eyes were closed, her posture supine, her expression — how do you judge the expression of a corpse? The muscles in her face were slack, which leant her a kind of peace. Her bloodless mouth had been pried open. She looked as if waiting to be kissed.

"How's your arm?" Ben asked.

"Hurts." I set it on top of the nearest supply cabinet and looked over at Kroon. "The hell did you do that for?"

"I am so sorry," he said. "I am so ashamed."

With my right hand I worked my cell out of my left pocket, tossed it to Ben. "His son's number's in the contacts."

"I don't want to live," Kroon the Elder said.

"Shut up. Sit there." To Ben: "Pair of cuffs in the trunk of the car. Grab them, will you?"

"Shouldn't we take you to a hospital?"

Through my teeth I said, "Faster you get the cuffs, faster we can go."

"All right." Ben ducked out.

I leaned back against the wall a few feet from where Kroon sat. The endorphins were slowly kicking in and the pain was almost tenable. Almost.

"I'm so ashamed," Kroon repeated. He blew snot on the front of his shirt. "In that cupboard there's a bottle of chloroform. Half a cup is fatal. I can't bear to see my son."

"Don't think about it."

"My whole life has been a waste," he said. "When I saw Ethel laid out there, I remembered seeing her in Church years ago. Tried to summon the courage to ask her out, but she was a year ahead of me, and always with older boys, and so very beautiful. After how many bodies over how many years, I saw her laid out and I thought, what a waste. I never had the courage, and I knew her husband hadn't made her happy." He wiped his nose. "And the others, all beautiful, all gone." He looked over at me. "I'm sorry about your arm. I am so ashamed. Please let me get to my cabinet."

Drops of sweat hit the floor. "Unless you named me in your will, you sit your ass down."

"What's going to happen?"

"I don't know yet."

Ben came back and tossed me the cuffs, which bounced off my good shoulder and hit the floor. I stared at him. He walked over, picked them up and clasped them around Mr. Kroon's wrists.

"Why?" Ben asked him, looking from the cadaver to the sobbing man on the ground.

"Missed his chance with the original victim," I said. "She could've been his first girlfriend."

Ben leaned towards me and said sotto voce, "Guess he made sure he was her last."

The Ethics of Extortion

A tired-looking doctor glanced at the X-rays and called it a hairline fracture of the ulna. A typical sports injury, she assured me, as common as a cold. My arm was cast by a nurse named Sunny who told me she'd personally set three other broken arms this week. I asked her in a city the size of Vancouver was that a lot or a little. She said she didn't know.

Ben drove me home and called a cab for himself. I made it downstairs, still reeling from the anesthetic, and found my bed in the dark. The dog inspected the cast. I pushed her snout away from the plaster. I lay sweating on top of the covers until sleep came. When I woke up in the late morning I found myself fully-dressed and still wearing shoes.

Upstairs I answered my grandmother's questions and drank orange juice. Once she was satisfied the person who broke the arm wasn't in league with the firecracker-throwers, she asked me if I'd be home tonight. I told her not to plan on it.

"You will pick up the candy, though? And the pumpkin?"

"I'll take care of it." I rinsed out my glass. "Should I get someone to stay with you?"

"Not necessary."

"You have my cell."

"Don't forget the candy."

* * *

Driving with one arm took getting used to. For the end of October the weather was balmy. A pleasant breeze stirred the laurel bushes. The sun shined through cloud cover. It would be a busy Halloween for the trick-or-treat crowd. Doubtless someone would go missing. A kid in a dark costume, garbage bag swinging against her legs as she strays away from the cluster of kids, eager to hit the next house and the next. The parents hanging back to gab with other parents or exchange sheepish smiles with the home owners as the kids trample through the garden to the house next door. Or maybe everything would work out for everybody. The dangers of Halloween are always over-stressed. Maybe what makes it an appealing holiday is just those dangers, that mockery of death and tempting of one's fate. Those were feelings that don't get expressed in the December holidays.

I ran the errands first, picking up a box of Cadbury's assorted miniatures and a pumpkin the size of a severed head. Ichabod Crane, Bing Crosby, and the Disney cartoon. I wondered if there were still assholes out there who handed out raisins and toothbrushes. Probably more than before. That was how the world was heading. Safe and joyless. Anyone who doubted that had only to turn on the radio. Sometimes it didn't seem so bad to go missing.

I parked in front of the funeral home, surprised to see that it was open and the weekend staff were going about their business. The younger Thomas Kroon noted my cast, smiled apologetically and led me to his office. He unlocked it, led me in, locked it behind us.

His father sat in a client's chair to the left of the desk, a nylon hockey jersey spread over his lap to cover the cuffs. I unhooked him and settled into the other chair. He massaged his wrists, left to take a leak, returned with a mug of coffee.

"You did all of them?" I asked him. He nodded. I turned to his son. "And you had zero idea it was him?"

"Would I have hired you if I knew?"

"Why did you hire me?" I asked the old man. "Didn't you think I'd find out?"

"I'm so ashamed," the older Thomas Kroon said.

"Don't start," I said. "The question is, what happens now?"

"What's your suggestion?" Younger asked me.

"First off and non-negotiable, this can't continue."

Both Kroons agreed it couldn't.

"He —" I pointed at Elder "— can't work here. He needs counseling and supervision."

"My therapist recommended someone," Younger said. "Funny. My father always said those people were full of shit."

Elder flinched when his son referred to him as if he wasn't there. It was curious to watch the two of them redraw the lines of power. A month earlier when they'd come to my office they'd resembled walking advertisements for old and new school: Elder patient, mannered, calm and commanding respect, Younger brash and smarmy, bridling at any insinuation he wasn't ready to take the reins. Now Younger looked burdened. He cast his eyes about the room as if looking for something to anchor him. He looked everywhere but avoided his father, whose eyes rarely left his, as if pleading to his son for reassurance, and the son unwilling or unable to give it. Discovering the identity of the Corpse Fucker had not only destroyed Thomas Kroon the Younger's image of his father, but that of himself as well. I wondered if having the same name added to the burden.

"I'll get him the help he needs," Younger said to me. "Now what about the police — should we involve them?" His voice free of indications of his own preference.

"When we started you told me you didn't want the publicity that law enforcement would bring. Is that still true?"

"I guess so. Yes."

"Then I need some things from you." To Elder I said, "First off, no more talk of suicide or how ashamed you are. You accept what you did and accept help. Any more suicide nonsense, word or deed, and it ends up page one of the *Sun*, with a letter going out to each of the victims' families."

"All right," Elder said. He looked hopefully to his son, who busied himself writing something on a sticky note.

"If the incidents are over and I don't have to worry about you offing yourself, then I can live with not involving the police. The only other matter is the sum of ten thousand dollars, which I'd like paid out over the next four months."

"You're shaking us down?" Younger said, perplexed.

"Call it atonement," I said. "I'm working a missing child case where there's a chance of finding the kid if we act now. The father can't afford to pay and I can't afford to work for free, and to be honest, you can't afford not to pay, so it works out for everyone, you subsidizing the search. If it wraps up in the first two months, I won't ask you for the other five grand. The only way I come out of this with a somewhat clean conscience is if I know Szabo gets the help he needs."

"Szabo? That was in the paper the other day," Younger said.

"I remember," Elder said, looking to the son who wouldn't look at him.

The son said, "We'll pay."

I shook their hands in turn. "Can you see me out?" I asked Younger.

On the walkway he lit a cigarette, offered me the pack. "Tempting but no," I said. He lit up and exhaled something more than smoke. "You're in your mid-forties?" I asked him.

"Forty-two this April. What're you, early thirties?"

"Twenty-nine," I said. "I have no place giving you advice, but that's not going to stop me. You'll be mad at him a long time, and he deserves that. But don't drag it out. Don't hate him."

"I can't hate someone I don't fucking know," he said. He coughed hard enough to extinguish the cigarette. He relit it. "My dad taught me the business. It's all I know. Now I find out at the centre of this is — " He spread his hands, to say, well, what exactly *is* this?

"Your attitude to him the next few months will affect his lifespan," I said. "You don't want him to kick off with some reckoning still owed between you." Kroon looked at me as if to say, "Is the lecture over now?" I added, hesitantly, "Fucked-up parents are better than none at all."

He finished his smoke, stubbed it out, and contemplated the butt as he worked it into the concrete with the toe of his loafer. My part in their family drama was over. I wondered if either of them would forgive the elder Thomas Kroon. I wondered if I'd ever know.

Katherine was at the office sending off the last batch of files to the lawyer. From the looks of things the lawsuit would proceed against the school. I'd thought of it as a scare tactic, but it looked as if the school would rather take the whole sordid matter to court than simply pay my fee. This presented me with the day's second great ethical dilemma. A lawsuit had the potential to ruin the reputation of a teacher who, to my knowledge, had never glanced sideways at a child. I had Katherine indicate that if it came down to such a scenario, we would drop the lawsuit before dragging the man's name through the mud. Hopefully the school trustees would pull their heads out of their asses and pay up before it came to that. I wasn't optimistic.

I put a call in to Gavin Fisk and tapped my pencil while I waited.

"Are you meeting Ben and I for a drink tonight?" I asked Katherine.

"Maybe," she said. "Who else'll be there?"

"Probably just us, Yeats if she wants to come."

"I can't make it, I just remembered."

"What do you have against her?"

"It's no use talking to you," Katherine said.

"Why's that?"

"Because. Anything I say will just make you defend her more fiercely, which means we're going to fight, and I don't want that."

Irrefutable logic if you took the first idea as truth. Amelia Yeats was beautiful, brilliant, talented, funny. What wasn't there to love? Drugs for starters. I hated to think of myself as a prude, but I'd seen too many ashen-faced zombies with no teeth and gouges out of their arms to be comfortable with dating someone into that. Yeats was also inexplicably rude to Katherine — maybe she could sense her disapproval. It was hard to imagine someone as self-reliant as Amelia Yeats falling into either of those traps.

I worried it over until Fisk returned my call. "Mister Holmes," he said. "I did promise to keep you informed. April 7th, Barbara Della Costa tried to use a credit card at a Shell station on Vancouver Island, a small town north of Nanaimo called Prosper's Point. Am-Ex hadn't received a payment from her in five months. Week later the card was used at a rod-and-gun store. Same town. Owners had the old manual imprint system, frequent problems with service out in the boonies."

"She bought a gun?"

"Six top-of-the-line fishing rods," Fisk said. "A pawn shop nearby confirms that a woman hocked two of them the same day. Brought the others back the next week but the shop owner said nothing doing. She gave him a fake address, naturally. I'm heading over Monday."

"No word on the other two girls?"

"None, but we have a name for one of them. Dawn Meeker. Co-signed a lease on an apartment with Barbara before they moved into the house on Fraser."

"Dawn Meeker. Dominique."

"Never would've thought of that, Sherlock. Glad there are PIs around to keep bumbling cops like me from missing the obvious."

"Can I tell Szabo?"

"I'd prefer to be there for that conversation," Fisk said.

"We're meeting Sunday morning."

"That's my day off," Fisk said. I said nothing. "Fine," he said. "Didn't want to sleep in anyway."

"Eleven in front of the police station."

"Try and get him to open up a bit to me," Fisk said. "Being forthcoming is in his interest more'n mine. Grouchy old bastard. How you got him to trust you is beyond me."

"My countenance enforces homage," I said.

"What?"

"Shakespeare. You wouldn't understand. See you tomorrow."

As we closed up shop, I said to Katherine, "If I promise not to argue with you, will you tell me what you have against Amelia Yeats?"

"We're back to that?"

"I guess I never left it," I said. "Are you worried she'll have me running the office off of star alignments and tarot cards?"

Katherine shook her head. "You're way too domineering for that."

"So it's just the name-calling?"

"No," Katherine said. "I didn't want to bring it up, but don't you think she's a little close to this investigation? One of the last people to see Django. Frequently did business with Cliff, and we know how reputable the people he deals with are. Contact with lots of lowlifes, like those punks that were in the stairwell. Plus you told me her father's insane."

"I'm trying to imagine the scenario you've come up with," I said. "She decides out of the blue she wants this kid so she hires Zak Atero to boost the car, hires the hookers to take Django and make it look like they left town with him, and all so that she can — what? Give him to her father? Grind his bones to make her bread? No," I said, locking the door behind us, "Yeats has her problems but she's not involved."

"Does she use drugs?" Katherine asked.

"What does that matter?"

"That's a yes," she said. "What's the connection between Zak Atero and Dominique?"

"You have a point," I said. "I'll ask if she knows them. But she won't."

"She only knows the good drug users?" I started to respond and she said, "Just look at her like you would anyone else, Mike."

I wondered if that were possible.

XX

The Paddy's Cure

From home I phoned Yeats to broach the subject of the Ateros. Before I could, she asked if I wanted to go to a Hallowe'en party at some club downtown. Before I knew it I'd re-arranged my night so I was meeting Ben at nine at Doolin's.

"What's your costume?" she asked me.

"It's a surprise. You?"

"Same. Pick me up at 6:30."

I helped my grandmother carve a jack-o-lantern, at least as much help as a one-armed man could give. When I'd finished dumping out the sheets of newspaper covered in seeds and pumpkin muck, I held up the felt pen she'd used to trace the facial features and asked if she wanted to be the first to sign my cast.

In contrast to the sardonic tags my friends would make, she wrote, in her elegant, slightly wobbly penmanship:

> *Dear Grandson, I hope you heal up quickly.*
> *Stay safe and out of trouble. Have a happy*
> *Hallowe'en. Love Gran.*

Before I left I phoned Mira Das and asked her to have a patrol car check on the house. I hoped the Ateros would be busy with their own celebrations.

* * *

"What're you 'sposed to be?" Yeats said as she slid in next to me. Her father had been tranquilized for the evening and put to bed. I waited for her in the car. She came out wearing an orange jumpsuit with numbers painted on the back and rubber manacles around her ankles. The suit was unzipped to her belly and showed a generous amount of skin.

"Couldn't think of anything," I said.

"No costume is the saddest costume of all." She pawed through an orange-knit handbag, her hand emerging with a pair of drugstore sunglasses. "Here," she said, sliding them into my pocket. "If anyone asks you can tell them you're Corey Hart."

There was no live music at the club, just a succession of DJs, none of whom seemed all that concerned with who they scared off the dance floor. I stuck close to Yeats, determined to ask her about Atero and not to let her out of my sight. Maybe it was insecurity, and maybe that was why I hadn't bothered with a costume, too uncomfortable in my own skin to layer something over it. Yeats's costume was both sexy and self-referential, poking fun at her mother's incarceration and maybe making that fact easier to deal with. I knew I wasn't there yet. I'd hidden behind ironic detachment, finding myself a vantage point where I could criticize others without being criticized. She was right, no costume was the complete failure of imagination and courage.

"Not really my scene," she said over the *boosh-boosh-boosh* of the house music. "Split?"

"Split," I said. We did, working our way down Granville, paying the cover when we had to or slipping in with a bribe to the bouncer.

I'd taken the Tylenol Threes the doctor prescribed and decided mixing them with alcohol would be a bad idea. After the first five dollar ginger ale, I changed my mind and ordered beer. Then some oily-looking executive sent over a tray of shots. By the time we'd worked from the Vogue to the Commodore to the Media Room, I'd decided that alcohol pretty much went with anything. A few painkillers and some watery club beer wasn't going to turn me into Samuel Coleridge, but it did give me a nice out-of-it feeling.

At the last club we arrived during the band's intermission. Yeats saw her friend Zoltan lurch out of the men's room looking nauseous. She asked me to stick with him for a minute while she touched base with someone backstage.

I propped Zoltan against the bar. He was dressed as usual: Nirvana tee, flannel shirt wrapped around the waist, ripped jeans. "Who are you?" he said, drooling a little on the bar.

"Mike," I said. "What's your costume?"

"I'm Eddie Vedder," he said, flashing a grin before stumbling and sending his drink into the lap of a seated couple behind us.

Zoltan wandered off. I circulated, trying to recognize people I'd been introduced to at other events. I tried to guess what the elaborate and occasionally wonderful costumes were meant to symbolize. The bar was tiny and packed with friends of the band, all of them artists, all of them political theorists and critics of pop culture. So-and-so's side band was total genius. The Beatles were overrated. The only real American writer is Bukowski. Like listening to a chorus of solipsists. When I couldn't take any more I pushed through the door to the side of the stage.

A skinhead with a thick orange goatee held me up at the backstage entrance. "You have a pass to be back here?"

"Security," I said, handing him one of my cards and scowling as if preoccupied so he wouldn't notice I was drunk. He looked skeptical but let me through.

Backstage wasn't at all glamorous. I found Amelia Yeats in a dirty corner underneath some pipes on the ceiling, crouching with two women and a man. The man was cutting lines of coke on the top of a road case. The band's name, Prawn Chow, was stenciled on the side.

She looked up at me, wiping her nose. "Dad's here," one of the other women said.

"I did warn you," Yeats said, trying for a self-effacing smile that wasn't quite there. "So don't act surprised."

"I'm not," I said. *Right.* "This makes you happy?"

She didn't answer. The ferret-faced man tried to duck out. I caught him by the jacket collar, spun him into the wall and frisked him, coming up with two more baggies, each marked with an Olympic-rings logo. Not a street brand I recognized.

"The fuck is this guy's problem?" one of the other women said.

"Is he a cop?" the other said.

"No," Yeats said. "Give those back to Max, Mike."

I looked over at Max, who wanted nothing more than to excuse himself from a situation he didn't understand. "Do you want these back?" I asked him. He shook his head. "What's the price on these?" No answer. I dug a hundred-dollar bill out of my wallet. "C-note do the trick?" He nodded, took the money and scurried out.

"Don't," Yeats said as I ripped open one of the bags.

I tapped out an amount on the back of my hand. Years of handling drugs and watching others use them and I still fumbled. "Up the nose?" I said.

"Mike."

"Here goes," I said, taking my first nostril-full of an illegal narcotic. In the shock I dropped the packets, which were scooped up by the other women on their way out. One even pinched up the coke that had spilled on the floor from the open baggie, reaching through my legs to do so.

"What did that prove?" Yeats said.

"I don't know."

'Intense euphoria' was a phrase from police drug literature that came to mind. I certainly didn't feel that. My nose felt sore and after a minute my nostrils went numb. After a while I felt like large shards of my brain had become unmoored and had begun to drift into orbit around my skull. Only willpower kept them from flying off completely. I spotted an orange exit sign and made for it. Yeats followed me out. Over before it began, I thought. My mouth felt dry.

"Do you know Zak Atero?" I asked her.

"Who's that?"

"Barbara Della Costa? Dawn Meeker?"

"Are these people you know who use drugs?" Standing in the doorway, arms crossed, both of us lit up by the marquee signs that cast shadows and light over the alley.

"Yes," I said.

"So I must know them, right?" Yeats shook her head, using the opportunity to wipe her eyes. "Never heard of them. I don't understand what just happened. I told you days ago what I did. I thought you were cool with that."

"I thought I was, too," I said. "Evidently not."

"You think you're going to stop me, or save me, or something like that?"

I leaned against the wet brick.

"I think, as much of an asshole and an idiot as I feel like now, I'd've felt ten times worse watching those parasites burrow into you and doing nothing. You have money and you hate yourself for reasons I can't fathom. They smell it on you same as I do, and they feed off it. I will walk back in there and apologize if you tell me any of them paid for that stuff 'sides you."

"It's not your business, Mike."

"Hell it isn't."

"You don't get a say in what I do, in any of it."

The music started up and our voices were almost lost. I watched the light reflected in the puddles ripple as the rain started up again.

"I knew you'd get like this," she said, smiling and shaking her head to herself. "I don't need you to protect me. I don't want you to try. Can't you respect that?"

"No," I said.

"Then fuck you."

She zipped up her jumpsuit, wiped at her eyes. I shrugged and pulled my coat around me. I felt the sunglasses in my pocket press against my breast and thought to give them back, but instead I heard myself say, "Look me up when you feel like making a change." I felt stupid. I started up the alley towards the bar.

As I lay down on the wood planks of the corner booth, I explained to Ben the reasoning behind what I'd just done. I found it made as much sense to him as it did to me upon hearing myself say it, namely, no sense at all. I attributed this to the coke and painkillers and bourbon and beer, and the half-dozen rounds of Bushmill's and Harp chasers we were in the process of putting away.

I find that when I drink there's a movement to jettison things which may, when sober, prove necessary, but under the influence seem more trouble than they're worth. No girl-friend? No girlfriend problems. Simple as that. A drunk can justify a lot of bad decisions that way. Maybe a few days out of the year that's good. When you start repeating that logic sober, though, you know you're in trouble.

Doolin's had the darkness and warmth of a traditional public house in the old country, or at least a humble Vancouverite's idea of what that might be like. I've never been to Ireland. I've never been anywhere. I was in Toronto once, for two weeks, on business. I was in no hurry to go back. I found myself repeating this out loud as Ben tried to unravel the chronology of my fight with Yeats.

"You tried to confront her drug use by snorting half her coke?"

"It wasn't nearly that much," I said. "I spilled most of it."

I heard Ben slam his empty shotglass on the bar. He had showed up dressed head to toe in black, head shaved completely, a copy of *From Ritual to Romance* crammed into his pocket. I'd been trying to figure out what his costume was, but after lying on my back for twenty minutes trying to will the ceiling not to spin, I was no longer sure what he was wearing. I sat up just to check.

"My heart's still racing," I said.

"I guess that would be the cocaine."

"You've never tried it?"

"A couple times in high school," he said. "Problem is, I'm fat and I like to eat, and that's not likely to change. If all those *Saturday Night Live* deaths taught us anything, it's that you can be fat or you can do coke, but you can't have both."

"Was John Candy a sniffer?"

"He was Second City," Ben said.

I downed the whiskey, killed the last of the Harp. At the bar the crowd segued from "Fields of Athenry" to "Rocky Road to Dublin." I banged my hand on the table in tempo.

"I should get a shillelagh and wallop the shit out of him," I said.

"Who?"

"Theo Atero. Who else was I talking about?"

"You haven't mentioned him all night," Ben said.

"So what was I talking about?"

"Amelia Yeats."

"Right," I said. "Anyway, I guess that's over."

"From the sound of things."

"I was looking forward to getting laid tonight."

"Probably shouldn't've pissed her off then."

"Not that that's the only reason I wanted to see her."

"Of course not."

"I'm serious."

From the bar, a crescendo of voices.

"Katherine thinks I'm in love."

"With her?"

"With Yeats."

"Ever consider she might be in love with you?"

"Yeats?"

"Katherine."

"She seems happy with her boyfriend."

"Maybe."

"Though I don't know why. He really is a dullard."

"Agreed."

"Want to go for a walk?"

"I'll settle up," Ben said.

We walked down to West Georgia, past the bank and credit card towers, to a row of three-storey office buildings with glass storefronts and canopied staircases. I knew the block I wanted but not the suite number, only that it was on the second floor and accessible by an outside staircase, just like my own office.

"Hamlet in chemotherapy," I guessed as I checked the office directory posted outside the main entrance.

"My costume, you mean? Guess again."

"Yul Brynner?"

"Kurtz," he said testily. "Brando? How could you not get that?"

"I sort of see it now," I said.

"Did you know Orson Welles almost made *Heart of Darkness* instead of *Citizen Kane*?"

"What does that have to do with your costume?"

"Nothing," Ben said.

On the side entrance I found the Aries Investigations logo stenciled on the door. The stairwell light inside was off. I unzipped my fly and hosed the door down.

"Real mature," Ben said.

I shook out the last drops and zipped up. "Guy's an asshole," I said.

"The handle's steaming."

"Someone's going to have to touch that," I said.

"Gross."

"Let's do some more drinking."

"That'll solve everything," Ben said.

As we walked back across Burrard the Night Bus let off its passengers. Two figures in black headed down towards the waterfront. I recognized one of them.

"Katherine," I said.

She turned. She was wearing a leather bustier, fishnets on her arms, a streak of red in her hair. Thick makeup, black and crimson over white, a pincushion's worth of piercings. Her companion I eventually recognized as Scott, wearing combat boots and goggles and a KMFDM hoodie drawn tight around his head.

"Jesus, you're drunk," she said.

"Happy Hallowe'en. Is this a costume or are you a goth?"

Underneath the corpse paint I saw her blush. "We're on our way to a club."

"We've got nothing better to do," I said, indicating Ben and myself. "Does this club serve booze?"

"It's kind of a private party," she said.

"Whatever. So you dress like this when you're not at work or school?"

Katherine looked embarrassed but didn't deny it.

"You know it wouldn't bother me, you showing up for work like that. The dress code is lax at Hastings Street Investigations. I mean it."

"Okay." Doubtful. "See you tomorrow. Happy Hallowe'en."

Scott nodded to us in turn. "Later."

"Enjoy your vampire romance," Ben said. "Have a glass of watered-down, de-wormwooded absinthe for me."

"Fuck you," Scott called back to him, his voice cracking.

"Kindergoths are so easy to wind up," Ben said as we made our way back toward Doolin's.

"My cousin went through that," I said. "Least they're not Nickelback fans."

"There's that," Ben admitted.

Through sheer luck I maneuvered my car from the parkade on Granville to the parking spot behind my office. Ben and I split a cab from there. I had the cabbie drop me on Oak, figuring the walk would either sober me up or tire me out. It accomplished both.

The jack-o-lantern on my grandmother's porch had collapsed in on itself, extinguishing the candle. The air around the porch smelled of burnt pumpkin. I was happy to see the new porch light snap on as I approached. The old girl had figured it out.

Inside I poured myself a glass of water, then another, and another. I took my shoes off and moved into the living room. Something rustled on the couch and I dropped my empty glass on the rug. *Atero,* I thought, *here to return the favor.*

Amelia Yeats sat up on the couch and threw off the Hudson's

Bay point blanket that my grandmother liked to offer guests. She was wearing one of my shirts. It looked better on her. She put her thumb and index finger into her mouth and pulled something out which she placed in a pink case on the lampstand.

"I wear a retainer," she said, somewhat embarrassed. "Feel like watching television?"

"Should we maybe talk?"

"It can wait for the morning."

I sat down next to her. She clicked through a few late-night movie stations, eventually settling on *Defending Your Life*. As we watched she leaned on my shoulder, moving down to rest her head on my lap. And then I was struggling out of my underwear as she took my cock in her mouth. When release came I pinned her beneath me on the couch and kissed down her torso till my tongue settled on the thatch of coarse hair and licked into the slit beneath it. Later, when the credits rolled and the movie started up again, so did we, finding a sweet rhythm beneath the rough wool of the blanket, sliding the cushions off the couch and finishing on the floor, with the only sound in the house our breath and blood.

It was jealousy, I told her. She said that Max and the others were friends and not even really that. Not sexual jealousy, I said. What other kind is there?

I told her I'd read a book once on the psychology of police officers. One of the reasons they tended to bend the law was a feeling of responsibility for things they couldn't possibly be responsible for. Justice weighs heavily on some people. They feel the entire city depends on them. They're aware of how flawed the system is and they can't change it, so they try to work around it.

She said, "What does that have to do with anything?"

"I don't want to be responsible anymore," I said. "I want to not care. People who don't give a shit about justice or about other people live happier lives. I've always felt that way. I see it on their faces."

"You think I'm like that?"

I told her I didn't know.

"Maybe that's true," she said. "I care about art. More than anything."

"It makes you happy?"

"Sometimes," she said. "What made you quit being a police officer?"

"I don't think I ever did."

"But why'd you resign?"

"I'll tell you in the morning."

"It's morning now," she said.

XXI

The Flight of the Wild Atero

I woke to the chirping of the house phone. I sat up. Yeats wasn't next to me. I was alone.

The clock read 11:37 a.m. The phone's ringing became a high-pitched jackhammer ripping up pavement in my frontal lobe.

I groped the floor, found my pants, found the phone and flipped it open.

Gavin Fisk's voice. "You forget you me and Cliff had an appointment?"

"Personal situation," I said, sitting up. My head throbbed and my stomach felt as if one of H.R. Giger's abominations had crawled inside to devour its young. "Start without me, I'll be there in ten minutes."

"Believe me I'd like to start without you. I'd like to be done by now. Only Szabo says he wants to talk to you before he'll talk to me. That better not be the sound of you getting out of bed, Mike."

"Ten minutes," I said.

It took me twenty-two minutes to wash and call for a cab and make the trip to the station. Fisk and Szabo stood by the door of the station in the light rain holding takeaway coffee cups.

Fisk banged a finger on his watch. I held up a finger in return.

"Minute with my client first," I said, leading Cliff to the crosswalk.

"We were waiting," he said.

"Yeah, I'm sorry." I rubbed the bridge of my nose.

"You look hungover."

"I am a bit."

"This is how you look for my son?"

"I'm sorry I was late," I reiterated. "I do have other cases, not to mention a life. And anyway, there's not much I can do till the police are finished. I know that's not pretty to hear, but it's a fact."

He shook his head, more hurt than angry. He spotted the cast on my arm. His temper cooled long enough for me to tell him about the Ateros, the tape, and the vacant apartment.

"These girls might have Django?" he said, his anger and mistrust directed away from me.

"Seems like."

"Why does Theo Atero want to hurt you if his brother doesn't have my son?"

"Family honour, I guess, which is stupid when you consider the family."

Szabo deposited his coffee cup in the first bin we passed. "He lends money, Theo. A shylock. He has connections."

"I'll watch out," I said.

We ran out of awning and turned back towards Fisk. Szabo popped an antacid tablet. "Constable Fisk is going to the Island?" he said.

"On Monday, yes."

"You'll go with him?"

"Tell him you think I should," I said. "I'm sure he'll appreciate it."

"My sister is sick," he said. "She needs me. Otherwise I'd go. But I trust you."

"It's important to me you do," I said, thinking it was better he wasn't coming with us. "And I am sorry I was late."

Fisk was on his phone. As we crossed the street he looked up, saw us, and said so I could hear, "He just came back. Want me to tell him?" He waited for instructions, then held out the cell for me. "Mira," he said. "Your car — I'll let her tell it."

"Mike," she said. Beside me Szabo and Fisk were conferring. "Mike, listen. Did you park at your office last night?"

"Yeah. Spent the night out, decided to park it there so I wouldn't do anything stupid like drive under the influence. Why, I get a ticket? I didn't leave it unlocked, did I?"

"Your car's been vandalized, Mike."

"How bad?"

"It looks like it was stripped for parts and then set on fire. Mark Eager is the constable in charge. He'll want to ask you about the Ateros."

"I'll make time for him." I'd never heard of Eager, but then I was out of the loop. Life seemed determined to push me ever further from my former job.

I had no doubt this was the work of the Ateros: trust the sons of a mechanic to strip parts from a car before torching it. I'd half-closed the deal with Chet Yates for the van. Now that would have to be fast-tracked, the van Air Cared and insured. Then there was the process of filling out an insurance form for the value of the Camry. Luckily my cameras and gear were in the office waiting for someone to catalogue and store the footage from the mortuary. I was out an overnight bag full of clothing and half a box of granola bars. Acceptable losses.

I passed the phone back to Fisk, whose expression had soured since beginning his talk with Szabo. He said, nodding at Szabo but looking at me, "You put your client up to asking that?"

"About me coming with you to the Island?" I shook my head. "His idea entirely."

Fisk poured his cold coffee into the gutter. "Not only do I get to deal with some local RCMP clown, but I get to hang with a half-assed private eye too. Lucky fucking me."

"You have an ability to bring people together, Gavin. Embrace it."

The major casualty of the fire was the Camry's leather interior. The contents of the trunk were undisturbed, save for the permeating smell of gasoline. The hood had been forced up with a crowbar and left propped open. The catalytic converter, the distributor pad, and a few other easy-to-carry parts were gone. Eager had canvassed the neighbourhood. No one had seen anything. I answered his questions but didn't elaborate on the Atero brothers.

Once the car had been towed and Eager placated, I hiked up to my office, made tea and flipped through the mail. From the small balcony I couldn't see around the corner of the building where the car had burned. I could, however, see the front window of Grayson's Diner. If a person wanted to watch both the car and office, the front window of that greasy spoon offered the best vantage.

The sun was positioned such that I couldn't see through the window of Grayson's on account of the glare. The Ateros could have been inside, could still be there. I locked up the office and crossed the street to find out.

A few sallow-faced patrons sat on mismatched chairs, eating and looking over the racing forms. I reckoned most of them were dealing with hangovers at least as severe as mine. Grayson stood with his back to the register, wearing a grimy smock over a brown polo shirt with loose threads hanging from the sleeves.

He fed carrots into a food processor which coughed the shredded remains into a bowl already filled with cabbage.

"The private eye from across the way," he said, catching sight of me. "Used to come here when you first moved in. Not so much after that."

"I brown bag it most days," I said. The menu was written out on a whiteboard hung over the prep counter. "Have anything that will cure a hangover?"

Grayson brought a tub of mayonnaise from beneath the counter and began stripping the plastic seal around the lid. "If I did I'd own franchises," he said, slopping two spoonfuls of mayo into the bowl and tossing the contents, the sailor girl on his bicep contorting as he worked the spoon through the mixture.

I waited until he was done to put in my order. "Grilled cheese and a Coke. Seen two guys in here, both white, brown hair and eyes, one about twenty-eight, lanky and fidgety, the other late thirties, stockier, balding?"

"Were they both maybe wearing T-shirts and jeans?" Grayson asked. He opened a package of brown bread and buttered two slices with a spatula. "Because that would describe three-quarters of my clientele."

"They probably would've been in late last night, around the time of the fire."

"Is that what this is about?" Mild curiosity on his face as he peeled a slice of American cheese, stuck it between the bread and dropped the sandwich onto the grill. "Was the younger one kind of pale? Druggy sort of look to him, like all he wants to do is score, and it's the bald guy keeping him from it?"

"Those are them."

Grayson scraped at a spot on the grill. He took a paper plate from the stack and added a scoop of fresh slaw and a quarter of a dill pickle.

"Younger one had a milkshake. Bald guy ordered a bacon cheddar. Threw a fit when I told him we don't serve fries past midnight. I told him the deep fryers are off at 11:30, says so on the board." Indeed it did.

"So they were in after twelve?"

"Squeezed in at 1:20," he said. "Left at 1:40, ten minutes past closed." I handed him a five dollar bill. He began to make change. I shook my head.

"Don't know what it is about me," he said, "but I've started to lose my nerve. Probably on account of having my balls beat off last year by a couple of crackheads."

I ate my sandwich standing by the counter. Undercooked but not half bad. I stood the ketchup bottle on its head for a solid minute and couldn't get anything out.

"Maybe you sensed they were going to make a move," I said.

"Maybe," Grayson said. "Hallowe'en does tend to bring the fruitcakes out of the woodwork. Closing time, people try all kinds of scams they'd never have the nerve for mid-day. Still, when I think back on them sitting there, me making a racket putting up chairs, hoping they'll take the hint, I can't help think to myself, why didn't you just tell them, 'Hey assholes, we close at half past one?'"

I had some of the slaw to be polite but left the pickle.

"You probably did yourself a favor," I said. "Those aren't two guys I'd start a fight with, I could help it." According to Katherine and McEachern, I thought, I'd done just that.

"Was that your car?" Grayson asked me. I nodded. "You think those two torched it?"

I tossed the plate. "More than possible."

I saw Ben walk up from the bus stop and enter my door. I crossed the street and found him at the top of the staircase catching his breath. I unlocked the door and let him inside. As usual he took the client's chair and let his eyes settle on the

Loeb file. Every time he did so it seemed to take him longer to find his way back to the present business.

"I heard about the fire," he said eventually.

"From the cops?"

"Yeah but don't worry, I alibi'd for you."

I poured us each a cup of tea. "You told Eager the truth," I said.

"I told him I was with you all night."

"Great thinking," I said. "I told him I was with you till I went home. Which is what happened. Which is what I expected you to tell them."

"But then they'd suspect you, since for part of the evening you were alone."

"I wasn't alone."

"Oh." A grin breaking out on his face. "You patched things up with Yeats?"

"Who was gone when I got up this afternoon." I sat in my chair but didn't tip it back. I wasn't yet sure the grilled cheese would keep down, and I wanted as direct a course to the washroom as possible should my stomach reject it.

"Are you going to phone her?"

"I was thinking I would." I spun the phone around so the receiver was within Ben's reach. "First, though, you're going to phone Eager and straighten out your story."

While he did that I checked the messages on the office line. Nothing from Yeats. One from a number I didn't know. No text or voicemail, just a phone call and the sound of hanging up. Time: 12:38 a.m.

I dialed the mystery number. On the first ring someone picked up. "Landmark Logistix?"

The warehouse where Theo Atero worked. I asked for him.

"Theo's out for the day. I could take a message or I could pass you along to the assistant floor manager."

"Message," I said. "Tell him I have proof he and his brother torched my car. Tell him not only will the police be given copies of the proof to aid their investigation, but I'll also be sending copies to the Better Business Bureau, Workplace Safety, Customs and Border Patrol. Not to mention all major news outlets in the Lower Mainland. Tell him starting tomorrow his place of business will be under more scrutiny than the Zapruder film. That's all."

"Are you saying Theo was involved in some sort of crime?"

"Search his brother Zak's name in the news and you'll see what sort of person Theo is."

I hung up. Ben was emptying sugar packets into his tea. "You don't have proof," he said.

"Nope."

"And you probably just cost him his job. Even if he was squeaky clean I wouldn't keep him on after that."

"It won't make a dent in his income, losing that job, but it's taxable. He'll have to find another way to declare the money he makes. It's a nuisance, anyway."

"Is that what you want to do to the guy?" Ben asked. "Be a nuisance?"

"I'm not going to burn one of his cars in retaliation."

"I don't see why not," Ben said.

At three a tired and disheveled Katherine, still in her goth attire, appeared on the stairwell monitor. "I left my clothes here," she explained. "I was going to change before going home."

"Your parents don't know you're a — " Ben searched for the right phrase, "— Bride of Lugosi?"

"They know," she said. "It makes things easier if they don't have to see it. How's any of that your problem?"

"It's not," Ben said, "but it's a silly subculture. And the music is awful. I can see Scott going for it because he's a dolt, but you, I thought, were smarter than that."

"Guess not," Katherine said. "My first choice was to lie around in my underwear all day playing Xbox and not getting laid, but I just wasn't up to the high standards you set for yourself. And as for music you're one to talk, Mr. Last-Concert-I-Went-To-Was-A-Symphony-Orchestra-Playing-Music-From-*Zelda*."

I told them both to shut up. Theo and Zak Atero and Zak's Asian partner had appeared on the monitor.

"Hide in the washroom," I told Ben and Katherine. Neither of them moved. I wasn't sure if that was loyalty or they disliked the idea of being trapped together in a confined space. I nodded to Ben to open the door for the Ateros. He did, and came back to stand next to me behind the table.

"I should throw you off the balcony for what you said to my boss," Theo said. "You know I'm suspended without pay?"

"Tough break. Clear your arson schedule and you could maybe find a night shift position."

"Too bad you couldn't see it," Theo said. "Next time I'll call you so you can watch from your office. Then you can jump off that balcony, doing me and my brother a huge favor."

"That's two balcony threats," Ben said to me and Katherine.

"You're keeping track?" Theo asked Ben.

"Counting to two isn't a full-time occupation for some of us."

Zak and his partner lingered by the door. Zak's foot was wedged against the frame as if to guarantee he'd have an exit. No one had weapons in their hands, although all three wore heavy enough jackets that something could be concealed beneath them. My Glock was within reach, but I had a feeling this could be solved without firearms.

Theo looked from Ben to me. "Your butt buddy thinks it's all right insulting me. Obviously he's not taking into account

I'm on an extremely short tether since my brother's face ended up on the CBC."

I asked Zak, "Do you think you got a raw deal?"

Zak shuffled foot to foot and shrugged.

"Leave him out of things," Theo said, inches from the table. I stood up, came around to stand eye to eye. I saw Katherine unplug and pocket my cell.

I was glad of the height advantage, but Theo seemed comfortable staring down people taller than him.

I said, "That's the last order you give me in that tone of voice."

"There an 'or else' attached to that?"

"How stupid can this guy be?" Ben said. Theo turned his head towards him. "Since you've met Mike you've lost a job, your brother's become a media star, and you've found out your boss won't back you in a fight. And Mike hasn't broken a sweat. How much worse do things have to get for you to back off?"

"I do my own fighting," Theo said. "I don't need Lloyd's permission. How 'bout you? Comfortable standing behind your friend's back?"

"Of course," Ben said. "I've got a great view for when he kicks your ass."

"You're a fat-titted schoolboy."

"Better than an unemployed Dennis Franz lookalike."

Theo's eyes met mine. When he spoke again it was at half the volume, like an exasperated teacher trying not to yell at a lazy dunce.

"My mistake was in treating you like a man," he said to me. "I thought a warning might be enough. All you had to do was back up politely and let me and my brother alone."

"Leave," I said to Zak and his partner. Zak looked to Theo, who nodded. Zak took a few cautious steps out the door. We listened to his footfalls on the stairs. His partner lingered for a few seconds before following Zak out.

"What does the Pacific Northwest Dennis Franz Lookalike Society charge in yearly dues?" Ben asked Theo.

"Shut up," I said to Ben.

Theo smiled and nodded. He turned to Ben. "Your friend's giving you good advice."

"I don't want to see you again," I said to Theo. "And if you answer me with another empty threat I'll send you to the emergency room at St. Paul's. Understand?"

I took a step towards him and he backpedaled towards the door. "I was you," he said, "before I ran my mouth, I'd take out life insurance." We took another collective step toward the door. His hand grazed the knob. He was still talking. With my good hand I grabbed the first object off the table, a three-hole punch, and buffaloed him across the forehead. Theo fell backwards into the door. I dropped the hole punch and shoved him hard down the stairs.

He didn't fall the entire flight, only about two-thirds. A scream of shock issued from him in the brief instant he was in mid-air. Then he landed on his side, heavily, moaning and uttering curses under laboured breathing.

I walked down to where he lay and grabbed a handful of hair, raising his head off the step. When I dropped his head his jaw clicked shut. I walked to the bottom and locked the street-level door. Zak and his partner stood by Theo's Mustang, passing a joint between them.

"Up we go," I said, seizing Theo by his collar and belt. I dragged him up, counting the stairs he'd fallen. Nine counting the top. There were sixteen in total. Theo didn't struggle as we climbed.

I propped him up against the door at the top of the stairs. He'd started to sweat. Ben and Katherine were whispering behind me.

"I hope that hurt," I said. "If it didn't I'll have to do it again. I don't want to, but I can't have you threatening me."

"Break your other arm," he said. "Fuck you up royally."

"That's exactly what has to stop," I said. I helped him to his feet.

"When you least expect it," Theo mumbled. "Gonna fuck you up. Gonna —"

"This is pointless," I said. I let go of his shirt, grabbed a hank of hair and pitched him back down the stairs.

He landed awkwardly and rolled almost to the bottom. I followed him down and put the boots to him. I held onto the rail with my casted left arm and kicked at his ribs. When his hands moved to protect his side I kicked him in the face. From the way he thrashed about I could tell he hadn't broken anything more serious than a rib or a finger. That made me mad. Old Man Kroon flails about in the dark and manages to fracture my arm, while Theo Atero escapes two trips down the stairs unscathed. Well, not quite unscathed.

I was gripping the rail with both hands now, stomping on him. Most of my blows caught his fleshy parts, thighs and arm. One solid drop of the heel found his ribs and I knew I'd broken at least one. I felt a pair of arms encircle my neck from behind and I shoved them away to deliver one last kick that caught Theo in the groin. He let loose with a howl of pain. I looked behind me, re-orienting myself. The arms had been Katherine's. I'd shoved her back into the stairs.

The sight of her and the look of fear on her face calmed me instantly. She looked pale. For a moment I thought I'd hurt her, but then I saw it was the makeup caking on her cheeks. I looked down at Theo Atero, wriggling towards the door. I stepped over him and unlocked it but let him crawl and reach for the knob. Theo spilled out onto the sidewalk.

Zak and his partner caught sight of Theo. They weren't the only ones. A long-haired panhandler across the street looked over, as did a young gay couple walking their dog. All six of us regarded the man in the street. Theo crawled to the curb where his brother bent to help him.

I slammed the door, locked it and headed up to the office, walking past the blood on the stairs and on the wall.

Ben had positioned himself by the balcony window, watching the Ateros' car speed away. Katherine emerged from the washroom holding a moistened paper towel to her elbow.

"Did I hurt you?" I asked her.

She shook her head. "It's just a scrape." We were both speaking quietly, using what teachers used to call thirty-centimetre voices.

"That was ferocious," Ben said.

"You're an idiot." Katherine flung the towel at him. It bounced off his breast and hit his shoe. "If you'd shut up maybe it wouldn't've come to that."

"Like he was going to be reasonable," Ben said.

She walked to her desk, picked up a stray napkin and clamped it over the elbow. "I quit," she said.

I wanted to tell her not to. I would have, but quitting would put her out of harm's way. I had no right to meddle with her safety. I wanted to, though.

I said to Ben, "There's a squirt bottle of bleach and water beneath the sink. Take it and one of those rags and go over the stairs, especially at the bottom. Keep your back to the door so anyone peering in can't see what you're doing. Make sure to disinfect anything that even remotely looks like blood."

To Katherine I said, "Could I trouble you to erase the last hour of security cam footage?"

She nodded.

"I didn't mean to shove you," I said. "I'm sorry it happened. I'm sorry about the whole thing."

"You would have killed him," she said.

"No. But I'm grateful you stopped me."

She moved to her desk and called up the camera application on her computer. "Sure about that?" Ben said, carrying the bottle and some stiff-looking rags. "If it was me I'd want a copy of that beating."

XXII

Prosper's Point

Monday morning I was up before dawn, packing a travel bag and a Thermos, two sandwiches, a case of water, and the first Mandarin orange of the season. It wasn't a long trip — half an hour to the Tsawwassen ferry terminal, two or two and a half hours on the water depending on the ferry, add half an hour for loading and unloading, and a ninety-minute drive from Schwartz Bay north to Prosper's Point. Five hours give or take. If we lucked out we'd be on the last boat back to the Mainland. More likely, though, Fisk and I would be spending the night.

When I reached the Tsawwassen terminal there was no lineup and the parking lots were practically empty. I pulled up next to Fisk's F350 in the Premium lot, a stone's throw from the water's edge.

"You know parking is five bucks cheaper over there." I pointed to the yellow barrier a hundred yards away that marked the start of the Econo lot.

"I like to leave quickly" was Fisk's reply.

We'd decided that since I might stay longer, I'd take the van over and he'd ride with me. Fisk had been in contact with a constable named Delgado who'd agreed to show us around. Fisk described him as "pissy." I chalked that up to VPD-RCMP police rivalry.

We were the third car onto the ferry. By seven we were having breakfast in the ship's cafeteria, watching through the portals as we sliced our way across the Strait of Georgia.

"Mark Eager told me something funny," Fisk said as he tucked into a plate of eggs benedict.

I'd brought tea bags with me, and set one down in a cup of hot water. I didn't answer. Fisk would get there himself.

"Some question of where you were the time of the fire," he said. "Your friend said you were with him all night, then called Mark back to tell him actually you weren't. He wanted it stated for the record — actual term he used, according to Mark — that you told him to tell the truth. Some people might think you put him up to lying in the first place, then realized we'd see through that."

I said, "That makes a hell of a lot of sense."

"Just saying, there are a few unanswered questions, least in Eager's mind."

"That's because I set the fire," I said. "I thought, 'Shit, I don't need the car, and wrangling with ICBC claims adjustors for months on end is enjoyable and productive.' Why wouldn't I want to do that?"

"What Mark also said was that you made no mention of your trouble with the Ateros."

"He knew their names. I said I knew them."

"But you didn't exactly volunteer the information." Fisk sopped up hollandaise with a triangle of toast. The beige concoction on his plate looked like it had been created in a laboratory rather than a kitchen. "If the Ateros aren't involved, who else could be responsible?"

"My money's on you," I said, blocking out the imaginary headline with my hands. "Bungling Cop Overcome by Jealousy, Sets Fire to Intrepid PI's Car."

"That's how you see me?" Fisk said.

"No."

"That how you see yourself?"

"Christ, it was a joke," I said.

He nodded. "It's early. I'm not a morning person."

Then he did something that utterly surprised me — he pulled a book out of his travel bag. I bent my head to look at the title. *The Green Hills of Africa*, an ancient yellowed paperback edition that looked identical to one I'd bought at MacLeod's years ago.

"What?" he said, looking up from the page. "You didn't think I read?"

"No, I just took you for more of a Fitzgerald guy."

"It was on Mira's shelf. It's about hunting. What's wrong with it?"

"Nothing," I said. "I must've left it at her place." I wondered what else he might have inherited.

"It always comes back to that," Fisk said. "It was almost two years ago. Can't you let it go?"

"It was more than two years ago, and I didn't bring it up." I finished my tea and fetched my own book, *On Boxing* by Joyce Carol Oates, which had been sitting on my bookshelf for half a decade. Sometimes you buy a book so that it's on hand when the moment arrives. But this wasn't to be that moment.

Fisk clapped his book shut and dropped it on the table. "Why don't you get it off your chest."

"Get what off?"

"You've been waiting two years to say it. What an asshole I am."

"You are an asshole," I said. "You're a shithead. Why would you do something like that to someone who was your friend?"

"Like if you were in my place you wouldn't've done the same thing?"

"No I wouldn't. Because I'm not a shithead."

The parents at a nearby table glanced at us, a tut-tut expression on the woman's face. Their kids paid us no mind.

"You beat the holy hell out of Theo Atero," Fisk said. "Eager told me he visited him in St. Paul's. Three broken ribs, a broken finger and a sprained wrist, plus the concussion."

"He's in a rough line of work," I said. "What does that have to do with me?"

"You beat him up, didn't you?"

I pointed to my cast as if that was proof I wasn't complicit. "Maybe he fell down some stairs. Twice," I added, unable to help myself.

"So how are you better than me?"

"I never thought that," I said, "until you slept with the woman I was engaged to. Things were a mess between her and me, but at least Mira apologized."

"Is that what you want from me, an apology?"

"I don't want anything from you except to find the Szabo kid and go home."

We each picked up our books.

"Sorry," he said.

When I looked up his face was buried in the page.

"Did you say something?"

"No."

"Just checking."

"Who the hell is Garrick?" Fisk asked after a few minutes of reading.

"In the book? One of the guides."

"I know that. Why does Hemingway call him that?"

"Name of a famous actor, I think."

"Guess that makes sense."

I read a little about boxing.

* * *

Before I'd left I tried to talk to Amelia Yeats, but her phone went straight to message. She wasn't at Enola Curious, and nobody answered when I rang the bell at Yates Manor.

Sunday night she emailed me. With her spelling corrected, this is how it read:

> Hey.
>
> I'm in Reykjavik right now, helping my dad record this heavy metal band that hasn't played together in forty years. They got offered a million dollars to re-form for the European festival circuit. Some of them haven't picked up their instruments in all that time. I guess there will be a lot of disappointed Europeans next year. But then most people go to shows to see a group, not to listen to them, so maybe no one will notice.
>
> I think if you took everything we said to each other and everything we did, and separated them, there would be two different relationships. I think some people talk out of fear but act out of love. I think we're both like that.
>
> I've attached that *Hooker'N Heat* album we talked about. I have the vinyl at home, but I downloaded this copy illegally. Don't hold it against me.
>
> The band and my dad are back from the pub. In Iceland they have this drink called Glögg. It's hot wine with cloves in it, served with raisins and almonds. Sounds gross, but once you get used to it it's really quite horrible. The bass player Nils is in Narcotics

Anonymous. Some of what he says makes sense. Don't get your hopes up.

Anyway, I have to go. I hope you find Cliff's son. I miss seeing them.

Love.

She hadn't signed it, just *love*. Love was enough.

The van's glove box yielded a treasure trove of demo CDs. Fisk and I listened to them as we drove. Most lasted about thirty seconds before Fisk hit eject and Frisbee'd them out the window. We listened to a passable metal band and a live recording of a his-and-hers folk duo who sung "Wade in the Water," "I'll Fly Away," and an original that had a call-and-response structure. The man would ask some sort of hippie-drivel question and the woman would answer "Yes, Yes."

Do we wish all people loved each other?
Yes, yes.
Do we wish more people hugged each other?
Yes, yes.

"Put a fucking bullet in me," Fisk said.

Do we believe that we can change, that governments don't have to fly their planes of destruction,
O destruction, let me hear you sing it now,
Yes, yes.

The other verses were even worse.

Prosper's Point was named for a hill rather than a coastal feature, and located in the interior of the island. We drove through

Nanaimo ("Would be the easiest city to police," Fisk said.

"Why?"

"Because it's built on a slope; all the criminals would run downhill.") and north through pasture. We passed isolated ranches whose barns, long empty, had been allowed to weather artfully but not fall into disrepair. In one fenced-in meadow a trio of Bay horses grazed. All three were wearing capes to ward off the chill. It gave them a kind of regal appearance but also looked stupid, like dogs in pink sweaters. We passed the turn-off for a trailer park

("I'd be shocked if there were less than three meth labs in there," said Fisk.) and turned on to a narrow road that cut through the Douglas Fir leading us to the top of a small rise. On the other side lay Prosper's Point.

The main strip had a McDonald's and a Country Cabin Motel, two gas stations and a selection of bars. The thoroughly modern glass-and-plastic RCMP station was sandwiched between a coffee shop franchise shaped like a teepee and a solid-looking blue brick building that housed the Prosper's Point Library, City Hall, and Chamber of Commerce. I pulled into the parking lot, climbed out of the van and stretched.

Fisk said, "How 'bout I go track down this twit Delgado while you get us a coffee?" I was too busy yawning to argue. He went inside the station and I walked over to the teepee. A heavily-freckled redhead and a dark-haired boy, both wearing yolk-yellow T-shirts carrying the franchise's logo, stood behind the counter. They looked about seventeen, the girl maybe older, in the full flush of her beauty, the boy gangly, acne-pitted, and awkward. He was in the middle of an anecdote that had put a smile of questionable sincerity on her face. The sum total of their relationship, and indeed their lives, was written in that tableau for any stranger to see.

The boy noticed me and put his arms on the counter. "How," he said.

"Please tell me your boss makes you say that."

The girl grinned. So did the boy, but only after checking her face and then only enough so she wouldn't think him jealous. His nametag read STEVIE, hers ABIGAIL.

"Guess a London Fog's out of the question," I said.

"What's that?"

There was no bill of fare posted in the small shack, just urns of coffee and hot water and a display rack of shrink-wrapped pastries.

"What kind of tea do you have?"

"Tetley's and Rose Red," Abigail said.

"Cup of hot water and a Double Double," I said. "That's coffee, two cream two sugar."

"I know what a Double Double is," Stevie said. He went about putting the drinks together. Abigail remained perched on the back counter.

"That your van?" she asked.

"Just bought it this weekend," I said. "Used to belong to a record producer-slash-engineer. He accepted it as payment from a bar band for doing their demo."

"Really?"

"Really."

Stevie put the drinks on the counter and made change from my twenty.

"In fact," I said, "were you to inspect the back of the van, you would find a piece of plywood. If you were to lift this plywood up, you would find a hole drilled in the floor of the van."

"What for?" asked Abigail.

I unwrapped my Twinings bag and dunked it in the water. Stevie seemed agitated that I hadn't left. I didn't want to cause him grief by wooing his girlfriend with tales of musicians and exotic beverages, but I felt that if anyone noticed who came and went in Prosper's Point, it would be her.

"The hole," I said, "is for a funnel and a hose."

"Like a beer bong?"

"Much like a beer bong, except it's used to get rid of fluids. When you tour Canada by van, you can't stop every time someone needs to piss."

"I don't believe it," she said.

"If you can abandon your post for a moment I'll prove it."

She hopped off the counter and came out the back entrance. I didn't need to look back at Stevie to know his expression.

I put Fisk's coffee on the roof, opened the back doors and pulled back the plywood. "One hole as promised. Now you can go to your grave having seen everything."

"Not quite," she said.

I sat on the floor of the van with my legs hanging out and patted the bumper for her to join me.

"My name is Mike Drayton and I'm a private investigator from Vancouver," I said. The last two words made her face light up. "I'm looking for three women who came here in March or April, either passing through or to stay."

"Why, what'd they do?"

"Do you want me to lie to you, or can I just say it's important to find them?"

"Mysterious," she said.

"They would've had a boy with them, maybe twelve years old."

"And they looked like what?"

"Blonde, mid-thirties named Barbara. Brunette named Dawn or Dominique. No description on the third one."

She shook out a cigarette from a pack she kept in the back pocket of her jeans. She offered me one, lit hers and blew out a mouthful of smoke with what passed for cosmopolitan non-chalance in Prosper's Point. "Three you said?"

"Any number, if they were traveling with the boy."

"The boy I don't know about," Abigail said. "I remember two women in a Jeep. They'd get gas across the street and one of them would come over for coffee and danishes, enough for three people. The weird thing was, it was the same woman who pumped the gas that got the coffee. The other one just sat in the car."

"Who got the coffee? Was she blonde?"

"Both brown haired, I think." Abigail flicked her cigarette butt into a puddle near the curb, disturbing the rainbow scum of oil. "The one in the car was a mousy brown, kind of thin. The one that got the coffee looked about forty. On the fat side, no makeup, only these really fake drawn-on eyebrows. You know those racist cartoons from World War Two, where Asian people's eyes are drawn as upside-down V's? That's what her eyebrows looked like."

"This is in April?"

"April and May, yeah."

"How many times did you see them?"

"A few times. I think they were living around here."

"Do you know where?"

"No clue," she said.

"Would Stevie know?"

"Why would he?"

"Different question: are there prostitutes in town?"

She raised one eyebrow. "Couldn't tell you."

"If there were, which bar would they frequent?"

Abigail thought it over. "Big Dave's is where the old people drink. Ace's is more upscale. Cops drink there. That leaves the Palatial. Lot of fights break out there. They even had a shooting two years ago. Yeah, I'd say the Palatial."

"'Preciate it," I said, handing her a twenty-dollar bill and a business card. "Think of anything else, let me know."

She folded the money and tucked it and the card inside the packaging of her cigarettes.

"Tell Stevie I didn't mean to step on his turf."

"You didn't," Abigail said. "And it won't matter, he'll be jealous anyway."

"Why's that?"

"Because you're more interesting than him," she said. "He'll sulk and then talk shit about you when I get back. So predictable. We hooked up like a year ago and he's obsessed."

"Probably not a lot of alternatives," I said. Then realizing how insulting that could be taken: "Not that you're not worth obsessing over."

"I'm eighteen in less than two months," she said. "New Year's Baby."

"Are you planning on leaving?"

"I want to."

"Then you should," I said. "Go waitress in the Big City. Be broke, live in squalor. Don't wait for some guy to take you out of here."

She tore one of the flaps off the cigarette pack, wrote something on it, and placed it on the plywood before hopping down and heading back to the teepee. I looked at the paper and saw it was a phone number and email, and her name, the *i* dotted with a heart. I left it on the floor of the van, locked up, and headed into the station.

When I asked where I'd find Sergeant Delgado, the receptionist said, "Willie's down in the morgue talking with Dr. Boone and somebody from the Mainland. Want me to page him?"

"If you could just give me directions," I said, showing her my credentials. A private eye license does not grant admission to an autopsy room, but either she didn't know that, or Fisk had already cleared me. She pointed to the elevator and told me I wanted Basement Two.

The coroner's office was on the right hand side of the hall as I came out of the elevator. The door was open. Inside sat Gavin Fisk, a ponytailed older woman in a suit, and a tall man in the dark blue RCMP uniform. Fisk looked up at me as I handed him his coffee.

"Mike Drayton," he said to the others. "Formerly VPD, hired by the father to make sure I dot my P's and Q's."

The Mountie stood up and extended a big hand. "Willie Delgado," he said. "This is Beth Boone, our corpse doctor."

"Pleased, Mike," Boone said, extending her own well-moisturized hand.

"Beth was telling us that the official identification will take at least a week on account of the lack of personal effects."

"Who's the deceased?" I asked. "I mean what's the description?"

"Unidentified woman, mid-thirties, black hair," Delgado said.

"Barbara Della Costa?"

"If they knew her identity, Mike, she wouldn't be unidentified," Fisk said. "'Sides, Barbara was the blonde." Before I could retort he added, "Not that she'd have any difficulty buying a tube of black dye, or that black couldn't be her natural colour."

I asked Dr. Boone, "Were her eyebrows drawn on V-shaped, very severely, maybe oversized?"

"She died several months ago, so that's hard to say. I can tell you for sure, though, that her face was regularly depilated." Her hand traced along her own silver eyebrows. "Faint razor scars, too. Only noticed them when she was on the table. I'll finish my coffee and get to the autopsy."

"Where was she found? What body position?"

"Upright behind the wheel of a late nineties LeBaron," Delgado said. "Parked in the shed on Lester Rusk's place. Lester's been dead eight years. His niece sold the spread to a Japanese concern. No one really goes there."

"You found her?"

"'Fraid so," he said. "Not my finest hour, I must admit. My new neighbours got this dog, which has been taking an interest in the rabbit hutch my daughters keep. A fence seemed like the solution, but I didn't own an auger — that's a tool to dig fence holes."

"I've used an auger before," I said, wondering why I felt the need to tell him that.

"Anyway, these days, who's got an auger? Then I remembered that Lester had all sorts of tools, 'cluding at least one auger. Man liked his flea markets. He used to leave his tools all over the yard, but after the sale, all that crap was thrown in the shed."

"Should I be writing this down?" I said, thinking, a policeman should be able to pick out a pertinent detail.

Delgado smiled. "Anyway, a couple months ago I head over to the Rusk place. The shed's been padlocked, but all the tools and whatnot have been piled along the side. I take the auger and think nothing of it, 'cause it's not like I'm technically 'sposed to be there anyhow. Then the other day when Mr. Fisk phoned about that missing boy, I thought to myself, that shed could only have been emptied out 'round the timeframe he mentioned, March–April–May. See, I'd been to the shed before that to return a little hand-cranked cement mixer."

"Sure," I said, hoping to cut the anecdote short. "So you took off the padlock and the car was inside."

"How it happened, pretty much."

I turned to Fisk. "Should we check out the Rusk place?"

"Unless the sarge has any leads on who killed her."

"What, not who," said Dr. Boone. "From first glance I'd say carbon monoxide poisoning. Looks to me like she killed herself."

XXIIII

The Ostrich Man

"I don't like this Delgado," Fisk said. "I don't like this town. I don't like the coroner sitting on her ass when that body might tell us something."

We were following Delgado's Interceptor up a gravel logging road. The road was so narrow that when a car approached going the opposite way, we had to stop and pull over so that the right-side wheels rested on the ribbon of grass separating the road from an algae-covered ditch.

"We know one thing," I said. "Barbara and Dawn came here for a reason. They weren't hiding out here at random."

"What makes you say that?"

Delgado turned left onto a strip of hard-packed dirt. He parked in front of a weather-beaten homestead, its ancient porch a gap-toothed smile of sunken and missing planks. Behind and to the left was a rusty aluminum shed, white with red trim, its doors hanging open. Police tape and an official notice were secured to the door.

I said, "If this was just a stop-over, Barbara would have bought the fishing rods here, then sold them somewhere else. Tofino, maybe. But she stayed here to try and sell them, meaning this was her base. If she did herself in, whatever was here was something she couldn't outrun or escape."

"Doesn't bode well for the kid," Fisk said.

"No it doesn't."

"She kills him, then kills herself?"

"Why take him in the first place then?"

"So what happened here?"

"I don't know."

"Something bad, probably."

"I don't know, Gavin."

He unbuckled his seatbelt as I stopped. "I don't like this place," he reiterated.

The ground was puddled and uneven. Delgado walked us toward the barn. "Anything in there?" Fisk asked, pointing at the house.

"Cleared, emptied and sealed up, just the way it was after Lester passed."

"But you guys unsealed it and looked inside." Fisk had stopped moving.

"Of course," Delgado said.

"Nothing tampered with?"

"Nope."

"No secret rooms or nothing?"

"There's a salt cellar."

"And what was in there?"

"Salt."

Delgado led us to the open mouth of the shed. The aluminum frame had been fastened onto a concrete slab using industrial screws. An array of shovels, axes, trowels, hoes, rakes, shears and machetes littered the ground by the right side, along with some larger tools including Delgado's borrowed cement mixer, bricks, pottery and other flotsam.

"You print these?" I asked him.

Delgado shook his head. "Don't see the point. I mean, some of my own prints would be on there."

"The point, Willie," Fisk said, "is that the car got in the shed somehow. Meaning whoever put the car in the shed took the crap out of the shed and dumped it here."

"Don't take a tone with me," Delgado said. "Beth believes this to be a suicide."

"Prosper's Point must have a different definition of the term," Fisk said, "'cause in Vancouver suicides don't padlock themselves in sheds after they off themselves."

"Easy," I said to Fisk, and turned to Delgado. "My colleague's concern is that we simply don't know all the details at this point. Given that, it makes sense to treat this like a potential crime scene. Which I'm sure you've done."

Delgado directed a pained look at Fisk. "As to the padlocking," he said, taking a sudden interest in his shoelaces, "I couldn't be sure someone from around here didn't see the padlock on the ground and lock the shed to prevent vandalism."

"Reasonable," I said, thinking just the opposite and wondering what Fisk was making of this. I hoped he wouldn't share his thoughts and make an enemy out of Sgt. Delgado. To his credit, Fisk kept dumb.

"To be perfectly honest," Delgado said, "I couldn't swear that it wasn't me who saw the car and put that padlock on. My thinking being that since the house wasn't disturbed, one of the new owners might have intended to lock the car in the shed and forgot. The lock was in its original packaging but the keys had been removed."

"Did you at least run the plates?" Fisk asked.

"I certainly did, when I came back the second time, after your call."

"Unbelievable," Fisk said. "I'm gonna check the house."

Once Fisk had removed the planks from the side door and entered, Delgado said to me, "Your — colleague? — could stand with a refresher course in getting along with people."

* * *

The autopsy wasn't finished by the time we returned to the centre of town. Delgado invited us for drinks and grub at Ace's. We settled our gear into adjoining rooms in the Country Cabin. My room had a stale smell to it. An old-style TV with knobs and dials, a phone, a painting of grouse above the headboard. I unpacked my clothing and appliances, plugged in the cellphone charger. In the bedstand drawer, instead of a bible, was a chapbook of inspirational poems from local authors.

I phoned Katherine. She gave me the number in Iceland I'd asked for. She also told me about someone who'd phoned the office.

"Loretta Dearborn."

"Don't know her," I said. "Potential client?"

"She phoned about the missing child."

"The Loeb case or the Szabo case?"

"Didn't specify."

"Could you find out for me?"

"I'll give you her number, Mike, but I meant what I said."

"About?"

"About not working for you anymore."

"For the next day or so, till I get back to the office and can sort things out, could you please check into it? Think of it like you're helping a missing child."

"You're a manipulative prick."

"Any sightings of the Ateros?"

"No, it's been quiet."

"Stay away from the office. Just use the answering service. If Loretta wants to meet, suggest a neutral, public place, coffee shop or the like. Any trouble get in touch with Mira Das."

"Look both ways before you cross the street, I got it. Enjoy your vacation."

"Kiss my ass."

I cleared off the student's desk that stood in the corner of the room and set up my kettle and grill. I lay down on the bed. My cast itched. I wondered what time it was in Reykjavik.

I'd dozed off on the bed with my shoes and coat still on. Fisk woke me when he opened the adjoining door. He looked over at the steaming kettle on the desk. "Planning on moving here?"

I sat up. He unplugged the kettle for me and looked at the other appliance. "That a George Foreman?"

"I was planning on walking down to the Overwaitee and buying the makings for grilled cheese," I said.

Fisk had a beer in his hand. "I thought we'd try out the famous Prosper's Point cuisine."

"I don't have money for that, and I can't stomach fast food more than once a day. You go ahead, I'll meet you back here later."

Fisk would have none of it. "I think I can put a couple of steak dinners on my expense account," he said. "Don't make me drink with Delgado alone."

Ace's had Molson and Bud on special. I forget what we ordered. By the second pitcher all was right between Gavin and Willie. They'd moved on to first names and were sharing war stories. We all ordered T-Bone steaks with fries. The two of them argued over who would pick up the check.

The autopsy had confirmed Dr. Boone's speculation: asphyxiation due to carbon monoxide poisoning, though she was waiting for test results on the carboxyhemoglobin-to-hemoglobin ratio in the dead woman's blood. No bruises on her body or any signs to suggest she'd been coerced. Moles on her left breast and both arms, a tattoo on her lower back of a butterfly, scars on her knees and hip. Dr. Boone wasn't ready to pronounce a definitive time-of-death, but she told Delgado that mid-June probably wouldn't be too far off the mark.

Fisk made a call from the payphone and came back having verified that Barbara Della Costa had a butterfly tattoo on her back. "Not that that clinches it," he said. We were all drinking from pitchers now. "You couldn't pick a more common tramp stamp."

"Almost as clichéd as barbed wire around the bicep," I said, knowing Fisk had that tattoo.

"Hey," Delgado said, as if about to broach a subject he'd given some thought to. "Either of you ever seen a pussy with rings and stuff in it? That common in the city?"

"Ask Mike about his cock piercings," Fisk said. He found this hilarious, almost falling off his chair.

"Is he serious?"

"No," I said, "he was born without a sense of humour. It's a side effect of being an investigative genius."

"I just don't understand why a person would put shrapnel in their privates," Delgado said, in what sounded like a punchline cribbed from a bad standup act.

"High self-esteem," Fisk said. "First girl I ever ate out had six piercings, including one in her clit. And I —" He laughed, unable to finish his sentence "— had braces."

A country band set up, bringing with them a small crowd. When Delgado left the bar for a smoke, I followed him out.

"Which way is the Palatial?" I asked him.

"Left to Third Avenue and down a piece," he said. "Don't know why you'd want to go there. Other than when the bikers come, it's pretty dead."

As I started off down the street, Delgado said, "Did it hurt?"

"Did what hurt?"

"Getting that cock piercing installed. Sounds painful to me."

I paused to think up an appropriate response, settling on, "Not as bad as you'd think." Sometimes the joke is on you, and it's best to just go with it.

As a structure, the Palatial was not a dive. In fact, it had points over Ace's. The bar itself was varnished mahogany, with the same for the banisters, stairs, tables and chairs. The room had been designed with thought given to table space, privacy, acoustics. Over this foundation, though, a layer of neglect and abuse had settled. Every surface had been gouged, burned, carved and graffitied. The floor was sticky and dotted with bottle caps crushed into the wood and bits of glass. None of which was as bad as the table in the far corner, its surface covered with specks of old vomit, or the overturned rat trap beneath the P.A. system.

The bartender was a woman in flannel who didn't look like a stranger to her own product line. She had a bright red cratered nose, small eyes and a broad, aimless smile.

"Set you up?" she asked.

"Pabst Blue Ribbon, and I'd like to open it."

She shrugged and fetched the bottle.

Other patrons floated through a cigarette haze. A native-looking couple sat drinking from the same glass in the quiet and relative cleanliness of the upstairs. A gent with a long beard and grubby overalls had parked himself at the end of the bar. He was talking to a man who looked comatose, but who rose up every few seconds to nod and slurp from his beer stein, which remained planted on the bar. Two women ate French fries by the door. They shot me looks of appraisal. I nodded back. Odds that at least one of them was on the game: even.

The bartender brought me the PBR and the glass. I ignored the glass. I wiped the lip of the bottle with my shirt cuff.

I sat down on a stool that seemed to have missed a few steps on the assembly line. I kept my feet flat on the ground. Serves me right, I figured, offering my clients that wobbly bench all those months. Thank God for Staples. One of the women leaned over the table to confer with the other in whispers. The one standing looked at me again. Thicker by far in the waist than the hips, smaller on top, black hair trimmed short. Her friend had peroxide cornrows, was a third the size, and had a malnourished pallor that made me wonder if she glowed in the dark. Odds that they were on the game: seven in ten.

I took in the bar so as not to seem interested. A man sat at a small table half-hidden by the staircase. He was drinking cider from a can and eating a BLT, fingers poised on either end of the toothpick. A boutique notebook sat open in front of him, six sharpened pencils rubber-banded together within reach. Sharing the table was a green bird in a cage.

The bartender picked up on the look I was giving the man and his bird, neither of whom paid attention to me.

"That's Jerry and Precious."

"Which is which?"

She guffawed. "Jerry's the one runs up his tab. Raises all kinds of birds, 'cluding exotics. Had a lovely pair of peacocks, some ostriches. That's the source of his nickname, the Ostrich Man."

"What does he raise them for?"

"Zoos, meat, I don't know."

The Ostrich Man wrote something in his notebook and looked up to see who was watching him. I nodded to him. He smiled.

"It's a green conure," he said, "case you were wondering."

"Beautiful," I said.

He opened the cage, brought Precious out, sat her on his arm to show how tame she was. "Completely domesticated," he said. "Conures make good pets. They like attention."

He walked to the bar and tipped Precious onto my arm. At that range I could smell the cider. The bird strutted down to my elbow, about-faced and hopped back onto Jerry's palm.

I said, "Next round's on me, if you'll have it." I looked at the bartender and pointed at the two girls at the table. "Include them, will you? And another Blended Splendid for me."

When the drinks came, the dark-haired woman sidled up to me. Odds: nine in ten.

"My girlfriend Di thinks you're a cop," she said.

"Ever know a cop to buy a round?"

She downed her shot of what looked like Jagermeister, picked up my beer bottle and helped herself. My next sip of beer tasted like licorice. Definitely Jager. Definitely on the game.

"Truth is," I said, "I came here to get away from cops. I was at Ace's earlier. Don't know if you're familiar with that establishment, but it's full of cops. What's your name?"

"Shoshona. Yours?"

"Wilbur. Glad to meet you."

The Ostrich Man had finished his drink and retreated with his bird to the table, probably all too aware of the kind of business Shoshona and I were conducting. As I walked to the girls' table I passed Jerry and Precious's table, stuck out a finger to the bird, who was content chewing on a branch, and caught a look of disapproval from the Ostrich Man.

Di headed to the washroom as we took our places. Shoshona pushed the fry plate away and downed the residue in Di's shot glass. "What line of work are you in, Wilbur?" Nodding over at the bartender to hit us again.

"Well, Shoshona, I'm a security installation consultant. I travel around this great province helping businesses optimize their security systems. Do you know, Shoshona, that thirty-six percent of all public buildings, and a whopping fifty-six percent of all small businesses, have insufficient alarm and security features?"

"Wow," Shoshona said. I held up two fingers to the bartender. Another beer, another Jager.

"Those numbers are based on an eighteen-month study using forty separate criteria. Not only did I oversee the study, but I designed the criteria myself. My bosses said that I showed tremendous initiative. They were right."

"I think you showed tremendous initiative too," Shoshona said.

"Thank you. Can I ask you something, Shoshona?"

"You're buying."

"In addition to tremendous initiative, I'm also blessed with a rather large cock, and a few extra dollars. I'd like to invite you or your friend, or both, for an all-expenses-paid trip to my shitty motel room down the road. How does that sound, Shoshona?"

"You can have me or Di, can't have both."

"Then I'd much prefer you. I'd be afraid of ripping her in two."

Before we left the Palatial, Shoshona told Di which room I was staying at. "It's just a precaution," she said as she rejoined me. "Can't be too careful."

Outside the temperature had dropped below zero. A wedge of moon hung in a cloudless sky. We crossed the street to avoid walking past Ace's.

"Born here?" I asked Shoshona as I brought out my keys.

"No. I've lived here for — let me see." She counted on her hand. "Six years." The number seemed to depress her.

"Know the place pretty well."

"I guess."

I followed her inside, closed the door, hit the lights.

"Off," Fisk growled. He'd passed out on my bed.

"What is this?" Shoshona said. "I don't pull trains."

"My colleague is drunk. He used the wrong room."

She saw Fisk's holster in the open drawer of the bedstand. I beat her to it and shut the drawer. Fisk sat up at the sound.

"You *are* cops," Shoshona said. "I fucking *knew* it."

"We have some questions for you," I said. "We're looking for a missing child who came here in March or April with three women, all in the same business as you. One was mid-thirties, blonde or black hair, another younger, brunette."

"Barb and Dom," Shoshona said.

"You saw them? You talked to them? Was the kid with them?"

"If I tell you, what happens to me?" Shoshona asked.

"Who gives a shit?"

She settled into the chair and lit a smoke. "I met Barb at the Palatial. She was really friendly, really genuine. She'd been in the business a long time. She said she and her friend were in town for a couple weeks. They weren't going to stay, just meeting someone. Till then they needed money. What I thought was nice was she asked us could they trick in our backyard for a little while. They didn't have a pimp, and they were planning on being out by May. That's what she said."

"What about the other girls and the kid?"

"Dom came in the bar with Barb. Only times she came in by herself was to score off me or Di. Barb was clean — been there, done that."

"The kid," I said.

"Right, Mungo or whatever his name was."

"Django?"

"Sure. Mungo, Django. Barb said he was Dom's, but I didn't buy that. I've had two kids, I know what it does to your hips and ass. Barb maybe I could see, or the other one, but not Dom."

"Other one?"

"Deirdre I think her name was. I saw her a few times but she didn't party, so we didn't really talk."

"So what happened?"

"Come May they left."

"All three of them and the kid?"

"They were renting this small house in town, corner of Fifth and Gardenia. Deirdre and Dom used to leave food out for the neighbourhood cats, but there are no neighbourhood cats. One day they were all there, then it was just Barb, and then she was gone, too."

"When did you see them last?"

"Really couldn't tell you," Shoshona said. "I assumed they went back to the Mainland. I do know that Dom scored a bunch of dope before she left."

"Are we talking about a selling amount?"

"No, just personal, but like she wasn't going to be able to get any for a couple weeks. When she came in the Palatial to pick that up, that might have been the last time I saw her."

"And the kid, how did he look?"

"Like a kid," she said. "Looked healthy, no broken bones. Always off in his own world. They got him one of those Game Station things, portable video games and movies. Kid barely looked up."

"No idea who they were waiting for? Someone local, someone passing through?"

"No idea. Can I go now?"

"Never said you couldn't," I said. "But we'll wait for your friend to show up all the same."

"What are you talking about?"

"She'll knock any minute now," I said. "Open the door maybe an inch and tell her to toss her gun inside. Then you can go."

Shoshona spent three minutes attempting to convince me I was wrong, but soon enough we heard a soft knocking.

Shoshona persuaded Di to toss the small pearl-handled revolver inside. "Now can I go?" she said.

"We've got a house to check," Fisk said. "People to talk to. Uh huh. I do understand that, sir. An extra day would be appreci— one more day. I understand. Yes sir. Goodbye."

"Bureaucrat," Fisk said after he'd set the phone down. He said to me, "The Superintendent doesn't see why I need two extra days. He said tomorrow's my last."

"I'll drop you at the ferry tomorrow night, then."

I was on the bed. Fisk stood in the doorway. My gun was at hand, Di's revolver in the bedstand next to the poems.

"The kid was still alive in May," Fisk said. "That ought to give you hope."

"It does."

"The suicide's tough to figure."

"He's alive," I said, startling myself with the words.

"You feel it, do you? In your bones?"

"No," I said, "I just think it. I haven't thought it before seriously but I think it now."

Alive.

XXIV

The Friends of Michael Drayton

Loretta Dearborn left two more messages. Katherine finally phoned her back Tuesday. With an hour before her French lab, she put in the call from one of the payphones in the Langara College atrium. She could barely hear Mrs. Dearborn's responses over the throng of students pushing to get in and out of the lecture theatres.

"I wish to speak to Michael Drayton and he alone," Mrs. Dearborn said.

"Mike is on the Island right now."

"They don't have phones on Vancouver Island?"

"You know what cellphone satellites are like," Katherine said, covering for my technological ineptitude. "I swear I'll pass whatever it is straight on to him."

"It concerns the disappearance on the news."

"Then Mike will want to hear it when I tell him."

"Has he checked the house on the 500 Block of Fraser Street?"

"What do you know about that house?"

"Young lady," Mrs. Dearborn said, "I was a secretary for the Toronto Dominion Bank for thirty-seven years. If I displayed telephone manners like yours, I'd've never been hired in the first place."

"I'm really, really sorry," Katherine said.

Before sharing her information, Loretta Dearborn told Katherine that she'd phoned the police several times a week until they stopped answering her calls. She tried to phone Mr. Szabo himself, but his phone manners were every bit as bad as Katherine's, in fact much worse. She tried to take into account the difficult circumstances, but that was no excuse for profanity and derogatory comments.

Next she'd tried Aries Investigations, who were handling the Szabo case. Roy McEachern she found utterly charming. He spoke like a gentleman, thanked her for her diligence and foresight, and assured her he'd act immediately on her tip. Unfortunately, Mr. McEachern became harder and harder to get hold of on the phone, and his manners became more brusque, until finally like the cops he broke off contact with her. A shame, because he seemed so nice and forthright.

So Mrs. Dearborn sat on her information until she chanced across a local news segment the other day. The handsome Indo-Canadian anchor was discussing the Szabo disappearance. She learned that Cliff Szabo had replaced Mr. McEachern with a Mr. Drayton. Mr. Szabo and the newscasters urged the public to come forward with information. Mrs. Dearborn decided to try one last time.

"I'm sure Mike and Mr. Szabo will thank you for all that," Katherine said. "If it's not too much trouble, could you tell me what you know?"

"I've lived on Fraser Street for fifty-one years, since driving out here from Morden, Manitoba, with my husband. I can tell you from observation that the neighbourhood is not what it used to be. Used to be families lived in those houses and I could name you each one. The Robinsons, the Russos, the Van der Meersches. Now they've chopped all these homes into separate apartments, and the ones living upstairs don't know the people below them."

"That's true," Katherine said.

"And so many Chinese."

"Ma'am, if you don't mind, could you get to the point?"

"That house on the corner of 500 Block used to belong to Gus and Louise Crane. A nicer couple than you're apt to meet these days. When they passed on, their son Martin took over the house. Then Martin moved to Saskatoon and sold it to a family named Bellows. I couldn't tell you how it passed into the hands of those prostitutes, but that's who was living there when the child went missing."

"What did you see?"

"I do not begrudge a person a cat, even two or three. I've owned my share over the years. But those women had four, none of them spayed. They seemed to play host to every cat in the neighbourhood. It was ridiculous. And when they left, they left the cats. Some animal lovers."

"I hate that, too," Katherine said, still looking for a means to speed the old girl up.

"Anyway, I tried to tell the policeman, a crass young man named Fisk, but he didn't want to listen. I saw the three women who lived there drive off in a very small car with a bicycle sticking out of the trunk. The trunk was tied down with that elasticky rope, I don't know what it's called. People use it to jump off bridges and other foolishness."

"Bungie cord," Katherine volunteered.

"The women had a boy with them. I didn't see him all that well, but I do know he had brown hair. I'd never seen any of them with a child before. I told that to Constable Fisk and to Mr. McEachern. They both said they'd look into it but they never did."

"Mike is a bit more thorough," Katherine said, or at least that's what she reported to me that she'd said.

"Then I saw the police cars out front of that place the other day and I thought, 'Finally.' And when Mr. Szabo mentioned Mr. Drayton on television, I decided to call."

"He'll thank you personally when he gets back," Katherine said.

"Did they talk to the one who returned, do you know?"

"The one what?"

"The girl, dear."

"One of the three girls came back?"

"She lives down the block from me," Mrs. Dearborn said. "The little yellow house on the corner. The MacReady's home, at one time. She rents the downstairs. I don't see her too often on account of the hours she keeps. Back to her wicked ways, I'm sure."

"And she's still there?"

"As far as I know, Miss."

"When did you see her?"

"June or July? I made a note of it, I could check."

"Just the one time?"

"A few times in June or in July."

"But not recently?"

"Well not yesterday, but four months ago is fairly recent."

"I promise I'll look into it," Katherine said, and hung up without saying thank you, a point of contention between them in the weeks to come.

Katherine tried my cell, couldn't get through, left a message at the Country Cabin Motel. Then she called Mira Das and explained the situation to her. Mira and another constable met the real estate agent at the yellow house. The name on the lease agreement was Deirdre Hayes.

The agent pulled up in a Suburban with a raised chassis and monster wheels. Mira described him as looking like a pro wrestler's manager. Mira asked him if he also rented the house with the cats. He explained that the company he worked for owned about fifty houses in Vancouver, most partitioned into suites. Because of the condition and small size of the suites, it wasn't uncommon for tenants to pick up on short notice, forfeiting their half-month's deposit. In some cases it took a few months to get in, clean things up, assess what renovations were needed, and get the suites back on the market.

"No landlord takes that long," Mira said. "You're saying you've had a vacant apartment, overrun with cats, that you didn't go inside for seven months? And you rented another suite to the same woman three months later? Hard to believe, sir."

"Believe what you like," the agent said.

He unlocked the ground level suite and let them inside. Mira was prepared for another horror scene. The suite was small and narrow, a single room with a kitchen at one end and a shower stall and toilet at the other. Fridge empty. Cupboards bare. A small bag of vet-approved gourmet cat food on the counter next to the hot plate. To Mira it looked like some-one had cleaned the place at least a month ago, and it had sat empty ever since.

"When was the last rent payment?" Mira asked the agent.

"I'll check the books," he said. He kept these in his truck. Mira and Constable Mander waited as he flipped through a big dirty binder covered in stickers.

"Post-dates through July of next year," he said.

"And the last few have gone through?"

He flipped. "Looks like."

"You know you're obligated to go through a rental suite once every six months," Mira said.

"Fifty houses. Eighty-seven suites. Think it's easy? Because it's not."

"And the other house?"

Flip. Gusts of air from the corner of his mouth as he found the page. "Post-dates to August. May's was the last that cleared."

"And you didn't follow up on that? And don't tell me about the fifty houses again."

"This isn't my area of concern," the agent said.

"It will be if I bring you to the station," Mira said. "You know this ties into the abduction of a child?"

That rocked him. "I just handle houses, okay?"

"Last time: why didn't you follow up when the check bounced?"

He shrugged and spread his hands. "They're whores. Do I really want to know the ins and outs of a whore's business? No pun intended."

"Either you got money from them off the books, or your boss told you not to pursue it. Maybe both."

"Hey," he said.

"Which was it?" Mira gave him a second. "Okay, let's go down to the station and discuss this further."

"All right," the agent said. "There's a guy who works for my boss name of Zak. He gave me six thousand dollars towards their rent and towards fixing up the place. I don't know if he gave it to me on instructions from his boss or it was his own idea, but I took the dough and did what he asked. I mean, I don't know that side of the business, just enough to know I don't want to know."

"Name of the business?"

"C and C Properties."

"What do the C's stand for?"

"Crittenden and Chow."

Deirdre Hayes, Dawn Meeker, and Barbara Della Costa leave Vancouver with Django James Szabo in March. Barbara and Dawn appear in Prosper's Point soon after. Maybe Deirdre was with them, but in any case she returned to the city in June. Perhaps she had a falling out with the others. Perhaps she wanted to check on her cats.

Deirdre rented the downstairs suite of the yellow house in June. There was no evidence she'd done more than drop her luggage by the door and her toiletries by the bathroom sink.

Dr. Boone's final pathology report would put Barbara Della Costa's death in early June. The evidence suggested that someone else moved the car to the shed in order to prevent the discovery of Barbara's body. Two missing women, one missing boy, one corpse. Only one other person seemed to know anything about Dawn Meeker.

Zak Atero's video confession was good television, but had no weight in court. His position, given through counsel, was that the tape was coaxed from an unwell man suffering from withdrawal. Atero declined to be interviewed and made it clear that all such requests should go through counsel.

There are ways around this, from coercion to deception to outright violation of a person's rights. Zak Atero wasn't smart enough to avoid these on his own, but with his brother to tell him to keep quiet and leave it to the attorneys, he might as well have been.

But Theo was out of the picture, until he walked out of the hospital Wednesday morning intent on killing me. On Tuesday night, though, Mira Das picked up Zak using one pretext or another and managed to maneuver him into an interview room and have him waive his right to counsel.

Mira is neither violent nor comfortable bending the rights of a suspect to secure a confession, which is probably why, unlike myself, she's still a police officer. She is, however, a brilliant interviewer. By the end of her talk with Atero, he had admitted to stripping and burning my Camry. He'd also given them as much as he could about Dawn Meeker, his fellow addict and sometime bed partner. He knew she was from a small town somewhere on the Island. He knew her parents were dead and had left her nothing. He knew her foster father had forced her to perform fellatio. He knew she had a brother and that the brother knew about the foster father's abuse. The brother promised her that one day they would have revenge. The brother lived on the Island but his work brought him to the Lower Mainland frequently. He didn't know names — hadn't, in fact, known that Dominique's real name was Dawn.

This was communicated to me on Tuesday night by Mira, at about the same time Zak was telling his brother what he'd just admitted to.

Getting out of the bed was the hard part. No doubt Theo's entire body still ached from the beating. The cracked ribs made it hard to draw breath. The sprained fingers made wielding a bat or a knife cumbersome. He could shoot a pistol left-handed, but to hit anything he'd have to be at arm's length to the intended recipient.

I'd seen his target pistol in his room, but that wasn't the weapon he brought to the office with him. Most likely he had a source for untraceable firearms, boosted from private residences or bought at gun shows. The weapon he brought was a .32 snubnose revolver with a blued finish, a weapon for personal defense, to be pulled from a closet safe or a handbag when the owner feels threatened.

He didn't stop at his house but wore the clothes he'd been admitted in, zipping up his suede jacket to conceal the blood on his shirt. He purchased a toque and a pair of gloves at the Bay and made one other verifiable stop at the Blue Papaya.

Lloyd Crittenden had washed his hands of the Atero-Drayton feud, but Theo had markers and called them in. I'd been wrong — Theo's job at Landmark Logistix was more than a tax dodge. It was a strategic placement, since a warehouse bonded to deal with shipping containers from overseas offered all sorts of possibilities. Theo would have preferred working with cars, his and his brother's passion. Doubtless he reminded Crittenden of this sacrifice.

He left the restaurant with David Chou, Zak's partner and fellow Crittenden bag man, and two other men, newly-arrived immigrants from Mainland China with criminal records there. Perhaps at this point he bought his toque and gloves, but I think it more likely they proceeded straight to my office.

Of course, on Wednesday morning I was far from the office — in point of fact I was in a field several kilometres outside of Prosper's Point, watching the house of the person ultimately responsible for keeping Django Szabo from his father. Katherine was at school, Mira had begun her seven-day rotation off, and my grandmother was sleeping in after a late night at the casino. Only Ben was inside the office. I've mentioned that he was drawn there. Like Katherine he enjoyed spending time inside, even when I wasn't around. Maybe especially then. Alone with a hot beverage and a book or a computer, the office could seem like a person's own Fortress of Solitude in the midst of the city.

He got the keys from Katherine on Tuesday, telling her that a present had arrived for me and he wanted to put it up as a surprise. Ben had pushed me to buy an Orson Welles poster for the office wall. When I reminded him what he'd said about *Citizen Kane* and *Speed*, he brushed it off as if it had never happened. One day he told me he was ordering a poster for me whether I wanted it or not. He pulled up the website on his PDA. He said I could choose between *Touch of Evil* and *The Stranger*.

"He's a corrupt cop in *Touch of Evil*," I'd said. "What is he in *The Stranger*?"

LAST OF THE INDEPENDENTS

"An escaped Nazi."

"Settles that, doesn't it?"

Inside, he thumb-tacked the poster crookedly and without smoothing it, so it hung off the wall like a sail full of wind. He made himself an instant hot chocolate with those vile de-moisturized marshmallows. He sat down at my table, to do what I don't know. I can guess. Before I'd left, I'd taken care to lock the Loeb file in the bottom drawer of the filing cabinet. When I returned to the Mainland and saw the damage to the office, I noticed that the bottom drawer was still locked, though the cabinet itself had been overturned. Parts of Cynthia Loeb's life had been strewn about the office, torn, crumpled, pissed on, along with other files and furniture. I suspect Ben opened the cabinet and was reading through the file when Theo Atero and the others broke in.

I'd told him in the first few days when we met that finding people was less about deduction than diligence. Even something as ephemeral as luck was in fact brought on by hour upon hour of intense scrutiny, legwork, brainstorming, list-making, canvassing, and conversation. The more time that went into the case, the greater chance of something new turning up — a witness's memory dislodging a vital detail, a surveillance tape popping up showing little Cynthia Loeb and whoever was with her when she disappeared. I told him, even if the connection between hard work and luck isn't apparent, it exists. I do believe that.

Maybe he had the file out hoping to strike gold, and maybe he had it out to add a few more hours' study to the case. Maybe he simply missed his sister, and reading through that mountain of recollections and facts was a way to connect with her, the spirit of her, if only in its absence. His attention wasn't on the surveillance monitor. He didn't hear the door chime. The first inclination he had about what was to happen was when Theo Atero's people broke down the upstairs door.

Theo was the first into the room. He already had his gun drawn. Ben stood up, the backs of his knees pushing the chair against the wall. He stood there as Theo took three steps into the office, creating space for the others to file past him. It was possible the others had guns, but they were wielding a tire iron and a camping hatchet and a lacrosse bat.

Theo recognized Ben. Ben recognized Theo. Both recognized the situation.

"Nothing funny you want to say? No other actors you want to compare me to? Say something, schoolboy."

"I can't think of anything," Ben said.

"Where's your friend?"

"Not here."

"Where's your friend?"

"I don't know. He's out of town."

Theo swept the computer to the floor with his bandaged hand. The Mac's mouse and keyboard clotheslined the Loeb file, spilling it across the table. Theo pointed the gun at the surveillance monitor and the two recent arrivals began disassembling it and Katherine's computer with the tire iron and hatchet. Theo ripped the phone from the wall socket and leveled the gun at Ben. David Chou overturned one of the file cabinets. The sound inside the office caused Ben to flinch. This made Theo laugh.

"Not so brave without your pal," he said. "Do you like to ambush people too?"

"No."

"Like to kick people when they're down?"

"No."

"So you're all talk, right?"

"Yes."

"Say it."

"I'm all talk."

"You're a fat-titted schoolboy. Say it."

"I'm a fat-titted schoolboy."

"Who talks a big game but doesn't have the balls to face a person one on one. Say it."

"Who talks a big —"

"Say it."

"I don't remember it all."

"Say it."

"I'm sorry."

"Get that tape," Theo said to the arrivals. To Ben he said, "Do you want the first one in the head or the heart?"

"Look, I'm sorry —"

"Take off your clothes."

"Look, I'm really sorry —"

"Strip, schoolboy."

Ben did, kicking off his shoes, then his pants, then his shirt and socks and finally his underwear. He'd begun to cry.

"Look at those tits," Theo said, laughing at the sight of his obese, hairless body. Ben, blubbering now, couldn't respond.

One of the arrivals said something to David Chou and pointed at Katherine's computer. The three of them conferred. Theo made Ben walk out from behind the table. He told Ben to sit in one of the client's chairs. Theo kicked over the other and produced a role of tape.

"Problem, boss," Chou said to Theo. "Camera application's backing up to an external hard drive."

"So smash the camera and then smash the drive."

Theo had taped one of Ben's wrists to the chair and torn off another piece with his teeth, which he put over Ben's mouth. The amount of mucous and tears kept the tape from sticking. He began ripping off a longer piece to wrap around Ben's head.

"I'd like to smash the drive," David Chou said, "but I can't see it. Must be wireless."

Theo turned to Ben. "Where's the drive?"

"I don't know," Ben said, the scrap of tape falling from his lips.

"Where would your pal keep it?"

"I don't know. I don't know."

The filing cabinet had been overturned in front of the stairwell door. When Theo crouched to look under the table Ben stood and turned, opened the sliding glass door and threw himself and the chair over the balcony.

He hit the pavement and broke his leg and sprained his wrist. He rolled off the sidewalk into the gutter. His vision was blurred. A car honked and slowed but passed him. He felt the rain pelt him. Another car stopped. The driver didn't get out but she phoned 911 and the next driver got out and asked him if he was okay.

Up in the office they gave up the search for the drive. They smashed the computers, pulled down the camera and overturned the other cabinet. Theo piled pages on the table and set them on fire. One of the arrivals threw parts of the camera into the puddle of piss where Ben and the chair had been. The papers burned but the table didn't catch and the fire was out before the four of them left. The driver who stopped saw them jogging up the sidewalk past the naked bloodied man in the gutter. None of this I knew at the time.

XXV

Specimens

The realtor for the house on Third and Gardenia remembered renting to a Deirdre Hayes. She had paid the extra hundred dollars for multiple tenants. Fisk and I paid the realtor a visit early Tuesday morning.

Duncan Perry was "The Island's Number One Choice For Realty Three Years in a Row," according to the ad on the back of the *Prosper's Point Free Press*. Perry's office was decorated with nautical memorabilia, including navigational charts of Vancouver Island and a lacquered oar in a display case. The office was cluttered and disorganized. Perry didn't seem to mind.

"Course I asked her who was staying with her," Perry said. "I made sure to get a name and a SIN number."

Fisk and I waited, arms crossed, as Perry dug it up. I noticed a ship in a bottle sitting on the window ledge. The ship had broken in two, the top of its paper sail no doubt part of the clutter on Perry's desk.

"Here we go." He held up a neon pink sticky note. "Had her write it down for me. Dominique LaChanteuse. Social Insurance number Seven-Three-Four ..." he paused. We looked at him expectantly. "Looks like there's only five numbers here."

"Meaning you didn't look too hard at the information she supplied," Fisk said. "Like checking to see does her SIN have nine digits."

"Miss Hayes checked out fine," Perry said. He continued to run his hands over the paperwork, less concerned with creating order than maintaining momentum. He was thin and had a ruddy face and a smile his mother wouldn't believe.

"So you figure why bother getting even a realistic alias from her friend?" Fisk took the piece of paper from him. "Dominique the singer? You fell for that?"

"So I don't read French good," Duncan Perry said.

"What I want to know," Fisk said to me, "was which one blew him?"

"My money's on Deirdre," I said.

"Then too bad for him."

"Why?" Perry asked.

"I don't want to get into anyone's venereal history," Fisk said, "'pecially not one as long and storied as Deirdre Hayes's. It's a Russian novel. Her STDs have STDs."

"You're bullshitting," Perry said.

Fisk turned to me. "What was her nickname, Mike?"

"The Specimen Jar?"

"Specimen Jar, right. On account of the smorgasbord of diseases she — "

"I only saw her friends the one time," Perry said.

"Friends plural?" Fisk acted mock surprised. "Are you saying Dominique La Chanteuse was such a convincing alias you felt it covered two people? She must give some crazy head."

"All she told me," Perry said, "was that the other girl and her son weren't going to be there for more than a couple days."

"And were they?"

"They might have been there a little longer."

We waited for him to name a number.

"A couple months," he said. "April and May. Maybe part of June. I meant to bring it up with Deirdre, but when I emailed her, she wrote back saying she was on the Mainland dealing with a family crisis." The sound of his fists clenching and unclenching was audible. "I know you're lying about her," he added. "Think I'm dumb enough to fall for that?"

I backhanded Duncan Perry with enough force to send him backwards into his chair. The move surprised all three of us. Perry looked up at me with "What'd I do?" scrawled on his face.

"I am sick of people like you doing the minimum and fucking things up for the rest of us," I said, trying to justify the blow. "Fucking kid's missing and all you could think of is getting a free half-and-half. I should beat the piss out of you. In fact — " I turned to Fisk "— how about getting a coffee and giving us a moment?"

"Easy," Fisk said, inserting an arm between us. You know you're out of line when Gavin Fisk becomes the voice of reason.

"Easy hell," I said, playing it up now. "The next thing out of this hump's mouth better be a lead on Dominique or I swear —" I took a step towards the desk and Fisk restrained me. Fisk turned to Duncan Perry, his expression saying, "Give me something to placate him with."

Perry said, "The three of them, and the kid of course, they were gone by late June. I checked on the house then and it was vacated."

"There's a case-breaker," I said.

"Barbara I know was in town until June. I saw her a few times at the bars, late at night. I said *saw*. We didn't interact."

"Keep going."

"They weren't living in town but they were still around town, at least Dominique was. I saw her at the supermarket. This would be late August. Before she moved she was wearing skirts and tank tops, sexy stuff. When I saw her in August she was more covered up."

"It's called fall."

"It was more than that," Perry said. "She was wearing this older-type clothing, like a frock, and she had her hair done Jackie Kennedy style. She had a fake pearl bracelet, costume jewellery."

"Not real pearls?"

"I buy those for my wife, I know real pearls when I see them."

"Did you say anything to her in the market?" I asked.

"That's the thing. I said hi and she kind of brushed me off, pretended not to see me. But I said hi again and asked about her friends. She said they were both fine. I said there was some paperwork to settle with Deirdre — waiver of deposit, lease-breaker, and so forth. She said Deirdre would be back next week and she'd settle everything then. Deirdre never showed. The paperwork's still around here." He made a show of searching for it.

"And that was it?" Fisk asked.

"My wife was with me, I didn't want to pursue it too much."

"Last you saw of her?"

"That was the last time, yes." Perry's gaze fixed on the broken ship on the ledge. "One thing I thought was weird. You know how when you go through a checkout line you give the cashier your points card and the cashier repeats your name back to you? Like, 'Thanks for shopping here, Mr. Perry?' 'Have a good day, Mr. Perry?' That sort of thing? Well, when she finished, the cashier goes, 'Thanks for shopping, Mrs. Meeker.' I'm behind her in line. I say, 'I didn't know you were married, congrats.' Dominique nods like she doesn't want to talk about it."

"What was she buying?" I asked.

He shrugged, what does it matter, but then the answer came to him and he said, "Bag of potatoes, bag of onions, canned goods, and prime rib roasts, which I remember were on sale that week because I bought a couple myself. The cashier asked if she wanted a hand out to her car and she said no. I was going to ask her but she just picked up the bags, no cart, and hoofed it. Hopped in the passenger's seat of a blue SUV and they drove off. I didn't get the plate, and I'm not good with makes and models when it comes to those big gas guzzlers. It looked pretty new, though."

"Did you see who was driving?"

"A man."

"Could you describe him?"

"He was wearing a coat." Perry shrugged. "The windows were tinted."

"Could it have been a woman?" I asked.

"Would have to be a large, manly-looking woman." Perry shook his head. "No, it was a guy, I'm sure."

"Let's get Delgado on that search," Fisk said to me. "Thanks," he said to Duncan Perry.

I nodded at Perry sheepishly.

"I could sue you," he said, sitting a bit straighter now that we were leaving.

Fisk turned back and said, "You're lucky I don't arrest you for attacking my friend the way you did. You're a vicious animal and should be locked away."

Perry watched us leave without moving from his desk.

Before meeting Delgado we tried the stores Barbara Della Costa had visited. The sporting goods store was under new management, having been bought by a franchise. The pawn shop owners remembered the transaction but couldn't recall any details, other than the woman was dark-haired and had severe eyebrows. "That was a fucking bust," Fisk said as we walked back towards the main strip. "Talking to them was only the entire reason we came over here."

Not the entire reason, I thought.

Delgado took the information and put one of his people on it. The three of us had an early dinner again at Ace's. Same gristly T-bone, undercooked fries and batter-soaked onion strings. Another few days of Prosper's Point cooking and I'd *be* Orson Welles.

"My thinking," Delgado said through a mouth full of beef, "is that if Dawn Meeker was staying around here and wanted to avoid people, the logical place would be the Rusk home. It's isolated and it's where her friend was found. Plus we know someone was on the property."

"I checked that house," Fisk said. "Nobody'd been in there since it was boarded up."

"Only empty building for a hundred klicks," Delgado said.

"That tells us she's staying with someone," I said. "Any other Rusks in the area? Any Meekers?"

Delgado shook his head. "Arthur Simons married Lester Rusk's sister. She's passed, but Arthur's still alive. Don't know where his son ended up. I could find out."

"Know anyone who drives a blue SUV?"

"Only about everybody," he said.

I skipped out on drinking and went back to my room. I phoned Mira and she told me about Deirdre's empty apartment. She suggested that Duncan Perry and her real estate agent might have been twins separated at birth.

I phoned the number in Reykjavik that Katherine had found for me. The hotel owner spoke English with a halting accent that I assumed was Icelandic. The owner told me the Yates-Yeats rooms had a Do-Not-Disturb order on them. She asked if I wanted to leave a message. "Nothing," I said. I wondered whether she took my meaning or she'd pass that on as the message.

I lay on the bed feeling homesick. There was an internet café down the block but the thought of staring at a screen made me nauseous. I put in my headphones and made myself a playlist, everything from Joni Mitchell to Memphis Slim, Hamza El Din to Isobel Campbell. Even music couldn't drown out my thoughts.

What if he's alive and what if he isn't and what if he is and what if he isn't?

I picked up the phone and dialed home. My grandmother picked up.

"How's the trip?" she asked. "This week's 'sposed to be wet and cold over there. Are you dressing for it?"

"Layers and everything."

"You always say that, but you're probably wearing one of those thin shirts under your coat. It's not enough, Michael. You need a scarf and toque. Maybe for Christmas."

"Anything but that."

"The season's right around the corner. Have you thought about what you want?"

"Not a thing. What about you?"

"My new wooden floor would be nice."

"Chrissakes," I said. "I'll deal with the dog when I get back, I promise. Could you put her on?"

"The dog?"

"Yeah, so I can say hi."

"Be serious."

I hadn't really expected her to hold the dog's head to the receiver. I wondered why I'd bothered asking. "Have fun at the casino. Say hi to the girls. Tell what's-her-name with the oxygen tank to go easy."

"You come home safe," she said.

I ran Fisk down to the ferry, two hours there and back. There'd been no word on the SUV list. Arthur Simons was living alone. He was happy to converse with the officers and let them look around his place, just to break up the monotony of retired life. His son had died of pneumonia — another dead end.

I slung Fisk's gear out of the van. The two of us shook hands.

"Don't tune up anyone who doesn't deserve it," he said. "See you back in civilization."

I watched him and the other passengers walk up the covered gangplank and onto the ferry. One more goodbye.

As I drove back to Prosper's Point, I played the last of the demo CDs. It featured a girl singing blues licks over synth drums and electric guitar and a haunting, tremulous Fender Rhodes. I recognized the backup vocalist's voice. Amelia Yeats. She sang lead on the fourth song. I listened to it on repeat. The song was another sort of goodbye, letting me know I'd gotten everything I would get from her. There'd be no more. The end had been written into the beginning and what was left were merely stray sensations. At some point in the future that might be a comfort, the way the memory of danger survived makes a person confident in dealing with what's to come. But it was too recent, thinking about it hurt, and listening to the song was driving salt into the wound.

I gunned the van down the hill, blowing past half a dozen hazard signs and through a desolate intersection. The van didn't handle all that well. At high speeds it shuddered. I had a vision of crashing over the traffic circles and slamming into the beige-painted wall of the elementary school. Maybe punch through it and drive to the coastline and swim back to the Mainland. Cheery thoughts for a late night alone in Prosper's Point.

As I turned towards the motel I caught the glint of metallic blue in the rearview. Stadium lights lit up a row of trucks, some of them blue. Price tags in neon over the windshields. Another dead end in a case that had seemed like a string of them. The Ramseys, the Ateros, Crittenden, Dawn Meeker, and now an elusive blue SUV.

I pulled into the lot, half-thinking that I'd check out the new Camrys and see if they were unobtrusive enough for work, and half-thinking that I didn't want to sit in the Country Cabin Motel any longer than necessary. I contemplated checking out and sleeping in the van, parking along the side of the road and reclining the chair. Or not even bother checking out, just leaving. I had my suitcase in the back of the van. All I'd be out were a few appliances.

I strolled the aisles of the small but densely packed lot. The new Camry looked fine, but I knew I'd end up buying a used one with low mileage. In TV shows PIs always drive Mustangs or Porsches. Try tailing a deadbeat husband in a bright yellow 911 slope-nose through industrial Vancouver. Even so, it would be nice to drive something with flair.

The big lights snapped off. I looked towards the office. A woman in heels was dragging the security cage around the inside of the showroom. She locked it into place behind the windows and locked the front door. She was walking to her car when she noticed me. Her smile was warm, but she grasped the strap of her handbag tight as she got closer.

"Were you still looking?" she asked. She was my height, around fifty, wearing a leather skirt and a frilly purple blouse with a plunging neckline. A big faceless watch on a platinum band.

"Just browsing," I said. "Sorry to startle you."

"Was there a car you wanted to look at? I can open up and get the keys, it's no trouble."

"No," I said. "It'll be a while till the settlement comes in."

Her Nissan was parked next to the van. As she beeped the doors open I asked, "Do you sell a lot of blue sports utility vehicles?"

She raised one eyebrow, no mean feat considering the amount of work that face had been put through. "Why blue?"

I held up a business card for her to read. "I'm trying to find someone. All I know is he drives a blue SUV."

"No year, no make, no model?"

"No."

"But you're sure he bought it in town?"

"I'm not sure it has anything to do with anything," I said. "Just a longshot."

"Well if he bought it in town within the last eight years, chances are he bought it from us." She pointed off towards the residential area. "I own the GM dealership, too."

"You keep records? A database of who you sold to?"

Bemused, she shook her head and smiled. "If you have to ask that, evidently you don't know much about the car business."

"Next to nothing," I said. "I used to help my grandfather buy cars at police auctions, but that was pre-onboard computers. Now, something goes wrong under the hood, I'm completely clueless."

"What's this for?"

"I'm trying to find a kid."

"A runaway?"

"Somewhere between that and an abduction. The motive is still fuzzy."

She nodded, looked at the office, at her watch, her Nissan and back at me. "Two hundred."

"Pardon?"

"You were leading up to asking me if you could check the database, weren't you?"

"I was hoping you'd offer to help out of pity."

"Not in this economy, kiddo."

The dealer's name was Alessandra Bock. We quickly found that it was easier for her to compile the search results. I stared over her shoulder, inhaling hairspray and Chanel, as she narrowed the list by make and colour and gender of purchaser.

"You'd be surprised how many women buy SUVs," she said.

After an hour she had it down to twelve names. I waited as she pulled the files.

"None of these leave the office," she said. She set the stack of files on the desk. She lit a cigarette in the small inner office and opened the window while I read.

The problem was, I didn't know what I was looking for. Twelve names, twelve SUVs. Irvin Singer, Rob Hargrove, Gerald Barton, Bud Schmidt. I looked over Singer's profile carefully, thinking that Dominique La Chanteuse might be an in-joke. But Singer had bought his Escalade in late September of this year, and Perry had seen Dawn in August.

"I could use a coffee," Alessandra volunteered.

While she readied the packet of instant, I read through Singer's paperwork again. Perhaps he'd driven an SUV before — but no, he'd traded in a four-cylinder Mazda towards the Escalade. I flipped to the end and stared at the photocopy of his driver's license. Singer was a harmless-looking seventy-year-old.

I flipped through Hargrove's and Barton's and the others. Something clicked. I went back through them slower.

Gerald Barton had bought his Grand Cherokee two years ago. No trade-in, no lease, payment in full secured by a loan from the local credit union. His business and home address were the same. Same phone number. Under the *occupation* space on the application he'd put *self-employed*. I knew from experience that that was never a point in one's favor when securing credit.

Alessandra put a mug of coffee in front of me and sat down at the desk. "So are you married?"

"No. You?"

"Not at the moment. Seeing someone?"

"Sort of." My attention was on the files.

"What does 'sort of' mean?"

I looked up. She was regarding me over the brim of her mug, which said *Proud Parent of a Bill Reid Secondary Honour Student*.

No sense in lying to her. I said, "It means we had sex once and now she's in Iceland."

Alessandra took a moment to process this and decided it was funny.

"Scared her off the continent, did you?"

Barton's driver's license photo showed a forty-year-old white man, average height, and slender build. I almost didn't recognize him without his glasses. Gerald Barton. Jerry Barton. The Ostrich Man.

I woke up Mira Das, had her repeat to me what she'd found out about Dawn Meeker from Zak Atero. Raised in a foster home. Brother missing. Was there any way to check if two people with different surnames had grown up with the same foster parent? Not at night, Mira said.

I wished Gavin or Mira had been with me, or Katherine or Ben. Someone who had my back and would speak up if what I was doing was reckless. But all my friends were other places.

I left Alessandra and the dealership with Barton's address in my pocket. My exit had been abrupt. It was late, and I knew where Barton would be.

The Palatial's parking lot was around back. The lot was half-full and poorly lit. No one milled about for a smoke or a private chat. I found the Cherokee. I peered inside. A large cage sat on the back bench. The cage was empty. Nothing but feathers on the seats.

I stabbed my knife into the front right tire, working it around. I did the same to the back right. As I extracted it the blade snapped. Taiwanese craftsmanship for you. Crouching, I moved back to the street and looked through the window. I couldn't see him inside, but I saw Shoshona and Di, mucking it up with a trio of bikers. I left before they saw me.

Barton's address was 622 Mason Lane. 400 Block and 800 block showed up on the road map. I used my cellphone's GPS to plot a course that I could follow in the dark. And it was dark. I drove down the same unnamed logging road, past the Rusk home, down to the crossroads and left of Mason. 400. 500. At 600 I killed the headlights and pulled onto the shoulder, stuck a hastily-scrawled GONE FOR GAS note under the wiper blades. My grandmother was right. It was too cold for just a shirt and coat. I felt my gun in my pocket.

Most of the addresses were attached to undeveloped tracts or farmsteads, their true size hidden from the street by thick second-growth forest. Driveways were long ribbons of hard-packed dirt or gravel. The addresses were marked on mailboxes or on boulders set by the driveways, almost impossible to see in the dark. Barton's drive had no indicator of address, not even on the rusty mailbox. I checked the GPS, then followed the driveway until the house came in sight. I cut east through the trees so that as I inched closer I was hidden from both the house and anyone coming down the drive after me.

The lights were off in the house save for a porch light, a naked incandescent bulb at midpoint over the stoop of fresh cedar along the front of the house. A white two-person rocking chair sat still beneath the bulb, burdened with coils of Christmas lights. A mosquito zapper hung beneath the eaves.

I followed the treeline to the side of the house. A stack of firewood beneath a moss-covered lean-to, blackberry bushes encroaching. A path of old car mats had been laid over the mud, leading to the rear of the house. The property rivaled Yates Manor in size, the difference being that here, nature had been beaten back instead of manicured and tamed.

The backyard was dirt, clumps of grass, and blackberry brambles; vegetation grew up through the old pens that formed a grid of posts and wire mesh. Half a chicken coop, gutted by fire. Behind the property was a knoll, steep and dotted with young pines. The moon reflected in the water-logged crevices and ditches of the property.

I knocked, entered, and turned on the lights. A kitchen, microwave door open, orange grease on the range hood, smell of pork in the air but not from tonight. A line of empty Grolsch bottles on the windowsill, an empty jam jar holding twist ties and feathers. Formica table, vinyl-upholstered chairs, and a booth done in naugahyde. A pack of cards and a cribbage board left out. A scratch pad, the logo of Duncan Perry Realty across the top. The page was divided into two columns, a scorecard, the initials F and D underlined at the top. *Django/Dawn/Dominique/ Dad/Duncan/Di.* And F — whose name started with F? Father?

The microwave clock read twelve past three. I moved room by room, turning on lights as I went. Living room, hallway, broom closet, bedrooms, all nondescript, showing signs of regular use. A coat rack by the front door, his, hers, and junior's rain slickers and galoshes arranged with military precision. Apple box full of old newsprint.

Wrong house, maybe. The basement door was locked but only with the kind of knob that prevents a person from walking into an occupied bathroom. Enough pressure and it snapped open without damage. The lights in the basement were already burning and it was warmer than the rest of the house. The smell of birds told me why. Down the stairs I saw cages everywhere, orange-light incubators for chicks. Some finches and some chickadees and another half-dozen green-winged conures whose beaks followed my hand as I waved it in front of them. More exotic-looking species in hand-built ventilated crates, stuffed with straw and heaters. No ostriches, though. Sacks of feed leaned against a mini-fridge which held Tupperware cartons of grubs and other wriggling things.

The Ostrich Man actually raised birds. Imagine.

I phoned the RCMP and talked to a Constable Snyder. She seemed reluctant to speak candidly over the phone. I dropped Delgado's name, and Fisk's, and when that didn't convince her I rattled off my old badge number and told her as a fellow law enforcer I expected her to extend the same courtesy to me she'd expect in my place, and not a bunch of god-damned rigamarole at quarter to four in the fucking morning. She actually apologized to me while she checked Barton on CPIC.

"Nothing but a disturbing the Peace complaint against Mr. Barton," Snyder said, "and that's seventeen years old."

"Worth a try," I said. "You know Barton?"

"By sight, not to speak to."

"He seems a bit standoffish."

"Well put, sir."

"'Preciate the candor. Sorry to gripe. Have a safe shift."

I'd been wrong before and was happy to be so again. For Christmas this year Jerry Barton would receive a pair of all-weather radials from an anonymous benefactor. As for breaking into his house and violating his privacy, chalk it up to caution and concern.

I almost missed the second door. The basement was painted beige and the stairs had been drywalled and painted the same colour. The door was behind the staircase, handle and hinges painted over, easy to overlook in the shadows cast by the orange light.

The door opened onto another staircase. Another basement. I remembered a Stephen King story, rat-catchers descending into basement after basement, each leading to bigger and more ferocious vermin.

Probably a salt cellar. Probably nothing. I pulled my gun just in case.

Down, down.

XXVI

DJANGO

You go far enough, descend enough stairs, and you come out where you started. At the bottom of the staircase, propped upside down on newspaper with the wheels in the air, was a blue Schwinn Stingray. Someone was in the process of replacing the inner tube of the back tire.

I expected horror or emptiness in this hidden basement with its low ceilings and painted brick walls. I didn't expect another home, but that's what I found. When the lights were on I saw a small kitchen and a study and a dining room with a hand-carved oak table and three chairs. Saran-wrapped leftovers in the fridge, stack of vinyl placemats and a lazy Susan. Dishes and crock pot drying in a rack by the sink. No Django, though.

The living room had no television, only a furnace and two bookshelves stuffed with primers and Dr. Seuss books, Funk & Wagnall's encyclopedias with yearbooks up to 1994. On the top shelf behind a glass case was a row of elegantly bound notebooks, Moleskines or the like, each with a date chalked on its spine. Games on the lower shelves, backgammon and chess. A child's wind-up record player. No dust on anything.

I was drawn to the notebooks, but first the door. Like the other it was built beneath the staircase. The light switch was nearby, but flicking it did nothing as the bulb had been removed. The door was unlocked. I pulled out my cell and used the screen's backlight for illumination. A captain's bed, neatly made and tucked in, glow-in-the-dark moons on the comforter. A chemical toilet and basin next to the bed. And in the corner a great cage stretching to the ceiling, a bed of newspaper inside that spilled out through the grille to the surrounding floor.

The phone's backlight flicked off ominously. I hit random buttons to keep it lit as I examined the cage. On the floor were two dishes, water and brown hard spheres. I recognized the smell of dry kibble.

Once I was sure I was alone, I moved back into the living room. I slid open the glass case and took down the first notebook. I flipped through. In legible block printing, the title page read:

REDEEMING THE FAMILY
BY
G.V. BARTON

A dedication: To James and Dawn.
An epigraph from Tolstoy.

> At a distance, evolution seems linear. Birds from winged reptiles, homo sapiens from apes. We think this way about society, too, as if we move through the generations from ignorance to enlightenment, from evil to good, towards perfection. These are but convenient fictions. In truth, society grows misshapen and deformed. The family, our social heart, has stopped beating. Not only have we not protested this erosion-from-within, we have

applauded it. We think technology and wealth will fill the void. Like flightless birds, we have lost our most valuable gift.

There is no progress without the family. By this I don't mean the 'nuclear family', that creation of a century's worth of advertising and propaganda. I mean a unit of people concerned with the welfare of each other, nurturing a spirit of community and love. All my life I pursued wealth and autonomy and excellence: I see now that all of this is fleeting and inconsequential without a family to share my blessings with, and to transmit my knowledge to.

I know my sister Dawn shares these feelings, even though we've never spoken of them. We have seen the horror of an empty and broken family, and we know that the only way to rectify things is to create our own.

As children I often held her at night in our shared bed, kissing her cheeks still slick with our foster father's semen. To reassure her I promised her that it wouldn't always be like this, that one day the old man would be gone and we'd have a proper family. Since arriving back in town, Dawn seems healthier than she has in years. Much of this is due to her young friend, James, who I presume has run away from similar horrors. How fitting that the three of us would find each other now.

What followed were dates and entries, some tending to the scientific, others journal-like.

Today I pitched my idea to the other women. Dawn remained characteristically silent. Barbara seemed reluctant to let Dawn and I adopt the boy, in part I think because she believes there is money in withholding her approval. Deirdre has bowed out, wanting nothing to do with us. She doesn't seem the type to betray her friends. I think she is eager to see her animals again. I can relate.

This morning Deirdre left and Barbara moved back into town. Dawn and James are sullen. I handed Barbara seven thousand dollars in exchange for "keeping her big yap shut," as she put it. A small price to pay to start a family.

I'd hoped it wasn't true, but it is: the missing child on television is unquestionably our James. He is quiet and often sullen, but I believe he is happy here. He wouldn't try to contact his birth parents, even if we did have a phone in the house. In any case, I can't risk our family on the whims of a child. Tomorrow I will clean the sub-basement and furnish it for him. This shouldn't be hard, as the sub-basement is well-provisioned and built to withstand the end of the world. Our foster father was many things, God forgive him, but he was not unprepared.

Starting on June 6th, the tone of the journals shifted and the handwriting became sloppy, lapsing into bursts of cursive.

The lock on the sub-basement was broken. He was hiding beneath the sacks of feed, as if I wouldn't notice a different configuration of sacks. I don't know what to do with him. I don't believe in parental violence, having been on its receiving end. I will be lenient this time. We will see what develops. Maybe his "escape attempts" are simply part of a developmental phase.

He was in the backyard, having snared his leg in wire from the ostrich pen. Thank God Dawn and I found him in time. That settles it. I cannot raise a beast like a human. I will put the old cage in his room, so that it is visible from the bed, and vice versa. He will have a choice.

Success! After a week in the cage James emerged meek and obedient. Dawn is buying food for tonight's feast, the boy's first hot meal in seven days. I knew there was a better way than the belt.

Today I gave James his first bird, a chick with a maimed wing and vestiges of its absorbed twin still grafted to its torso. It won't live long, but it will teach James how to care for something, and allow him to observe nature taking its course. In the real world, kindness and cruelty are often intertwined. On a personal note, it feels wonderful to have someone to share my hobby with.

I am glad I was the one to find the body and the note. "Sick experiment" indeed! Fine sentiment from a career prostitute. My dear sister fell into low company before I intervened, and this "sick experiment" has made her happier than she has ever been. The child is safe and loved. All we need is a respectful distance kept by those who would meddle. Perhaps Barbara's decision to end her life is for the best. It does beg the question of Deirdre.

It's done and I'm back home. God will forgive me or he won't, but the three of us are safe. Maybe Deirdre would have kept her word, but I doubt it. Cleaning her apartment I found her own diary. She shared the same apocalyptic perspective that Barbara had. I didn't read it before shredding it. God can judge me, History can judge me, but I will not be naysayed by those with no grasp of the importance of my work. Don't they realize that if Dawn and I are successful with James, there will be a blueprint for others to follow in rehabilitating their own families? My sole comfort is that time has exonerated other visionaries before me. And if we are unsuccessful? I gave it my all and have no regrets.

Today Dawn left. I found drug paraphernalia in her abandoned room. Has she been in a stupor the entire time? I feel weary. Everything is off-balance. How can she prefer that life to this one? I must gather my wits. James is my responsibility now. If I set the correct example she will doubtless come back.

In the last book, the dates late September:

> Life is funny. I sit at my table, alone with Precious, night after night, maintaining the illusion that I'm a harmless eccentric. "The Ostrich Man," they call me. As if, to these drunks and harlots, I'm a kind of mascot. A pet. I cannot wait for posterity to vindicate me. The books they will write: "Barton's first great work was written in peculiar circumstances." If only I could live to see that.

> All great advances are predicated on failure. I wonder how much of my work I could salvage if circumstances forced me to flee. I love James. I consider him my son. Sometimes, though, I think of the mistakes I've made with him and I want nothing more than a clean slate. Maybe this is how Dawn felt. We are both hopeless dreamers. Sometimes the world seems so drab and mundane compared to our designs. Why can we not say to hell with the world and live in these designs instead?

I pocketed the first and last of the notebooks and headed out of the sub-basement. Nothing had been disturbed in the aviary. The house was still, save for the clicks and groans and hums that empty houses make. I went to the bedrooms on the main floor and tossed them. Gerald Barton was meticulous in his bookkeeping and kept a tidy room. Dawn Meeker's was filthy, and judging from the dust on the bedsheets, had been vacant at least a month. I wondered if they fucked and where.

SAM WIEBE

I left the house via the back and retraced my steps past the wood pile. I noticed built into the side of the house a wooden hatch with a bar across it. I didn't have the stomach for another basement. I unlatched it and peered inside, once again using the cell as a flashlight. The door didn't lead down but sideways, in a narrow crawlspace that ran beneath the kitchen and living room, between the first basement and ground level.

A water barrel on its side. A long slim zippered pouch. I recognized the latter as a rifle case. I bent and reached inside, clutching the gun by the barrel through the bag. A lever-action Winchester 30-30, some sort of limited edition with elaborate scrollwork on the metal. I checked to see if the rifle was loaded. It was. Foolish to store a gun that way.

I bent and straddled the entrance, leaning inside the crawlspace. I righted the barrel and used my free hand to work off the lid. I leaned in and hugged the barrel and twisted the lid, which came off in my hand. The barrel tipped towards me.

That smell of human meat decaying, liquid sloshing out, soaking the crawlspace, soaking my shirt and hands. A yellow eye, stringy black hair, and that smell.

I fell backwards out of the crawlspace, landing on wet grass. My cell was out of my hand, lost somewhere. I grabbed the rifle, tried to push myself to my feet and gave up.

So there he was. Dead for over a month judging from the decomp. No indication how.

I couldn't look at him again. I wrote off my cellphone and sealed the crawlspace, my hands and torso soaked in Django James Szabo. I knew what came next. I picked up the rifle and flung the wet case into the bushes.

I sat on the edge of the porch out of the light and I waited — two hours? Four? Tears on my face, my clothes drying solid in the cold air. I froze but didn't care.

The first inkling of morning shone through the trees. Eventually I saw high beams down the path. The Cherokee stopped in the patch of dead grass that served as a driveway. I heard the door thunk closed, another open and then close. The Ostrich Man was whistling.

He reached the door to the house. He set down the conure's cage and fumbled with his keys. He stopped, maybe sensing something out of place. I crossed the stoop with the gun at my hip and stepped into the halo of the porch light so he could see the son of a bitch who was about to kill him.

Recognition on his face. Terror. A glance towards his truck. I stepped off the porch, cutting off his escape. He ran for the opposite side of the house. I shot from the hip like a fucking amateur and missed, the report louder than fury.

I followed him around the side of the house where there was no light. He cleared it, racing across an open stretch of backyard. Our feet made rude noises as we worked them free of the mud. I took another shot but missed him again, transferred the rifle to my left hand and came out with the Glock. I took two shots at him as we ran. I stopped and let the rifle fall and aimed two-handed with the Glock and squeezed off the rest of the clip, slow and with regulated breathing. He dropped but came up immediately and I knew I'd winged him but not killed him.

I tossed the pistol in frustration and bent to take up the rifle, the smooth shoulder rest covered in mud. My cast made it awkward to grasp the barrel. I held my breath and sighted on his back and fired. In the fraction of time between noise and impact I prayed to whatever God would listen please let me kill him. I saw the shot catch him almost square in the back and propel him down into the grass, scant feet from the base of the knoll.

I ran towards him through the mud with the gun held over my head like some kind of trophy. He was facedown, still alive. He managed to turn onto his back and look up at me. I saw the dark splotch of the exit wound above and to the right of his heart. His right hand held the knife blade which he'd worked out of the tire, clamped in a dirty linen handkerchief.

It took him almost a minute to drag out a full sentence. "I can explain if you'll listen."

I pulled the notebooks from my pocket and held them in front of his face. He clutched at them and I lifted them just out of his fingers' reach.

"I did not kill him. Swear I didn't."

"Your sister then?"

"Neither of us. We're not murderers. Not a hair on his head."

"This isn't your house?" I kicked him. "Not your barrels?"

"I loved James," he said.

"How'd he die?"

"Fell."

"On the stairs?" A nod. "You push him?"

"He tripped."

"You're lying."

"He fell."

I ripped the title page out of his book.

"I swear to God he fell."

Crows settled onto the high branches along the edge of the property. Barton's eyes flicked to them reflexively. Without meeting my gaze he said, "He was trying to escape. He fell down the stairs in the dark. He hurt his head. I tried to help him but there was nothing I could do."

"You take him to a hospital?"

His eyes on the birds. "No."

"You just, what — hoped he'd get better? Look at me."

Tears. "I didn't kill him."

"Where's your sister?"

"I don't know. Swear to God."

"You hid Barbara in that shed?"

"To protect us."

"And killed Deirdre for the same reason?"

"To protect James. He could've been happy here. Swear to God."

With his free hand he reached up for the book. I tore it up the spine and knelt down with the rifle pointed at his chest.

I said, "I want you to know that after I kill you I'm going to burn this book and the others. All your papers, all your notes. Whatever fame you think you're entitled to will vanish. You'll be just another sick bastard. If the world says anything it'll say good riddance."

I believe I was grinning when I said that. It seemed to take the heart out of him. He didn't react when I worked the lever on the rifle and chambered another round.

"You don't have to do this," he said.

In fact I felt like I already had. I tried to find words to tell him this.

"This is a nice country," I said. "We're not set up to deal with people like you." I stepped on his chest and pulled the trigger.

The gun jammed. Barton rolled away, putting me off balance, sending me into the muck. He swiped at me with the broken blade. I felt the skin tear below my eye. He swiped again but there was no force behind the movement. I regained my feet and took the rifle by the barrel and stove his head in.

XXVIII

No Redress

It took what felt like an hour before I could hear anything besides tidal waves of blood crashing into the rocky coastline in my skull. I stood over him feeling self-righteous as hell until I began to feel the cold creep up through my muddy sneakers and pant legs. The morning sun brought faint showers and no warmth. I tucked my coat around me and began to think rationally. It was my first killing and I found this hard.

I used my coat to bundle everything — guns, shell casings, knife blade and linen, all but the notebooks. I even waded back into the crawlspace, the child's bodily fluids underfoot, and pulled my cellphone from the slime. While inside I noted the other barrels beneath a tarp, like great blue eggs. Someone else's to discover. I righted the barrel with Django's body in it and sealed the lid.

Barton I left for the critters.

In the house I opened the birds' cages and dumped the feed out in a pile on the basement floor. Under the kitchen sink upstairs I found a jug of bleach. As I walked back to the van I stopped to break the rifle on the ground, douse the pieces with bleach and toss them into the forest. Cars came along the road. I turned my back to them and made like I was pissing.

At the van I stripped and dressed in yesterday's clothes. I'd left my appliances at the motel but figured I could live without them. I made a pile of all the artifacts and emptied the jug above them. I tossed them into my suitcase. The notebooks I hid in a crevice of the van. I used the water I'd brought to wash myself as best I could, using a bleach solution to mask the smell of death.

There is an air taxi from Nanaimo to Vancouver which takes less than an hour from takeoff to touchdown. I was tempted, but I needed to bring the van back over. I wondered how much time I'd have.

I had lunch in the same cafeteria booth that I'd sat in with Fisk on the ride over. Ferry ice cream is better than it has any right to be. I had a dish and some tea, hoping a spike in blood sugar would sort everything out. I felt a dull pain from my arm and wished I'd brought my painkillers.

I phoned Katherine from a phone on the boat that charged an extortionist's rate. She told me about Ben and about the office. I didn't share my news.

Halfway across the Strait of Georgia I walked down to the vehicle deck and opened the back doors of the van. I slid out the suitcase and closed the doors, eyed a spot near the stern where there were no security cameras or crew members, and heaved the case over the railing and into the churning white water behind us.

What hadn't been destroyed by Theo Atero and his crew had been stolen or vandalized by the Hastings Street locals, who treat yellow police ribbons as invitations to help themselves. The vultures even took the toilet seat. I worked off the wall panel and found the contracts and the wireless drive and the drawstring Crown Royal pouch I used in lieu of a cashbox. I tore up the Szabo contract and flushed it. I pocketed the pouch. I'd come straight from the ferry terminal to do this, knowing the Ateros could be lurking around and that I'd just pitched my gun into the ocean.

I took the stairs down and crossed to the van and heard someone call my name and turned. Gavin Fisk and Mira Das were walking towards me from the corner. We met at the van.

I held my hands over my head. "I know what this looks like, but officers, please, I swear I'm just holding for a friend." Only Fisk laughed.

Mira said, "You're lucky you're not dead."

"There's a good chance you're right."

"You've heard about your friend Ben?"

"Heading to the hospital right now."

"Where's this going to end, Mike?"

"What 'this' are you referring to, Mira?"

"You and the Ateros." Her expression saying, "What other 'this' could I mean?"

"It's played out, far as I'm concerned."

Fisk said, "She's worried you'll go after them with guns blazing. You're more of a nightstick guy, is what I told her."

"I'm sorry about your office," Mira said.

"It'll fix."

"And your face?"

Barton's blade — my blade — had left the faintest of marks. "Cut myself," I said.

"Your friend Katherine told me you were coming here. She asked us to watch out for you."

"I didn't tell her I was coming here."

"She must have assumed it then." Mira patted my shoulder. "Go home and see your grandmother. And clean yourself up. You need a shower in the worst possible way."

* * *

The main hall of the church was in use, but Pastor Flaherty set aside one of the meeting rooms for us. The carpet had cigarette burns and the one window looked out on the building next door. Cliff Szabo was waiting, holding two cups of coffee.

I wanted to confess everything to him. He deserved it. At the same time there was self-preservation to think of, and his own culpability. I pulled two folding chairs off the stack and set them facing each other. I sat him down and told him his son was dead. I'd never seen him emote beyond frustration and anger, but he bowed his head and the tears came, along with a whimpering sound from his throat.

"How?"

"Accident which went untreated," I said. "I'm sorry as hell."

I gave him his money and told him to rip up his copy of our contract. A silly precaution given that he'd announced I was working for him on the nightly news, but the less evidence the better. I told him to tell people that I'd been on vacation, that he'd never asked me to accompany Fisk to the Island. I wondered if Fisk would tell what he knew. Hard to say.

"In a week or so," I said, "you'll get two books in the mail. They're written by the man responsible, in his own hand. They spell out what happened. If I was you I'd burn them, but you deserve the option." I stared at my hands clasped in front of me, avoiding his face. "I don't think he suffered," I added.

"What happened to the man responsible?"

I told him.

Ben was lying with his back to the door when I entered the bright hospital room and took in the stale, flower-scented air. I figured he was sleeping and that I'd sit for a while, maybe rustle up a Ludlum or a Travis McGee from the hospital's lending library. But he turned over and I saw the tears on his face.

"Feeling okay?" I said, once again trying to comfort someone to whom the idea of comfort was obscene.

Both legs cast, bandages on his face and hands. "How can you ask me that?"

"Want me to get the nurse?"

"I have a button if I need it," he said. "Anyway, I'm pretty high right now. That's why there might be tears. Side effect of the drugs."

"Right."

He repositioned himself on his back. "How'd it go?"

"Not well," I said, laughing despite myself at the understatement. "About the same as things here."

"So he's dead?"

"Yes. No miracles."

Ben nodded and invented pretexts to wipe his face. I turned away for a moment and pulled a wicker chair closer to his bed.

"That's how Cynthia ended up, didn't she?"

"I didn't find her body there, though I'm sure that's the first thing your mother will ask me. The cases aren't connected."

"But that's what happened to her, isn't it?"

I began to lie but couldn't summon the effort.

"Probably," I said. "Almost certainly."

"Some evil bastard just took her and did what he wanted and killed her."

"They're out there," I said, "and there's nothing you can do about them, nothing that can make it right. And that applies to the person that put you here."

"I gathered that," he said.

I handed him the wireless drive. "The attack will be on here. No way Theo walks after the police see it."

Ben nodded and let it fall on his bedsheets. He said, "Until I ended up in here I don't think I ever felt the emptiness of not having Cynthia, just as a presence on the planet. It sounds stupid, but I think I was keeping her alive by writing about her. That's why I write, you know — to keep dead people alive. Magnus Kane started out as this ultra-powerful version of me who could do whatever he wanted, but as I started fleshing him out, he became my brother. And Rosalind, she was just a hostage to be rescued in the first game, but then she grew and became Cynthia. It wasn't so much about rescuing her as about what she'd do once she was rescued, the life she'd lead. The further I went, the less it felt like the real people were really gone. And I can't write anymore because I see it for what it is, a poor substitute, and not fair to their memories."

"Maybe it'll come back," I said. "If not, there's a secretary's position open at Hastings Street Investigations."

Mrs. Loeb opened the door, arms laden with styrofoam containers and parcels. "Any news?" she asked me.

"None. Sorry."

She nodded and focused her attention on Ben, wheeling over the meal tray. "Chicken soup with kreplach from Cantor's," she said. "There's enough for three if you're hungry, Michael."

"I should leave you two alone," I said, thinking of my bed and my dog, and a woman who wouldn't be there.

Mrs. Loeb handed me one of the containers. "Have a couple of spoons just to be sociable. I can always get more. And I did want to talk with you about something concerning Cynthia."

"You already asked him if there was news," Ben said. "Can't it wait?"

"Of course, but I don't see why it should. If you'd rather not hear it, Mike and I can go down the hall."

Ben flung the napkin she'd spread to the floor. "Mom, she's not coming back. She's dead or worse."

His mother paused, the soup-lid half-removed.

"I understand you're upset," she said.

"I understand you want to believe Cynthia's alive but she's not, she's not coming back, because some sick fucker picked her up and probably took her across the country and raped her and sodomized her and tortured her and kept her in a dog kennel, and once she was dead cut her into pieces and tossed them into a well or ate them. And probably you'll never find out. And I know this and the cops know this and Mike here knows. The missing persons groups and those stupid support groups you go to, they all know it too. And you know it, Mom, don't you? Deep down? So why don't we cut out the lies and stop pretending she's alive and well and just forgot to call these last years? Could we do that, put these illusions aside, at least for a while?"

Estelline Loeb put the soup down on the moveable tray. She set out plastic cutlery, including a superfluous knife and fork and individual packets of salt and pepper. She'd bought a box of crackers and pulled one of the packages out of the box and tore it open for Ben to help himself. She unfolded a fresh napkin and made to tie it around Ben's neck, but he flinched and she smoothed it and set it on the tray next to the bowl.

When that was done, she said to me, "Let's go outside and let him eat."

I followed her to the end of the corridor, where a window looked down on Burrard Street.

"Ben said the file was destroyed by those hooligans," she said. "Is that right?"

"I have a copy with my lawyer, but it's about two months old. I have most of the rest on file. I'll be able to put everything together as it was, minus my margin scrawls."

"Forget it," she said.

"You're sure?"

"I am."

"All right," I said.

"Because, you see, a lot of the problem I think is that we've had the material but haven't been able to look at it fresh, and evaluate the original evidence with everything that's come to light. What we really have to do is start at the end and work back. I think that will help us see the original statements with new eyes, and maybe banish some of the fogginess that creeps in when we deal with so much information. Or, tell you what, you could start at the beginning and I'll start with the most recent, and we can spend maybe an hour or two each week comparing and discussing what we've looked at, to see what connections can be made. Do you think there's any sense in that, Michael?"

"Abso-fucking-lutely," I said.

Epilogue

It struck her as sad how far the scope of her life had been reduced. She regretted never learning to drive. Before retirement she'd counted on the bus, and her husband, on his days off, had always been willing to drive her. One of his better qualities. Now two floors in one house contained her, aside from the occasional foray with her grandson or the ladies from Come Share. She found herself confined with the animal and noted its decline with much more scrutiny than her grandson did. Blindness from affection is still blindness.

In the morning she came downstairs and turned on the kettle and stared at the dead TV screen, knowing if she turned that on too, that was what she would do for the day. The house was too quiet so she turned on the radio and listened to one of the disk jockeys jabber about parliament while she had her porridge. She did the dishes humming to the songs on the oldies station.

At noon she let the dog out of the basement. It drank water and nuzzled her leg. It smelled rank. She let it into the yard and cleaned her silver while watching the dog from the window. The dog did nothing.

She vacuumed the carpets but the smell of sick dog was worked into the fibers now. The dog lay in the yard. *Damn you,* she thought. *Leaving that thing for me to look after, unwilling to face what will happen regardless, and unwilling to make it as painless as it could be. Still a child in some respects. Too many.*

Look at it, she thought. *Even it knows it's time.*

He'd left his gun with her. He'd taught her how to use the big shotgun, but cautioned her that firing it would probably break her shoulder. No. Guns weren't her business. Her husband's, her grandson's. Not hers.

He'd left his pain medication behind as well. She opened a can of Fancy Feast — the dog preferred cat food for some silly reason, and he'd indulged it — and ground three of the pills up and worked them into the food. She took the bowl out to it with one hand, her knife in the other. Placed the bowl on the grass. Watched it bow its head, sniff the bowl and begin to eat. When it had eaten its fill she slit its throat the way she'd done with pigs more than half a century ago on her father's farm, a strong deep cut, the kind that would elicit a nod of approval from her father. All the gold stars and report cards never pleased that man as much as watching one of his daughters make a clean kill. When it was over she dug the grave, the shovel too long and heavy. Falling on her knees, she used the dog's food dish and a rusty trowel. Her arms hurt and she had to break for food and to return circulation to her knees and elbows. By nightfall she still wasn't done but she kept digging. By midnight, an hour that rarely saw her awake, she had lowered the body and the clumps of blood-stained grass that served as evidence into the ground. She packed the earth over the body and rolled a few stones onto the grave. She stood up and wiped her hands on her knees, then went back inside to sleep and eat and wait for his call.

OF RELATED INTEREST

Pumpkin Eater
A Dan Sharp Mystery
by Jeffrey Round

Following an anonymous tip, missing persons investigator Dan Sharp makes a grisly find in a burned-out slaughterhouse in Toronto's west end. Someone is targeting known sex offenders whose names and identities were released on the Internet. When an iconic rock star contacts Dan to keep from becoming the next victim, things take a curious turn. Dan's search for a killer takes him underground in Toronto's broken social scene — a secret world of misfits and guerrilla activists living off the grid — where he hopes to find the key to the murders.

Birds of a Feather
A Jack Taggart Mystery
by Don Easton

Lily Rae is on holiday in El Paso, Texas, when she's kidnapped by a Mexican drug cartel. El Paso borders on one of the most dangerous places in the world — Ciudad Juarez, Mexico — a city caught in the grip of a war between cartels.

Her disappearance is investigated by undercover Mountie Jack Taggart, who discovers a Canadian link to the cartel and penetrates the organization. Taggart is sent to El Paso, where he is partnered with special U.S. Customs agent John Adams. Neither Taggart nor Adams know they have been paired together for a secret purpose.

Taggart has strict orders to stay out of Juarez, but his gut instinct directs him otherwise. The investigation seems to be going smoothly — until the cartel discovers his true identity.

Practically torn from the headlines, *Birds of a Feather* will keep you on the edge of your seat and leave you questioning right and wrong.

Twilight Is Not Good for Maidens
A Holly Martin Mystery
by Lou Allin

Corporal Holly Martin's small RCMP detachment on Vancouver Island is rocked by a midnight attack on a woman camping alone at picturesque French Beach. Then Holly's constable, Chipper Knox Singh, is accused of sexually assaulting a girl during a routine traffic stop and is removed from active duty. At another beach a girl is killed. An assailant is operating unseen in these dark, forested locations.

The case breaks open when a third young woman is raped in daylight and gives a precise description of the assailant. Public outrage and harsh criticism of local law enforcement augment tensions in the frightened community, but as a mere corporal, Holly is kept on the periphery. She must assemble her own clues.

Available at your favourite bookseller

DUNDURN

Visit us at
Dundurn.com
@dundurnpress
Facebook.com/dundurnpress
Pinterest.com/dundurnpress